"Take my hand!" he shouted, reaching into the wreck.

Nadia grabbed his hand. His fingers wrapped around her wrist, and they felt like the only warmth in the world. She let him tow her upward, helping him by climbing as best she could. Rain spattered against her face and hands as she emerged from the wreckage, and her rescuer slung one arm around her waist to pull her away from the car, onto the nearby bank of the ditch they'd crashed into.

As they flopped onto the muddy ground, lightning crashed again, painting his face in eerie blue. He must have seen her more clearly, too, because he whispered, "Oh, my God. It's you."

Also by Claudia Gray

EVERNIGHT
STARGAZER
HOURGLASS
AFTERLIFE
BALTHAZAR

FATEFUL

STEADFAST

SPELLCASTER

CLAUDIA GRAY

HARPER TEEN

HarperTeen is an imprint of HarperCollins Publishers.

Spellcaster
Copyright © 2013 by Amy Vincent
www.epicreads.com

Library of Congress Cataloging-in-Publication Data
Gray, Claudia.
Spellcaster / Claudia Gray. — 1st ed.
    p.   cm.
    Summary: "Descended from witches, high school senior Nadia can tell as
soon as her family moves to Captive's Sound that the town is under a dark
and powerful spell. Then she meets Mateo, the teenage local whose cursed
dreams predict the future, and they must work together to prevent an
impending disaster that threatens the entire town" — Provided by
publisher.
    ISBN 978-0-06-196121-2 53333489 03/14
[1. Witches—Fiction.   2. Magic—Fiction.   3. Blessing and
cursing—Fiction.   4. High schools—Fiction.   5. Schools—Fiction.
6. Family life—Rhode Island—Fiction.   7. Rhode Island—Fiction.
8. Horror stories.]   I. Title.
PZ7.G77625Spe 2013   2012025331
[Fic]—dc23
Typography by Torborg Davern

14   15   16   17   18   LP/RRDH   10 9 8 7 6 5 4 3 2 1
❖
First paperback edition, 2014

SPELLCASTER

1

BEFORE ANYTHING ELSE, NADIA FELT THE CHILL.

She wasn't sure why. Her father already had the car's heat on because of the awful weather. Her little brother, Cole, was too engrossed in his game to have rolled down any of the windows. The only sounds were the *slap-slap* of the windshield wipers, Cole's thumbs tapping on the tablet screen, and Dad's classical music—some piano concerto, notes rippling and rolling over them, not unlike the driving rain outside. It was just like the other countless hours they'd spent in this car today.

There was no reason for the trembling cold that snaked its way along Nadia's skin. No reason for her head to swim as all her senses heightened.

No normal reason anyway.

Nadia straightened in her seat—in the back, next to her brother. The passenger seat in the front was always left empty, as if Mom might suddenly return at the next rest stop. "Dad, where are we?"

"Almost there."

"You said that three states ago," Cole chimed in, never looking up from his game.

"I mean it this time," Dad insisted. "We should get into town any minute now. So hang in there, guys."

"I just mean—my head hurts." Honestly explaining what was wrong was out of the question. Nadia already knew that the strange sensations washing over her weren't physical or emotional.

They were signs of magic.

Dad turned the piano music down to a soft wash. "You okay, sweetheart? There's painkillers in the first-aid kit; we could pull over."

"I'm fine," Nadia said. "If we're almost there, let's not stop now."

Even as she spoke, though, she felt as if she had made a mistake—as if she ought to have said, *Yes, pull over, let's get out of this car as soon as possible.* Everything within her told her that they were traveling closer and closer to a source of magic—unlike any she had known before. But instinct alone told Nadia this magic was . . . primal. Powerful. Potentially overwhelming.

Her eyes flickered over to the empty seat next to her father. Mom would have known what to do—

Well, Mom's not here, Nadia told herself savagely. *She's still back in Chicago, probably off drinking cocktails with some guy she just met. I'll never finish my training. I'll never be able to use magic the way she did.*

*But we're headed into something dangerous. I have to do some-*thing.

But what?

Nadia glanced sideways at Cole, who remained wrapped up in his game. Like her father, he was oblivious to the forces they were approaching; like all males, they were magic-blind. Quickly she closed her eyes and settled her left wrist in her right hand. On her left wrist she wore what Dad called her charm bracelet—and it did look like one, at a glance.

Even after Mom had left, ruining their lives and all Nadia's hopes, Nadia had kept wearing the bracelet every day. It was too hard to let it go.

Her fingers found the small pendant of ivory, the material she needed to balance her spell.

Silently, she went through the spell for illumination of magical shape. The ingredients came back to her faster than she would have thought.

> *A winter sunrise.*
> *The pain of abandonment.*
> *The knowledge of love.*

She went deep within herself, calling up the ingredients, experiencing each more powerfully than real memory—as if she were living them again—

The sun rising on a sharp, cold morning when the snow was high enough to sink into knee-deep, painting the sky a pale pink, while Nadia shivered on the balcony.

Nadia standing dumbfounded in the door of her parents' bedroom as Mom packed a suitcase and said, "Your father and I think we should live apart for a while."

Waking up in a violent thunderstorm to find Cole curled next to her wearing his footie pajamas, in silent, total confidence that his big sister could protect him.

The emotions and images coursed through her, reverberating through her powers, bouncing off the ivory until Nadia could see—a barrier. They were headed straight toward . . . what was this? . . . Was it meant to keep out any other forms of magic, or warn someone else if magic entered this space?

Nadia's eyes widened. She'd be able to pass through the barrier—limits on magic didn't apply to magic users—but that wasn't her biggest problem.

Oh, no, she thought. *The car.*

In the trunk, in her suitcase, wrapped in her clothes, was her Book of Shadows.

"Dad?" Her voice was tight and high with fear as they came closer to the barrier; she could almost feel it now, like static electricity against her skin. "Dad, can we pull over?"

He'd been too lost in his own thoughts to hear her. "What's that, sweetheart?"

And then—impact.

The road seemed to jerk beneath the wheels of the car, as if the earth were being sheared away beneath them. Nadia slammed into the window as her father struggled for control of the wheel—in vain. She could hear the squeal of brakes and Cole's scream as the world turned over, over again, thrashing her in every direction at once. Something hit her head, and then she couldn't quite see, couldn't quite hear. Yet Cole was still screaming—or was it her? She didn't know anymore—

They crashed to a halt, the impact throwing her forward and backward so hard that her seat belt felt like a club smashing into her chest.

She slammed back into reality, and wished she hadn't.

Nadia cried out as the window beside her—now beneath her—splintered, and mud and water began oozing in. Above her, Cole half dangled from his booster seat, wailing in panic. She reached up with a shaky hand to touch him, comfort him, make sure he wasn't injured. But her head was still reeling.

The Book of Shadows—it hit that barrier, and it was like—like an explosion or something—

"Cole! Nadia!" The inside of the car was almost entirely dark now that the lights were as dead as the engine, but she could make out the shadow of her father trying to clamber into the backseat with them. "Are you all right?"

"We're okay," Nadia managed to gasp.

"The water—"

"I see it!" Already the muck was rising—or was the car sinking? Nadia couldn't tell.

Dad stopped trying to get in the back with them; instead he managed to push open the passenger-side front door and climb out of the car. For one moment, Nadia felt crazy terror stab her—*he's left us, where's Dad, where's Dad?*—but then Cole's door opened and Dad reached inside to pull her little brother free.

"Daddy!" Cole wailed as he clamped his arms around their father's neck. Raindrops fell into the car now, hard and stinging. Nadia managed to undo the straps of his safety seat, so Dad could lift him.

"That's right. Daddy's here. Nadia, I'm going to get Cole out of this ditch and come right back for you. Right back! Hang on!"

Nadia nodded, too quickly, because her whiplash-stung neck ached. She clawed at her seat belt, freeing herself just as the water rose high enough to wash over one of her legs. The seat belt had been keeping her out of the mud, and she tumbled into it. It was cold—so cold the mere touch of it numbed her to the bone. A long scrape along her forearm stung tears into her eyes. She was clumsy now, and even more afraid than before. But it didn't matter as long as she could still climb out.

She braced her feet against the armrest and tried to stand; she was dizzy, but she could do it. Where was her father? Was he all right?

Lightning flashed. In the blaze of that sudden light, Nadia glimpsed someone above her.

He was her age, perhaps. Dark hair, dark eyes, though she could tell nothing else in the night and the rain. But in that flash of lightning, she'd already seen that he was beautiful—so much that she wondered if the crash had dazed her into seeing phantoms, delusions, angels. Thunder rolled.

"Take my hand!" he shouted, reaching into the wreck.

Nadia grabbed his hand. His fingers wrapped around her wrist, and they felt like the only warmth in the world. She let him tow her upward, helping him by climbing as best she could. Rain spattered against her face and hands as she emerged from the wreckage, and her rescuer slung one arm around her waist to pull her away from the car, onto the nearby bank of the ditch they'd crashed into.

As they flopped onto the muddy ground, lightning crashed again, painting his face in eerie blue. He must have seen her more clearly, too, because he whispered, "Oh, my God. It's you."

She drew in a sharp breath. This guy knew her?

How could he know her when she didn't know him?

Next to them were Dad and Cole. "Thank you," her father breathed, clutching one side as if in pain; Nadia only then realized he'd been injured.

"Dad! Are you okay?"

"I'm fine," he said, though his whole body was stiff with pain. "I was able to call 911 while our new friend—what's your name?"

"Mateo."

Nadia turned back to him, but Mateo was already looking away from her, as if unwilling to meet her eyes. He, too, was gasping for breath; the rescue couldn't have been much less frightening for him than the crash had been for her.

But how could he know her? *Did* he know her? Was she imagining things in the aftermath of the wreck?

"While Mateo helped you. We'll—we'll be all right."

"What happened?" Cole sniffled. He clung to his father as if afraid he might fall in the ditch again.

Nadia scooted closer to them so she could take her little brother's hand. "It's okay, buddy. We're okay. We had a wreck, that's all."

"Sometimes cars hydroplane during a storm." Dad breathed in and out through his nose, hand still braced against his ribs. "That means the tires are actually on the water instead of the road. It can be dangerous. I really thought—I thought we were going slow enough to avoid that—"

"You weren't doing anything wrong." Nadia wished she could have told her father not to blame himself, but he could never understand what had just happened to them, or why.

She turned back to see her mysterious rescuer—Mateo— but he was gone. Peering through the rain and gloom, Nadia tried to make out where he might be. He couldn't have gotten far. But she couldn't find him; it was as if he'd vanished.

Her father, distracted with pain and Cole's fear, didn't seem to notice that Mateo had left. "We're okay," he kept repeating, rocking her little brother back and forth. "We're all okay, and nothing else matters."

In the distance, sirens wailed, and she could make out the beat of red-blue lights from a far-off police car or ambulance. Help was on the way, yet Nadia shivered from the cold and the adrenaline and the pent-up fear.

She glanced upward to see that they'd damaged a sign in the wreck. Leaning to one side, rocking back and forth in the wind of the storm, was a placard emblazoned with the words WELCOME TO CAPTIVE'S SOUND.

She's real.

Mateo stood in the woods, his back to a tree, as he watched the police see to the family he'd just helped. An ambulance had pulled up for the father, but there didn't seem to be any particular rush for them to get to the hospital. Nobody was hurt too badly. Good.

Despite the darkness, he could see the girl sitting in the backseat of the police car. A pale blanket had been wrapped around her shoulders. It helped to think of her warm and safe.

Lightning streaked through the sky overhead again, and Mateo remembered dimly that standing next to a large tree was probably not the smartest thing he could be doing right now. But shock had numbed him past the ability to move.

Besides—he knew he wouldn't be killed by lightning tonight.

He *knew.*

All day, he'd tried to ignore the dream he'd had. He'd told himself that it was a nightmare like any other—the vision of the storm, the crash, the beautiful girl trapped in the wreckage. But when the sun had set and the rain had come, Mateo had been unable to ignore the dream any longer.

He'd come out here in the hopes of proving to himself that it wasn't true. For hours, he'd stood in the rain, watching and waiting, pissed off at himself for even believing this was possible, yet more hopeful as time ticked on and nothing happened.

And then—right when he'd begun to believe it really was only a dream—everything had happened just as he'd known it would.

She's real, he thought. *If the crash happened like I saw it would, then so will everything else I've seen.*

Shaky and cold with horror, Mateo closed his eyes against the realization that he was doomed.

And if the girl from his dreams didn't stay far away from him—she'd be doomed, too.

2

DESPITE WHIPLASH AND THE BANDAGES ON HER SORE arm, Nadia got to work unpacking right away. Dad couldn't manage much with his ribs broken, Cole was way too young to help with anything besides putting away his toys, and besides—there were certain items she wanted to be positive nobody else saw.

Like, say, her witchcraft supplies.

I could come up with an explanation for the glass jars, like, they were for makeup or something, Nadia mused as she unwrapped them from wads of newspaper. *But the powdered bone? Forget it. Dad would probably think I was on drugs.*

It felt stupid to have kept everything. Without Mom, there was no hope of continuing her training; witchcraft was a closely held secret, passed down between female relatives in the rare bloodlines that had the power. Mom had never revealed the other members of her coven to Nadia—which was just how things were. Nadia wouldn't have expected to learn any of their names until she was a true witch herself and able to join the coven in her own right.

Still, she'd thought one of them might reveal herself after the divorce—come forward and offer to teach Nadia, or at least give some advice—

But nothing. Mom probably hadn't even told them that she'd abandoned her own daughter half-trained, with only enough knowledge to get herself in trouble, not nearly enough to solve any of her problems.

No matter how good a student she'd been, no matter how hard she'd worked her whole life—Nadia would never get to become a witch now. Mom had taken that with her, too.

Even as her throat tightened with unshed tears, Nadia tried to snap herself out of it. *You know enough to do some things. It's still useful, right?*

Useful enough to get us in a car crash. If I'd faced facts and ditched my Book of Shadows—

But no. She could never do that. A Book of Shadows—even one as new as hers—had power. You couldn't leave that lying around. And she didn't have the heart to destroy it.

Despite everything, Nadia didn't have the heart to walk away from the Craft yet.

As she thought of the wreck, the images of that night swept over her so vividly that it was like she was back there in that ditch. The way the storm had crashed and rolled overhead. The terror of feeling herself sliding down into the cold muck, not knowing whether she could escape.

And Mateo's face, outlined by lightning, as he reached in to save her—

Nadia's breath caught in her throat. Who was he? And how had he known her?

But that wasn't the biggest mystery of that night, and Nadia knew it. The biggest mystery was—who had put up that magical barrier around Captive's Sound?

And why?

"Make a Mickey Mouse one!"

Nadia poured the pancake batter into three circles, two small ones for the ears and a big one for Mickey's face. "No whipped cream for the smile today, buddy, but you're going to eat him too fast for that, anyway, aren't you?"

"Definitely." Cole walked to the kitchen table with his glass of milk—way too full, Nadia saw, but he didn't spill any.

"What's this?" Dad came into the kitchen of their new house; he was moving easily now, without pain, but the stark white of his bandages still showed through his dress shirt. "I was going to make you guys breakfast. To celebrate the big day."

"Nobody celebrates the first day of school," Cole said as he took his seat, tiny sneakered feet now dangling above the wood floor. He was in such a good mood—so confident and easygoing—and Nadia and her father exchanged a look. Cole was finally doing better; maybe the fresh start was working precisely like they'd hoped.

"Making breakfast is no big deal," Nadia said. "Anyway, I'm a better cook than you, and you know it."

Dad nodded, acknowledging this, as he took his seat. "But how else am I going to learn?"

Cooking wasn't a chore for her; it was a hobby, even a passion. She'd filled some of the hours that had once gone to her witchcraft lessons with studying cookbooks and experimenting. Still—one way or the other, she wouldn't be at home full-time after graduation, so maybe she ought to teach him a few things, just to make sure they wouldn't starve. "I'll give you lessons. Wait and see."

Although Dad looked like he wanted to protest, he'd also caught sight of the bacon she'd put on the table. Distraction provided; discussion over.

The kitchen in their new house was one of the few things about it Nadia didn't like. In their Chicago condominium, they'd had the best and brightest appliances her father's big-law-firm salary could buy, and oceans of counter space. Here, everything was old-fashioned and a little shabby. But what she disliked in the kitchen was precisely what made the rest of the house so awesome. It was an old Victorian, two stories not counting the large attic she'd claimed as her private space—the perfect hiding place for her Book of Shadows and the supplies for her magic. She'd expected Cole to pitch a fit, but he was so thrilled by having a real, true backyard of his own that he showed no signs of coming indoors of his own free will ever again. The oaken plank floors creaked comfortingly, and a stained-glass window let cranberry-tinted light into the stairwell. If it was all slightly run-down, it was also beautiful—and as big a change from their high-rise condo as she could imagine.

Nadia didn't want any reminders of their life before. She wanted to seal her family into a place where nothing could hurt them—not memory, not her mother, not whatever weird magic was at work in this town. This house seemed to provide a chance, and she knew just enough of the Craft to help that along.

So she'd whispered the spells, encircled it with the best protection she knew. She'd slipped out in the night to bury moonstones next to the steps; she'd begun the work of painting the attic ceiling blue. *To make it cute,* she'd told her dad. The real power of that particular shade, what it meant for a home to be protected from above—those were things he never had to know.

Great, Nadia thought as she stared at her new high school, Isaac P. Rodman High. *Just great.*

Just the fact that it was a high school was bad enough. On top of that, it was a new school for her senior year. She'd accepted they needed the move, but that didn't mean she was looking forward to navigating completely new people and teachers and cliques for the nine and a half months before she'd graduate and be free again. Her new school was far smaller than the one she'd attended in Chicago, but in some ways that was more intimidating, not less. Everyone here knew one another, and probably had for their whole lives.

That made her the odd one out.

But beyond that, there was something else. Something shivering just beneath the surface—once again, something magical, though it was different from anything else she'd ever known. Precisely how it was different, she couldn't say, but this energy was familiar and unfamiliar at once. Nadia could feel it coursing all around her, that static-electricity thing all over again.

This was . . . a complication.

What is going on here? It's not like someone is using magic near me—even if I could feel that, I don't think it would feel like this. It's more like some source of magical energy is kept here. But shielded—encased—in a way I don't understand.

Nadia clutched the straps of her backpack tighter as she hurried inside the registrar's office. *Don't think about it now,* she told herself. *You can figure it out later. Besides, there's nothing you can do about it without Mom around to help. For now? All you have to do is get through the day.*

Even waiting for her class schedule was almost more than she could take.

"So, like, Jinnie's just standing there, like nothing is going on, even though we both know what's going on, so I'm like, *hey, Jinnie,* and she's like, *hey, Kendall,* and I'm like, *what's up,* and she's like, *nothing.* I swear to God, she is so fake." The girl in front of Nadia somehow managed to talk into her cell phone without pausing, even though she was chewing at least half a pack of gum at once. "And she's all, *did you have a good summer,* and I just went, *yeah,* because I'm

16

so not getting into that with her."

Nadia prayed for the ancient secretary behind the counter in her lilac polyester suit to find whatever the heck it was this girl wanted so she'd leave already. Or shut up. Either way.

The door opened and shut behind her; Nadia didn't bother turning around. The girl in front of her did, her sandy hair falling over her shoulder. Almost instantly, her freckled face went from pleasant to nasty, her expression from vapid to mean. "Speaking of total fake bitches," she said into her phone, far too loudly, "that skank Verlaine just walked in."

Nadia couldn't help but turn back to look.

The first word that came into her mind when she saw Verlaine was *Goth*. But that wasn't right. The black dress she wore wasn't lace or leather; it had puffed sleeves and a wide belt at the waist like something from a 1950s movie, and her shoes were cheerful kelly-green Converse sneakers. Her complexion was so white that Nadia had assumed she was wearing that stuff Goths used to come across like porcelain dolls or ghosts—but Verlaine was really that fair all over. And her long hair wasn't an elaborate wig or even a dye job, unless she'd been thorough enough to even do her eyebrows. Instead, it was really, truly, totally silver-gray, though Verlaine seemed to be no older than Nadia herself.

The most striking thing about her, though, was how . . . hopeless she looked. Like people were mean to her all the time, and she no longer even dreamed of anything better. Her only response was to roll her eyes and say, "Kendall, give it a rest."

Kendall said, "I have to go. If I don't get out of here soon, the skank overload will kill me." She stowed her phone with another withering glance toward Verlaine; Kendall's bubbly personality seemed to have changed in an instant. "You'd think having two fags for dads would mean at least somebody would tell you what to wear."

Nadia couldn't hold it back any longer. "You'd think anybody wearing *those* shoes would know they didn't have the right to tell anybody else what to wear."

Kendall, caught up short, stared down at her shoes like she was trying to guess what was wrong with them. They were fine, as far as Nadia could tell, but with fashion, attitude was half the battle. Verlaine's face lit up; her smile looked uneven, as though she didn't get much practice.

"Here you go, Miss Bender." The secretary shuffled out with a manila folder, which Kendall snatched from her hands before stomping out. "And you are?"

"Nadia Caldani. I'm new. You should have my records from Chicago."

"Oh, yes. We have your schedule—right back here—" The secretary wandered toward the back room, still in no hurry.

"Thanks," Verlaine whispered. "Kendall was being such a witch."

Nadia tried to brush aside her momentary annoyance. "I prefer *bitch*, actually. Most witches are perfectly nice people. Sorry—pet peeve."

"No worries. About time somebody else with some

attitude got here. Captive's Sound is mostly a graveyard for the living."

"Wow, you make it sound awesome."

"I'm exaggerating. Graveyards are more exciting."

Nadia smiled, but talking to Verlaine felt—weird. She didn't want to make any friends. After the way everybody had started avoiding her in Chicago—like her bad luck was catching—well, "friendship" obviously didn't mean what Nadia had always thought it did. And there was just something about Verlaine . . . something she couldn't put her finger on. . . .

There was no time to think about that, though. By the time the secretary finally waddled forth with her class schedule, Nadia was already almost late for her first class. She politely waved good-bye to Verlaine, who didn't really react, only nodded; then she rushed toward what she thought was the right building. Forget the locker—that she could find later, and it wasn't like she had any of her books yet.

"There he is," whispered one girl excitedly. "Holy crap, he got even hotter over the summer. I didn't think that was possible."

"He's nice to look at," said another whisper, "but he's bad news. You know that."

"It's a bunch of crazy gossiping old people. That's all that is."

"Oh, yeah? Well, how come you never talk to him, either?"

"Shut up."

Nadia couldn't help but turn her head to see who the whispering was about—and her eyes went wide.

Mateo. He was here, in her school—letter jacket on his shoulders, dark hair brushed back, even more gorgeous in the daylight than he'd been in the dark. In those first terrifying moments, she'd assumed he was a couple years older than she was, but apparently he was a student at Rodman, too.

For his part, when their eyes met, he froze in place. It was almost as if the sight of her—scared him.

But that couldn't be right. He'd saved her from the wreck, which was the single bravest act she'd ever witnessed. Why would he be scared of *her*?

Nadia said, "Mateo, hi. I didn't realize you went here." Was that a stupid thing to say? It wasn't like they'd talked a lot about school or anything else.

He said only, "Yeah. Hi. Are you okay? You and your family?"

People were staring at them openly: the new girl and Mateo, who was for some unknown reason "bad news."

"They're fine," Nadia said quickly. "Dad cracked a couple ribs, but not too bad. He's already feeling better. Started work today." Like he even cared about her father's job. Words seemed to be coming out of her mouth for no reason.

"Good. That's good." Mateo ran one hand through his dark hair, as though he was self-conscious; now that she saw it in daylight, Nadia realized it wasn't black like hers but the deepest possible brown, just like his eyes. His skin was as tan as hers, maybe even darker. He wasn't supertall, but a couple inches over her—which was of course perfect—

"So. Okay. I'll be seeing you." Nadia started to walk past him, then realized she'd forgotten to mention something. "I'm Nadia, by the way."

"Nadia," he said, his voice soft. Something about the sudden light in his eyes told her he'd been wondering about her name for a long while.

He knows me—I wasn't imagining things—but how is that possible?

Yet he turned away and pushed through the crowded hall, surrounded by whispers that were almost as loud as the slamming locker doors.

She knew she needed to hurry in the opposite direction, but she found herself watching him go all the way down the corridor to the broad doors that led outside, until he pushed them open and was swallowed up in the light.

Mateo walked across the grounds—walked faster—and broke into a run. He had to get away from her, even more for her sake than for his. And yet something in his mind kept repeating the name. *Nadia.*

"Hey!"

He skidded to a stop only a moment before he would have run into Gage Calloway, who had four inches and about twenty pounds of muscle on Mateo. That would've hurt. His brain had obviously checked out. "Sorry."

"Any particular reason you're running out of here like the proverbial bat out of hell?" Gage grinned. "Not that

I wouldn't rather be escaping, too, but I figure we gotta graduate to make that work in the long term."

Sighing, Mateo ran one hand through his hair. "I need a sec."

"All right. I'll take a sec here with you."

That was fine with Mateo. They weren't exactly close friends—they'd only met when Gage transferred to Rodman last year—but Gage at least treated Mateo like he was a normal person. Gage didn't know any better, at least not yet.

Mateo saw that instead of cutting his dreadlocks over the summer, as some teachers had suggested, Gage had drawn them back into a neat bun at the nape of his neck, which brought him just into compliance with school rules. Although he was handsome and athletic—and not afraid to be himself in conformity-obsessed Captive's Sound—Gage wasn't one of the more popular kids in school. He was probably too independent for that, not to mention too discriminating to hang out with jerks like Jinnie and Jeremy. Instead he was content to hang out on the sidelines and do his own thing. Mateo was grateful for that; only someone who didn't follow the herd would hang out with him.

Then Gage's eyes widened, and his normally carefree expression switched into pure, abject devotion. "Which means maybe I get to talk to Elizabeth."

Mateo looked across the grounds to the edge of campus, where Elizabeth stood. Her long chestnut curls ruffled in the breeze, as did the simple white dress she wore. She was so unlike any other girl at school—her face clean-scrubbed, her clothes anything but fashionable, and yet there was no doubting her beauty.

She was his oldest friend. His best friend. There was no one else he could ever have told about Nadia—and until this moment, he hadn't realized how badly he needed to talk.

Elizabeth came toward him, and though she spoke softly, he heard every word. "Mateo. You look troubled."

"It's not a great day," he answered.

Gage tried to cut in. "Since when is the first day of school a great day? Am I right?" He laughed a little too loud, then gave Mateo a look that clearly meant, *Why am I talking like an idiot?* The poor guy was so into her it scrambled his brains. Sometimes Mateo thought Gage might stand a chance with Elizabeth if he'd try shutting up occasionally.

But at the moment, Elizabeth showed no signs of even noticing that Gage was there. Her attention was only for Mateo. "Do you need to talk?"

"I kinda do. But I don't want to make you late for class."

"You're gonna be late to class, too," Gage pointed out. "Remember the part about escape through graduation?"

"They worked it out so my study hall is first period. In case La Catrina closes late." Mateo spoke more to Elizabeth than to Gage. "Unless you guys are in study hall, too—"

"I can skip," Elizabeth insisted. Her gentle voice could sound so firm sometimes. "This is important."

Gage obviously wanted to think of a reason he should stay as well, but came up blank. "Okay. So. Catch you later?"

"Sure thing." Mateo watched Gage lope off across the grounds, grateful there was one guy he could hang with. But he had only one real friend: Elizabeth. She alone understood him; she knew Mateo's soul.

As they walked together to the broad elm at the very edge of school property, Mateo wondered once again why he wasn't in love with Elizabeth. He should've been. Instead she was like the sister he'd never had. In childhood, when the other kids shunned him for being Lauren Cabot's son, Elizabeth had played with him. Together they had climbed trees, made cookies, watched TV. She alone was loyal. She alone accepted him no matter what.

They sat side by side, their backs against the elm tree, as the bell rang. When it stopped, Elizabeth said, "Have you been having the dreams again?"

"Yes. Except they aren't only dreams, Elizabeth. They're real."

"You don't know that."

"I do." The next would sound unbelievable, but the proof was here, now, walking the halls of Rodman High in the form of a girl so beautiful she stopped his heart. "I've seen her. The girl from the dream I told you about."

"That could have been anybody in the wreck. It was dark and rainy—you had to be in shock—"

"You keep saying that, and I kept trying to believe you, but she's here at Rodman High. Today. Her name is Nadia."

"Nadia. Do you know her last name?"

"No." He only barely stopped himself from saying *not yet*.

24

Elizabeth took a sip from her bottle of water, obviously taking a moment to consider this. "You're sure she's the same one?"

"Positive. It's her. How else would I have known to be there before the accident?"

"Coincidence."

"I could've believed that before today. Not anymore." Mateo kicked at the ground with the heel of his sneaker. "I'm seeing the future. Just like Mom. Just like all the other Cabots."

"They only *thought* they saw the future—"

"That's what everybody always believed. I always believed that, too. But now I know it's for real."

Which meant the rest of the "Cabot curse" was real as well.

It stretched back through generations of his mother's family—for hundreds of years, since Rhode Island was a colony and the first Cabots settled here. Maybe it went back to England, too; nobody knew for sure. All anybody knew was that, once a generation, a member of the Cabot family began claiming to know the future. That was how it always began. It always ended like—like it had for Mom.

At first she had been merely distracted. Staying up late at night, mumbling over breakfast with dark circles under her eyes. Yet over the next few months, Mateo's mother had . . . disintegrated. There was no other word for it. Her temper had become quicker; she said things that didn't make any sense. Mom stopped bothering with dressing nicely or brushing her hair, and when she came to pick him up from school, he was ashamed of her. He hated himself for that feeling now. She was his mother, and he shouldn't have cared what anyone else thought.

Before long, Mom didn't remember to pick him up from school in the first place. Dad would try to talk to her, tell her to get help, but she'd sob brokenly, telling him there was no help for her and they both knew it. They'd known it from the start.

She'd taken a rowboat out on the ocean. There was no telling for sure whether it was an accident; Mateo thought she'd planned it that way, so maybe he wouldn't know what she'd really done. He knew anyway.

Elizabeth turned toward him, more intent now than she had been before. "Focus. It's important. If you saw this girl— what did you see? Have you seen anyone else you know? Have you seen me?"

"Not you. Not since that dream I had a few weeks ago." It had been a weird one, something about them running through a haunted house; he wasn't even sure that was one of the visions, since it could have been only a regular dream like any other. Mateo leaned his head back against the tree. Weak sunlight filtered through the elm's spindly branches. "I see a lot of things I don't understand. Rainstorms that seem to have been going on for weeks. Hospital rooms—lots of those. Jeremy Prasad trying to have a serious conversation with me, which absolutely can't be the future, right? Because that would never happen. That girl with the gray hair, what's her name, except maybe she was also glowing? That one was probably just a weird dream like any other weird dream. But Nadia—I've definitely seen her, and more than once. In one dream, she's lying at my feet in the aftermath of this blazing fire. In another, I see her being sucked down into—mud, maybe quicksand, I don't even know what it is, but it has her. I see her fighting something—something not human. But in a lot of the dreams, she's in danger. Elizabeth—sometimes I see her dying. And when she dies, I'm with her." He sought Elizabeth's blue eyes. "What if I'm the reason Nadia's going to die?"

She shook her head sadly, and he leaned his head on her shoulder. Neither of them said any more; what else could there be to say? The future was rushing toward him—his future, and his curse. Nothing Elizabeth or anyone else could do would stop it.

But maybe—maybe if he stayed away from Nadia—he might have a chance to save her.

A large crow landed on the grass near them, cocking its head. It flew away in another instant, so Mateo couldn't be sure, but for a moment it had looked as though there were milky cobwebs where its eyes should have been.

Crazy, he told himself. *You're going crazy. It's already begun.*

3

"SO, LET'S SEE—NADIA CALDANI." THE GUIDANCE counselor shuffled through the file quickly. "Transfer from Chicago. For your senior year only?"

"Unless I flunk."

The counselor—whose desk nameplate read FAYE WALSH— gave her a glance that clearly meant, *we can joke around, but not right now.* "I meant, it's unusual for students to move to a new school and new state for their senior year. Work thing for your parents?"

"My dad wanted to quit working for a big law firm. Sick of the crazy hours, the corporate crap, all of that." Was she going to get lectured for using the word *crap*? Apparently not. Ms. Walsh remained unruffled. She was unexpectedly chic for a school counselor, or really for anyone Nadia had yet seen in Captive's Sound: close-cropped hair, big silver jewelry, and a white sheath dress that set off her dark skin.

This was somebody who had a life outside Rodman High; Nadia could respect that. "He took a job here in Captive's Sound—public-interest law. Representing lower-income workers who have disputes with their employers for back pay, workplace injuries, things like that." Dad always claimed to be a do-gooder at heart, but Nadia had been kind of surprised when he stopped talking and did something about it. "And they'll let him work from home sometimes, so he can be around for me and my brother."

"That's a definite plus," Ms. Walsh said. She ran one perfectly manicured nail along the edge of the papers spread out on her desk. "Your dad's the one who signed all the forms and consents."

Oh, great—this was one of those counselors who expected to actually counsel you instead of just handing you college brochures. Nadia decided the quickest way out was to explain it all and move on. "My mother left my father several months ago. Didn't ask for custody or alimony or anything. So she's out of the picture."

"How often do you see her?"

"Never," Nadia said. "I see her never. She doesn't want visitation. She doesn't pick up the phone when we call, and I don't think she so much as listens to our voice mails. I used to email her some; I think my little brother still does. But she never answers. Mom is—gone. Past tense. So Dad's the one handling all the college stuff." Hopefully that would be enough to shut Ms. Walsh up.

Usually it wasn't, though. Other people who had heard

this story, like her former friends back in Chicago, would pile on the questions: *Really? Never? That's so awful. That's so weird. Did she have a nervous breakdown? Did your father hit her when he got mad? Was there, you know, somebody else?* These questions always made Nadia want to scream. She had no answers, none, and Nadia didn't see why she was responsible for explaining why her mother was such a loser.

Ms. Walsh didn't ask any more questions. She only nodded. "You don't have a lot of extracurriculars in your record."

Nadia had more extracurricular interests than nearly anyone, but witchcraft wasn't something you could put down in your college application. Honing her skills in magic, reading the ancient books her mother had given to her—it didn't leave much time for show choir or the debate team. "Guess I'm not a joiner."

"We should try to get you into something this year, though. To show colleges that you're well rounded."

"I'm not even sure I'm going to college. I'd rather look at culinary schools."

"A chef, huh? You should have told me. If I'd known baked goods were involved here, it would've changed everything."

That was almost funny. Nadia didn't let herself smile. "Anyway, culinary schools don't care about extracurriculars. They care about your flaky pie crusts and your béarnaise sauce."

"You could always go to college and then culinary school."

"Oh, yeah, more years of school. Fabulous."

Ms. Walsh cocked her head, studying Nadia closely. "I realize how that sounds. But you strike me as a young woman with a great deal of potential. If you go to culinary school without getting any other education, you're eliminating a lot of possibilities for your future. Never limit yourself like that."

"Is this the part where you tell me there are no limits besides my dreams?" *Gag.*

But Ms. Walsh started to laugh. "Oh, no, Nadia. There are plenty of limits, and trust me, the world will smack you down and teach you where they are. But make the world do that. Don't do it to yourself." She snapped the folder shut. "Enough for today. Check in with me soon, okay? And let me know what I have to do to taste this pie crust for myself."

Bribing school officials with pie: well, there were worse ways to get out of show choir.

The rest of the day passed more or less without incident. Mateo turned out to be in her chemistry class right before lunch. He sat all the way across the room and never even glanced at Nadia—if anything, she thought he was ignoring her—so she only learned two things about him that whole time.

One, his last name was Perez. Two, he apparently had a girlfriend.

Which was disappointing, even if she hadn't intended on going after him. *But not surprising,* she told herself. *Mateo's a gorgeous guy, apparently an athlete—plus he goes around saving people from disasters in his spare time. He could be with anybody he wanted. Of course he's already with someone.*

And Elizabeth Pike looked like the kind of someone he'd pick. She was beautiful—not the shallow kind of beautiful most people could buy with stylish clothes and good makeup, but the kind that shone from her even with a bare face and a plain cotton dress. The same fluorescent classroom lights that made everyone else look like zombies made her perfect skin peachy, and her reddish-brown curls shone as if she were in a shampoo commercial. She and Mateo had a lab table together, and she was superattentive to him—watching him almost every moment, sitting in the desk next to his. It was pretty obvious what was going on.

While Mateo never looked over at her, Elizabeth did once. Her blue eyes met Nadia's steadily. There were no "stay away from my boyfriend" vibes there; she just seemed interested in the new girl. Maybe Mateo told her about the wreck.

And he hadn't said anything to make Elizabeth jealous. So, okay. Nadia figured at least she knew where she stood.

The mystery of how Mateo seemed to know her would have to remain unsolved. *Probably that was something I dreamed up because I was stunned in the wreck,* she decided. *Something like that.*

Her heart told her that wasn't all there was to it—but her heart told her lots of stupid things these days. Things like *Mom will call soon,* or *You'll find another teacher in the Craft somehow.* She didn't need to add *Mateo will leave his gorgeous girlfriend for you* to the list.

Besides, there was that feeling again—that static-electricity feeling that told her magical power was near, very near. . . .

Nadia found herself glancing down at the floor of the chemistry lab, as though she would be able to literally see that force for herself. Which was ridiculous—magic didn't glow green or anything like that, not unless you were a Steadfast, which she wasn't. And yet the force was so near—so vivid——as though it were directly beneath her feet.

Under the floor of the chemistry lab? *Come on. You're so freaked out about not having a teacher any longer that you're . . . making up stuff. Trying to create a crisis where there isn't one, so you'll have something to tell Mom that would make her come back.*

And yet she felt it. Whatever this odd power was simmering beneath the surface—Nadia couldn't ignore it. Couldn't wish it away.

After school, Mateo parked his motorcycle at the bottom of the hill . . . the Hill, always capitalized by people who lived in Captive's Sound. This was where the wealthy and privileged lived, in great houses with iron gates. At the very top of the Hill, shining white as though it were made of marble, was Cabot House.

Yours, someday, his father would always say, like that was a good thing. But Mateo found Cabot House creepy as hell and tried to visit as little as possible.

That suited his grandmother fine, most of the time. Mateo wondered if another guest had crossed the threshold of that house anytime in the past five years. Maybe not since Mom's funeral, and even then, people came more to gawk than to sympathize. Not once had he ever dropped by unannounced.

Today, though—Mateo needed to learn more about what was happening to him, and there was nobody else who could possibly know.

He walked up the Hill. If she didn't hear the motorcycle's engine, then she wouldn't know he was coming, wouldn't have time to tell the butler not to let him in. The neighborhood was weirdly hushed, as if the residents kept noise out along with the poor people. Jaguars and Mercedes gleamed in the driveways, and more than one person had hedges cut into weird shapes. Who paid someone to cut a bush into a cone shape? Mateo figured that even in a world where he had infinite money, he wouldn't see the point.

On the step, in front of the enormous black door, Mateo took a deep breath before swinging the brass knocker heavily, twice, three times. After way too long, the door opened and the butler stood there, blinking. "Young Mr. Perez," he said, his voice creaky. "To what do we owe the pleasure?"

"Just wanted to drop by and see Grandma." Mateo stepped inside without waiting to be told whether or not he could. The butler hesitated, but no doubt he didn't want to offend the so-called Cabot heir.

"She is in the music room," the butler said. "Follow me."

It had to suck to be him, Mateo figured as he walked behind him. Musty suit, Grandma for a boss, almost nothing to actually do; he was less a butler and more somebody paid to stand around being stiff all day until Grandma finally died, when he'd be the one to phone the undertaker. Probably he was hoping to inherit something in the will. Mateo had half a mind to sign Cabot House over to the guy when the time came. That way, he'd never have to live here himself.

The music room was as dry and joyless as the rest of the house. Ceilings stretched up twenty feet, hung with chandeliers gone cloudy, layered with dust. The heavy black woodwork scrolled and curled along every wall and column, like some kind of mold run amok. An enormous grand piano was even dustier than the chandeliers, and a few brass music stands clustered together in one corner, forgotten. No music had been made in this room for a very long time.

Seated by the far window, staring out at her own back garden, was Grandma.

"Your grandson, Mrs. Cabot," the butler said. Without turning her head, she glared in their direction, and the room seemed to become ten degrees colder instantly. Right away the butler backed out, leaving Mateo to face her alone. Maybe Mateo wouldn't give him the house after all.

"Mateo." Her voice was hoarse with disuse. "To what do I owe this visit? It can't be your birthday again already. I don't have a savings bond for you."

"That's not till January," Mateo said. She usually inspected him once a year, on his birthday, and they left it at that. "I, um—I wanted to talk."

"To me?" That seemed to amuse her, for all the wrong

reasons. Though she didn't turn her head, showing him only her perfect white cameo profile, she smiled coolly. "That would be a first. Don't tell me your father's restaurant has failed to be profitable enough to build up a college fund for you."

Mateo balled his fists in the pockets of his letter jacket. Later. He could let his temper out later. "We're doing great." *Great* was overstating it—Captive's Sound never had anything like the kind of summer business it should have had—but they more than paid the bills. Mateo had been helping with the books since last year.

"Then why are you here? The pleasure of my company?" The acid in her voice made it clear she knew precisely how unpleasant she was, and liked it.

This was harder to get out than Mateo had expected. He swallowed hard, shifted his weight from foot to foot, swallowed again. "I—I wanted to talk to you about—about the curse."

Grandma sat up very straight in her chair. "Has it come upon you, then?"

"No!" Mateo lied. She'd throw him out of here if he said anything else. "No way. I don't even believe in it. You know I don't."

Until he'd seen Nadia that stormy night, he hadn't.

"Then why talk about it? If it's just a story, like you pretend."

"Because I want to understand. Because every kid in school acts like I've got AIDS or something." Only Elizabeth and Gage treated him like a human being, and in Gage's case, that was only because he'd moved to Captive's Sound too late to grow up with all the stories about the mad, dangerous Cabots.

"The children have heard the stories from their parents. Who heard them from their parents. It's always the same." She laughed mirthlessly. "They are frightened of the Cabots. Then they get older, decide the stories are only folklore. Tales to scare the foolish. Then the next Cabot goes insane, and they see the truth for themselves. Just as they saw when your mother degenerated so abruptly, and drowned herself in the sea. Just as they saw when your grandfather did this to me."

She turned toward him then, showing him her full face, not only the profile. While the left side of her face remained pale and normal—smooth for a woman of her age, maybe because she never went outside—the right side was a ruin. Deep red slashes ran through her skin like fault lines; crinkles of scar tissue surrounded gouges in flesh that had never healed. Her blind right eye showed milky white, with one twitching red spot of blood that never, ever went away.

"You look pale." Grandma smiled. It was a terrible smile. "I should think you'd be used to it by now. But I'm still not used to it myself, so how can I blame you?"

"What happened?" Mateo tried to plow on. "What made Grandpa do this?" He'd never known his grandfather, who'd been institutionalized long before Mateo was born. But Mom had always said he was a loving dad . . . at least, until that final year.

"The curse is what happened. Scoff all you like. I used to. Franklin Cabot was handsome, wealthy, kind, courteous—all the things a young man should be. So I ignored the stories I'd grown up with, the warnings of my own parents, and married him. Had his child. For the first decade, all was as it should be." Her voice softened for a moment, like she was remembering what it had been like to be happy. "Then the dreams began."

Mateo wished the butler had brought in another chair for him to sit on. "Dreams?"

"He thought they showed him the future. Or so he claimed. I noticed he never mentioned these predictions until *after* they'd come to pass. At first I thought it was no more than a mania—a terror of becoming what his mother had been before him—and that he would get over it. I told him all would be well. But he became more and more fixated on the dreams. Stayed up for days on end in an effort to keep himself from dreaming."

He remembered that—the way Mom would pace for hours at night, and how he'd laid awake, pretending he didn't hear her, that everything was actually okay.

Grandma, oblivious to Mateo's unease, kept talking. "Your grandfather's frenzies became worse and worse. Then came that day when he was up in the attic with the old oil lantern, and I dared to interrupt his ranting and pacing. That was the day he did this and set the rafters on fire." She put two fingers to her ravaged cheek. "They acted faster to save the house than to save my face."

Sleep deprivation could drive anyone crazy, Mateo figured. Maybe that was all it was. "That doesn't prove anything."

"Generation after generation, the Cabots try to convince themselves of that. And generation after generation, they're wrong. I tried to end it with your mother, you know. I told her never to marry or have children, and for so long she obeyed. Then your father moved to town when she was forty—even I thought it might be safe by that point—but here you are." Grandma leaned back in her chair, as though exhausted; this was probably the most talking she'd done in a year. "You can break the cycle, Mateo. You can end this by refusing to father children. Don't adopt, either. It will only be crueler for them when you go mad."

"I won't." The words came out louder than Mateo meant for them to, so loud that her eyes widened. He tried again. "I mean, it's not going to happen to me."

"But it will," she said quite calmly. "You are the only one of your generation. There is no rescuing you." Her bony hand reached out to ring the small silver bell that summoned the butler. "A pity, really. You were such a lovely child."

Then she turned back to her window, and the butler came, and there was nothing for Mateo to do but leave, even more freaked out than he'd been before.

As he stumbled out into the sunlight, which now seemed too strong to his eyes, the countless other questions he had welled up inside: *Why did Mom go on for so long without it happening to her? When did it begin? What were the first signs?*

And why was Nadia mixed up in it all?

But there were no answers, only the sure knowledge that tonight, when he slept, he would dream again. Once the madness began, it never stopped.

Nadia hung around after school as long as possible, speaking to no one, in hopes of slipping back into the chemistry lab. Of course, she didn't have her materials with her, the various powders and bones necessary for more complicated magical work . . . but there had to be some kind of simple spell that would reveal the force underneath more completely.

"Hey."

Startled, Nadia glanced over to see Faye Walsh standing at the far end of the hallway, a patent-leather file folder in one hand. "Oh. Hi."

"Looking for something?" In other words, *Do you have a reason for loitering on school grounds, or do you want to get a move on?*

She'd have to try again another day. "I was just . . . finishing some stuff up. I'm headed out."

Ms. Walsh nodded. "Have a good evening." At least she did Nadia the courtesy of not watching her the whole way out.

So Nadia started home; the walk wasn't too far, and though she'd only traveled it once, she figured this town wasn't big enough to get really lost in. It was kind of weird, though, being surrounded by trees and quiet instead of the bustle of city life. Nadia felt safer in crowds. This kind of setting—with nothing but the sky overhead, nobody much around—she associated with trashy true-crime TV. They always put the abduction reenactments in settings like this, showed the cell phone or purse abandoned on the ground.

Nobody's going to snatch you. Besides, you could protect yourself if they tried. She knew those spells backward and forward, could do them if she was drugged or stunned or anything. That was basic witchcraft self-defense.

Nadia cut across the running track on her way toward the road that led back to her house. There was a little patch of trees back there—probably where the stoners hung out, though right now nobody was around. Somebody's ancient car, a maroon land yacht from the 1970s or something, was parked nearby but empty. No sound broke the eerie stillness that surrounded her.

It's not eerie, Nadia reminded herself. *Outside Chicago, you can actually hear things like the wind through the trees. Or—wait, what is* that?

The rumbling sounded like an earthquake, or at least what Nadia thought an earthquake might sound like. Then the ground began shaking beneath her feet.

Earthquakes in Rhode Island? Nadia grabbed at the trunk of the nearest tree, right at the outskirts of the grove, to steady herself.

But it wasn't an earthquake.

The ground just—sank. In front of her, an entire trench opened up, dirt flying and trees tilting, all of it sloping into the new ditch. Nadia gaped as the lone car tilted onto one side and slid down into the trench.

Then, as soon as it had begun, it ended.

Breathing fast, Nadia didn't let go of her hold on the tree; obviously she couldn't even trust the ground here. What was that? What had just ripped a hole in the earth?

Her mind went first to supernatural explanations. Nadia thought again of that weird feeling she'd had, that something might be lurking underneath the chemistry lab . . . but she didn't sense that same energy here. Nobody else seemed to be around, which meant no witches to cast spells. Nadia didn't know of any magic that could work to rip the earth out from underneath; that didn't mean no such magic existed, but it seemed doubtful. Besides, what could be the point of a spell like that? Would a spellcaster bother trashing people's junker cars?

Nadia sighed, now more annoyed than alarmed. Had that been a sinkhole? An underground tunnel or room collapsing? Great, now she lived in BFE *and* it was collapsing in on itself.

Sucks to be the owner of that car, she thought. All that remained visible was the back bumper. *When they get back, they're gonna be ticked.*

And then she thought—maybe they didn't have to know.

Maybe it was because she'd found herself wishing for something more to be at work, something magical, so she'd have a test for her skills. Maybe it was because Ms. Walsh had made her promise not to limit herself. Maybe she just missed spellcasting.

And a lot of it probably had to do with the fact that this was what she'd wanted to do when her family was in the wreck—but couldn't while Dad and Cole were there, not unless their lives were in true, inescapable danger.

Whatever it was, it made Nadia decide, *I'm going to get that car out of the ditch.*

Moving physical objects was surprisingly difficult; witchcraft had more to do with insight and influence than brute strength in the physical world. Nadia had never lifted anything as heavy as a car before, had never even tried. But she knew the spell.

People would surely come running soon to see what had happened. If she was going to do this, she had to try it now.

Nadia glanced around—no, nobody was around yet. The school grounds were deserted; no traffic zoomed along the streets. So she took hold of the sliver of ivory on her bracelet and put the ingredients together:

> *Terror so great it paralyzes.*
> *Hope so desperate it aches.*
> *Courage so strong it survives.*

Nadia closed her eyes as she brought them fully into her mind—tried to wrap her consciousness around the memory and somehow around the car, too. Weirdly, it seemed to her that she could feel it, the bulk and metal of it balancing against her mind—

Lying in the wreck of the car that night, hearing Cole shriek and not knowing for a moment whether her baby brother was hurt, or how badly.

That first night after Mom left, when the phone rang, and she and Dad looked at each other in wild hope before she dove for it— but it wasn't Mom, only some survey that wanted to know if they were buying a new television this year.

Getting up the morning after that, not crying once, and making breakfast for Dad and Cole like Mom used to, and how they all ate together like it was normal, like it was fine, because they were going to be fine without her somehow.

Nadia heard a solid *thunk* and the creaking of old shock absorbers. Tentatively she opened her eyes to see—the car, still rocking back and forth in its new place next to the ditch. She grinned in triumph.

And then her face fell . . . as someone sat up in the driver's seat.

Verlaine.

Who was now staring at Nadia in a way that made it absolutely clear that, even though she might not have known what just happened, she knew exactly who was responsible.

She'd been caught doing witchcraft.

ONE MINUTE, VERLAINE HAD BEEN HANGING OUT IN HER car, stretched out on the old-fashioned front seat, trying to work a tangle out of her hair and watching videos on her phone. She'd planned to stay late enough that Uncle Gary and Uncle Dave would think she had friends to spend time with; that way they wouldn't worry so much, or at least they'd stop nagging her about being alone so often. The next, the ground had swallowed her car. She'd been too startled even to scream.

And that wasn't even the freakiest thing that had happened to her today—not compared to the part where her car *flew out of the ditch again.*

Or where that new girl was the one responsible.

She dropped her hand right away, like that would make Verlaine not suspect her. Maybe it was kind of a crazy thing to suspect somebody of. But, hello, the car just flew, so welcome to Crazyville, and besides—she *knew*.

The new girl said, "Hey, are you all right?"

Verlaine had to swallow hard before she could speak. "How did you make the car fly?"

That first split second—that was the tell. Yeah, the new girl, Natalie or whatever her name was, she tried hard to cover. But her first reaction had been total guilt and horror, which made her awkward smile afterward that much more unconvincing. "Wow, you must have hit your head."

"I didn't hit my head."

"You must have! Because, you know, cars don't fly. Obviously."

Verlaine tried the door; it still worked, and she stepped out on shaky legs. "Then how did it get out of the ditch? Do you have a forklift or a crane or something hidden around here, Natalie?"

"It's Nadia. And of course I don't. Your car never went into the ditch."

"Um, yes, it definitely did."

"It only tilted to one side!" Nadia looked . . . weird. Like, chugged-a-Butterfinger-Blizzard-in-ninety-seconds-and-got-on-the-Tilt-A-Whirl weird. But she was trying hard to sound reassuring. "Probably it *felt* like you went into the ditch, but you didn't. I'm sure it was crazy scary. Can't believe you didn't scream! I would definitely have thought anybody in the car would have screamed. Definitely. But you—didn't."

"If my car didn't fall in the ditch, why is there dirt in

my hair?" Verlaine grabbed the ends of her nearly waist-length hair; now there were twigs and leaves caught in it, too. "Why are there pine needles all over my backseat? And, oh yeah, why do I *remember* falling in the ditch?"

Nadia went on the offensive then: "Why are you pretend-ing cars can fly? How would I even make that happen?"

Two very good questions. But Verlaine said only, "I know what I know."

"When you go home and think about it, and talk about it with your dads, you'll get it straightened out," Nadia replied, as if she very much wanted to believe it was true. "If you're okay, well, I'm going home."

In silence, Verlaine watched her go. Nadia never once glanced back. Wouldn't anyone normal glance back after something like that?

Verlaine considered whether this Nadia was in fact severely abnormal. She hadn't looked like a weirdo; Nadia was beau-tiful, even a little glamorous, with the kind of designer jeans and funky custom-made jewelry that didn't appear in the halls of Rodman High very often. But making cars levitate out of a ditch? Definitely not average.

Then a moment of doubt crept in . . . levitation, flying, all of it sounded like stuff from comic books or fairy tales. It didn't seem possible for Nadia to do that—and besides, why even assume Nadia was responsible? Yes, she'd been stand-ing right there, and holding her bracelet and her hands in that odd position, but that hardly meant she had powers over gravity. She was also the first person Verlaine had met in a long time, possibly ever, who had even been—well, nice to her. Normal. She didn't know why Nadia treated her nicely, any more than she knew why everybody else treated her like dirt. What she did know was that it had been a relief to talk to someone like it was no big deal, and maybe that politeness meant she ought to give Nadia the benefit of the doubt.

But the car had flown. For sure. Verlaine didn't doubt that for a second.

And there was no reason for Nadia to deny that it had, unless she was the person responsible.

Maybe Verlaine was dreaming it. Making it up.

But she didn't think so.

Something weird was going on. Deeply weird. And Nadia was at the heart of it.

In other words—something interesting was *finally* happening.

Standing there next to her banged-up car, dirt and leaves still in her hair, Verlaine started to grin.

Nadia rushed blindly away, her head whirling. *She knows. Don't be stupid, she doesn't know. Unless she's stupid, she knows. You did magic in front of someone outside the Craft, and then you got too upset to cover your tracks, and now you're exposed.*

But she had to stay calm. Mom had always said that most people exposed to magic ended up explaining it away. They didn't believe in supernatural forces, so experiencing them made them wonder if they were going crazy. Nobody wanted to think they were going crazy. So they made up lies to believe in instead. *I was imagining things. A trick of the light. Just the wind.*

Steadier now, Nadia adjusted her backpack and tried to figure out how far she was from her house—only to realize she had no idea where she was.

She'd thought it would be easy to get back home, and it should have been. But Nadia hadn't been paying attention when she dashed away from Verlaine, had taken a wrong turn, and now was in a totally unfamiliar area. Not surprising, given that almost all of Captive's Sound besides her house, the high school, and the grocery store were unfamiliar at this point. But she'd thought it was too tiny to even get lost in. Apparently not.

Okay, she told herself. *No big deal. This whole town would fit in Lincoln Park. Walk long enough and you'll see a place you recognize.*

Of course, in Chicago she could have hopped on a bus, or hailed a cab. . . .

Never mind. If worse came to worst, she could call her dad to pick her up, but that would only make him feel like he had to worry about her. Dad had enough to deal with. She was supposed to be taking care of him and Cole, not the other way around.

So she wandered through the streets of Captive's Sound, the first time she'd ever explored it on foot.

And as she went, she realized more and more . . . something wasn't right. The weirdness she'd sensed here didn't begin with the magical barrier or end with whatever was beneath the chem lab. No, the entire town was—sick.

The grass had a yellow cast, and lay limply upon the ground. Every tree seemed to be on the verge of death, with straggly branches and chipped, grayish bark. The sky was darker than it should have been in midafternoon, though maybe that was because it looked likely to rain anytime now. Signs of disrepair were everywhere: The pavement was cracked, the curbs overgrown with straggly weeds. The dank mood seemed to have affected the residents, too; only a handful of houses appeared to have been painted in the last twenty years. Most of the homes, however apparently large or elegant, were chipped and faded. Nobody cared about how it looked. Nobody cared about Captive's Sound.

Nadia remembered the magical barrier at the edge of town. She looked again at the battered, depressed town that surrounded her.

From the crash, she'd known something powerful was in this town. But what if that powerful force was . . . draining Captive's Sound? Dragging it down?

In her mind flashed the image of the ground caving in beneath Verlaine's car, and she shuddered.

A motorcycle's engine growled along behind her, slowed as it drew closer, and then came to a stop beside her. Nadia's eyes widened as the driver removed his helmet and she saw Mateo.

"Hey," he said. "You look—lost, I guess."

"That obvious, huh?"

Given everything she was attempting to deal with, it should have taken more than a hot guy to make her smile. Yet Nadia knew she'd started smiling.

Mateo didn't appear to be equally thrilled to see her; in fact, he couldn't quite meet her eyes, like he was trying to avoid Nadia's gaze. But he'd stopped for her, hadn't he? "Okay, tell me where you live. I could—I can give you a ride. And then you'll know how to get back home after that."

Nadia tucked a lock of her long hair behind one ear. "So, do you do this rescue thing full-time?"

That made him grin—but only for a moment, because he quickly glanced away again. "I was going to drop by and see Elizabeth." Mateo pointed at a house farther down the street, off by itself and even more gray and lonely than the rest. "But I've got a minute."

Of course he was going to see his girlfriend. Because on top of being hot and courageous, Mateo was also an awesome boyfriend. Of *course*.

Still, it was stupid to pass up a lift home, right?

"You're on," Nadia said. "I live on Felicity Street—right by the park. And thanks."

"No problem. Hop on." Mateo paused, then held out his black helmet. "You should wear this."

"Thanks." Nadia slid the heavy thing onto her head, wondering if it made her look dorky—but there was no way she'd turn down an offer that chivalrous. Then she slipped one leg over the bike and settled into the seat right behind

Mateo. Her legs were pressed against his legs, her belly against his back.

"Hang on," he said just before he gunned the engine back to life, and Nadia brought her hands to his waist, tangling her fingers in the belt loops of his jeans. Then they were rolling—and to her, it felt like flying. Mateo's deep brown hair ruffled in the breeze, and Nadia wished she lived farther away so the ride could last longer.

Much farther away. Say, maybe, California.

Stop it, she told herself, even as they rounded a corner and she slid her arms around his waist to hold on tighter. *He's not available.* Nor was he likely to be, seeing as how he was devoted to his gorgeous girlfriend.

But at least she could enjoy the ride.

Mateo found her house disappointingly fast, bringing his motorcycle to a stop right in front. "You guys took this place, huh?" he said as Nadia tugged the helmet off and hoped she didn't have crazy hat hair. "I've always liked it."

"Yeah, it's great. Kind of old and creaky, but that makes it cozy." Their house was a little run-down, too, but it looked more comfortable than ratty, unlike the rest of Captive's Sound. Then again, other people's houses probably looked like that to them.

Her father appeared at the front door, and while he didn't do anything as embarrassing as walking out and demanding an introduction, he did wave.

"Gotta go," she said in a hurry. "Thanks for the rescue. Again."

"You'll be able to find your way from now on." Something about the way Mateo said that sounded so weirdly final—but he simply lifted one hand in a farewell before putting the helmet back on and driving off.

Dad came up beside her as she watched him go. "Honey, I'm not sure about you riding a motorcycle."

"I had on a helmet," Nadia protested. "We weren't going fast."

He nodded in a way that told her he was willing to let it go . . . this time. "So, I see you've already made a friend. A *guy* friend." Dad smirked, like this was teasing her instead of checking the guy out; really, it was both.

"That's Mateo. From the night of the wreck."

"He goes to your school?" Dad peered after him. "You should've asked Mateo in, honey; I'd have liked to thank him. That was amazing, what he did that night."

"He was in a hurry," Nadia said, walking toward the door with him. "I just caught a ride."

"Well, if that's the kind of boy you're going to be bringing home, I approve."

"*Dad.* Mateo's—it's not like that. He has a girlfriend already." For the first time, Nadia realized her father was wearing an apron. "And hey, I told you I'd be home in time to make dinner."

"I keep telling you, I'm capable of making dinner."

Nadia frowned. "Then why do I smell smoke?"

Her father made a face. "Let's say that maybe turkey tetrazzini was . . . overly ambitious."

Despite everything weighing on her mind, Nadia had to laugh. "Come on. Let's see if we can save it."

Nadia.

Standing alongside the road, her hair fluttering in the breeze—so black it was nearly blue, shining even in the dim light. Behind him on the bike, her tiny frame snug against his and so warm—

Mateo groaned as he flopped back onto the bed. He'd stayed up for hours past the point when his father would think he was asleep—late enough that the alarm tomorrow was going to seriously hurt—but maybe this way he wouldn't dream.

And yet when he spent those hours thinking about Nadia, it was just another kind of torture.

He'd known from his dreams that she was beautiful, with the kind of quiet beauty that most people wouldn't see right away. He'd known she would have enormous dark eyes and a heart-shaped face. Some of the dreams had even told him what the heavy silk of her hair would feel like in his hands.

So many of them had showed him how she might die.

Why did I stop for her today? The temptation had come over him, even though Mateo knew better. None of the dreams showed her dying on a motorcycle, so that was probably safe, he'd decided. Everything had turned out fine. But when would he make one excuse too many to be near her, and put her in danger?

If the dreams showed him there when she died, and he refused to be anywhere near her, then Nadia would be okay. At least, none of those dreams could come true—not if he didn't let them.

Mateo tugged his blanket over his head, closed his eyes, and willed himself not to think about her any longer. He'd done that at least a dozen times that night.

This time, though, he was finally exhausted enough for it to work. He fell asleep.

And dreamed.

Their surroundings were so murky he could barely make her out amid the green-gray swirls. Nadia drifted above him, her black hair streaming out all around. In that first instant, Mateo could only think how amazing she looked—like some kind of angel descending to Earth—until he saw the chains.

Were they chains? Whatever they were they were heavy, and dark, and wrapped around her ankles. Nadia was reaching upward, her fingertips straining toward something overhead and out of sight, but she couldn't escape.

Nadia's eyes met his, a silent plea for him to help her, to save her. Mateo grabbed the chains, but they were loose, slippery, and they fell from his fingers—

He awoke with a start, panting, desperate for air. His head buzzed and his ears rang; Mateo realized he'd been holding his breath in his sleep.

The next day, in chemistry, Nadia was determined to ignore Mateo.

Well, not *ignore*. It would be rude to ignore a classmate who had given you a ride home, not to mention rescued your whole family a week and a half ago. But she was going to be friendly. A *just-friends* kind of friendly. That was how you treated a guy who had a girlfriend.

Yet she knew the minute he walked in. Her head lifted from her lab table at that moment, her eyes drawn to Mateo as if by some irresistible force. Whatever it was, he felt it, too; their gazes met, and in that first second, she couldn't even breathe.

Nadia broke the glance, though, and Mateo went quickly to his lab table, where Elizabeth was waiting for him.

She pushed aside her disappointment and tried to focus . . . not on chemistry, but on the magical power she felt within this room. Beneath it.

Something is buried here, Nadia thought. *Buried deep under the foundation of the school—so there's no chance I can find out what it is.*

Whatever it was, its power was almost eerie. Not unlike the weird barrier they had collided with on the edge of town. Magic, but twisted and gnarled from its rightful shape. This wasn't a power Nadia or any other witch could call upon. It was a power that . . . drained. Subtracted. Withered. A power that wanted something it didn't have.

She thought again of the gray skies and dead trees in Captive's Sound. Was this why? Because the town was near—this, whatever it was?

And, of course, if something was buried, someone had

done the burying. At one point, there had been witches in Captive's Sound. Surely they couldn't be here any longer, but back in the town's history, there had to have been powerful witches at work. A coven, even.

Nadia sat up straighter in her seat, suddenly energized. *There's going to be a whole history of magic here. I don't have any idea how to find it yet, but there has to be a way, and—it's something I could learn, right? Something I can teach* myself.

It was the first time since Mom's departure that Nadia had thought about striking out on her own. Always, before, the task of training herself in the final, most complex stages of witchcraft had seemed impossible. She *still* thought it was impossible. And yet—even if she couldn't take herself all the way, maybe she could at least take herself further.

Yes, there had to have been many witches here, and gifted ones, to control, capture, and bury something this powerfully dark. . . .

Witches, or a Sorceress.

A chill swept through Nadia. Then she told herself she was being stupid. There had only been a handful of Sorceresses in the whole history of witchcraft, which went back to the dawn of civilization at Uruk. A Sorceress broke the One Absolute Law. She was outcast, soulless, beyond what anyone could call "wicked" or "evil"—so complete was her dedication to destruction.

A Sorceress had sworn allegiance to the One Beneath.

Once again, Nadia shivered.

"Cold?" murmured a tall, good-looking guy who sat near

57

her. Before she could answer, he smirked. "Nice thin T-shirt shows that off. I like it."

Gross. "Die in a fire," Nadia muttered.

She hugged herself and tried, belatedly, to pay attention to her chemistry teacher, even to the sniggering jerk next to her, to anything at all besides the idea of a Sorceress and the horrible writhing power lurking underneath her feet.

5

VERLAINE FLATTENED HERSELF AGAINST THE WALL, where she was hidden by the lockers. Then she wondered if she looked like an insane person.

Well, it wasn't like people at this school could hate her any more even if she were crazy. Everybody knew Mateo Perez was basically a big old ticking time bomb of crazy, but nobody went out of their way to be unkind to *him*.

Maybe she actually *was* nuts—but there was only one way to find out.

Peering out from behind the lockers, Verlaine could again see Nadia Caldani, who was putting away her books. She looked like any other girl in school, getting ready to go home like everybody else, and about the only thing that stood out was her really great hair. Verlaine glanced down at her own prematurely gray locks and sighed.

Was she really going to challenge Nadia about this? Was

she willing to stand up and say she believed something that bizarre?

My car flew, Verlaine thought, and decided to trust her gut.

Just as she darted forward into the crush of people in the hallway, Nadia lifted her head and saw her. As soon as she did, she turned away from Verlaine, obviously eager to escape, but Verlaine quickened her steps to catch up.

Then Jeremy Prasad appeared. Verlaine's heart did that thing it did whenever she saw him—that stealthy thing that felt like turning over and constricting at the same time. It wasn't that she liked the guy; Jeremy's personality defied any reaction but total contempt. But oh, God, that face—those shoulders—

"So you're the new girl," he said to Nadia, who was now glancing back and forth between Verlaine and Jeremy like she was trapped. "Need someone to show you around? We ought to be friends, you know. The benefits—we can add those later."

Sensing her opportunity, Verlaine pounced. "Sorry, Jeremy. Nadia and I are headed out." She folded her arm possessively in Nadia's, and Nadia was either too surprised to resist or too desperate to get away from the oily sheen of Jeremy Prasad.

"Hanging with the freaks already?" Jeremy said to Nadia. He shrugged, and damn it, the movement of his muscles showed through every inch of the tee he was wearing. "Have it your way."

As he wandered off, Nadia muttered, "Who is that loser?"

"Jeremy Prasad? He's pretty much the king of the hill around here, and he knows it. As rich as his family is, and with a face like that, I guess he figures he can pick up any girl he wants, no matter how disgusting he is." Verlaine hated that she'd said anything nice about him. "It's not like I *like* him or anything. I just wish—sometimes—it were possible to pour somebody else's soul inside that body. You know?"

"It would have to be an improvement." Then Nadia tensed, and Verlaine knew she was about to try to dodge her again. Maybe it would be good to get her off her guard.

"How do you like the Piranha?"

"The Piranha—oh, is that what people call Mrs. Purdhy? I can kind of see it. The thing with the teeth—" Nadia made a face instantly recognizable as Mrs. Purdhy's clenched jaw. She seemed to have decided that talking about anything but what happened yesterday might be a good idea . . . as if Verlaine would just forget about it. "Hey, cool dress."

"Oh . . . thanks. Glad you like it," Verlaine said, genuinely surprised. Most people in Captive's Sound didn't understand vintage style, though of course that meant Verlaine got to comb through the local thrift stores and secondhand shops without having to compete for their treasures. Today she was wearing a mod dress from the 1960s with big black-and-white squares, exactly the kind of thing most people here made fun of. Verlaine had told herself she didn't care about the ridicule anymore, but all the same, it was nice to have someone actually get it.

Obviously Nadia thought the danger was past, because

she had begun to relax. "The shoes are kind of different, though."

"I stick to Converse." Today's pair was black. "Real period shoes are expensive, and they never turn up in sizes big enough for my boat feet. Besides, if I wore heels, I would go from being the third tallest person at this school to the actual tallest, and yes, I'm including everyone on the men's basketball team." They were out on the quad now, away from some of the other students; Verlaine decided it was about time to make her move. "So, yesterday, what was that?"

Nadia whirled toward her, too caught off guard to hide her shock. She tried to recover, though: "What are you talking about?"

"Last night, I narrowed it down to three possibilities." Verlaine counted them off on her fingers. "One, you have some kind of superpower, but you're trying to hide it because you have a secret identity; maybe there's a Justice League scenario, et cetera. Two, this is more supernatural or occult, like witchcraft, maybe. Three, you're an alien. I know that's a long shot, but then all of these seem like long shots even though they're the only possible explanations. So, can't exclude aliens. If you are from another planet, I want to say, welcome to Earth, and if you have a starship or a transporter beam or whatever, as long as I can still call my dads once in a while, I'm totally ready to ditch this planet and try it somewhere else."

After a long moment when they stared at each other and Verlaine's heart thumped crazily in her chest, Nadia breathed out in a sigh. "Not here, okay?"

"Okay." Wait. Did that mean—she was right? This really was something out of the ordinary? The surreal was becoming real, at last? *Yes.* It was all Verlaine could do not to jump in the air and cheer.

Glancing around nervously, Nadia said, "Is there someplace we can talk?"

"Not at school. Let me think—someplace quiet—"

"No. Someplace loud." Nadia seemed very sure about this. "People overhear you in quiet places. Nobody overhears when it's loud. Mom—my mother would talk about it in the mall, or at Cubs games, places like that."

Her mother was a—whatever she was—too? This was getting better and better. And for once, Verlaine was absolutely sure she knew the right thing to suggest. "If you want loud, we should go to La Catrina."

La Catrina turned out to be the only Mexican restaurant in town, or at least the busiest. Even though Nadia had yet to taste the food, she could understand why everybody came here; this was pretty much the first cheerful public place she'd seen in Captive's Sound. It was warm and welcoming, with pressed-tin panels on the ceiling, dark gold walls, and tons of woodwork stained a deep red. Brilliantly painted carvings hung on the walls—all of them skeletons, though they were the happy kind, grinning merrily, wearing sombreros or colorful dresses, and apparently having the time of their afterlives.

Verlaine leaned over the table, obviously starting to digest everything Nadia had told her. "So, you don't look like a witch." She glanced around, but the din of laughter, conversation, and jukebox music made it obvious they wouldn't be overheard. "Either the haglike, warty, green variety or the mystical pagan sexpot variety."

"Uh, thanks, I guess."

"You're not going to try to recruit me, are you? Is this one of those things where you learn about the witchcraft and then, that's it, you're trapped in it for life?"

"No. I can tell you about it, and that's fine. But you really shouldn't tell anyone else." There were spells Nadia could use to make sure Verlaine didn't tell anyone—spells of silencing or forgetting—but they were drastic measures. Messing with another person's head that way was nasty work, something you only did if you had no other choice.

But Verlaine said only, "Who could I possibly tell? Nobody would ever believe me." Then she frowned. "Wait. You can teach me some spells, right? Without me being sworn to witchcraft for eternity or anything. I really want to stress that last part."

"It's too late for me to teach you," Nadia said.

"You mean—too late today, or what?"

"I mean, too late ever." Nadia made the words as gentle as she could. What would it be like, to discover that witchcraft was real but you were left out? "You have to start learning in childhood. The earlier the better, my mom always said. And not every girl can be a witch. If witchcraft doesn't run in your family, you probably don't have the blood for it. And even if you did, by now, you would have lost the potential."

"Oh." Verlaine frowned. "That leaves you with the power, then, doesn't it?"

"Pretty much." It was the truth; why should she apologize for it?

"How do I know you won't turn me into a newt or something?"

"Honestly, where are you getting this? Listen. Most of what's in pop culture about witchcraft is crap. What I practice doesn't have anything to do with being Wiccan, either; that's a religion of its own. I think the Craft I practice might have been linked to it way back when, but they parted paths a long time ago. And in neither of those is there any turning people into newts."

Verlaine didn't seem comforted in the slightest. "I wasn't specifically afraid of newthood. What I mean is, it's kind of freaky to know somebody has power over you that you can't understand."

Nadia shrugged. "Yeah. It throws a lot of people off. Which is exactly why we try to keep it secret. But you wanted to know. And now you do."

After an awkward pause, Verlaine said, "Okay, no newts. But what kind of stuff can you do?"

Nadia felt weird—beyond weird—talking about this with someone who wasn't a witch herself. Mom was the only witch she'd ever known well; Grandma had been in the Craft herself, of course, and had taught Mom, but she'd died when Nadia was eight and had learned only the basics.

Not every witch was so isolated—some cities and even small towns had active communities—but Mom had stuck to her one secret coven in Chicago. Nadia had never been introduced to them, and had not expected to be; usually you only met witches outside of your family once you were grown and fully possessed of your power. And while it wasn't forbidden to reveal witchcraft to a woman who didn't practice, it was something you were supposed to do as little as possible . . . which Nadia now understood completely.

Secrecy is important, Mom always said. *Secrecy is what protects us from the ignorant and the hateful. Secrecy is the first and most precious rule.*

Well, Mom always said she loved us forever, Nadia thought savagely. *So who cares about her rules?*

"The only real limit on what a witch can do is how much she's learned so far," Nadia said. "Well, that and the First Laws, of course."

"What are the laws?" Verlaine asked. But that was the moment the waiter strolled up to their table.

"Hello there and welcome to . . ." Mateo's voice trailed off as he recognized them; his eyes widened as they met Nadia's. But he barely paused in his spiel. "La Catrina."

"You work here?" Nadia asked, then felt stupid. He wasn't walking up to their table in a black apron because he was trying to set a fashion trend.

"This is my dad's restaurant. I help out after school, on weekends—that kind of thing." Mateo took out his order pad and stared down at it as if he was unwilling to meet her eyes one moment longer. "What can I get for you guys?"

"Not dinner, sorry. Maybe some salsa and chips, though," Verlaine said cheerfully. "Oh, how about two virgin margaritas? What do you think, Nadia?"

"Sure." Nadia never stopped looking at Mateo; he never looked back at her.

"Got it," Mateo said, scribbling it down. "Have that right out to you."

As he walked away, Nadia said, "Did it seem like Mateo was, I don't know—trying to ignore me?"

"He always ignores me. Which makes him one of the nice guys. I mean, at least he's never mean to me." Verlaine stopped. "Wait. How do you know Mateo? I thought you just moved to town."

"I don't know him, really. But I met him when—when he pulled me out of a car accident."

"*What?*"

Nadia retold the whole story while Verlaine stared, open-mouthed. Only when it was all over did Verlaine manage to say, "That is *wild*."

"I wish I knew why he acted like he knew me that night," Nadia said. "Or why he acts like he wishes he didn't know me now."

"Well, probably because he's crazy."

With a shrug, Nadia said, "Like all guys are crazy?" The ones she liked never seemed to be the ones who liked her.

"No, I mean, *crazy* crazy." Verlaine glanced over her shoulder to check for Mateo. "I wouldn't want to hurt his feelings.

Like I said, he's always been nice enough to leave me alone. But his mother was a Cabot, and everybody knows all the Cabots eventually lose their minds. It's the family curse."

Nadia didn't hear those words; she felt them. Literally felt them as a sudden sickening drop in her belly, like she was riding a roller coaster that had started to plunge downward. "What did you say?"

"They all go insane. Apparently it's hereditary or something. They've lived in this town since the beginning of time—well, the 1600s. And they've been going crazy ever since. I feel bad for him, but it's not like anything can change your genes." Verlaine glanced toward the bar, where Mateo was grabbing a tray of sodas for another table. "Why does it always happen to the hot ones?"

"The family curse," Nadia repeated. Maybe it was only a saying. Maybe it was the small-town version of an urban legend. For Mateo's sake, she hoped so.

Verlaine clearly was ready to get back to the subject. "So, come on. Tell me the laws of witchcraft."

The First Laws were so familiar to Nadia—so often repeated to her, so much a part of her—that the words seemed to flow out almost without her thinking about it. "The most unbreakable one is that you must never be sworn to the One Beneath and do his bidding. Besides that—you must not reveal the Craft to anyone who would betray it. You must never speak of witchcraft to any man. You must never attempt to divine your own fate. You must never bear a child to the son of another witch. You must never command the will of another. You must never suffer a demon to walk among mortals." Her eyes sought Mateo as she spoke the last remaining law:

"You must never cast a curse."

"Switch tables with me, will you, Melanie? Trade you eight for eighteen."

Melanie Sweeney, the senior waitress at La Catrina, glanced past him and frowned. "Eighteen's just two kids. Girls. Cute ones, too. So why do you want to wait on those six jerks at eight? Wait, don't tell me. You asked one of the girls out; she shot you down."

"Love hurts," Mateo said, which was enough like a yes without being a lie.

"No worries, buddy. I got 'em." Melanie grinned. "But you better take those guys their empanadas PDQ."

As he hurried to table eight, Mateo's mind remained focused on one thing alone—Nadia. If his dreams were really telling him the future—and because of the car crash, they had to be at least partly true, didn't they?—then the danger surrounding Nadia was very real. And whatever it was, Mateo himself was a part of it.

But his plan—"Stay Away From Nadia for Her Own Good"—was clearly useless. What had he been thinking? This was *Captive's Sound*, a town the size of a flash drive. He ran into almost everyone in town at least once a week; with Nadia in his chemistry class, he was guaranteed to see her almost every day. Now that she turned out to like Mexican food—forget it. Game over.

So what the hell was he going to do?

Would Nadia believe him if he tried to explain? Most people wouldn't, even if they hadn't grown up in Captive's Sound thinking he was guaranteed to turn out insane. And even if she believed, did he know enough to protect her? If he frightened Nadia, convinced her that she should fear for her life, then failed to prevent any of his nightmares from coming to pass—that would be worse than anything else he could do.

No, he decided. *That's not the worst thing I could do. The worst thing I could do is nothing.*

There have to be ways I could look out for her without talking to her about the visions. I can . . . watch from afar. Guard her as best I can without putting her in danger.

But is that even possible?

Right as he was trying to work it all out, table eight decided they each had a complicated special order—no refried beans here, extra guacamole there, so on and so forth—and Mateo was too busy to do anything but hurry back and forth between his tables and the kitchen for the next half hour. By the time he was able to look back at Nadia's table again, she was gone, and Melanie was wiping it down to get it ready for the next customers.

Okay, fine. She was home. That had to be safe, right? Maybe not, though. He hadn't taken a close enough look before to see whether it resembled the setting of any of his dreams. Why hadn't he done that?

"Hey, Mateo." Melanie held up a cell phone. "One of them left this. You too brokenhearted to take it to her at school tomorrow?"

"I can handle it," Mateo said.

Maybe he'd get his chance to look out for Nadia after all.

Nadia had never realized there could be so many questions about witchcraft; she didn't remember asking this many even when she was a little kid. Then again, she'd grown up in the constant company of her mother's powers, naturally understanding so much of it that there was no need to ask.

Verlaine, on the other hand, felt the need to ask everything.

"Can you fly?" she said as she and Nadia walked along the main strip of Captive's Sound, Nadia trying her best to be sure she knew her way home. "I don't mean on a broomstick, Gryffindor-style. That would be stupid. Unless you do use broomsticks."

"No broomsticks," Nadia said. "I can't fly. There are spells—really advanced spells—they could let you, I don't know, defy the laws of physics for a while. Sort of souped-up versions of what I did to your car. But I'm not that skilled yet. Not even close."

"So your mom was a witch?"

"Yeah. She taught me."

"Will she be mad that you told me?"

"Mom's not in our lives anymore. She left my dad back in the spring, and she pretty much washed her hands of me and Cole then, too." The facts were harsh enough, but somehow

71

they sounded even worse spoken aloud like that.

Verlaine bit her lip, less confrontational than she'd been at any other point during this endless interrogation. "I'm sorry. That sucks. I mean, I don't even remember my mom and dad—but it would be worse to remember them and then lose them. At least, I think so."

So, actually, I'm not the only person who's had it bad. Nadia felt like a jerk. "It sucks either way. But it's okay. We're still here, right?"

"Right."

"And here is—three blocks from my house, if I turn left at this corner?"

"You've got it! Congrats. You've learned your way around all ten square feet of Captive's Sound. Once you get all the gossip down, nobody will be able to tell you from the native population."

The one piece of gossip she'd learned—about Mateo Perez—echoed in Nadia's mind again. *The family curse.*

A cool breeze stirred past them, tangling Verlaine's silvery hair, which already stood out in the early-evening gloom. After spending most of her life in Chicago, Nadia had thought she was pretty much winter-proofed—but cold came early here, and it cut to the bone. Slowly she said, "Has the town always been like this?"

"Like what?"

"Not right." Then Nadia said what she really thought: "Dead inside."

Verlaine stopped. For a long moment they stood there

beneath one of the streetlamps, the first fall leaves scudding across the cracked sidewalks. "I always thought—I figured it was just because I hate it here. The same way a lot of people want out of their hometowns, you know? When I looked around and only saw the bad side of it, I thought it was, like, me being in a mood. But it's not, is it?"

"No. It's not."

"Then what is it?"

"I'm not sure. But I think it has to do with whatever's buried beneath the chemistry lab." As Verlaine's eyes widened, Nadia said, "I have no idea. All I know is, it's dark and it's strange and some other witch has to have buried it there a long time ago. It's dark enough to poison this town. To hollow it out."

Verlaine took that in for a few moments. "Is it—dangerous? I mean, beyond sucking the life out of Captive's Sound, assuming it had any life to begin with." Her ghostly skin somehow became even paler. "Can it get *worse*? I would've thought that was impossible, but—you know, the sinkholes—"

"I don't know that those are related," Nadia said. Then again, she didn't know that they weren't. Was it possible that she'd arrived just as things took a turn for the worse? As the thing buried beneath Captive's Sound finally . . . got out?

"Is there a spell we can do to find out?" Verlaine drummed her fingers against her notebook, nervous energy crackling from her almost like static electricity.

Slowly, Nadia answered, "We could try to tell the future."

"You can tell the future? *Awesome*. Do I ever—wait. No. You can't tell the future. That was one of the First Laws, wasn't it? That you're not supposed to do that."

"You have a good memory. Yes, that's one of the laws. But there are a few ways around it." Deep in thought, Nadia tried to remember what Mom had said about when you could work with that rule, bend it without breaking it entirely. "If I tried to tell my own future, or yours, it would break that law. Also, it would seriously mess us up, mentally, but— never mind. What we could do is tell the *town's* future. See what's happening to Captive's Sound. That's distant enough from us that it's allowed, and that would be enough to tell us whether—whether something serious has begun, or whether the way things are is permanent. Not changing."

"Probably the latter," Verlaine said, "with my luck. Nothing ever changes around here."

There were worse things than not changing, Nadia thought. "I should probably do this spell alone."

Verlaine's dark, silvery eyebrows knitted together as she scowled. "Oh, come on. I know about magic, remember? So why can't I watch? I want to see! Something besides flying cars, anyway, even though that was excellent."

"You shouldn't watch because it's dangerous."

To Nadia's astonishment, Verlaine grinned. "Do you have any idea how long I've waited for something interesting to happen to me? I don't care if it's dangerous. I don't care what it is. Bring it."

6

THE CROW SWOOPED OVER CAPTIVE'S SOUND, WINGS outspread. His cobweb eyes saw nothing and everything.

They saw two girls walking together along the street, one's hair black and one's nearly white, one short and one tall, yet not opposites. Not apart as they should be.

They saw the girls go toward a large house the color of the sky at dawn in early spring. The house glowed from within with a force that flickered like candlelight but had the potential to become a flame.

Beyond anything else they saw the dark ripples through the earth, tracing rings beneath every street, every house, every human being in Captive's Sound. The energy leaped and sparked as it found the deep lines of power that underlay this town, but those lines couldn't stop the web from being spun. They only made it stronger.

Something else looked through the crow's stolen eyes and

recorded it all. The crow flew on, unknowing, enslaved, and blind.

"Can I go now?" Mateo asked as he loaded the final pitchers into the dishwasher.

"You haven't touched the Bissell, and I don't see any chopped peppers in this fridge." Dad crossed his arms. "What's up with you? You've been trying to escape for twenty minutes, and you know your shift isn't up for another fifteen. Not like you to ditch the job."

That was the problem with having your father for a boss; not only was he judging you as harshly as any other boss would, but he also wanted to psychoanalyze you in the bargain.

And Dad was the absolute last person he could talk to about any of this stuff.

At least he had a reason for wanting out that his father would understand. "One of the customers left her cell phone here. A girl I know from school. I wanted to run it by her house."

"Ahhh. There's a lady in the case. Might have known."

"*Dad*. She really left her phone. See?" Mateo held it up as evidence.

"That's why we have a lost-and-found box." But his father seemed more amused than anything else. "About time a girl got your special attention."

Mateo went for the knife and the peppers. The quicker he finished up his side work, the quicker he could escape both work and the interrogation.

"Here I thought you were going to play the field forever," Dad said as he continued stirring the *sopa Azteca*. "Not that a handsome young fellow like you shouldn't play, hmm? But there's more to life than that."

Girls would "play," sure. Mateo had learned that early. They were attracted to him, flirted with him. At a party, sometimes they would hook up with him, making out just long enough for Mateo to start to hope things were finally changing. But that was it. Girls in Captive's Sound thought he was *dangerous*; kissing him, letting him touch them, was something they did only for a thrill. Nobody was foolhardy enough to stay with him—to let herself care. After a beach bonfire early in the summer, when he'd realized this one girl had gotten with him only because her friends dared her to, Mateo hadn't bothered trying again.

"I spent my time as a bachelor," Dad said.

Oh, great. Mateo hoped he wouldn't vomit on the peppers.

But Dad wasn't going to launch into stories about his swinging single days; it was worse than that. "From the week I moved to Captive's Sound—the day I met your mother—it all changed. So beautiful. So lonely. Nobody in this damned town ever gave her a chance." Bitterness had crept into his father's voice; it usually did, when they talked about Mom. "Crazy, they called her. They *drove* her crazy with their stupid stories about a curse. That's what did her in, Mateo. As far as I'm concerned, every gossip in this town has her blood on their hands."

This was the point in the speech where Mateo usually

mouthed the final words along with Dad's voice: *blood on their hands.*

Today, though—with his own knowledge of the dreams Mom had seen, too, with his grandmother's scarred face still fresh in his memory—that blood seemed way too real.

Nadia had hoped she and Verlaine could slip up to the attic without being noticed, but there was a downside to having her father working from home.

"Well, who have we here?" He smiled as he rose from his desk; already stacks of papers were spread around him like he was building a nest. Within a week, the chaos would be total.

"Verlaine Laughton," Verlaine said. She didn't seem to mind meeting Nadia's father; the weird defensive edge she had most of the time had vanished. "Nadia and I go to school together. Thanks for having me over. This house is amazing. Is it, like, a hundred years old?"

"A hundred and fifteen, according to the realtor. Did you say your name was—"

"Verlaine." Obviously she was used to repeating it. "One of my grandmothers was named Vera, the other one was named Elaine, so my parents put them together." Her cheery expression clouded. "I like to think they'd have chosen something else if they'd known Verlaine was also a famous poet who died of syphilis back in the day. At least, I hope they would've."

"At least it's original." Dad laughed, though he was clearly distracted; Nadia could tell she'd have to remind him of Verlaine's name again.

"We'll be upstairs, okay, Dad?" Nadia hurried Verlaine out as smoothly as she could. For his part, Dad settled back into work; when he got his head into legal questions, he usually didn't resurface for hours. Cole, meanwhile, had only looked away from the Disney Channel long enough to wave.

Verlaine followed her up to the attic, obviously wary, but when she got there, her reaction was almost deflated. "I thought this would be all, you know, spooky and mysterious."

"Sorry to disappoint you." Nadia stowed her school stuff in a corner. Already she'd set up a couple of card tables; someday soon, around the end of the month, she'd go Dumpster diving and see if she couldn't find something sturdier to replace them with. Her various ingredients were stored in test tubes and flasks she'd ordered from medical-supply catalogs, along with a few apothecary jars that had been in her family for a long time, left behind by Mom when she went, probably by accident. Her Book of Shadows might get to look mystical in time—as they gained power, apparently, they could change appearance and practically take on lives of their own—but right now it looked like an ordinary leather-bound journal propped on a windowsill.

But it wasn't all science. She had some oversize pillows to sit on, the protective blue ceiling like a cloudless sky overhead, and a secret stash of chocolate. Some materials and ingredients had the power to conduct and focus magic, and weirdly, wonderfully, chocolate was one of the best.

As she tossed Verlaine one of the mini candy bars, Nadia said, "So, you need to really listen to this, okay? Think long and hard before you say you want to stay. It's serious."

"What's serious?" Verlaine said around a mouthful of chocolate.

"If you're here when I cast a prophetic spell—which I'm going to admit right now I've never done before—there's a chance you'll do more than watch me. There's a chance the magic will . . . change you. Change us. It could make you my Steadfast."

Verlaine scooted closer. "What's a Steadfast? It sounds important."

"It is." Nadia had to go through it all, so there would at least be some chance Verlaine knew what she was getting into. "A Steadfast is a woman who isn't a witch herself, but who has the ability to enhance a witch's powers through her presence. A Steadfast doesn't have magic of her own, but she amplifies everyone else's magic. By that, I really mean everyone—any witch who's near the Steadfast, whether they know about her or not—but the effect is infinitely more powerful for the witch she's bound to."

"Whoa." Verlaine's face lit up, which told Nadia she wasn't explaining this well enough. "That's fantastic. Beyond fantastic. Do you have, like, dozens of Steadfasts?"

"What? No. Never. You can only have one, and it's a serious thing. A sacred thing. A witch and a Steadfast are truly bound together in the most profound way. Lots of times, it's a witch's sister who doesn't have the gift, or a daughter.

Someone who's always going to be there, no matter what."

This was crazy, taking a chance like this with someone she'd known only a couple of days. Of course, it wasn't much of a chance. Some witches cast prophetic spells dozens of times with their closest friends, hoping to be bound as Steadfasts, without it ever occurring.

But Mom had always said, *You never know. When you open yourself to prophetic magic, you open yourself to the primal forces of the universe. It's unpredictable, and it's dangerous, and your soul reaches out, like casting anchor in a stormy harbor—*

Nadia didn't need an anchor, though. She didn't need Verlaine, didn't need anyone. Well, Dad and Cole—but really that was more like they needed her.

"What does that mean, enhance your powers?" Verlaine grabbed another couple of chocolate bars.

"It means if I cast a spell when my Steadfast is nearby, that spell will be stronger. More effective. It will last longer. That person's presence might make it possible for me to cast spells that might otherwise be beyond me at this point. I'd probably advance faster, too, if we spent enough time together." Nadia took a deep breath. "So for me, it's all positive. For the Steadfast, it's not. Steadfasts can see magic in ways I can't—in ways no one else can. Apparently that can be, well, disturbing." Nadia sighed. "It's probably not going to happen with you. Seriously. We just met."

"You never know. I have really crappy luck, so if this is actually dangerous and bad, I bet I get it on the first try." Although Verlaine had been joking, Nadia could see her expression shift as she considered the possibilities more seriously. "How long does it last? Being a Steadfast."

"Until the witch and her Steadfast end it, or die. So hopefully a really long time. And the bond's strongest when it's newest; it would be really hard to break in less than a couple of years." It might be hard even after ten. Or more. This was one of those things Mom hadn't reviewed in full.

The one part about a Steadfast that Mom had stressed most was that person should matter to you. Deeply. The power a Steadfast gave to a witch was in direct proportion to the capacity for love and loyalty between them. It was a bond more profound than any other, as enduring as that between parents and children—

—so, maybe not that profound, then.

"It's not going to happen for us," Nadia said, trying to push aside the swell of anger within her. "So forget it. Never mind. Don't be freaked."

Verlaine had evidently gone from being excited at the possibility to relieved that it was unlikely. "Okay, I get it, you were just—giving me the 'in case of emergency' speech. Like on a plane. They always tell you where the life jackets are, and show you how to *calmly* put on the oxygen masks— like if those masks fell out of the plane ceiling you wouldn't all be screaming bloody murder."

Nadia had to laugh. "Yeah, pretty much." She pointed with her whole hand, flat like a blade, the way stewardesses did. "That way is the emergency exit."

"Got it. Okay, so—show me what you've got."

Nothing for it now but to start the spell.

She took down her Book of Shadows, because she still needed the instructions for a prophetic spell. It probably looked pretty impressive as she scattered a circle of whitish-gray powder on the floor. Even better would be the cleansing flame, which was violet and hovered slightly above the powder, glowing brilliantly.

"What is that?" Verlaine whispered.

"A cleansing flame."

"What's it cleansing?"

"The air. Also the bone."

"Bone?"

Nadia pointed at the powder on the floor. "You can buy it in some fertilizer stores."

"Ew. Um, no offense."

"None taken. There's a lot of grossness in witchcraft."

The cleansing flame began to do its work; the bone powder looked precisely the same, but the light in the room seemed to disappear. Really, it was all being drawn into the one violet flame, which grew larger, brighter, tongued with more forks of fire. It was a blaze now, illuminating them both. Nadia took her seat on the floor across from Verlaine, who obviously realized the moment was near.

"We're about ready," she said. "Spellcasting is silent, usually. You can speak spells aloud if you really need to keep yourself together, but mostly it works better when the focus turns inward. So I'm going to go through it without speaking. Okay?"

"Okay." Verlaine hesitated. "If I do turn into your Stead-fast, how will I know?"

"You won't be my Steadfast. I'm, like, ninety-nine percent positive."

"Yeah, but just in case of a water landing, tell me where to find my life jacket."

Nadia grinned despite herself. "There would be a—flare. A surge in the flame. And you'd start to feel it not long afterward."

"Got it." Verlaine straightened herself, clearly ready. Nadia hoped she was, too.

Looking straight into Verlaine's hazel eyes, her fingers closing around the pure silver dangle on her bracelet, Nadia began to go through the ingredients of the fortune-telling spell:

> *The sight of something wondrous, never before seen.*
> *The breaking of a bond that should never have been broken.*
> *Cold beyond desolation.*
> *Loyalty beyond life.*

These were mostly very powerful ingredients; only at this point in her life, she realized, would she have had any chance of casting this. Nadia pulled the memories together and thought them, felt them, as deeply as she possibly could:

The first time she'd seen Cole—when he was still in Mom's belly, the one time her parents let her come to the sonogram, and suddenly all the boring talk about this baby brother she didn't really want turned into something real, someone real, her actual true brother practically waving to her before he was even born.

Mom standing at the door, a suitcase next to her, saying, "It's better this way," and the horrible sight of her father unable to speak for his tears.

Chicago that year they'd had the "thundersnow," when the winds had been hurricane-strength and two feet of snow had fallen amid bolts of lightning, and she'd opened the door to the balcony just to feel the storm's fury, and the wind had nearly torn her away—

Dad on the night of the wreck, crawling through twisted metal and broken glass to grab Cole, never hesitating even though his own ribs were cracked and he had to be in incredible pain—

The magic turned over inside her. Rippled around her. Nadia drew a line in the remaining bone dust and envisioned Captive's Sound—every street she'd seen, every moment she'd spent here—recreating the place as best she could within her mind and demanding that fate show her what was in store.

Her eyes widened as the bone dust blackened, began to radiate an unearthly heat that seared her outstretched hand—

The attic door opened. "Nadia?"

Startled, Nadia turned to see Mateo poking his head up into her attic.

The violet flame flared—and vanished. Instantly the room's light looked normal; the magic she'd felt had gone . . . someplace. The bone dust was just so much black gunk on the ground. Verlaine jerked back, clearly not sure what to do.

Mateo frowned. "Whoa. What was that?"

"What was what?" Nadia answered, too quickly. She tucked her hair behind one ear, glanced back at the pile of bone dust on the floor, and adjusted herself so maybe he wouldn't see it. Did it look like she was acting weird? Probably.

"Sorry to barge in; your dad said it was okay." But Mateo's attention remained on what he'd seen. "I meant, what was that—purple light, and all the sparks?"

Verlaine was doing a much better job of acting natural. "What purple light?"

He paused, then shrugged. "Guess it was something about—you know, it's dark in the hallway and then you come up here—"

"Like how you see red after a camera flash," Nadia agreed. "Definitely. Happens to me all the time. By the way—what are you doing here?"

Did that sound unfriendly? She hoped not. But it was a pretty good question.

"Does this look familiar?" Mateo held up a cell phone identical to hers—*wait*.

"I never took it out of my backpack!" Nadia protested, going to pick up her pack to prove her point. That was when she discovered a brand-new hole in the side pocket. "Oh, great. Wow. I'm glad it fell out at La Catrina instead of on the side of the road or something." Blushing—in embarrassment, in the shock of near-discovery, because Mateo was near, for a dozen reasons—Nadia gave him a sidelong glance. "Thanks."

He smiled, but awkwardly. "So. I should get going. It's late. I told my dad I'd be back to help close up. But we should, um, talk sometime. Yeah. Right?" Mateo sounded so awkward, and yet nothing like the guys at school who had no idea how to ask a girl out. There was something else behind his hesitation, something heavier. Nadia could sense the barriers he put between himself and the world, and how hard it was for him to reach past them. And there was something about his eyes—something lost, something hunted.

Something she wouldn't understand tonight. So maybe she should stop staring at the guy.

"Definitely. We'll talk. See you around," Nadia said.

And then Mateo was gone, back down the attic ladder, the door shutting atop him.

Verlaine said, "Do the two of you usually affect each other like that?"

"Like what?"

"You know—big Bambi eyes, all bashful, kind of gooey—"

"I wasn't gooey," Nadia protested as she took her seat next to Verlaine again. "Wait. Did you think Mateo was, um, gooey?"

"We'll figure it out later," Verlaine said impatiently. "The flame definitely flared. Completely. You saw it, right? Am I your Steadfast now?"

"I—don't know. I doubt it." But Verlaine was right; Nadia had seen the flare for herself.

"Wouldn't I feel it? I don't feel any different."

Nadia shrugged. "We'll have to check to make sure."

Something quick and simple would be best: Reigniting the cleansing flame, maybe? Nadia pinched a bit of the bone dust between her fingers; it was still warm. Bone had a slight oiliness to it that set it apart from sand or ash, a reminder that it had once been alive.

If Verlaine were her Steadfast, even brand-new, then the flame would flare up instantly, and brighter than ever before. Nadia snapped her fingers, feeling the bone crumble and spark between them—

—but a spark was all she got.

"It didn't take," Nadia said. "We'll have to try again."

Verlaine shook her head, suddenly panicked. "What if it took, but it's Mateo Perez instead?"

"Impossible."

"What are you talking about? He came in just when the flame went *foomp* and flared up. He could be your Steadfast now!"

Nadia shook her head. "Couldn't happen. No man can ever be a Steadfast, no more than a man can be a witch. They're magic-blind, all of them."

"All of them?" Verlaine didn't look convinced. "You can't be sure."

"I can be absolutely sure, and so can you. It's one of the absolute truths of witchcraft. It's been true as long as there have been witches, so about as long as there's been human history. No men. Not one. Not ever. Some people say it's because a witch went evil and cursed them all way back at the start of civilization, but that would have been one badass curse. There's all kinds of theories. But the old books all say 'no man conceived of woman' can ever know or use magic. And it's true."

Verlaine frowned. "Isn't that sexist? You know, reverse sexism?"

"I don't know, and I don't care. We have bigger problems, okay?" Nadia kept staring down at the black, oily smears on her fingertips. "The spell."

"Oh, right. Yeah! You told the fortune of Captive's Sound, and . . . that is not a good expression on your face."

Slowly Nadia shook her head.

"I would call that a bad expression. Very bad." Verlaine began twisting the ends of her long, silvery hair between her fingers, her nails tugging at a small tangle there. "But—you didn't see much. You couldn't. It just turned black, that's all."

"It turned black," Nadia said. "Nothing more. That means there's only one thing waiting in this town's future."

Verlaine's eyes were wide. "Which is not good."

"Which is *destruction*. Complete and total." Nadia stared down at the black oily soot on her hand, which was about as much as would be left of Captive's Sound in the end. "I don't know when it's coming. And I don't know why. But it's coming."

Anxious to be done with his work for the night, Mateo tied off a bag of garbage in the back room at La Catrina and stepped out into the alley.

His eyes widened, and the garbage bag slipped from his fingers, landing on the pavement with a wet crunch.

Mateo couldn't pay any attention to that, or to anything else besides the fact that the world had apparently gone mad.

7

MATEO STARED AT SOMETHING NOT OF THIS EARTH.

Precisely what it was he couldn't have said. The first word that popped into his stunned mind was *ox*, and the second was *wolf*, and yet it seemed to be a man, too. As it crouched over the dank asphalt of the alleyway, it lifted its heavy, horned head; eyes that burned with white flame stared at Mateo—through him—and he felt a chill so deep that he thought he might actually freeze. Its fur bristled; even though it stood in shadows, Mateo could see that much.

Before he could say or do anything else, though, the thing—disappeared. Which was the only way he could describe how it went from being solid to transparent to just not there.

Within five seconds Mateo was as alone in the alley as he'd ever been, with no other sound but a can skittering along the pavement in the nighttime breeze. The harsh glare of the streetlamp nearby cast its usual stark shadows. He hadn't thought to check whether the horned thing had a shadow or not.

Mateo went back inside La Catrina, shut the back door, and leaned against it.

I'm not insane. I'm not. Easy to say. Hard to believe, given that he had just seen a monster, which had then vanished in a way he associated more with science-fiction movies than real life.

But whatever he'd just seen—it didn't *feel* like one of his dreams. He was awake. Aware. That hadn't been a vision of the future, or even a nightmare. It had been very solid. Very near.

Except for the part where it vanished, he told himself. *Come on. That couldn't have been real.*

Quickly he turned back to his final tasks at La Catrina for the night. If he concentrated on his chores, then he wouldn't have to think about what he'd seen. Or not seen. Maybe he could even forget about it.

Side work finally done, Mateo folded his black apron and hurried back out to his motorcycle. Right now all he wanted to do was get home. He didn't see the horned thing again; at first he thought whatever weird thing had happened to his brain had ended.

But things weren't back to normal.

Something about Captive's Sound had . . . changed.

When he looked upward, it was as if there were a film between him and the stars overhead—like a grimy window between the town and the sky. And it was as if there were a deep, dark line in the ground, curving along the street as far as he could see in either direction. A fault line, he wanted to call it, except that it was visible and invisible at the same time. Mateo stretched one foot toward it, a kind of experiment, but the road felt perfectly smooth underneath. Yet there was this odd sensation, almost like vibration, that came up from it.

A stray cat nearby hissed at him and darted away. Mateo often put milk or leftover scraps of the fish tacos out at the end of the day; the strays knew him, sometimes curling about his legs so fondly that he had to shoo them off before he could straddle his motorcycle. Did even the cats see that something was wrong with him?

Is this what it's like? Going insane?

Mateo put on his helmet, got on the bike, and revved the motor. He needed to get home. Once he was home, he'd feel better. He had to.

The ride was even weirder, though. The farther he drove through Captive's Sound, the worse it seemed. Those strange lines in the roads—they were everywhere, and he had to remind himself to focus on traffic instead of the ground to keep himself from having a wreck. And some of the houses had a strange, watery light around them, as if they were melting. It was like being in a Van Gogh painting: colors too bright, perspective skewed, and the sense that everything was being broken down into pieces.

Except Mateo had liked Van Gogh when he took art

history. Van Gogh was beautiful. Captive's Sound was grotesque.

This started at Nadia's house. Once again Mateo thought of what he'd seen when he looked into the attic—like a flash, a purple flash of light surrounded by all those dark red sparks—and then there had been that incredible shiver when his eyes met Nadia's. But the shiver . . . well, that was just Nadia's dark eyes. The light, though—

Seriously, what do you think purple light had to do with this? Why would that make you feel so weird? Either you're going crazy or you're coming down with the flu. Or you're going crazy and coming down with the flu for extra fun.

Somehow he got home, pulling up to his house right as he thought he couldn't take it anymore. The ocean roared even louder in his ears—or was that his own blood rushing through? His heart was beating fast, his skin sweaty, all of it adrenaline overload.

At least Dad wasn't home yet. Mateo slammed the door behind him and stumbled to the bathroom to splash cold water on his face. It wasn't much, but it seemed to help.

At least, until he stood up and looked in the mirror.

His face was the same, but around it was—Mateo would have called it a halo, except that it was dark instead of light. Within it twisted shapes, too foggy and indefinite to be identified, but his mind supplied suggestions. *Snakes. Broken glass. Thorns.*

Water dripping from his forehead and chin, Mateo lifted his shaking hands to try to touch the halo. Would it feel like slime? Like razor blades? It couldn't be anything good; it had to hurt, but somehow he had to prove to himself that it was really there.

Instead his hands passed right through it. Mateo felt a slight chill against his fingers, but nothing else.

In his reflection, the halo swirled around his fingers, seeming to stick to them like tar.

Mateo bolted from the bathroom and ran from his house, scrambling down the rocky slope that led from their back-yard down to the beach. Gritty sand dragged at his boots as he stumbled toward the ocean—toward the vast darkness where nothing had changed, nothing was sick, and every-thing remained sane.

Is that why you did it, Mom? Is that why you decided to drown? Was this the last place left you could get any peace?

But the waves weren't dark any longer. Out in the dis-tance, not far from the lighthouse, a beam shone up from the water like a spotlight aimed at the stars. It gleamed a vivid pale green, more steadily than it should have for something submerged in the ocean.

Hugging himself against the chill, staring at the eerie light, Mateo fought back the urge to vomit. The fear that had been haunting him since the dreams began was on him now, like a bird of prey on its kill, and he felt paralyzed. Numbly he thought that he should call Elizabeth—one of the handful of numbers saved in his phone, by far his most called. She'd know what to do. She always did.

But Elizabeth still believed he was sane, and he couldn't

bear the thought of her giving up on him like everybody else.

Soon everyone would know, though. Dad, Gage, even Nadia—

Nadia, the girl he'd thought he might be able to keep safe. What a joke. Maybe his insanity was the reason she was going to die.

Then, once more, he remembered the light in her attic—the light that had surrounded her.

Which was a stupid thing to be thinking about, except that something about that light—some quality it had that he couldn't name—was sort of like the halo he'd seen in the mirror. The difference was that the halo was hideous, and that light had been beautiful. But they were *alike*.

And both of them were like the strange green glow he saw out in the sound.

How was that possible?

And what did Nadia Caldani have to do with it?

Even taking time to make waffles for Cole and double-check that he had all his art supplies, Nadia got to school early. She hoped to have a chance to sneak into the chemistry lab.

Something was buried there—long buried, sunk deep. Whatever it was, it held enormous power.

Was that power linked to the darker fate she saw in store for Captive's Sound? It had taken Nadia the better part of an hour to calm Verlaine down, to explain that the devastation she saw could be either a week or a century away, or anything in between. But as Verlaine had said—that meant "one week" was a possibility, and so they'd better figure some things out sooner rather than later.

Rodman High wasn't deserted, even this early; a few teachers on morning duty stood around clutching go-mugs of coffee, and a couple of cheerleaders were putting up posters about the first football game. But none of them paid much attention to Nadia as she darted inside. Despite the uncertainty churning inside her, she continued with her plan to investigate the chemistry lab.

Great. All I have to do is throw my stuff in my locker and figure out a question to ask the Piranha if she shows up in her room early—

Halfway down the hall, Nadia froze. There, sitting on the floor with his back against her locker, was Mateo. To judge by his rumpled hair and the shadows under his eyes, he might have been there for hours, even all night.

At the echo of her footsteps, Mateo looked up. "Nadia. Hey."

"Hi." She started walking toward him, her backpack off one shoulder, unsure what to think. But when she saw again how exhausted he looked, she said, "Are you okay?"

"No." Mateo pushed himself to his feet. "Listen. I know how this is going to sound. I've gone over this in my head about a thousand times, trying to make it make sense. It never does. But I've got to ask you." He took a deep breath as she reached him, and they were face-to-face. "Last night—when I looked into your attic and saw that light—"

Oh, crap. Nadia tried to think of another, better explanation than she'd been able to come up with last night.

But then he said, "Did you do something to me?"

"Do something to you? Did it—did the attic light hurt your eyes?" Maybe cleansing flame was damaging to people who weren't prepared for it? Nadia had never heard of anything like that, but maybe it was only one of the countless things Mom hadn't gotten around to explaining.

"After I left your house, for a while I felt kind of dizzy—disoriented—"

Which could happen to a Steadfast, but that had to be a coincidence.

"—then I started seeing things." Mateo's hands were clenching and unclenching at his sides, like he had to force himself to get through this. "As in, strange phantom animals in the alleyway. Weird lights and stuff around houses. And the sky—it's all over town, and I thought it might be better when the sun went up, but it's not. It's like Captive's Sound is completely surrounded by something dirty and cloudy and—and *evil.*"

This can't be happening, she thought. *There's no possible way.* It was like things falling upward. Or suddenly needing to breathe water instead of air. Men didn't possess magic. They couldn't. That rule was absolute.

"Were you maybe—I don't know—cooking some kind of drugs? Something that makes you trip? The purple flame—that could be a hallucination, maybe." He held up his hands. "I swear I won't report you, or anything like that, but if that's true, please tell me the truth so I'll know this is going to get out of my system."

Nadia shook her head no, even though that lie would have been her best out. As she did so, the brief hope in his eyes died.

"You think I'm crazy." Mateo smiled grimly. "Of course you do. You've been in town, what, almost two weeks now? So people already got to you and told you that I'm—that my family—they told you, right?"

"The family curse," she whispered.

Mateo raked one hand through his dark brown hair, clearly trying to hold himself together—and failing. "So you think I'm insane, like everyone else does. Maybe I am. I guess—I guess—" He seemed to remember where he was, and the look of regret on his face cut her to the bone. "I'm sorry I bothered you about it. Could you just, maybe, not tell anybody about this?"

She nodded. He started to walk away, his shoulders slumped, utterly defeated.

No, he couldn't have become her Steadfast. But if the curse on his family was real, was it possible that there had been some strange reaction between the curse and the Steadfast spell? That didn't make any sense according to the magical theory she knew, but the visions he was describing sounded all too familiar. By now she knew that what he'd seen—the shroud of evil hanging over this entire town—was very real.

And if there was any chance that she was responsible for

what he was seeing, then she couldn't let Mateo walk away thinking he was going mad.

"Mateo?" He only half turned, so she took a few steps closer to him. "What you saw—in the attic—"

"Yeah?"

You must never speak of witchcraft to any man. One of the First Laws—but maybe there was a way to bend that rule without breaking it. "It wasn't drugs. But it—it wasn't only the light."

Slowly he came back toward her. "Then what was it?"

"I can't tell you." Before he could protest, Nadia held up a hand. "I mean it. I can't."

"Did it do this to me? Whatever it was?"

"I'm not sure. I can find out, though. If it did, maybe I can undo it."

Mateo's eyes lit up with desperate hope. Though he clearly had no idea what she was talking about, he was clutching at any possibility. "Come on. You have to tell me."

"I can't," Nadia insisted. "Mateo, please. I know this is hard for you—"

"Thinking I'm going crazy like my mom? The one who drowned herself in the ocean? You have no idea how hard that is for me."

Almost on instinct, Nadia laid one hand against his chest to comfort him. He instantly stilled at her touch. It was amazing to think she could do that just by touching him.

Quickly she said, "We have to trust each other right now, okay? We have to . . . take some things on faith. You just have to understand—I believe you about everything you say you've seen. *I believe in you.*"

Mateo's lips parted slightly. Was it that astonishing, thinking that somebody really might trust him?

Nadia finished, "So I'm asking you to believe in me right now. Let me work this out. If I had anything to do with what's happening to you—I'll know soon."

He nodded. "Today? This week?"

Right away, Nadia wanted to say, but already people were starting to mill around in the hallways—only a few, but enough that she no longer felt safe to experiment in the lab uninterrupted.

But there was something she might be able to try even in the middle of class—quiet, simple, something nobody would even notice her casting—and she needed to do this right away, during the next class period they shared.

She looked back at Mateo and gave him the most encouraging smile she could manage. "Sometime during chemistry."

"Obviously we need to review how to write a lab report," the Piranha said as everyone began assembling their materials. "I've put an outline on the board, which should prove useful to those of you who have learned how to read. This is apparently a minority."

Nadia had finally been assigned a lab partner, which would have been bad news for her today no matter what. The fact that she'd been stuck with that slimy Jeremy Prasad made it worse. She didn't care what Verlaine said; as far as

Nadia was concerned, the view wasn't worth it, no matter how hot he was.

"She's such a bitch," he said as he handed Nadia the sodium bicarbonate for their experiment.

"The Piranha?" Nadia shrugged. She kept glancing over at Mateo, who looked as exhausted as he had this morning, though apparently it was comforting for him to be near Elizabeth. Every time their eyes met, he smiled. *They must really be in love. How awesome for them.* "Basic teacher snark, if you ask me."

"She shouldn't talk down to us. Somebody should teach that woman her place. *We* pay her salary."

Nadia wondered how many checks Jeremy had written to the school board lately. "We're supposed to write down our impressions of all the equipment and materials for the experiment."

"We get to write down our impressions of baggies? This is supposed to be a good use of our time?"

"If you do that part, I'll do the harder stuff later," Nadia promised. Not that Jeremy deserved a break, but she had better things to do.

Once again she turned her attention to the power she sensed underfoot. The burial was deep underground; that meant she was unlikely to be able to get to it through non-magical means. Which meant that if she wanted to use magic to get the buried thing out again, she would be taking it out sight unseen, with no idea what the source of that powerful magic was. That was an extremely bad plan. Possibly whoever had buried this . . . whatever . . . had had a very good reason.

And yet—she was tempted. Nadia itched to discover it, even if it were likely to blow up in her face like Pandora's box.

To have power—real power—beyond anything Mom had ever known, to be able to stand up and say, *See what you walked away from? I'm stronger than you. Stronger than anyone. You shouldn't have left me behind.*

Nadia blinked, shook her head. The shudder of vengeful fury that passed through her was gone in an instant, but the uneasiness it left behind lingered.

And she realized—that fury hadn't entirely been her own. It had belonged, in part, to whatever lay beneath the lab.

Now Nadia understood that mysterious presence as she never had before. It did not merely wait there: It lurked. It *seethed*. It longed to break free—

—and wreak vengeance.

Vengeance on what, she didn't know. She no longer wanted to. The only thing she understood was that it couldn't be directly causing any devastation in Captive's Sound; it lacked that power, and she was grateful.

Whatever lay imprisoned beneath the school had been put there for good reason. The entity she sensed was buried beneath any retrieval, and they were safe from it, and that was actually all she needed to know for now.

Besides, at the moment, her attention should be focused on whatever she'd done to Mateo.

It wasn't as if she could cast any elaborate spells right here in the middle of class. But something basic might be effective, if Mateo's problem was what she suspected.

If he was cursed—truly cursed, the inheritor of a dark magic hundreds of years old—then that meant he might potentially react to magic in a different way. Nadia wasn't exactly sure how that would work, but it seemed plausible.

And a basic spell of liberation might make the magic . . . unstick.

Well, it was worth a shot, anyway.

Nadia's fingers found the small ivory drop at her bracelet, and she put the ingredients together:

> *Helpless laughter.*
> *Washing away what cannot come clean.*
> *A moment of forgiveness.*

The first two were easy —

Her thirteenth birthday party, when they put a pair of Cole's Pull-Ups on her best friend's Boston terrier and they all got hysterical, rolling on the floor.

Taking her first shower in the new house, three in the morning after the wreck, mud under her fingernails and a piece of car glass in her hair, feeling like it would never, ever all rinse clean.

But forgiveness? Nadia dug deep.

Weeks of wondering if Dad had driven Mom away, if there had been an affair or something Nadia hadn't known about, all ending the moment she tiptoed to the kitchen late at night and glimpsed her father bent over the table, his head in his hands, so miserable that she knew, just knew, *he hadn't seen any of this coming.*

It was enough. She felt the spell swirling outward, invisible but powerful—

—really powerful—

"You know what?" Jeremy said loudly. "I'm sick of this." With that he shoved all the lab equipment off their table; it fell to the floor with a crash.

"You know what I'm sick of?" The Piranha put her hands on her hips. "You. All of you. This entire school. I could be in yoga right now instead of trying to pour information into the sieves you call your brains."

Several students started laughing. One girl started crying. Another reached around her own back and unfastened her bra through her sweater, groaning in relief as it went slack.

What the—

Another girl and a guy started making out. So did two guys in the far corner. Jeremy started tearing up his chemistry book, ripping pages out in hanks, then shredding them one by one. The Piranha kicked off her shoes and took a one-footed position that Nadia remembered from her own yoga class as Tree Pose.

Mateo sat up straight. "What's wrong with people?"

"I don't know," Nadia said. But she was starting to put it together. A spell of liberation could make people feel a little, well, uninhibited. But that was normally a minor side effect, enough to maybe give someone the giggles, not to make an entire roomful of people completely forget where they were.

The spell had been more powerful than usual—no, more powerful than *ever*.

That wasn't the effect of whatever lay beneath this room. If anything, that would have dimmed the spell, not enhanced it.

That—that was the kind of boost you could only get from a Steadfast.

Verlaine was nowhere near here, and besides, Nadia already knew the spell hadn't worked on her. Which meant the only option—the only possibility—

It can't be true, Nadia thought wildly. Everything she knew about magic was built on a few fundamental principles, and the most fundamental principle of all was that men couldn't hold magic. A curse was one thing—you didn't hold that; it held you. So men could be cursed. But being a Steadfast should be as impossible for a man as the sun circling the Earth.

"What's going on?" Mateo said. He was clearly unaffected by the spell—another sign. Steadfasts weren't as susceptible to simple magic. Then he turned toward Elizabeth—who remained still by his side—and gasped out loud. "Oh, my God. My *God*."

Mateo started backing away from Elizabeth, and the expression on his face was the last thing Nadia would have expected to see: utter horror.

Elizabeth made a swift, fluttering gesture with one hand; for the first time, Nadia noticed that she wore little rings on each finger—rings made out of the same materials Nadia wore on her bracelet. Mateo swayed once on his feet, then snapped out of it, turning again to Nadia. "What's going on?"

All around them, the kissing and laughter and even singing continued unabated. The Piranha, instead of calling for order, was on the floor in Low Cobra Pose. Nadia didn't look at any of it; she could only stare at Elizabeth. Meanwhile Elizabeth held her hand out over the floor—parallel to it—almost as though she were trying to calm an animal or a very small child.

Or, Nadia thought, *something buried beneath the school.*

That was ludicrous, wasn't it? Surely it had to be. Probably Nadia was freaking out because her spell had spun so wildly out of control, and because she'd just learned the incredible truth that Mateo was her Steadfast. Her imagination was running away with her.

But she wasn't imagining Elizabeth's reaction.

Elizabeth didn't look confused by any of this. Instead she took a gulp from her water bottle, and then her sweet, clean-scrubbed face shifted into a smile that was anything but sweet.

It felt more like—a dare.

Nadia's stomach dropped as she realized that Elizabeth wasn't any other girl in her class.

She was another witch.

8

CLASS ENDED WITH THE SECURITY GUARD TALKING ONE girl down from the top of the file cabinets, demerits for almost everyone, the Piranha on report, and people starting to complain of headaches or blush as they realized what they'd been doing. Nadia grabbed Mateo's arm to hustle him out of there as fast as possible.

"What just happened?" he said, his mouth so close to her ear that she could feel his breath.

"Let's get out of here first, okay?" Nadia hurried out, Mateo by her side. She glanced over her shoulder to look for Elizabeth, who stood there in the middle of the mayhem, very still, watching them go. A small smile played on her lips.

She knew that Nadia knew. And she didn't care whether Nadia knew or not.

As they went down the hallway toward the cafeteria, she

muttered, "Tell me this. What did you see when you looked at Elizabeth?"

"What are you talking about?"

"When you looked at her, right after everybody lost it. You seemed—panicked, almost."

Mateo frowned even as he pushed the door open for them both. "I don't remember looking at Elizabeth once. There was a lot more to see." He started laughing. "The Piranha's— really bendy. And Erik's been out since sophomore year, but I had no idea Charles was gay."

He'd forgotten; whatever Elizabeth had done to him to make him stop seeing had also made him lose his memory of it. She had acted quickly, and her counterspell had been completely effective.

With a rush of horror, Nadia thought, *The dark magic in town—it's her! It's Elizabeth; it has to be.*

But no. How could Elizabeth be behind everything happening in Captive's Sound? According to the increasingly worried Google searches Nadia had been running lately, the problems here seemed to go way back—since long before Elizabeth would even have been born, much less practicing magic. Plus, she and Nadia were about the same age, which meant they were only just now coming into their power.

Still—any other witch would have reached out at that moment. When Elizabeth saw that Nadia's spell had misfired, she should have helped to quiet it, and sought Nadia afterward. The secrecy that bound the Craft didn't extend that far.

Instead, Elizabeth had given her that cool, appraising

smile, covered her tracks with Mateo, and slipped away.

So maybe she wasn't the cause of everything going wrong in Captive's Sound. Yet Nadia knew, deep down, that whatever it was twisting things here up in knots—Elizabeth was in the thick of it.

As they got into the cafeteria line, Mateo said under his breath, "Okay, either you were cooking some kind of drugs that can make the whole school start hallucinating at once, or something else seriously strange is going on. Because I did *not* imagine that. Are you going to explain what this has to do with what happened last night?"

She reached for her tray on autopilot, thinking fast.

One of the First Laws was to never, ever reveal the secret of the Craft to a man. Any man.

Every principle of the Craft also said that it was impossible for a man to be a Steadfast. Yet she couldn't deny that this was exactly what Mateo had become.

Nadia might never understand how that was possible, but as long as it was—then he had to be told. It was wrong that this had happened to him without his knowledge or consent, wrong that someone already so troubled had been forced to carry that burden. The least she owed him was the truth.

"I'll tell you," she promised, feeling almost light-headed. It was like skydiving, terrifying and liberating at once. "I'll explain everything."

Elizabeth went home.

Her teachers would remember her being in class, whether

or not she attended. Really, going to Rodman was something she did only to be near the Chamber once in a while, and these days also occasionally to keep Mateo Perez soothed and unquestioning. Today she finally had something new to think about.

Nadia Caldani was a witch. Elizabeth had suspected as much, given the family's arrival in town immediately after the night of the storm, when her barrier had torn and shrieked as it was pierced through. What she had not suspected was that Nadia would possess such extraordinary magic.

Powerful—but undisciplined. Elizabeth had to smile as she remembered the ridiculous scene in chemistry class. Nadia must have suspected some magical hold on Mateo Perez; her crush was so painfully obvious, the way her eyes flickered over to him countless times during their lessons. Had she thought to free him with a spell of liberation?

The curse on the Cabots was far too old and too strong to be shaken loose by such feeble methods. She smiled around the rim of her water bottle.

And what ridiculous overkill. Clumsy, stupid, to have cast that spell with such force that it affected the entire class. Obviously Nadia was raw and new to the Craft. Her inherent abilities weren't matched by technique.

Yet she had, however briefly, somehow allowed Mateo to glimpse Elizabeth's true hold on him—and that wouldn't do. Elizabeth wasn't quite done with him yet.

Elizabeth reached the pale gray house, opened the door, and went inside. When one of her rare guests came here—Mateo, or the delivery service with her cases of bottled water—they saw whatever it was they expected to see. Mateo had commented once on the paintings; his mother had always talked about how soft the carpet was underfoot.

In reality, the creaking wooden boards of the floor had long ago been painted blue, and they were overlaid with decades worth of shattered glass.

Her feet wove through the shards easily; the gaps for her steps were as familiar to her as everything else in Captive's Sound. The yellowed plaster walls were all but bare; one held a mirror, draped with heavy old red velvet, which she could rip away in case of emergency. A few pieces of furniture from various centuries slumped against the walls, their wood crumbling, their upholstery threadbare. Elizabeth had no idea whether any of them could still bear her weight. In one corner was the old cast-iron stove, which as always glowed with a heat that was bright and constant, even beautiful, in the same way that a spectacular tropical bird could be beautiful even when kept in a cage too small for its wings. Between two of the walls hung the rope hammock, piled high with quilts and coverlets. The most powerful spells of imprisonment always worked from the ground up, and Elizabeth did not intend to be caught while sleeping.

On every surface sat empty bottles—water bottles, mostly, though there were some for soda, some for the green tea that seemed to be popular these days. Once every few months or so, Elizabeth would get rid of them, but she accumulated them so quickly that it was pointless to throw each out in turn. The thirst—the terrible thirst—it cracked and dried her from within every single moment, as it had for almost as long as she could remember. Even now she tossed aside the bottle that had seen her home and took up another one, gulping the water down desperately.

She'd tried drinking almost anything over the years, to see what might help. She'd drunk mud. She'd drunk wine. She'd even tried blood a few times, before she realized it was too salty to be any help.

Not long now, Elizabeth told herself. It was her only comfort.

Her hand rested on the knob of the door to the back room, the only room of her house she no longer really considered hers. That room belonged to something else.

Elizabeth looked inside. She felt as though her Book of Shadows looked back at her.

It shook free of the cobwebs with difficulty; it had been a long time since Elizabeth had consulted its pages instead of merely drawing upon its inherent power. For a moment she wondered whether it had become illegible, whether it had finally become a book no longer, but the fragile pages fell open to the correct page instantly. Her Book of Shadows still wished to do her bidding, no matter what.

Mateo sat at the cafeteria table, pizza untouched on his tray, staring at Nadia Caldani, who had turned out to be even crazier than he was.

Beautiful. Persuasive. But nuts. She was telling him stuff nobody could ever believe was real.

And yet he believed her.

"I'm sorry about you becoming my Steadfast," she said yet again, stabbing at her lasagna with her plastic fork like it was somehow responsible for this. "If I'd had any idea it could affect you—any man, ever—I'd never have cast a prophetic spell in my own house. And I still don't understand how it could be you."

"Yeah, yeah," he said, repeating the words she'd been over a couple times already, like he was on autopilot. "No man conceived of woman can hold magic. I remember that part."

"It's like finding out that every action doesn't have an equal and opposite reaction," Nadia protested. "But, still. Here you are. You're my Steadfast, and that's a pretty powerful bond, so we're going to have to learn to work with it."

"Hey there!" Verlaine Laughton came up to Nadia, skinny and strange as ever; she'd used two pencils to twist her silver-gray hair into a knot at the back of her neck, and wore the same kind of bizarre clothes she always favored—today, a peasant blouse and bell-bottomed jeans that had orange flower appliqués. She seemed to have been transported directly from 1972. That was about as much as Mateo had ever noticed about her; there was something about Verlaine that almost kept you from paying any attention. Like wherever something interesting was, Verlaine wasn't. But she seemed to know Nadia pretty well. Verlaine's face fell as she saw Mateo. "Oh, sorry, am I interrupting?"

Nadia looked up at her. "Mateo's my Steadfast."

Verlaine practically slammed the tray onto the table in vindication. "I *knew* it!"

"Are you a witch, too?" he said. Were there witches everywhere? Was the whole world about a thousand times weirder than he'd ever dreamed?

"Nope. This is all about as new to me as it is to you." Then Verlaine frowned at Nadia. "Wait. I thought you said men couldn't be Steadfasts. That they couldn't know about magic."

"Well, it turns out they can be Steadfasts," Nadia explained, "so I figured Mateo needs to know about magic. We're kind of working off-book here."

"No men ever, you said." Verlaine leaned across the table, peering at him. "Mateo, are you maybe—well—transgender? Intersex? No prejudice here. Just support."

Mateo would have started thudding his face against the table in frustration if his pizza hadn't been in the way. "I'm a guy."

"We'll take your word for it." Verlaine started in on her salad. "I was the only one who was supposed to be in danger of being . . . Steadfasted, or whatever you want to call it. I even kind of wanted it to happen. And now you stole it. Accidentally. But still."

"I wish it were you," Mateo replied. "This is really—weird." He glanced around, wondering whether anybody was overhearing them; the last thing he needed was for the school to have yet more reasons to write him off as crazy. But the din of a hundred students eating and talking at once drowned out their words. Also, the cafeteria looked more normal than any place he'd been since the . . . Steadfast thing began. Apparently the cafeteria was completely devoid of magic. This would come as no surprise to anyone who'd eaten the meatloaf.

Then Nadia reached across the table and tentatively laid her hand along his forearm. The touch shocked him out of his confusion. For a moment he could only look at her dark eyes, accepting in a way almost no one else's had ever been. "Tell me more about what you've been seeing. We'll figure out what it all means. It won't be as scary if you understand it."

She didn't make him feel bad about being scared; she acted like that was a totally natural way to react. Mateo hadn't realized how much that could help.

Where to begin? Worst things first, he decided. "What freaks me out the most is that—halo around my head. Halo's the wrong word, because that's something gorgeous and holy, and this is terrible. But I don't know what else to call it."

"What halo?" Verlaine was staring at his head.

"I see it in the mirror," he explained. "Since the . . . spell last night." Of all the freaky things he'd witnessed, including the weird horned thing, the halo was by far the most disturbing, because it was a part of him.

However, Nadia didn't seem disturbed at all. Very softly she said, "I suspect that's the curse."

The word *curse* always made Mateo's skin crawl—but it was different, the way Nadia said it. Everyone else made it sound unspeakable. Contagious. From her, it sounded real.

The curse was real.

The curse was *a curse*.

Hereditary insanity: He'd prepared himself for that. Superstition: what he'd assumed for most of his life. But an honest-to-God, or maybe honest-to-Satan, curse? Actual, supernatural evil that had been sunk into his family since the dawn of time and now had him, too?

"Excuse me," Mateo said as he rose from the cafeteria table. "I need a minute."

Then he stalked through the cafeteria, cut through the gymnasium and the dressing rooms—where he ran into Jeremy running down Charles for his make-out session with another guy, which was as good a reason as any to shove Jeremy into the lockers.

"My dad knows the city council! I'll have your rat-ass restaurant shut down!" Jeremy yelled after him. Mateo ignored this. First of all, Jeremy regularly threatened to have people's businesses shut down; by now everyone knew that if Jeremy's dad actually even listened to him, the city council didn't listen to Jeremy's dad.

Second, it didn't matter. Nothing mattered. Because he was *cursed*.

Finally Mateo reached the very back room where they kept the boxing equipment. He grabbed a pair of gloves, pulled them on, and started hitting the nearest bag. Punching it with all his strength. Whaling on it. Every blow jarred him all the way to his shoulder; the solidity of the bag almost seemed to hit back. But he punched over and over and over again, with all his strength, fighting the thing that had haunted him now that he'd finally seen it for what it was.

Verlaine said, "So, that went well."

Nadia groaned. "I'm making a total mess of this. But—I don't know what to do! Nothing like this has ever happened before, and I mean ever, as in since the dawn of time."

Verlaine tapped her fork against her tray. "Well, hey, why don't we transfer it over? Turn me into your Steadfast instead. Not that it sounds like so much fun, but—if Mateo can't handle it—I mean, he's already got a curse to deal with. I don't. Anyway, I still think it sounds cool. Can you switch us, Nadia?"

Nadia shook her head. "No chance."

"There's no fail-safe? Come on." Verlaine's eyes narrowed as she folded her arms; she seemed almost suspicious again.

"You remember how it worked. It's not something I control. It's something that happens of its own accord, because of the powers of prophetic magic." Nadia's head throbbed. She should never have cast that spell. All she'd done was scare them and turn Mateo into something he never, ever should have been.

"You have to have an out."

The lone possibility swam in front of her, simultaneously as tempting and as traitorous as a mirage in the desert. "I could end my bond with my Steadfast if I broke all my ties to magic and the Craft—"

"Why didn't you say so before?" Verlaine demanded. "That counts as an out!"

"Did you hear me? I'd have to break all my ties. I wouldn't be a witch any longer. Wouldn't be able to cast any spells, ever again."

When had she gone from assuming the Craft was lost to her to wanting to hold on to it with all her strength? Was she just fooling herself now? Nadia couldn't be sure—of anything. Magic itself had changed around her. Who knew what would be next?

After school—and a few more hours during which he was able to cool down—Mateo sought Nadia again. She and Verlaine were in the parking lot, sitting on the hood of Verlaine's enormous maroon car. Verlaine was the one who waved at him cheerily, like they were pals and this was any other day. "Hey! We were wondering if you'd show!"

"I've showed." He glanced around, but people were emptying out of the parking lot, and the school itself, as fast as possible. Usually Mateo did the same. If you wanted to be left totally alone, hanging around Rodman after 3:30 p.m. was a good way to go. The only person who seemed to be paying them any attention was Ms. Walsh—but after a glance in their direction, she slipped into her car to drive away. "Sorry for freaking out."

Nadia shrugged. "No worries. The news was pretty freak-worthy."

The wind played with her shining black hair; she could

look so casual discussing this, a literal matter of life and death. But it wasn't that she didn't take it seriously—Mateo could tell that much. It was more that Nadia could handle it. There was a center to her—a purpose, a definition—that Mateo had almost never sensed in anyone else. It drew him as strongly and inexorably as gravity pulled them to the earth.

Nadia continued their lunch conversation as if they'd never broken it off. "Like you said—yeah, I've already been in town long enough to hear about the family curse. I'm afraid curses are very real. Witches aren't ever supposed to cast them, but it can happen. If your family has been cursed for generations, then a very powerful witch laid this down long ago. Can you tell me more about how it works? I know it's supposed to lead to insanity, but there could be lots of reasons why."

Mateo straightened. Nobody had ever given him a chance to explain. "We start seeing the future. Or, up until recently, I thought it was that people believed they saw the future and that was the first sign they were losing it. But—I've been having dreams, and they've started coming true."

"Oh, this is unbelievable," Verlaine breathed, but she wasn't trying to move away from him. She only wanted to hear his side of the story. She wasn't so bad, really. "This is not good news. Nadia was explaining this just last night! Seeing the future makes people go *loco*."

"Tell me about it." Mateo's mother had rowed out to sea so she could drown. His grandfather had died in the house fire he himself had started, the one that had scarred

Grandma for life. His great-grandmother committed suicide in City Hall with a shotgun. So it went—on and on, further and further back—a string of suicides, homicides, and self-destructive behavior that had marked at least one Cabot in every generation all the way back to their arrival in the New World when Rhode Island was still a colony. They'd all gone crazy—because each and every one had seen the future, just like him.

"You dream of the future. Okay." Nadia still seemed totally calm. "What are your dreams?"

Mateo couldn't speak at first. *I've seen you lying dead in my arms.*

But he couldn't say that to her. Not yet and maybe not ever.

So he went for the simplest thing first. "The night of the wreck? I dreamed about your family's car going into that ditch. That's why I was there. I had to see if the dream would come true, and it did. I knew I'd have to pull you out."

Once again Nadia brushed her hand along his forearm. She had such small hands. "Half the burden is not being believed. Maybe not believing in yourself. But you know the truth, and now we do, too. And you're strong, Mateo. Strong enough to take this."

He had to laugh at her then, though he instantly regretted it. "Sorry. I mean, it's nice for you to say that. But you don't actually know me. So you don't have any idea whether I'm strong or not."

"You have to be. Your whole family has to be. Otherwise

you wouldn't be able to bear it at all. That's probably why your family was cursed in the first place—because you guys could endure what nobody else could."

All his life, Mateo had heard people speak of his Cabot blood as tainted, sick, even twisted. Never before had anybody said that they might be strong. That *he* might be.

As she absentmindedly tried to work a tangle out of her long hair, Verlaine said, "So why did somebody curse the Cabots?"

"So they'd know the future and reveal it," Nadia said slowly. "That way, the witch gets to know what the future holds, and the Cabots are the ones who endure the consequences. Mateo, who do you tell about your dreams?"

"Nobody. I mean, nobody besides you guys, today, and Elizabeth, of course."

Nadia's hand instantly went tense, and she pulled back from him, suddenly rigid. "About Elizabeth—"

"What about her?" Was there something magical after her, too? Mateo wasn't sure he could take it if anything happened to Elizabeth. He'd have to warn her. The next time they talked, he'd be able to tell her all of this—that the visions of the future really were true, that the curse was true, too, but there might be a way for him to deal with it. Being able to say all this to his best friend felt like the greatest relief imaginable.

But then Nadia said, "Have you ever noticed anything odd about her?"

"What do you mean? No. Of course not." Mateo smiled

fondly. "The only unusual thing about Elizabeth is how kind she is. She's the most understanding person in this entire town."

"That's so true," Verlaine agreed. "Everybody loves Elizabeth."

He hadn't even realized they knew each other. Pretty much nobody paid attention to Verlaine, but if anybody would, it would be Elizabeth. She had seen someone on the fringes and reached out, like she always did.

Nadia looked back and forth between them. "I'm guessing neither of you knew that Elizabeth is a witch, too."

Verlaine laughed out loud, kicking her heels against the chrome bumper in delight. "Oh, my God. She got even cooler. I thought that was impossible."

Mateo wasn't as sure how to feel about that. His first impulse was that Nadia had to be wrong—but if this witch-craft stuff was true, and it seemed to be, then she'd know another witch, wouldn't she? Still, Elizabeth? His best and oldest friend? It seemed unreal to him that he wouldn't know about such a huge part of her life.

Or that she wouldn't tell him curses were real, that the dreams truly could be glimpses of the future—

But she couldn't, could she? Nadia had said the witch laws or whatever didn't let them talk about it with men. So Elizabeth couldn't have told him, even if she'd wanted to. "She'll be relieved that I know," he said, starting to smile. "She's probably wanted to discuss it for a long time now."

"I doubt that." Nadia's full lips pressed together, as if she was holding back words but for only so long. "Listen—I know she's your girlfriend and everything—"

"Elizabeth's not my girlfriend."

Nadia paused, obviously caught short. Verlaine said, "Wow, I always thought you guys were together. Or did you break up?"

"We're just good friends," Mateo insisted. "She's like the sister I never had."

Quietly Nadia said, "Well, she's important to you, so this is still going to be tough to hear. I don't think Elizabeth is just any witch. I think—I think she might—know a little about what's going on here."

Mateo stared at her. "What do you mean, 'what's going on here'?"

"Some of the darker stuff happening in Captive's Sound." Although Nadia was clearly nervous, she continued, "I don't think Elizabeth plays by the rules."

The anger spiked again so fast there wasn't even a chance to hold it back. "That's ridiculous," Mateo said. "Elizabeth's a good person. Really good, deep down. There aren't many people like her. If she does perform magic—whatever, there's no way she does anything evil. It's impossible."

"You saw something frightening in her," Nadia insisted, but this made no sense. "In chemistry class, right after I cast the spell of liberation, you looked at Elizabeth and nearly panicked, before she got to you."

"What are you talking about? That didn't even happen! You're making it up."

"She made you forget." Nadia folded her arms in front of her. "I know this is hard for you to accept, but I know what I saw."

Mateo had heard enough of this. "You know what you saw. A few seconds in a room full of people who were all acting crazy, thanks to you, and that means you know my best friend—practically my only friend in the world—you think you know her better than me? You don't know her at all."

Nadia's dark eyes blazed, like she had any right to be angry. All she said was, "How about you come back and talk to me when you're ready to face facts?"

"How about you come and apologize when you realize you're not right about everything?" Mateo shot back. He grabbed his stuff and stalked to his motorcycle. Once he'd gunned the engine, he wouldn't have been able to hear Nadia even if she did call after him. He drove off without ever looking back.

It should have felt good to get away from Nadia and her lies about Elizabeth, but still something gray and wicked roiled overhead, between Mateo and the sky.

9

"I ONLY WANT TO ASK ONE QUESTION, OKAY?" VERLAINE'S voice sounded tinny on Nadia's cell phone. "Is this maybe a stupid thing to do?"

"I'm walking through my new neighborhood. There's still almost an hour of daylight. I already made dinner. It's baking in the oven, and even my dad can handle taking a casserole out when the timer goes off. So what's stupid about it?"

"You're going to confront another witch, who you don't even know for sure is a witch, but who might be evil? For no reason in particular?"

"Well. When you put it like that." But Nadia didn't turn back.

The entire length of Captive's Sound could be easily walked in half a day, and Elizabeth's home wasn't even a mile away from her own. She remembered the way well enough from her trip on Mateo's motorcycle—

—for a moment she remembered the way it had felt to put her arms around him, and her breath seemed to catch in her throat. Then she shoved that aside, replacing it with the way he'd driven off angrily after school. He'd rather accuse her of being paranoid or crazy than believe one word against his precious Elizabeth. Even though she wasn't his girlfriend after all—a revelation that had briefly filled Nadia with hope so sharp it hurt—Elizabeth mattered more to him than anyone else. More than Nadia, anyway.

Which of course made sense given that Elizabeth was his best friend and Nadia was a girl he'd known for a few days before she started babbling about witchcraft. But still.

Verlaine kept talking. "I just think maybe this is something you could do later. Or never. Never also works."

"I'm not confronting her," Nadia said as she made her way along the cracked sidewalk. Weeds jutted up from every chink in the concrete. Twilight had begun to deepen the blue of the sky, but she had time to get there and back before dark. "I'm simply—checking out the situation."

"So you're going to go to her house and sneak around, while hoping she doesn't catch you in the act. That's either dangerous for you or creepy for her. Possibly both."

"Listen. I know she's a witch. If she's not dangerous—and maybe she isn't, I don't know—then she's a potential friend, okay? Someone we need to know."

Unconvinced, Verlaine said, "If you want to make friends with someone, I'm pretty sure snooping around her house at sunset isn't the way to go."

She had a point. Nadia knew it. But she couldn't shake the idea that something was seriously not right about Elizabeth Pike, and if Elizabeth was in any way, shape, or form part of the darker forces at work in Captive's Sound, then a direct confrontation was a bad idea—at least until Nadia knew more about who she was dealing with. "I swear, I'm not going stalker on her. But if I walk up to her and start talking about witchcraft, and she doesn't know anything about it, then that's even worse than my taking a look at her house, right?"

"Maybe."

"And remember—there's trouble coming to town. Big trouble. If Elizabeth knows anything about it, we should find that out sooner rather than later."

"Okay, okay." Though Verlaine didn't sound enthusiastic, she gave in. "Text me the second you're done, all right? Which should be soon."

"A few minutes. That's all. Promise. I'm going now, all right? Catch you later."

Finally Nadia slid her cell into the pocket of her jeans. Within another couple of blocks, she'd reach Elizabeth's home, and she needed to concentrate. There were certain basic protective signs to look for—plantings by the front or back door, certain stones, things like that; Nadia had done a little of this around her family's new house already. Maybe she could spot Elizabeth's own wards against evil. In the end, though, she thought she might end up peeking through Elizabeth's windows like any Peeping Tom.

Was that weird and creepy? Even if she was doing it for a good cause?

But Nadia didn't know what else to do.

Just as she got within a couple blocks of her goal, though, she saw Elizabeth.

She sat on a cast-iron bench in a weedy, bedraggled garden—a public garden, Nadia now saw from the chipped sign. Before, when she'd gone past it, she had assumed it was an abandoned lot. Swiftly she ducked behind one of the overgrown hedges, so she wouldn't be seen.

To herself she said, *You know, this is definitely going over the edge into stalking.*

Elizabeth's white cotton dress was painted periwinkle blue by the dusky sky, and her curls blew softly in the breeze. In one hand she held a bottle of water, which caught the last rays of sunlight. Nadia heard an engine's roar—a familiar sound. Peering through the leaves of the hedge, she saw Mateo's motorcycle zoom down the street toward her.

No. Toward Elizabeth.

He braked his bike, shut it off. The look of rapt adoration on his face as he took off his helmet—it cut Nadia deeper than she would have thought possible. Elizabeth held out her arms, and Mateo went to her. Their shadows became one as he was enveloped in her embrace.

Nadia couldn't look anymore. For one split second, she was angry with him; then she was angrier with herself.

Why are you upset? Why are you even surprised? He cares about her. Something horrible has just happened to him. Of course Mateo would turn to Elizabeth.

No doubt Mateo was telling the truth about him and Elizabeth. But even if they weren't together—maybe he cared more for her than he'd revealed. Maybe even more than he realized.

Nadia started walking back the way she'd come—then running. As the pavement slapped beneath each step, she felt like more and more of an idiot.

Why would Elizabeth be connected to the evil force behind everything in Captive's Sound? Okay, she didn't freak out today. So what? You're pretty sure she's a witch—that's all—and so you ought to be making friends with her. Not spying. Not having some kind of a freak-out because she's being nice to Mateo, the guy she's known her whole life.

Holding Mateo—

Admit it. You wanted *her to be evil, because you wanted to get her away from him.*

Why am I so stupid?

Nadia came to a stop just short of her own house and braced herself against a neighbor's car, breathing hard, until the flush in her cheeks cooled and she felt like she was in control again. Dad and Cole couldn't see that she was hurting; they didn't need her to break down. They needed her love. They needed dinner.

For a moment she imagined how different it could be, how it ought to be. She would run inside to find Mom there, smiling and steady and smelling of her perfume, Dad's arms around her waist as he hugged her from behind. Nobody would have to worry about Cole. She could ask Mom what it all meant—what was sick in this town, what Elizabeth

might or might not be, how Mateo could be her Steadfast—
and Mom would know, because she always knew. They'd
figure it out together.

The longing swelled inside her until it felt like it would
bend her ribs outward, crack them, swallow her heart.

But Mom wouldn't ever be home again.

Stupid, Nadia thought again. *So stupid.*

Then she pulled herself together and walked inside with
an almost-believable smile.

"So, like, I felt like everybody else was doing it, okay? And
it's not like I actually wanted to steal Jinnie's phone. It's not
even that good a phone." Kendall was the last one taking her
turn around the circle in what was usually chemistry class.
Today, it was a weird therapy session about not acting on
inappropriate urges, and mob mentality, or something like
that. "But, like, everyone else was doing something, and I
figured I ought to do something, and that's what I did."

Nadia sighed. The overwhelming sense of unease she usually felt in the lab had been completely buried by boredom.
Everyone in class, including the Piranha, had been forced to
come up with some reason why they'd lost it yesterday. Since
nobody knew the real reason was a magic spell, their excuses
made no sense whatsoever. Some people blamed their ADD
meds; one guy thought they might have accidentally made
some kind of drug using the chemicals for their experiment,
though the Piranha said this was impossible.

Faye Walsh crossed her arms in front of her. With her

chic aquamarine wrap dress and high heels, the only sign that she wasn't totally confident and in charge was the little worried line between her eyebrows. "Okay. I don't know that we got at the root cause of what happened here, but this isn't about blame or punishment. Somehow, somebody got out of control, and everybody else went along with that. What was needed here was a little more self-discipline. Maybe somebody with the courage to stand up and say, 'What's going on?'"

Nadia hugged herself and glanced directly across the circle—where Mateo sat. He was already looking at her. Their eyes met instantly, and the doubt she saw there pierced her through.

But he had to have noticed the same thing she had: Elizabeth wasn't in chemistry class today. As far as Nadia could tell, she simply hadn't shown up for school.

And neither their teacher nor Ms. Walsh had said anything about it.

The bell rang, and Ms. Walsh said, "Okay, everybody, good session."

"Tomorrow we're picking up the labs where we left off!" the Piranha said loudly.

From his place next to Nadia, Jeremy Prasad muttered, "She thinks she can get her dignity back if she shouts enough."

"You're the one who started taking your clothes off," Nadia said, grabbing her stuff.

Undaunted, Jeremy grinned at her. He really would have

a gorgeous smile if he weren't such an ass. "You noticed, huh? Guess you liked the view."

"Spare me."

She'd assumed Mateo would be avoiding her, but as she walked toward the door, she realized he was hanging back—waiting for her. Nadia hesitated, but only for a moment. "Hey," she said, as he fell in step beside her.

"Hey. Listen—yesterday—I'm sorry I freaked out like that."

Was he starting to doubt Elizabeth after all? Had she left too early last night? A wild, painful thumping quickened in Nadia's chest.

But then he added, "You're wrong about Elizabeth. But I can see why you'd have to ask. Weird things are going on, Elizabeth's the only other wi—the only other, um, *w-i-t-c-h* you know of around here, and so you'd have to figure out if they're connected. But they aren't."

Nadia managed to smile. "I think most people can spell *witch* by now." Mateo laughed once, more in surprise than anything else, though he glanced around to see if they were being overheard. "Don't freak about it. Remember the cafeteria yesterday? You'd be amazed how much people aren't paying attention to what happens right in front of them."

"Okay."

They stepped onto the grounds together, the big quad between the school's buildings. Different groups were gathering for the lunch break—the rich kids from the Hill glossy and bright around one of the picnic tables, the jocks laughing loudly about a stupid joke, the drama geeks gathering around somebody's tablet to watch some video or other. Nadia didn't know whether to go into the cafeteria, or to stand there and wait for Verlaine, or to start talking; the tension between her and Mateo still crackled like static electricity. Amid all this noise and activity, they were motionless. Together alone.

Mateo finally said, "Do you think it's possible Elizabeth's in trouble?"

Be objective, Nadia told herself. "It's possible," she admitted. "At this point, anything's possible."

He didn't hear the warning in her words. "Like you said, girls aren't supposed to tell guys about witchcraft. So Elizabeth can't tell me what she knows. And she couldn't tell me if she were in danger from whatever is going on in this town."

"That could be completely true." Nadia wondered how she'd feel if it really were true. The important thing was to keep an open mind until she knew more—but it was worth finding out how much Elizabeth herself knew. "Did you tell her? About your being a Steadfast, about finding out about magic? About me?"

It was so easy to imagine—that clutch in the twilight, Elizabeth in Mateo's arms as he confessed everything—

But Mateo shook his head. "I wanted to. But—I know it's not only my secret to tell. It's yours, too. I think we can trust Elizabeth. You have to think so, too, though. When you're sure, we'll go to her together."

That seemed—epically unlikely. But Nadia remained focused. "We need to get more information first. About the curse, about witchcraft in this town, all of it. I've been mean-ing to dig into it for a while now. Really, I'd like to learn the history of your whole family, as far back as the curse goes. Do you have any older relatives who know more about it?"

"My grandmother. And no, you don't want to meet her. Trust me on this."

The suddenly haunted look in his eyes convinced Nadia not to argue, at least for now. "So what do we do? Hit the library?"

"We search through the newspaper archives—with the help of the intern," Mateo said. When Nadia gave him a questioning look, he pointed across the quad, where Ver-laine was loping toward them. Her expression was still wary, but Verlaine was taking it for granted, by now, that they would all hang out.

While it was still only her and Mateo, Nadia had to ask: "So, where's Elizabeth today?" When Mateo frowned in apparent confusion, she added, "Since she wasn't in class."

"Oh, yeah. I guess not." The question just rolled over him; even though he was worrying about Elizabeth being in danger, standing up for her honesty and goodness, Mateo didn't seem to take any note of whether she was there or not.

Like he's been told not to notice when she comes and goes, Nadia thought. *Like he's not able to notice. Like someone has stopped him.*

Elizabeth walked along the street, staring down at the pave-ment where the blood drops fell. A couple of times, she heard cars come up behind her, but they always slowed down, steered neatly around her, and moved on. None of the drivers would remember anything about it later.

Overhead the crow flew, the beating of its wings entirely regular; the small cut she'd made should not have weakened it greatly. Even if it had, though, she'd commanded the bird to fly on, no matter what.

The blood trailed off the main road, spattered onto the curb. Near someone's front step.

When she looked up, she stood in front of the house on Felicity, the Victorian that had been painted pale blue sometime in the past forty-five years. Even with Nadia at school, the outline of the building glowed slightly to Elizabeth's eyes, a sinuous violet shade—the sign of magic at work.

The mother, she thought. *It can only be the mother.*

Nadia was too young to be a true challenge to Elizabeth, and yet already she showed signs of extraordinary power. Only a few possibilities allowed that to be true—and the most likely was that the greater power came from Nadia's mother. She was the one who would have taught Nadia; she was the one who had tapped into her daughter's potential.

And she was the one who would have to be eliminated first.

As the crow fluttered into a nearby tree to rest, Elizabeth went up the steps, noting the slight reverberations around her as she did so; the usual wards and charms were in place, but nothing else. Elizabeth expected no response when she rang the doorbell, as it was the middle of the day—but then heavy footsteps came close, and a man in his forties opened the door. He was tan-skinned, dark-haired, pleasant despite the rolled-up sleeves and absent expression that suggested he'd been working. "Can I help you?"

"Are you Nadia's father?" Elizabeth gave him her most endearing smile. "I'm a new friend of hers. From school. Elizabeth Pike."

"Shouldn't you be in—" The question died on his lips as she brought him into her spell; from now on, Mr. Caldani would be no more likely than anyone else to question where she went, or when, or why. Nadia might be immune to that glamour, like other witches, but no one else could be. He grinned easily. "I'm glad to see that Nadia's met so many people right away."

"Captive's Sound is a really friendly town. Can I come in?"

He didn't ask why. Didn't wonder why. He only stepped aside and let Elizabeth walk right in.

Immediately she could tell that most of the spellcasting happened above her head—the attic, no doubt. Good. If the mother were up there, she wouldn't be able to get past Elizabeth. She was enclosed. Trapped. Tilting her head, smiling sweetly at Mr. Caldani, she said, "Is your wife at home?"

His face fell. For a moment he struggled to find words. "She . . . Nadia's mother and I recently divorced. She lives in Chicago."

"Oh. I'm so sorry." Elizabeth made sure her expression appeared sympathetic. It was best to give people the occasional real memory of her behaving in a thoughtful way; such memories reinforced her illusions. "I didn't mean to pry."

"It was a natural question. You didn't know. But don't talk about—no. I won't say that. If you and Nadia talk about it, be careful. Obviously it's a painful subject for all of us."

"You want to protect her," Elizabeth said. "Of course." He was a kind man, and a sensitive one. She could use that, if it came to it.

But she didn't think it would. Without a mother to guide her, Nadia was all power, no progress. She would never be a serious threat to Elizabeth's plans.

Peculiar that the mother would leave at the most sensitive part of the daughter's training—but most people were short-sighted. Elizabeth didn't suffer from that particular handicap, not any longer.

It would be simple now to go up to the attic and take Nadia's Book of Shadows, all her ingredients, everything, but what would be the point? Best to go. "I stopped by hoping Nadia was home," Elizabeth said. Mr. Caldani would never ask her, or himself, why Elizabeth would expect Nadia to be at her house during school hours, any more than he would again ask why Elizabeth was here herself. "I should go. Let you get back to work."

He managed a smile for her. "Well, it was nice to meet you, Elizabeth." They parted at the door almost as friends.

Swiftly she walked home. Would Mateo come by again tonight? He demanded so much time and care, and right now—when the dreams were still so unfocused—she was learning little.

Soon it would all be worthwhile, though. Very soon.

She walked into her house. The afternoon sunlight glinted on the broken glass on her floor as she paused, staring at the center of the room. There her crow shuddered on the floor, its wings beating desperately against the boards, twitching in its final throes. It had come back here to die, though not of its wound. The magic had strangled the bird, of course; it always did, sooner or later.

When at last it went still, she touched one of her rings and went through the spell almost without thinking it; that one was familiar to her now. Instantly the crow disappeared in a flame that lasted hardly more than a second. Only the smallest scorch mark on the floor showed where it had been.

Elizabeth reached amid her jars and pulled out the one filled with grayish liquid, the one where all the other dozens of eyes from the earlier crows still floated. She'd need it soon. Then she went to the windowsill, lifted up her arm, and made all the crows believe she was singing, singing to them, and it was only a question of which one came to her first.

"Technically I'm an intern," Verlaine said as they walked up the steps of the Captive's Sound newspaper, the *Guardian*. "But there's not that much to do here."

"Really?" Nadia looked askance at the dusty front office. "This seems like a town with a whole lot going on."

"Not anything normal people know about." Verlaine took out the heavy key and unlocked the door; the musty smell was comforting to her by now. "The paper publishes once a week. They used to be more newsy back in the day, but the paper was bought by some out-of-town people who only care about putting advertising circulars in it. Not much actual reporting going on, and the editors never let me do any of it. That's why all my work—and all the real news in town—goes to the *Lightning Rod*."

"The *Lightning Rod*?" Nadia looked confused.

It was Mateo who answered. "The school's news site. It was a paper until about six years ago. All the journalism students work on it."

"My honors project is making the back issues digital. Well, what back issues they have, thanks to that weird fire back in 1999." Verlaine dimly remembered that. What were the odds of lightning striking the chemistry lab twice? Well, Captive's Sound had a way of beating the odds. Now she finally understood why.

This town really was as strange as Verlaine had always thought. It was incredible how vindicated she felt, how justified. Every creepy nook and cranny of Captive's Sound was possessed by magic—the secret underlying the whole world, the element that proved wonderful, bizarre, impossible things could really happen.

And the way people were always so mean to her—well, all right, maybe that wasn't magic, but it wasn't inevitable. It wasn't the way her life would be forever. Only a couple of days into her senior year, and already it felt like her world had started to transform. She and Nadia . . . well, they weren't quite friends exactly, but they told each other their secrets, which was as close as Verlaine had ever come to friendship. Through Nadia, Mateo had suddenly noticed her, didn't seem crazy in the slightest, and seemed to like her just fine. After a life of near-total isolation, Verlaine found it almost dizzying to think of having not one but two people to spend time with.

Plus they had a mission! A real, true magical quest or investigation or whatever you wanted to call it, which was one hundred percent more interesting than anything else Verlaine had ever done in her life.

Of course, she'd probably have to give Nadia and Mateo some time alone occasionally. The way Nadia unconsciously bent toward him every time he talked—the light in his dark eyes whenever he looked at her—well, it was pretty obvious what was going on.

Verlaine didn't resent it. Not exactly. Or only a little. While she'd never been in love herself—had never even kissed a guy yet—she'd had plenty of chances to observe romance from the sidelines. People got incredibly stupid right before and right after they hooked up with someone they really liked, and that was all there was to it. If Nadia and Mateo were going to be way more into each other than they were into her for a while, she figured she could deal. Yes, she wished the first friends she'd ever had were more focused on her, but at least their absorption in each other wasn't a way of rejecting her. Verlaine had learned pretty much all the ways to get rejected by this point, and that wasn't what was going on. This was just hormone overload.

Right now, though, all three of them were . . . questing. Or whatever you wanted to call it.

So they got to work in the front office, aka the only office; the *Guardian* was old-fashioned enough to still have its printing presses in the back room. The front room was already a mass of papers and old photographs, the kind that had been printed on thick, shiny paper. They couldn't make it any more disorganized than it already was. Verlaine tugged out the bound back issues and let them all start searching through.

"What are we looking for?" Mateo asked, coughing as yet more dust drifted up in clouds from the back volumes.

"Anything that could point to witchcraft, or magic." Nadia began thumbing open the pages of *Volume XI: 1865–1870*. "In other words, anything weird."

"No shortage of that here," Verlaine said.

But it quickly became clear she hadn't understood the half of it.

The church fire in 1995? Not the first church fire in Captive's Sound. Not the second, or third. It was the *twenty-fifth*. Verlaine knew more buildings used to burn down back in the days of dry timber and no fire departments, but twenty-five churches seemed . . . extreme, even over a span of more than three centuries.

As for the sinkholes that had begun in town earlier this

year—that had happened before, too. Only once, and that back in the 1810s, but sinkholes were almost unheard of in this part of the United States. (Verlaine had researched this for the *Lightning Rod*, which was way more on top of the issue than the *Guardian*—not that anyone paid attention.)

The part that got to Verlaine was all the news about animals. She had a tender heart for animals—not just her beloved cat, Smuckers, but all of them, alpacas to zebras. Since age eleven she'd been a vegetarian. So her eyes blurred with tears every time she read about a mass death of crows, all of them found twitching and dying in a heap of feathers on the street. Or foals born with three heads, a bizarre genetic event that apparently happened in Captive's Sound once every twenty years, like clockwork. Or a dog found without its head on the steps of City Hall. Who could do that to a dog?

A witch, apparently. Not like Nadia. The other kind of witch, the one behind whatever was going on here.

"I can't believe we don't know about more of this," Mateo said after they'd all been at it for more than an hour. "I mean, they actually thought a 'freak wave' could pick up a whaling ship and just drop it in the middle of town? Even back in the 1700s, you'd figure they knew better than that."

"They probably did," Nadia said absently. "But what were they supposed to report? The truth?"

"Well, *yeah*." Verlaine took journalism seriously, even if everyone else thought it was just tabloid stuff and spin. There was a place in the world for people who told the unvarnished truth. At least, she hoped so.

"The part that weirds me out is the rain of toads," Nadia said.

At last, a question Verlaine could answer. "Oh, that's actually not magic. Not even weird. Sometimes tornadoes pick them up, and they get dropped down through a rain cloud somewhere else."

Nadia shook her head. "It rained toads *inside*. In several of the houses on the Hill. All of a sudden, *plop*, toads rained from the ceiling."

"Ew." Okay, Verlaine decided, that was definitely not tornado-related.

Mateo cut in, "What about the Cabot house? Did it happen there?"

Suddenly Nadia looked embarrassed—as though she'd like to sink into the ground to hide. Verlaine was very familiar with this feeling. "No. It didn't. But they—well, they said there were questions about whether a Cabot was involved. Some people suspected a prank by the 'eccentric' Millicent Cabot—"

"My great-great-grandmother." Mateo leaned back in the creaky wooden chair, shutting his eyes too tightly, like someone with a headache. "She lasted for decades, crazy as hell—at least, according to Grandma. Most of us burn out after only a few years of the visions. Millicent ran mad for almost thirty years, until finally one day she—well, she hung herself from the rafters in the attic." He tried to smile, but it was an odd expression, tense and tight. "Another reason I really never want to live in that house."

After a few moments of awkward silence, Verlaine tried to lighten the mood. "Hey, at least we weren't here for the ice storm in July. Or the time everyone at a screening of *How To Marry a Millionaire* started bleeding from the eyes and they blamed CinemaScope."

"I have a feeling—before this fall is through, we'll *wish* that's all we had to deal with," Nadia said, which in Verlaine's opinion wasn't helping the mood one bit. But Nadia remained focused. "What I can't get over are how many reports there are about witches, witchcraft, et cetera. All the reports are about rumors—'town lore,' that kind of thing—but it seems like witchcraft has been a pretty open secret here for a long time."

Verlaine pointed out, "Some of that is just New England for you. I mean, you have the Salem witch trials—women who fled Massachusetts because they were scared by the witch trials—that kind of thing."

"Right, of course," Nadia said, "but this goes way past that. So there have to be other witches in town, besides me and—and Elizabeth."

As Nadia spoke, she glanced over at Mateo, but he didn't argue. His arms were folded, and the expression on his face was strange—almost sad. He noticed both of them watching him and sighed. "I'm still wrapping my head around the fact that the curse is real. And looking through these records—do you see how often all the weirdness in town gets blamed on one of the Cabots? Not just Millicent. Any of us—almost all of us. Sometimes it was true, because of the curse. Sometimes it wasn't true, because of the witchcraft. It's like I have to rewrite everything I know about my family. About myself."

"It has to be rough," Nadia said softly. "I'm sorry." They gave each other a look then, one of those looks that seemed to raise the room's temperature by a few degrees and make Verlaine feel like she ought to find an excuse to leave.

Instead, she slid over the volume that read *1815–1820*. "I only found one report about witchcraft, actually. This one."

"This is almost two hundred years old?" Nadia began turning the pages, but very gingerly.

"A reproduction. The really old issues are too fragile now; they made copies of a lot of it back in the nineteen-fifties. But it's all verbatim."

They all gathered together, shoulder to shoulder, as Nadia found the correct issue. It took awhile to locate the story they wanted—newspapers were different then, with tiny type and vague headlines and no sections dividing the news by topic. But within a couple of minutes they had it:

"'The sailors met their mischance while diving off the lighthouse for so-called "buried treasure," perhaps believing it brought by privateers returning from the Caribbean,'" Verlaine read aloud. "'But such treasure is well known to be only the possessions of one Goodwife Hale, an early settler of Captive's Sound. Rumormongers and gossips claimed she had fled the Salem witch trials, and to be sure, she was a peculiar character, known for home medicines and squirrel-ing away odds and ends not valuable to any rational mind. Yet she was a poor woman who never owned the gold or jewels that the sailors boasted they might find. Compatriots in the tavern who overheard the doomed men's braggado-cio about treasure tried to tell them better, but they paid no heed—and have paid the price.'"

Nadia sighed. "Gold. Jewels. The stuff a witch would have possessed—it would have been worth way more than any of that junk, at least to me."

"How do you know she was a witch?" Verlaine had stud-ied the Salem hysteria in school; none of those people had really been witches.

"Well, I can't be totally sure," Nadia admitted, "but it sounds right. The bit about the home medicine—that's a clue. And keeping odds and ends that nobody else thought were useful? They could have been for spells. Plus, the article talks about her hiding stuff here and there, so—who knows? The sailors who died probably heard something third- or fourth-hand that was based on the truth. If she really did hide something out in the sound, it could've been . . . I don't know. Something amazing. But it has to have washed away years ago."

Mateo straightened in his chair, an odd expression on his face. "Or maybe not."

"What do you mean?" Verlaine said.

"After I became your Steadfast—when I could see—" He stumbled over the word before getting it out. "When I could see *magic* for the first time, I saw something shining up from beneath the water. Right around the lighthouse. Something brilliant green, and strong, like a spotlight."

"Green," Nadia murmured. "That sounds good." Apparently she could sense Verlaine's confusion, because she added, "Different kinds of magic often hold different colors. Black magic—misused magic, evil—that's usually a shade of red. Something green is either harmless or very, very helpful."

They all looked at one another. It was funny, Verlaine thought, how you could actually *see* an idea make its way around the room, illuminating each of their faces in turn.

"What's down there?" Verlaine finally whispered.

"No idea." Nadia started to grin. "But I intend to find out."

10

THE MAGICAL POSSESSIONS OF A WITCH FROM MORE THAN three centuries in the past—what could they be? What had Mateo seen shimmering in the depths of the sound? There could be tinctures and potions in sealed jars or bottles. Her bracelet or rings, whatever materials she had used to help her cast spells, which over time would acquire certain glamours of their own. Or anything, really, once mundane but enchanted by the mysterious Goodwife Hale.

By far the most tantalizing possibility, though, was that it might be Goodwife Hale's Book of Shadows.

The water burial would make sense. A Book of Shadows acquired too much power and individuality to simply be burned on a witch's death, but was a dangerous thing to leave lying around. Most witches either willed theirs to a younger witch in her family or were buried with them. Goodwife Hale might have chosen another path.

What would a centuries-old spell book look like? Nadia knew that most spells evolved over time, from community to community, from generation to generation. What would spells that ancient call for? How powerful must the book have been for it to need burial at sea?

"You've got that look again," Mateo said as he stood beside their table. They'd all decamped to La Catrina so he could be there for his evening shift, and she and Verlaine had made themselves comfortable in a far corner. But it was a quiet night at the restaurant, and instead of the bedlam she'd expected, they were surrounded by the murmurs of conversation at the few tables that were occupied, and delicious smells—black beans, roast chicken, fresh-cut tomatoes. Best of all was the way Mateo was smiling at her. "That gotta-have-it look," he said.

"It's important," she insisted. "Something extremely strange is going on in this town—a magical artifact from way back in its history could tell us a lot."

And if it is a Book of Shadows, it would teach me so much—maybe some of what my mother should've taught me and never will—

"No arguments here," Mateo said. "You know this stuff; I don't. It's like . . . it makes you light up. It's cute."

He'd called her cute. Her cheeks felt warm. Nadia dropped her gaze from his face, bashful, but found herself staring at his hands instead. They were nice hands—square and solid, and she remembered how he had held them out to her on the terrifying night of the wreck—

"Um, guys?" Verlaine glanced up from her laptop, which was currently atop their dinner table and casting a greenish light on her face. Her eyes were wide, and her voice shook. "I think you might want to see this."

"What is it?" Nadia said as Verlaine turned the laptop around so they could see.

"Okay, last year everybody who got detention had to help scan and catalog all the school annuals going back to the first one in 1892. So now there's an online version alumni can look through, stuff like that." With a nervous look at Mateo, she said, "I thought I'd run a search on Elizabeth. If she's a witch, maybe some people she spent time with the past couple of years might be witches, too, right?"

Nadia nodded; given the signs she'd already seen of a long history of witchcraft in Captive's Sound, it seemed unlikely that Elizabeth would be the only one. Although Mateo frowned and crossed his arms in front of him, he didn't protest.

Verlaine continued, "Look at the index."

She turned the screen around for them to see. Elizabeth Pike was pictured in last year's Rodman High School annual. And five years before that. And three years before that. And on and on—Nadia scrolled down to see that the list of images went back and back, never skipping more than seven years, all the way to 1892.

"It's a family name, I guess," Mateo said.

"But look." Verlaine flipped the computer around and started pulling up images. "Here's from last year—she didn't get an official picture taken, but there's this—" A photo showed Elizabeth on the quad, drinking a soda, just one of several students caught in a random shot. "And there's this from 1963."

The 1963 image popped up on screen, and Nadia gaped. The caption said it was "Liz Pike" standing in line for the new water fountain—but it looked exactly like Elizabeth. Her hair might have been in a little sprayed bubble and the clothes she wore might have looked like something out of a black-and-white movie, and maybe there was something about her face that made her look a bit older, but the resemblance was beyond uncanny.

Mateo shrugged. "So that's her grandmother. What about it?"

Verlaine said, "And 1930."

This image was of some kind of school dance. Standing behind the punch bowl in a ruffled formal dress and a big corsage at her neckline was another Elizabeth, equally identical to the one they knew—"Betsy Pike," maybe a year or so older than the one from 1963.

"Now 1892." Verlaine brought up one more image, a formal portrait. The caption again read "Elizabeth Pike"; the face was again unmistakably similar. Even with a lacy, high-necked shirt on and her hair caught atop her head in a prim bun, it was undeniably the exact same face. Only one change was obvious: The version in the earliest photo was the oldest. In 1892, she was listed as a teacher, not a student—a young one, perhaps, but no teenager.

For a long moment, nobody could speak. Finally Nadia said, "I don't understand."

"It's a family name," Mateo insisted. "Has to be."

"There's no way four generations all look that much alike." Nadia's mind was working fast.

She'd never learned any black magic—never wanted to. Once you started dealing with those kinds of spells, you were in league with demons, maybe with the One Beneath. But she knew enough about it to recognize it when she saw it.

Something like this—it was darker, and stronger, and scarier than anything she'd even heard of before.

"Elizabeth's family has to have been a part of this for a very long time." They would all have been witches, of course; the Craft was handed down mother to daughter.

Verlaine said, "A part of what?"

"Black magic."

Mateo's eyes darkened; his lips pressed together into a thin line. After a long moment, he said, "You can't know any of that from pictures in the yearbook. Come on."

"You've seen the pictures," Nadia insisted. "The same as we have. That's not a normal family resemblance, at all. It goes beyond that. It's almost like Elizabeth . . . like she's being born over and over . . ." But how would that even work?

"Okay, I don't know what the explanation is, but there has to be one," Mateo protested. "A joke by the kids in detention, Photoshopping some of us into old pictures, maybe. That doesn't mean she's evil."

"But this isn't as simple as Photoshop. I'm sure of it." The memory of Elizabeth smiling at her coolly while the entire chemistry class had a meltdown burned in Nadia's mind, constant as a gas flame, the one real proof she had that Elizabeth was far more than she seemed. What was going on?

Mateo said only, "I'm tired of blaming Elizabeth all the time. Let's just get this magic . . . thing you need and go on from there, okay?"

Right then, his father strolled over to them; he had his son's coloring but a pug-ugly face that suggested Mateo's aquiline good looks came from his mother. "Mateo, it's nice that you're spending so much time with the lovely ladies, but you should also spend some time with your other tables. Especially table eleven, the nice men whose fajitas are ready?"

"Sure, Dad. Nadia and Verlaine were just leaving," Mateo said. He didn't sound angry, exactly, but obviously he was glad to have an excuse to end the conversation.

As Verlaine and Nadia walked away from La Catrina afterward, Verlaine said, "Is that possible, what you said? Someone being born over and over again?"

"Well, I'm not sure. I never heard of a spell like that." If she could only talk to Mom for five minutes . . .

"If you never heard of that spell before, then why do you think that's what's going on?"

Nadia shrugged, suddenly uncomfortable in the early fall chill. Dark visions drawn from her mother's few whispered warnings about black magic swirled in her mind, and it seemed to her that underneath her feet she could feel the unsteady shifting of demon-haunted ground. An illusion, of course—but an illusion that might have meaning.

To Verlaine she said only, "With powerful enough magic—anything is possible. Anything at all."

That night, Mateo fell into bed, exhausted, but he couldn't sleep.

As he lay there, stretched atop his covers with his jeans still on, his mind raced. Even walking down the streets of Captive's Sound was different for him now; he knew the places he saw the glimmer were places touched by magic, knew the grime between him and the sky was proof that the entire town labored under some malevolent force. And even washing his face meant having to look again at the swirling, sickly blackness that haloed his head.

His curse was as loathsome to look at as it was to endure.

He shook a few extra Tylenol PM into his palm; he knew you could overdo these, and even trying not to have the dreams wasn't worth frying his liver, but he'd looked up the maximum safe dosage online. With one fist he tossed them into his mouth, gulped them down with water, and hoped again to rest too deeply for dreaming.

With his brain in complete overdrive like this, though, he didn't see how even regular sleep was possible. Mateo thought he could handle everything he'd learned about magic and witches; it was the stuff about Elizabeth that churned his guts and made him want to be sick.

No, Nadia's weird theories couldn't be true; he knew

that. But all those pictures—all those generations of women named Elizabeth Pike—

Why had Elizabeth never mentioned that she had a family name? That she looked just like her mother and grandmother? It was the kind of thing people brought up from time to time, or told jokes about. And he and Elizabeth were best friends. They shared everything.

Slowly he took up his phone and hit her name on Contacts. As always, she answered on the first ring. "Mateo. What's wrong? Did you have another dream?"

"Haven't fallen asleep yet." He curled on one side, imagining—like he often did—Elizabeth lying next to him. It wasn't a sexual fantasy, merely comforting—the idea of her so gentle and sweet and close.

And yet now he envisioned her as "Liz Pike," the sixties coed, or in old-timey Victorian clothes—

"I was thinking about when we were little," Mateo said. "All the fun stuff we used to do together."

"Those were good times, weren't they? Maybe you can think about those while you try to fall asleep."

"What was your favorite? Out of all those memories." He needed to hear that—to remember it through her, to know that she treasured those experiences as much as he did.

Elizabeth said, "All of them, of course."

"Pick one."

"Oh, I don't know."

Why was she being so vague? It couldn't be that she didn't cherish those memories as much as he did—that was impossible. Elizabeth had proved, time and again, how much she cared about him. If Elizabeth could forgive him for being a freak, then Mateo could forgive her for keeping a few secrets she felt she had to keep.

But I'm not a freak, he reminded himself. *The curse is real. What happened to Mom, to all the other Cabots—that was something done to us.*

Her soft voice said, "You'll call me if you have another of the dreams, won't you? Right away. I don't want you to worry."

If she is a witch, the way Nadia says, she knows the curse is real but won't tell me about it. Not even to make me less afraid of going nuts and killing myself.

"Okay," he said. He couldn't picture her lying next to him any longer. "Good night."

"Night," she replied. Funny, how he'd never noticed before now that she never added the *good* in front.

That night, despite all the Tylenol PM, he dreamed.

The entire world was fire.

Floor. Ceiling. Walls. Doors. Every breath burned in Mateo's lungs. Red, yellow, orange: They all glowed and flickered around him, strangely alive, as if heat itself could hate him enough to kill.

Nadia lay at his feet, her dark hair just another burn in the scorched world that now enclosed him.

Mateo wanted to go to her—to save her, to hold her, something, anything—but he couldn't, because he was in someone else's arms.

Why couldn't he let go?

From her place on the floor, Nadia whispered, "You shouldn't have kissed me."

Desperately Mateo tried to reach her, but he remained held fast—those weren't arms holding him, they couldn't be—they were chains—

He awoke with a start.

Then swore.

Then rolled over in bed, punching his pillow, to wait out the long, sleepless hours until dawn.

"You're positive?" Cole whispered, his covers drawn up under his chin.

Nadia closed the closet doors. "Inspected it top to bottom. No monsters. Absolutely, one hundred percent monster-free."

He smiled a little, and she came to his bedside and ruffled his hair. As Cole relaxed, he said, "Can we have mac and cheese tomorrow?"

"Tomorrow is a pizza night. I won't be here. But I bet Dad will order all the toppings you want. You should pick some crazy ones. Like—pineapple and anchovy!"

"Ewww." Cole wriggled in delighted disgust. "Where will you be?"

Diving in the sound for God knows what. "Out with some of my new friends. I'm lucky to have met so many people right away. What about you, buddy? Do you like the kids at school?"

Cole started telling her all about his new friends, and a birthday party he had this weekend; Nadia felt her phone vibrate in her pocket but ignored it, letting her little brother go on and on until his words came slowly, and his eyelids had begun to droop. He was worrying about the monsters less and less now. Maybe he was finally back to being a normal little kid. She hoped so. He deserved it. Mom had taken enough away from her and Dad—it wasn't right if she took away Cole's ability to feel safe ever again.

Only when he was conked out and she'd shut his door behind her did she look down and see that she had a message from Mateo. Instantly she hit Call Back. "Hey. What's up?"

"Hey." He sounded almost as sleepy as Cole had. There was something about his voice when it was sleepy—warm and not quite controlled. Nadia found herself leaning against the wall, making little circles on the floor with her foot. "Sorry we left things so weird. We seem to keep doing that."

Nadia forced out the next: "I don't mean to say anything bad about Elizabeth."

"Listen, I admit—Elizabeth hasn't told me the whole truth. I know she can't. I get that. I also know you're not making all this up. Before I can talk to Elizabeth, really talk about this, I have to know what she's dealing with. The more I know, the more she's likely to tell me. Right?"

"Right." Why did he have to be so focused on Elizabeth? Nadia focused on the most important thing. "I want to go diving near the lighthouse. To search. Tomorrow night, if I can."

She expected him to argue. Or hesitate. To come up with reasons they should ask more questions first.

All Mateo said was, "I'm with you."

All day, Nadia's mind was on the night's dive. Her body, unfortunately, was stuck in school, and every class seemed to drag on and on forever. A counseling session with Faye Walsh seemed likely to bore her to actual, literal death, until Nadia came up with the idea of telling her that she was working with Verlaine on digitizing the back issues of the *Lightning Rod*—that was an extracurricular project, right? Apparently it counted, at least enough to get Ms. Walsh off her back for the moment.

Her head still in the clouds—thinking of what to wear, when to go, what to tell her father—she drifted down the hallway toward her last class, when suddenly Elizabeth stepped directly in front of her.

Nadia stopped short. Elizabeth regarded her without malice or curiosity. With her chestnut curls long and loose and her unfashionable airy dress, she ought to have looked unkempt, even tacky. Instead, there was an incredible stillness to her. Her beauty was so precise that it might have been plotted on a sketch pad with compass and protractor, every measurement ideal and yet impersonal. Looking at Elizabeth was like looking at a statue of some ancient goddess that could smite you at a glance.

"Your mother is gone," Elizabeth said.

How did she know that? Nadia struggled for words. "That's—none of your business."

Elizabeth cocked her head. "Your father forgot to mention my visit, didn't he?"

Wait—Elizabeth was in my house? Nadia felt her arms tightening around her books, as if using them to shield her heart.

"People often forget where I've been," Elizabeth continued. "I prefer it that way. Once they're aware of me—of what I can do—it's harder. But I could make you forget about me. Forget my name. Forget your own name, if I chose."

Every bad thought she'd had about Elizabeth was true. Nadia remembered Mateo—the danger he was in because of the curse, how vulnerable he was to Elizabeth's manipulation—and that plus her fear for her dad seized her, turning her fear to rage. "Tell me what you're doing to this town. What are you after? What do you want?"

"Nothing I haven't earned."

"Then what are you doing to Mateo? You're friends. You have to care about him, at least a little. Why haven't you told him about the curse? Why aren't you protecting him from it?"

To her surprise, Elizabeth smiled. The expression was fond, in a patronizing way—like how she might look at a puppy before she petted its head. "You're very young. You don't have your full power yet, and you have no teacher to guide you. So you'll never be a real witch. You and I both know that. So why are you prying into my life? And Mateo belongs to me in ways you could never even begin to understand."

"He's not your property," Nadia shot back.

"Oh, but he is. You know I can make people forget, Nadia. I can also make people remember. If I wish it, Mateo will 'remember' that he's in love with me. That he always has been. He'd be so intensely in love with me that he'd do anything I asked, as quickly as a snap of my fingers." Elizabeth's eyes crinkled slightly at the corners, like someone remembering a good joke. "They say it's better to have loved and lost than to have never loved at all. But you've loved and lost, haven't you? You know how it hurts. Are you going to keep investing all that emotion in Mateo, knowing I can separate you two forever at any moment I please?"

Loved and lost. Nadia had gone out with guys, had cared about a few, but she'd never truly fallen for someone—not the way she sensed she could fall for Mateo. The only love she'd lost was her mother's love.

And that loss had gutted her beyond anything else Nadia had ever experienced or imagined. It still hurt so badly, every single day—

The thought of setting herself up for that kind of pain again made Nadia feel faint. She put one hand out to steady herself against the cinder-block wall of the school. Elizabeth's chin lifted—she'd seen Nadia's weakness, and Nadia hated herself for it.

Elizabeth said only, "For your own sake, you should move on. From me, from this town. Keep your family safe. Haven't you been through enough?"

Then she simply walked away.

Would that warning be sufficient?

Elizabeth thought so. She doubted a slip of a girl like Nadia Caldani represented any real danger in the first place; any complications from Nadia's crush on Mateo would be minor and easily corrected with spells of forgetting or compulsion. Nadia would never tell Mateo about magic, or therefore about Elizabeth's own witchcraft—someone so earnestly self-righteous would never break one of the First Laws.

And yet Elizabeth had to think of another besides herself.

Were Nadia to turn her avid curiosity away from Elizabeth and onto the magic she must, by now, have sensed beneath the chemistry lab—

No, that would not do.

Quickly Elizabeth cast a simple spell to shield the chemistry lab better. No magic on earth was capable of shielding that much power for very long, but she only needed another few weeks now.

I protect you, she thought to the last One she would ever love. *I stand between you and all who would oppose you, weak or mighty.*

The spell shimmered out across the school, settling deep within the earth, where it could do the most good.

Now, to cover her tracks. Briefly Elizabeth considered having Nadia forget everything about her. It would be cleaner—but probably short-lived. If Nadia had figured out this much already, she'd probably manage to figure out that Elizabeth was a witch again—and again—and again. Repeated confrontations: What a bore.

Besides, Nadia's knowledge was no more threat than Nadia herself, now that the Chamber was protected. Elizabeth needed only to ensure that would continue.

So she sent out a spell of forgetting, highly targeted, highly specific—and sufficient to make sure Nadia Caldani could do nothing to interfere with Elizabeth's plans, in even the slightest way.

Nadia stopped in her tracks, books in her arms. *Did I forget something?*

She'd been freaking out about Elizabeth facing her down that way—so much that apparently she'd lost track of something else. And it was important, too. Did it have to do with chemistry class, maybe?

I bet there's an assignment I forgot to write down, she thought, and sighed. She'd have to ask Mateo about it later.

The neighbors looked at Mateo warily when he asked to borrow the boat, but then, that was how they always looked at him. As soon as they said yes, he texted Nadia: *Meet me at sunset at the boathouse. Is Verlaine coming?*

I didn't tell her about it, Nadia replied, and Mateo felt slightly relieved. It wasn't that he didn't like Verlaine—he kind of did, which surprised him, since as long as he could remember, she'd been the only kid more outcast than he was in Captive's Sound. But whatever they found in the ocean— if it explained more about who Elizabeth really was, what she was keeping from him—then he wanted to talk about that with Nadia, alone.

Already he felt like he could tell Nadia everything.

What was it about someone that made you know, just know, your secrets were safe with them? Mateo had come to know Nadia first in his dreams, and in those dreams he'd felt—protectiveness, trust, even something that might be love. But those had been only nightmare visions, the emotions experienced there as fleeting as sleep. What was stirring between him and Nadia now—that was real. It could endure. Could he trust that feeling, and trust her?

Walking out to the water that evening made him shiver. Not from the chill in the air—though it was coming, fall already threatening to turn into winter with September not even quite over—but from the view, the look at his hometown that revealed all the evil he'd always sensed but never before seen.

Being a Steadfast meant more than strengthening Nadia's powers. It meant facing the world for what it really was—filled with magic, more dangerous and far stranger than anyone could ever guess.

Even during the daytime, the sky overhead was different than it should have been. Dingier. Lower. When he looked at it, Mateo had the uncanny sense that it was looking back. At first he thought he could even see the reflection of that gloom on the waters, but then he realized they were poisoned in the exact same way. Staring at the ocean, the waves seemed not blue but a slick, iridescent black, as if in the aftermath of an oil spill.

As the sun lowered enough to touch the eerie surface of the ocean, Nadia appeared at the boathouse. Her figure was all but obscured by the heavy fleece top and sweatpants she wore.

It wasn't like Mateo hadn't noticed before then that Nadia had an incredible body. He was a guy. There was no chance he'd miss that. But he hadn't realized he was already in the habit of checking Nadia out every single time he saw her. Maybe he should think about that some more later, he decided as he straightened up. They had a job to do.

"You got a boat?" she said. "Good work."

"No big deal. Pretty much half the population of Captive's Sound has a boat."

"How come you guys don't? No time, with the restaurant?"

Mateo hesitated. "We had one. Mom took it when she— when she drowned herself. Dad never bought another." He'd never known what became of the boat. Had it washed up, been found and disposed of by some neighbor quick to burn something that had touched the Cabot curse? Or did it drift out to sea? It might still be there, floating in the middle of the ocean, empty and alone.

Nadia's hand briefly rested on his shoulder. "I'm sorry. I didn't mean to bring that up. I should've thought."

"You didn't know." He took a deep breath. "Come on. Let's get going."

"Hey, do we have an assignment in chemistry?"

"No homework I can remember. Why?"

"Huh. No reason."

The motor gunned on the first yank, and soon they were skimming across the shining black water. Going out at dark like this was risky, he knew, but they couldn't be seen;

165

diving was way more dangerous than boating, and if anybody caught them at it, they'd get hauled back in.

Besides, he figured—they were heading straight for the lighthouse.

It still ran most nights, its golden beam sweeping around the water in wide circles. As the sky overhead darkened, the lighthouse turned on; the first time the beam swept over their boat, it was as if they momentarily dissolved in brilliance.

"Will the lighthouse keeper see us?" Nadia shouted over the roar of the engine. Her black hair streamed behind her in the wind.

Mateo shook his head. "It's automated. We're safe."

Then his eyes widened, and he didn't feel safe anymore.

Because once again he saw the magic burning bright beneath the water.

Finally the sky was dark enough for Mateo to take it in as he had before. The steady, greenish glow was a few dozen feet from the lighthouse. The churning surface of the waves, this close, meant that the illuminated water leaped and moved as though it were alive somehow, twisting and writhing as if to enclose them.

He cut the motor. Their boat continued forward propelled only by momentum. Nadia frowned at him. "Why are we stopping?"

"We're almost there. Can you not see it?"

"No. Tell me."

Mateo pointed at the heart of it, only a few feet away now.

The light seemed to form a wreath around their boat, as if they were caught in its net. "Right there. That's where I need to dive."

"You mean, where *I* need to dive."

He turned toward her, startled. "Nadia, are you crazy? I can see it. You can't. Being in the ocean—it's not like being in a pool, you know."

"But it's not that different from being in Lake Michigan," she insisted. "I'm a good swimmer. Even did Red Cross lifeguard training."

She had him there; Mateo had never been a great swimmer, and he'd given it up altogether after Mom's death. But he said, "I should still be able to dive for it if I can see it."

Already she was peeling off her sweatshirt; Nadia gasped softly, probably from the cold air hitting her skin. Next came the thermal undershirt, and then he could see the slim black one-piece she wore beneath. It was a lifeguard's suit, or a competitive swimmer's, not the usual brightly colored bikini girls wore to show off on the sand. And yet something about the purposeful way she moved, the simple grace of her, captivated him more than bare skin ever had.

Oblivious to his distraction, Nadia said, "Mateo, whatever is down there is powerful magic. There may be enchantments protecting it. Nobody but a witch would be able to do this. Besides—you're my Steadfast. You make me stronger. That's why I need you up here."

"I don't like it," he said, but if what she said was true—he was stuck with it. He tossed the anchor over the side; cold water splashed his arms as the chain snaked down behind it. Fifteen feet deep, maybe a little more: That wasn't too bad. "Okay. Just—work as fast as possible."

"Trust me, I intend to." Nadia had kicked off her sweatpants and shoes, too; she wore only the swimsuit and hugged herself as she looked over the edge. Mateo tried not to stare, at least not to drool like that jerk Jeremy Prasad would, but it was hard not to—she was so close to him, close enough to touch.

For a moment he found himself remembering last summer at the beach, and the girl who'd hooked up with him on a dare. But now, in his mind, he imagined that this time it was Nadia lying on the towel with him beneath the pier, her fingers tangled in his hair as he ran one hand along her bare leg—

Jesus, she's about to do something seriously dangerous, could you concentrate for a second? Mateo handed her the wrist flashlight he'd brought for his own use. "Here. And if you run into trouble, flick the light off and on really fast, okay?"

"Good idea." Nadia slipped it on, tested the switch, and took a deep breath. "Point to where you think it is—exactly where."

He leaned next to her, so that they were shoulder to shoulder, their foreheads touching. Nadia took one sharp breath that made the boat seem to rock and bob even more strongly beneath them. Lifting her hand with his, he made it so that their fingers pointed together to the core of the greenish fire. "Right there."

"I've got it."

Nadia turned to him as she spoke, and for one moment they remained like that—face-to-face, only inches apart.

Then she said, "Wish me luck."

Before he could do that, or say anything else, Nadia gulped in a breath and went over the edge, diving into the chilly sound without hesitating. The boat rocked beneath him.

And then—only then—did Mateo remember the dream of her floating overhead, writhed in the murk, her hair flowing around her. He'd thought she was suspended in midair, amid the fog.

But what if the dream had showed her underwater?

The cold stabbed into Nadia through every inch of her skin, and it took all her will not to open her mouth and gasp water into her lungs. She slapped on the wrist light, pointing the beam ahead of her—and thanks to Mateo's guidance, she saw it almost immediately. In a nest of seaweed lay a chest, half-dissolved by time and tide, its ancient boards warped free of the metal framework. A crab scuttled by in the murk, the light glinting off its shell.

With a few strong kicks, Nadia propelled herself toward it. With any luck she could grab whatever was in the chest right away and get back to the surface within seconds. Then she could put on her clothes, dry her hair, and be warm again—be ready to explore this thing—

Water stinging her eyes—ugh, she should have brought goggles, but what a time to think of it—Nadia reached the trunk. She couldn't pry the lid up, but no need: The side of the trunk fell away even as she touched it, and a crab scuttled out. Nadia hoped for no more crabs but put her hand in half expecting to be pinched.

Instead, she pulled out—*yes!*—a book. A Book of Shadows.

It was huge—so big she could hardly wrap her hand around it. Despite its centuries of immersion in water, the book remained intact; when she opened it, Nadia suspected, the pages would remain dry.

No charms showed themselves; no more spellwork was required. And only one breath! Triumphantly, Nadia began kicking toward the surface—only to feel seaweed winding around her legs.

Tight.

So tight it was like being tied down.

Nadia kicked, then thrashed, but the seaweed only increased its hold.

The Book of Shadows had been protected after all—and by magic she didn't know how to break.

FIRST, MATEO FELT IT—A QUIVER ALL AROUND HIM, as if the air itself were twisting away. At that moment, the unearthly glow beneath the water changed; it brightened sharply, then dimmed like someone had covered it. The darkness around them seemed almost complete, as if it were the dead of night instead of just after sunset. Without understanding *how* he knew, Mateo knew that a boundary had been crossed.

Again he thought of Nadia in his dream, floating, frightened, and trapped—

—and he had to trust the dream. It might be part of his curse, but it was also his only chance of keeping Nadia safe.

He was stripping off his sweater even before he saw the tiny beam of the flashlight go on, off, on, off. Nadia was in danger, and he had to get to her, now.

Mateo dove in. The biting cold that surrounded him,

sliced into him, was less important than what he saw. Nadia struggled underwater, one arm wrapped around an enormous book, the other clawing at the seaweed tangling around her ankles. But even as she would pull one tendril loose, two more would writhe along her foot and hold her even faster. Her eyes were wide and desperate; she had been down for a while now. Way too long.

Quickly he broke for the surface again, took in the largest mouthful of air he could hold, and plunged in. Mateo kicked toward her, caught her shoulders in his hands. The panic in Nadia's eyes was terrible to see. He pressed his mouth to hers, opening it—then blew the air into her lungs, giving Nadia precious oxygen. As he did, he felt Nadia realize what he was doing and inhale deeply; for a moment they remained tangled like that: two people, one breath.

Then he let go of her and kicked downward. His Swiss army knife had been in the exact same pocket of his jeans pretty much every day for the past five years; his fingers found it instantly, and he flicked out blades at random, the better to hack at the seaweed. Slash, rip, tear—his hand around Nadia's calf, the seaweed still trying to twist around her but increasingly unable to. Then Nadia finally wriggled free, and Mateo followed her, both of them racing toward the surface.

When he broke the water, cold air slapped his face, burned his lungs. Next to him he could hear Nadia choking and gasping as she struggled to stay afloat without letting go of the book.

That book—the way it gleamed, like it was made of liquid metal, the lone light in the dark sound—was both one of the most frightening and most beautiful things he'd ever seen.

As was Nadia's face, water beading on her full lips and flushed cheeks, still terrified but so determined, despite everything.

Mateo slung one arm around her and began pulling them back toward the boat.

Nadia sprawled on the floor of Mateo's house, wrapped in his father's heavy white bathrobe. She couldn't go home with her hair soaked through—Dad might be preoccupied with his job or Cole, but he'd notice if she walked into the house wet as a drowned rat. But apparently the Perez men didn't need a hair dryer. So she leaned back against the padded ottoman, hair streaming out behind her to take in the heat of their gas fireplace, as she propped Goodwife Hale's Book of Shadows on one bent knee.

Every page was dry and fresh; the binding showed age, but only the many years it would have belonged to Goodwife Hale, not the centuries between then and now. It crackled with a pleasant, warming energy; Nadia felt as if she were between two gentle fires. Although the handwriting was spidery and strange, with old-fashioned spelling that was sometimes difficult to read, already Nadia was getting the hang of it.

The spells were going to be amazing, she could tell—but what she wanted most now was the history. And the Book of Shadows had it.

"One cup of Aztec hot chocolate coming . . . up." Mateo stood in the doorway that led from the kitchen, staring at her with an odd expression on his face.

"Does the Book of Shadows look incredible to you?" She could only imagine what the world of magic looked like through a Steadfast's eyes. Maybe this book could even teach her how it was possible for a guy to possess that kind of power.

"I—uh—yeah."

Nadia suddenly realized how much of her leg he could see with her knee bent like that, and she tugged the robe around her snugly as she sat up and accepted the cup of hot chocolate. The water's chill still clung to her despite the nearness of the fire, plus chocolate was *always* a good idea—but this stuff was amazing. There was a spiciness to it that made it utterly delicious. "Wow. Aztec?"

Mateo shrugged as he sat cross-legged in front of her; the warm light painted his dark brown hair. "Aztec by way of my dad inventing the recipe. A little chili and ginger to add some heat—well, people at La Catrina like it." His hand rested on one of the fluffy towels still wrapped around her foot. "This book—this is important? The kind of thing you were hoping to find?"

"And then some. Goodwife Hale—she knew what she was doing. She has a lot of history in here, too; I'm looking through that right now. If she was a witch here when Captive's Sound was founded, then there's no telling what she might know."

"History? I thought you said this was a book of spells."

"It is," Nadia explained, "but she has journal entries in here, too. Some witches only put spells in their Book of Shadows; others use them like diaries. Some people sketch. Most people do a mix. There's no one right way. Luckily for us, Goodwife Hale was heavy on the diary entries. See, this talks about her fleeing Salem—this one mentions which shells she could use for spellcasting, which I definitely need to know—"

Nadia straightened. Her hand froze at the place where she'd been scanning, and her eyes read the words over and over without being quite able to believe them.

"What is it?" Mateo leaned forward to look, which spared her having to say it aloud.

Together they read the name: *Elizabeth Pike*.

From four hundred years ago.

"So her family goes way, way back," Mateo said, which seemed obvious, but Nadia could tell even he was freaked out by finding the same name yet again. "Well, what does it say?"

"Let's see." Quickly Nadia skimmed through the words. "A witch of great power; led the coven here—I *knew* there had to be a coven once, but then—oh."

The scariest words in all of witchcraft were written there: *the One Beneath*.

Mateo craned his head to look. "What does that mean?"

"Elizabeth Pike's husband was dying," Nadia whispered. "No natural or magical means would save him. So she swore herself to the One Beneath."

"Who is that? The devil?"

"Maybe you could call him that. I don't know how ancient he is, where he comes from. All I know is that he's the prince of black magic. The one who rules over the world of demons, which can never—and I mean, never, ever, *ever*—cross over with ours. He has no name, no laws, no limits. No witch can swear herself to him and share in his power. That turns her into something inhuman. Something . . . beyond evil."

Obviously Mateo had some trouble taking that in. Nadia had always tended to think of the One Beneath as something like a monster from a story—not anything she had to worry about. Yet here he was, woven into the history of Captive's Sound.

And maybe not just the history. Maybe he was part of the skin over the sky. The rumblings underfoot. Maybe the One Beneath held dominion here.

"But she did it for a good reason," Mateo said. "Elizabeth's ancestor—she was just trying to save her husband."

Nadia shook her head. "There's no good reason to swear yourself to the One Beneath. Whatever love or kindness or decency you had in you when you made the deal—he takes it. He hollows you out. Only the worst of you will be left behind."

Mateo didn't look convinced, but he nodded toward the Book of Shadows. "So what happened to the first Elizabeth Pike?"

"Her husband survived, but he became afraid of her. He wouldn't live with her, and she didn't seem to care." Nadia's fingers ran along each line of handwriting, and despite the nearness of the fire, a chill ran through her. "Then—over the years—she began to change. Her hair became less silver—her back unbent—and very slowly she became . . . younger."

The photographs they'd seen on Verlaine's computer suddenly flickered in front of her eyes like film on an old-style projector. They weren't several women with the same name; they were one person. One person growing younger, instead of older, with the years—with the centuries.

Could a spell make someone live that long? Make someone become younger, ever so slowly, going on backward through the centuries?

It was impossible. But it was also true.

Elizabeth Pike was four hundred years old. Elizabeth was sworn to the One Beneath. She would be the most dangerous witch Nadia had ever heard of—maybe the most dangerous one there could ever be. She was a Sorceress.

And she had her claws sunk deep into this town. She'd walked in Nadia's house, spoken to her defenseless, unknowing father.

She was using Mateo.

Nadia looked up at Mateo; obviously he understood at least some of what she was thinking. "That can't be the same Elizabeth."

"With dark enough magic, anything is possible," she repeated.

"But I remember growing up with her! Baking cookies. Climbing trees."

"Do you?" Elizabeth had suggested that people forgot what she wanted them to forget; maybe they also remembered what she wanted them to remember. Nadia asked, "What trees did you climb? Where? Were they in her yard? The park?"

"I—I don't know. Why would I know that? Nobody remembers everything from when they were five."

"What about the cookies? What kind of cookies were they?"

Mateo frowned. He was trying to remember, the effort written on his face, but the memories were empty of details. "What does that matter?"

Nadia leaned forward, very close; this would be hard for him to accept—Elizabeth was someone he thought was one of his only friends in a harsh world. But he had to understand. "Of all the memories you have of Elizabeth, are any of them bad? Did you ever, I don't know, fight over LEGOs? Did she ever puke on an amusement-park ride? Did she fall down and scratch her knees? If you've been friends your whole life, then you'd remember something about her that wasn't perfect. Nobody's perfect all the time. But if the memories are fake—if they're just pretty pictures she put in your head—then they'll all be ideal. And blank. And meaningless."

It was heartbreaking to see how hard Mateo worked to come up with one memory, just one, that was imperfect enough to be genuine. He found nothing.

Instead he said, very slowly, "She always asks me about my dreams."

"You mean your visions—the ones that tell you the future."

Mateo nodded. "I thought she asked because she cared. But she doesn't, does she? She knows the curse is real?"

"Worse than that." Nadia hated to say the next, but it was written there in Goodwife Hale's spidery handwriting. "It says—it says that she cursed George Cabot and all his line so that she might know the future without suffering the consequences."

Mateo said something so obscene Nadia had never before heard it spoken out loud. "You're telling me *Elizabeth* cursed my ancestor. My Elizabeth."

"That's what it says."

"So she cursed all of us. Every one of the Cabots. Right down to me."

Nadia nodded.

"*Elizabeth* did this to me. She pretended to be my friend, but she did this to me. And—*Mom*—" He swallowed hard. "Do you know how many years I've been angry at Mom for rowing out into the ocean? And it wasn't her fault. None of it. It was all Elizabeth."

Mateo's voice cracked, and Nadia remembered what he'd told her about his mother rowing out into the ocean to drown herself, leaving her young son behind. She'd done that because she'd been driven to insanity and despair, all so Elizabeth Pike could cheat time and fate yet again. Now the anger he'd felt toward his mother was cracking apart, leaving only the pain.

He turned away, hugging his knees to his chest. Yet she glimpsed the firelight glinting off one tear tracing down his cheek. He wouldn't want to be seen crying; guys usually didn't. Nadia longed to comfort him, but what could she say? She couldn't think of anything that didn't sound empty or stupid. This was about his mother being driven crazy and killed by the person he'd believed loved him. No words could make that seem any less horrible than it was.

Instead, she leaned against Mateo—her back to his back, so he had his privacy but knew she was here, that she hurt for him. After a moment, he let his head lean back onto her shoulder, but Nadia knew better than to touch him in any other way. Maybe it was enough just to be near.

On the far wall, the firelight cast the shadows of the two of them together, as though they were one person with two faces, one looking forward and one toward the past.

Finally, his voice hoarse, Mateo said, "That's why Elizabeth asks me about the dreams. She's using the curse to see the future without having to go crazy herself."

"Right." Nadia hated adding this, but better for him to hear the whole thing at once. He'd been lied to so horribly; she wouldn't hide the truth from him any longer. "I'd be willing to bet that pretty much every memory you have of Elizabeth is fake. She wouldn't have had any reason to pay attention to you until you started having the dreams. Anything you remember that goes back further—it probably isn't real."

"None of it," he whispered. "I thought she was the only

person besides my dad who cared about me. But there wasn't anybody. Not in all this time." His whole body went tense, like he was guarding himself against remembered pain.

Nadia had to turn to him then. "You have . . . friends now. You have us. You know that, right?"

What she really wanted to say was, *You have me.*

It was a long moment before Mateo met her eyes.

The betrayal there, the desolation, was almost more than Nadia could bear to see. How could he endure feeling it?

Only then did she realize how much of that betrayal— that anger—was for her.

He asked, "Is this what witchcraft is? One big trick you people play on the world?"

You people. He didn't see any difference between her and a servant of the One Beneath.

"A witch isn't the same thing as a Sorceress—"

"Stop it! I don't want to hear anything else about the—the First Laws or what a Steadfast is or any of it!" Mateo sprang to his feet. "Whatever it is you do, it's part of what screwed over my whole life before I was even born."

"Mateo—Mateo, I'm sorry—"

"For someone who's so sorry to hurt me, you've done a really good job of dragging me and Verlaine into it. Who else's life are you going to ruin?"

That wasn't fair. It wasn't.

Was it?

Whether that was true or not, the worst part was—Nadia didn't blame Mateo for being angry.

Why would anybody trust a witch, any witch, after learning *this*?

"I should go," she said quietly.

"Yeah. You should."

Mateo gave her a ride home, the same way he would have before, but he never spoke one word to her, not once the entire time. As he drove away, she wondered whether he ever would again.

Verlaine had suspected that something was up for Nadia and Mateo tonight. What she didn't know was whether it was a magical something, in which case she felt kind of left out and would consider going all the way to *annoyed*, or a dating something, in which case, fine, she could get all the details from Nadia tomorrow.

She sighed as she rolled back on her bed. After years and years of being treated like a social pariah, Verlaine was still wrapping her head around the idea of having . . . okay, maybe *friends* was too strong a word. But they were people to hang out with. People she expected to tell her about their days, and people she found herself waiting to talk to. It was more than she'd had in far too long. So shouldn't she be *less* lonely, instead of *more*?

But now that she could dream of not being alone—all the dreams she had about finding love, about some guy finding *her*, had come rushing in.

College, she'd told herself. *I'll find somebody in college. The guys won't be such jerkwads then. They'll be more mature. I'll meet somebody awesome.* Verlaine didn't even know exactly what this awesome guy would be like; she imagined him looking a little like Jeremy Prasad but acting way, way nicer.

Now, though, Verlaine was done with being alone. Done with being a patient good girl. Her life had started changing, and she wanted it to change completely.

One thing at a time, she thought. Nudging her cat, Smuckers, to one side, she pulled her cell phone out from under him; it was warm and dusted with orange fur. Verlaine brushed it off, deciding that just texting Nadia to check in wouldn't be too intrusive, even if she and Mateo *were* together—

—which was when the screams started outside.

Verlaine leaped up and ran for the front door, only a couple of steps ahead of her uncles in their bathrobes. "What the hell?" Uncle Dave yelled. "Are Claire and Bradford fighting again? If they damage our truck one more time, that's it. We're calling the cops. I don't care whether Claire's in anger-management therapy or not."

"That's more than two people out there," Uncle Gary replied. "Maybe they got their families in on it? Man, we live near some trashy people."

But then the ground shuddered slightly, and the three of them stared at one another. "What's going on?" Verlaine whispered.

Uncle Dave put his arms around her protectively while Uncle Gary ran for the door. When he flung it open, Verlaine saw—not fighting neighbors, not some summer-movie disaster, but Dave's beloved truck.

Buried halfway in the ground, tail end first.

"Oh, no, no!" Uncle Dave hugged her even tighter. "What the hell?"

Uncle Gary swore. "Not again! Not here! Dammit!"

What had happened was another sinkhole—or so they called it, though to Verlaine's eyes it looked more like a trench than a hole. This one went beyond any of the others in town, even the one that had nearly swallowed her car. The long, curving trench cut an arc through their street, ripping out yards, the Duxburys' garage, and unfortunately for the truck, a big chunk of their own driveway. Everybody was running around in their pajamas, looking to see what had happened to their homes and their neighbors.

"Do you have any idea what this is doing to our property values?" Uncle Gary said. Uncle Dave sighed.

Her heart fluttered faster in her chest as she remembered what it had been like when she fell into one of these herself— the whole world tilting sideways, the blank, silent terror that had made her claw at the steering wheel to keep from tumbling downward. But Verlaine forced herself to stay calm. She had a job to do here.

While Uncle Dave paced around the truck in horror and Uncle Gary called the insurance company, Verlaine went up and down the street with her phone, taking photos and footage to post on the *Lightning Rod*. Disaster in Captive's Sound! That was a good headline. Here, a shot of yet another family freaking out. There, the hollowed-out street. The overall scene—

—Verlaine lowered her phone and frowned.

For some reason, every tree on the street had birds in the branches. Dozens of them. Hundreds. Lines and lines of crows peered down; a few perched on the eaves of houses or hopped around on the ground.

"Beyond Hitchcock," she muttered.

One crow in particular hopped closer to her, cocking its head. But—what was wrong with its eyes—was it blind? They were gray, filmed over with some kind of webbing.

Poor thing, Verlaine thought, but in an instant it had taken off and flown away.

"Hope I didn't interrupt anything important," she said to Nadia on the phone twenty minutes later, as she finished coding the breaking news update for the *Lightning Rod.* "But I was wondering whether this was witchy stuff or just, you know, bad roads."

"I wouldn't be able to tell—I mean, it looked normal to me that first time, when your car fell in. Mateo could, maybe, if he—" Nadia sighed. "Nobody got hurt, right?"

"I don't think so."

"And what did you mean, interrupt anything important?"

"You know. You and Mateo. You guys were together tonight, right?"

"I didn't mean to leave you out." Nadia sounded apologetic, so Verlaine decided not to get irritated about it. Well, not *more* irritated, anyway.

"Don't be stupid. Of course you did. I get it. You and Mateo want some alone time."

"It's not like that," Nadia said, surprising Verlaine. "We're just friends—maybe we could've been more than friends, and I thought we might—until he found out—well. You should know what he found out."

And that whole set of revelations was so astonishing that Verlaine had to stop typing and just hang on to her phone and listen for a long time. At last she said, "Holy crap."

"Mateo's really crushed, obviously. So be careful how you talk about it with him."

"Elizabeth—she's dangerous. Seriously, seriously dangerous. That's what you're saying."

"Yeah. She is."

"Then would you go to the *Lightning Rod* site? Because if she's behind this, and my yard is already caving in? I want to know."

Verlaine had already charted tonight's craziness on a map of all the various road and bridge collapses around Captive's Sound in the past year. Most people thought that the roads commission must have hired bad contractors or pocketed the money for themselves; everyone in town knew there had to be a problem.

But what she saw now was a pattern.

"Are you clicking on it?" Verlaine enlarged the image on her screen. "Do you see what I see?"

"Concentric circles."

"Mouse over each spot—that gives you the date."

"It looks like the circles are tightening as time goes on."
Nadia's voice sounded like she was trying very hard to remain

calm, but the taut edge of her words gave Verlaine chills. "That space in the middle—you know Captive's Sound better than I do. What is that?"

"It's Swindoll Park." Why would the park be so important? "Nothing's there. Just, you know, trees and a duck pond and the carousel. They have a cookout on the Fourth of July. The Halloween carnival. That kind of thing."

"Did you say Halloween carnival?"

"Yeah. How does that matter?" It was mostly a costume contest rigged in favor of the mayor's kids and games like bobbing for apples, which was just about the stupidest so-called "fun activity" Verlaine could think of.

"Halloween is an important night for witches. That's one thing the movies don't lie about." Nadia was thinking it out as she said it, but she sounded terrifyingly sure. "If these circles are drawing close to this location—this place where all these people are going to be on Halloween night—"

Verlaine bit her lip. "What's going to happen?"

After a long silence, Nadia said, "I can't say for sure. But some spells—the darkest spells, those that serve the One Beneath—they require more than magic. They require blood."

"Halloween," Verlaine said. "That was—two months from when you did the fortune-telling spell."

"Exactly."

It's like a target, Verlaine thought as she looked at the map. *And we're in the bull's-eye.*

12

AT FIRST NADIA THOUGHT THEY'D WORK IT OUT AT school.

Mateo had to show up for classes, and they shared chemistry together, so meeting up was inevitable. He'd be furious for a few days, but sooner or later he'd want to talk this out—right?

But he cut class the next day.

And the next.

And the next.

When the Piranha marked down that third absence, she quipped, "Looks like Mr. Perez is dying to repeat his senior year."

Unable to resist any longer, Nadia raised her hand. "What about Elizabeth Pike?"

The Piranha frowned, genuinely confused. "What about her?"

"She's out, too." Just like she had been ever since that last confrontation they'd had in the hallway—a week now? More? Nadia found it difficult to remember, for some reason.

For a moment the Piranha thought about that, dismay creeping over her face . . . but then her eyes went kind of misty as she smiled. "Elizabeth's absence is excused. Her parents sent a note. And maybe you should mind your own business, Miss Caldani."

People giggled. Kendall glanced over her shoulder and muttered, "How come you're telling on people?"

"I was just mentioning it." Nadia tucked her hair behind her ear. She could feel her cheeks flushing hot.

Jeremy leaned across their shared lab table. He was a tall guy—lean and lithe—with sharp cheekbones that looked like they could cut glass, tawny skin, and dark curly hair that was as long as it could be and still look great instead of messy. All at once she totally got how this guy could get to Verlaine . . . if you only ever saw him at a distance, *wow* . . .

Then he said, "God, you're a tight ass." Grinning, he added, "I like a tight ass on a girl."

"Too bad for you I don't like slime on a guy."

His black eyes glinted with anger—real anger—but he just turned away from her to surreptitiously text someone. Even from where she sat, Nadia could read the words *stuck-up bitch*.

Nadia wondered whether there really were spells for turning men into toads. Probably not. But thinking about it helped.

"Maybe we should go check on him," Verlaine suggested after school.

Nadia shrugged. "I don't think so."

"But why are you assuming he's cutting class? I mean, Elizabeth could have confronted him—or he could have confronted her—and he could be, I don't know, a hostage in her house. Imprisoned!" In her mind, Verlaine saw this scenario as something suspiciously Disneyesque—Mateo seemed to be wearing a cape, even—but there was a black cave and bars over the windows and plenty of scarier elements that seemed totally like they might be Elizabeth's modus operandi.

"No, he's okay. He was working his shift at La Catrina last night."

Verlaine paused, the keys in her hand hovering just short of her car door's lock. "Wait, you saw him? You guys talked?"

Awkwardly Nadia said, "Well, I saw him."

Through narrowed eyes, Verlaine said, "You're spying on people again." Nadia didn't deny it. "Remember how I said that was maybe not such a great idea?"

"You were the one who said we should check on him! That's what I was doing. Just . . . covertly."

Verlaine shook her head as she unlocked the car. Her old land yacht might be beaten up and ancient and slightly stinky, like French fries were always in the glove compartment, but at least it was a little bit of a haven away from the rest of the school. When they were both inside, doors shut, Verlaine said, "You just spied on the restaurant?"

"Yeah. I sat in front of the barbershop across the street. Hey, does the woman who works there—is she not friendly?"

"Oh, that's just Ginger. She never talks." Verlaine didn't let herself get sidetracked. "What about his house? Did you spy there, too?"

"No. Give me some credit, okay? I just wanted to know he wasn't in danger from Elizabeth. More danger, I mean." Nadia raked her fingers through her black hair, and Verlaine realized her hands were shaking. Whoa. She'd known Nadia was worried about Mateo, but not that she was truly scared for him. Seeing Verlaine's face, Nadia sighed. "Elizabeth said—she told me Mateo was hers to control, anytime she wanted. She said she could make him love her, even believe that he'd always loved her. Which—I hate that idea, I *hate* it, but I'd rather think about him being with Elizabeth than the alternatives."

"What alternatives?"

"Think about it. She can control him, if she wants to. What if she's making him—do something crazy, even criminal, so everybody turns against him? Or she could have turned him into a puppet, somebody who's just sleepwalking through life while she waits for him to have another dream. Elizabeth could even tell him to kill himself." Nadia's voice trembled. "Think about it. His mother did, right? We've been assuming that's because the visions drove her crazy—but what if going crazy meant she just wasn't useful to Elizabeth anymore? Elizabeth might have tossed her aside. Wadded her up and thrown her away like scrap paper. She could do it to Mateo, too."

Okay, all of that sounded . . . extremely bad. But also

extremely theoretical. "Hey. Mateo was at La Catrina last night. So none of that scary stuff has happened. It's going to be all right. You know?"

"No. I don't know that."

"Yeah, Elizabeth's a powerful witch, but now you've got this badass old spell book, and your own magic, and we've figured out where and when her big plan is going down—"

Nadia snapped, "But we don't have any idea what it is, and even if we did—Verlaine, what do you think I can do about it? My magic is nothing compared to hers. *Nothing.* She's hundreds of years old! By now her Book of Shadows could probably take me out by itself. If she figures out that we're trying to get in her way—you get that this is dangerous, right?"

"Hey, don't bite my head off, okay?"

"Sorry." Nadia breathed out, then said it more like she really meant it. "I'm sorry. I'm just scared for Mateo. For all of us."

Fear curled up inside Verlaine's belly, cold and slithery. She remembered the map she'd posted on the *Lightning Rod* website, where anyone could see it (but, of course, no one ever looked). Again she thought about the target and envisioned herself standing in the center of it, looking up at an arrow swooshing down at her out of the sky.

But there was no running from what was coming. It was aimed not just at Verlaine, but at her uncles. Her house. Her closet. Smuckers. Everything she held dear and everything she hated—everything she knew.

What else was there to do but try to fight?

It seemed obvious to Verlaine, but as she watched Nadia curling up in her car, pulling on her headphones to try to shut out the world, she wasn't sure Nadia remembered that right now.

Mateo didn't blow off his shifts at the restaurant. The last thing he needed to deal with was Dad freaking out at him.

But other than that—he was free. At least until the school called his father, Mateo was free to do whatever he wanted.

And what he wanted to do was find out exactly how badly Elizabeth Pike, his supposed best friend, had screwed him over.

He started at home. It was easy enough to head back to the house after Dad had left to start getting ready to open La Catrina for lunch. Harder to go into the storage space beneath the house where Mom's few remaining possessions were boxed away in a corner, behind Mateo's old bike and a few sombreros left over from the restaurant redecoration seven years ago.

Mateo stood staring at the boxes, a crooked tower of cardboard. They were dusty. Nobody had ever opened them, not since the day his father had crammed them down here. As fondly as Dad remembered Mom, he never went through her old things; that wasn't his way. Mateo had thought it wasn't his, either. But now he began opening the boxes, one by one.

For the most part, they didn't tell him much. He'd been

hoping for a diary, something like that. Instead he found Mom's clothes—neatly folded once, but now crumpled almost past recognition. And yet he remembered that green dress—she would wear it to Christmas parties. The pink sweater . . . Mateo had no one specific memory of it, but he knew he'd hugged her while she wore it.

Hesitantly he lifted the sweater to his face and inhaled. But it didn't smell like Mom any longer, not even her perfume. It just smelled musty, like the back room at the Goodwill.

There were a few other things: some junky pieces of exercise equipment—she'd always had a bad habit of ordering them off television commercials, then never using them. A box filled with her costume jewelry. A folder filled with drawings he'd made for her when he was little; Mateo had to laugh at the crayoned image of him, Mom, and Cookie Monster all hanging out at the beach.

Mom had kept every one.

He hadn't learned anything by going through the boxes, but for a moment, Mateo thought it didn't matter. Being surrounded by Mom's stuff had been comforting rather than painful—a reminder that her life hadn't been all bad. Most of it had been great. How long had it been since Mateo let himself remember the good times instead of the awful end?

Just as he started repacking the final box, though, a card fell to the floor.

Mateo stooped to pick it up. It was in a lilac-colored envelope, and at first he assumed it must have been a Mother's

Day card he'd sent her. But then he saw his mother's hand-writing on the envelope: just one word, a name. *Elizabeth.*

Slowly he opened the envelope. Inside, a brightly colored card with glitter around the letters read *FOR A VERY SPECIAL GIRL!* Mateo read the inscription in Mom's cursive:

> *I'm so glad we've become friends this year. Nothing has ever made me so proud as the day that you said I was like a mom to you. Well, you're like a daughter to me! I hope we'll always be this close.—Lauren*

The date was only two weeks before her suicide. Maybe she never got around to sending the card. Maybe she forgot about it, because Elizabeth had wanted her to forget.

She hadn't just made Mom crazy. She'd made Mom love her. Some of the love that should have been Mateo's had been stolen away by a girl who was "like a daughter."

Mateo looked down at his pile of pictures that he had colored for Mom long ago. None of them had made his mother as proud as the illusion of something Elizabeth was supposed to have said.

They were friends. At least, Mom had thought they were friends—the same way he had. Elizabeth must have been hanging around the house all the time when he was little, but Mateo and his dad didn't remember a bit of it . . . because Elizabeth wouldn't let them.

Damn her. *Damn* her.

Stuffing everything back in the box, Mateo prepared to confront Elizabeth at last.

He tore out of the house, got on his bike, and sped toward Elizabeth's neighborhood. It was a gloomy day—the sky dark and low with rain that wouldn't quite fall. Mateo felt as though night had been draped over the daytime to blot out the sun.

Elizabeth's house stood out in the darkness. He could see magic now, and wondered how he hadn't seen this before. How could anybody not see that this house was deeply, sickeningly *wrong*? It glowed—no, flickered—it was like firelight, in a way, but not comforting or warm. Instead it looked . . . the way fever felt. Hot and sickly and inescapable.

The words Mateo wanted to say kept bubbling up inside him, but they changed from moment to moment, contradicting one another over and over:

You killed my mother. You ruined my life.

I thought you were my friend. Make me understand.

I'm going to destroy you if it's the last thing I do.

Can you shut this Steadfast thing off? Please just end the curse and leave us alone.

If I were ever going to murder any human being, it would be you.

Were any of my good memories of you real? I want at least one to be real, so I know I had at least one real thing.

I hate you. I never knew what hate was before, but now I do.

By the time he'd reached her front steps, he still didn't know what he wanted to say. Standing this close to her house was like standing within a bonfire; the sickly hot light surrounded him now. Mateo tried to imagine it burning the halo away, but he knew that wouldn't work. In fact, it seemed to him that he could almost feel the halo now—the circle of thorns cutting into his flesh—

"Mateo." Her voice came from within the flames. He couldn't actually see Elizabeth yet. She sounded as gentle and sweet as ever; of course, she wasn't in school either. "I've been worried about you."

All at once, he remembered Nadia so strongly that it was like she was right there with him—close enough to touch. She'd told him that he'd reacted to Elizabeth, that his Steadfast abilities had allowed him to see something unearthly in her. Something true. But when he'd reacted to that, she'd made him forget.

Don't react this time, he told himself as the hallucinatory flames flickered and parted. *No matter what Elizabeth looks like. No matter what she really is. Don't react.*

Elizabeth stepped closer to him, and he saw her—really saw her, for the first time.

She wasn't the aged, withered thing she ought to have been after four hundred years. No, her body looked like hers—if anything, she was even more beautiful.

But she was hardly even human.

Her skin seemed to be made of molten gold, shining and swirling and dripping along her bare limbs. Her curly chestnut hair was now a truer fire than the imaginary flames that surrounded him. Smoke swirled around her, forming her garment and her shroud. The lines of her face—while recognizably hers—were altered, with the nose almost flat and the cheekbones higher; the eyes were too large, and tilted like a cat's. It was as if she were half-transformed into some kind of animal—a hunter, a predator. He could imagine blood dripping from that smile. Nothing he had yet seen as a Steadfast—not the scum over the sky, not the strange horned beast in the alleyway behind La Catrina, not even the halo of soot and blades around his head—had disgusted him as much. Or frightened him as much.

Mateo didn't react. His face remained totally expressionless, and he kept his voice even. "I'm sorry I haven't called. It's been—scary."

"You know you can always talk to me." In her voice he could hear the rustling of dead leaves, the slithering of snakes. Her wet-gold hands cradled his face, and Mateo had to fight not to flinch. Yet she didn't burn him; her touch felt just the same. "Tell me about your dreams."

All the words he'd meant to say to her were gone now. Mateo knew he was powerless against this . . . thing that had masqueraded as his friend, as a regular human being. There was no point in shouting his hatred at her, or in begging her for explanations. Something like this didn't explain. It took what it wanted and destroyed everything that got in the way.

Which meant she could never know Nadia was in the way.

So he went to his last dream and focused on that, only on that. "I dreamed of fire."

Her eyes glinted as in triumph. "A terrible fire?"

"Yes."

Elizabeth cocked her head to one side, a gesture so like the friend he remembered that his blood ran cold. "Does the fire kill Nadia Caldani?"

He remembered the sight of Nadia lying amid the fire, her dark hair curling like smoke. "Yes. It does." Was he making Nadia sound too important in the visions? Would that make Elizabeth go after her? Desperate to protect Nadia, he improvised quickly. "Not only Nadia, though. I dream of everyone here in town—everybody dying."

"Even me?"

Let Elizabeth be scared along with everyone else for a while. "Yeah. Even you. That's why I haven't called. I didn't want to tell you."

She flinched. "But you never dream of me any longer. You said so."

Crap. He'd gotten it wrong.

Elizabeth's eyes narrowed, and he knew she'd realized he was lying.

Mateo tried to find the words to correct himself, to come up with anything to cover his tracks. But he couldn't speak.

Literally, he couldn't. His mouth wouldn't open; air wouldn't move through his larynx. He felt as if Elizabeth's fingers had curled around his throat so tightly it was impossible even to breathe—but she just stood there like before, the same blithe smile on her face.

"Tell me the truth," she said.

"No, I didn't dream of you in the fire. I only said that because I wanted you to be scared." *What the hell?* Mateo tried to stop himself, but he couldn't. It was as if he were a puppet in Elizabeth's hands.

"Why would you want me to be scared? We're friends."

As desperately as Mateo attempted to keep his mouth shut, it was impossible. "No, we're not. You just use me."

Elizabeth cocked her head. "Who told you that?"

"Nadia." *Damn it!*

"Still meddling."

But the look on Elizabeth's face was more amused than alarmed. She might as easily have found one of her cats burrowing into the clean laundry. Mateo's heart sank as he realized that Elizabeth wasn't afraid of them or of anything they could do. They weren't a threat as far as she was concerned—and he figured she was probably right.

Her fingertips smoothed along his cheek, half a caress, as she whispered, "Go back to the dream about the fire."

Wait—where was he?

Mateo stumbled and barely caught himself from falling. As his vision cleared, he saw Elizabeth standing in front of him—golden, inhuman, horrific—and just barely controlled his panic. *What did I tell her? Something about the dreams. I told her that I saw her in my dream of the fire, that she died, too. Did she believe me?*

Apparently she had. Elizabeth turned around, smoke billowing around her, and walked back into her house without another word.

Probably she'd always dismissed him just like that, and he hadn't remembered.

Legs shaking, Mateo made his way back toward home. He got all the way to the beach before the cramping in his gut took over, and then he fell down and retched and retched. And yet even when he couldn't vomit any longer, when he lay there with sand on his face, he knew he hadn't gotten all the poison out.

Late at night, Nadia sat up in her attic, both Books of Shadows open in front of her.

Every time she deciphered one of Goodwife Hale's old spells into modern terms, she jotted it into her own book. Not only would it be easier to reference this way, but the spell's power would also become part of her Book of Shadows.

So she ought to have felt more confident as she transcribed more and more of it. Instead, the fear only got stronger.

She understood so little of this. When she'd been working with her mother, Nadia had felt confident. Mom swore her power was exceptional; she'd studied hard and practiced every single day to make sure that power reached its full potential. All Nadia had ever wanted was to be a real witch, the best one she could possibly be.

Well, now that she didn't have a teacher, it looked like the best witch she could possibly be sucked.

This book of Goodwife Hale's—the one she'd thought could give her so many tricks and tips—most of it was completely incomprehensible to her. The terms used were centuries old, archaic. Some of the items needed for more complex spells were things nobody had today—a "spindle from a wheel"?

Good luck getting her hands on that. "The first butter from the churn"? Probably Parkay wasn't going to work.

Even worse, sometimes Nadia could work through the old-timey language enough to realize that complex, intricate magic was described in the book . . . but she didn't have the knowledge that would allow her to understand it, much less use it.

Like the final journal entry Goodwife Hale had ever made—it was either far over Nadia's head or it was nothing but nonsense.

She tried to put it in her own words, to see if she could parse it out. "Magic forms the bars of the cage. The bars of the cage lie beneath us all. To cut through the bars, the magic will be stolen, and only magic can replace it. The strongest force is not in opposition; it is in . . . partnership. Or something."

What was that even about?

Head aching, she turned back to the last spell she'd managed to decipher—one for forecasting weather, which would be handy if not exactly life-altering—stuck in a bookmark, and slammed the covers shut. It was well after one a.m.; tomorrow was going to be a four-Diet-Cokes day. Nadia lowered the attic stepladder and made her way down—

—then stopped short as she saw her father standing in the hallway, in pajama pants and an old Northwestern T-shirt. His arms were crossed in front of his chest as he leaned against the wall, obviously waiting for her.

"Did I wake you?" she whispered. The attic steps were close to the door of Cole's room.

"No."

Nadia glanced toward Cole's door. "Oh, no—did he have another nightmare about the monsters?"

"Cole's fine. I was worried about you."

She tried to smile for him. "You know I don't need as much sleep as normal humans."

But Dad wasn't going for the joke. "It's not just the staying up late. You've been on edge all week. Are you okay, sweetheart?"

"Yeah. Of course."

"You know you can talk to me, right?"

Like she could ever talk to him about any of this. She'd *had* to tell Mateo about magic, but he was the only guy she would ever, ever be able to discuss it with. Her dad was totally cut out of this part of her life, forever. And it wasn't just the magic, either; Dad had spent more time at his law firm than his house until Mom left and forced his hand. He hadn't been around for virtually any of the most important moments in Nadia's life. Why did he even pretend to understand her?

Before she could stop herself, she shot back, "The person I need to talk to is Mom."

His expression crumpled. Nadia had thought it was impossible to feel stupider than she had while getting lost in those ancient spells—but she'd been so wrong. Now she felt stupid and evil.

"I'm sorry. I'm really sorry, I just—I need to go to bed." Nadia pushed past her father to get to her own room. He didn't follow her, or knock after she shut the door.

So she was alone as she lay there in bed, tears streaming down her face. It was weird how hurting someone you loved was even worse than being hurt. That stayed with you longer, and weighed you down all through the night into dawn.

"SO, ARE YOU WEARING A COSTUME TO THE HALLOWEEN carnival?"

Mateo looked up from the stuff in his plastic cup. "What?"

Kendall Bender—who was the one throwing the party, or at any rate was the one who brought the cooler now holding the beers—shouted over the music. "Are you, like, wearing a costume? Because I know sometimes guys are like, that's so gay, not gay as in actual gay but gay as in not cool, except I guess maybe some costumes are actual gay if they're, like, drag and makeup or something, but then on the other hand some guys like to wear, like, horror costumes and look all badass and so I was wondering if you were going to maybe do something like that?"

He shrugged. Halloween was too far away to care about.

Somehow Kendall took this as encouragement. "I'm going to go as a geisha girl, but, like, a sexy geisha girl, so

205

the kimono is, like, all short and stuff, and I saw the costume comes with this wig, and I was going to do this makeup with my eyes but then somebody said that was racist, and I went, um, you are way too PC, and, like, you have to think for yourself. Right?"

"I wouldn't treat someone else's race as a costume."

Her face fell. "I forgot you aren't white. Sorry! Do you want another drink?"

He did, badly, even though he wasn't even halfway done with this one yet. But he wanted Kendall to leave him alone even more. "I'm good."

"Okay, well, bye." She jogged through the sand to the main group, where the music and laughter were loudest, and the light from the dock shone more brightly. Mateo figured the shadows suited him better.

"You think she'd forget *I'm* not white?" Gage appeared at his side; Mateo had almost forgotten he was still around. "Doubt it. Anyway, don't you count as the Caucasian persuasion? You're half, like, Pilgrim."

"The other half is Mexican, and in this uptight town? People notice."

Which was true enough. But of course it was the Cabot half everybody saw when they looked at him, the part they couldn't get over. That was the reason Kendall was laughing with her friends now, making that little swirly gesture beside her temple that meant *crazy*.

He was cursed, not crazy. Mateo was reminded of that every time he looked in the mirror and saw the storm cloud writing around his head. And he was reminded that the person who had cursed him was—

Mateo closed his eyes tightly against the pain.

"You're kinda slamming them back, there," Gage said.

"Looks like a cup you've got in your hand."

"This is *Sprite*. Even if I did have a beer, I'd just be chilling. You're—it's like you're trying to get yourself to pass out or something. Again."

"I'm fine."

"You won't be for long, if you keep that up." Gage shifted his weight from foot to foot, awkward now. "Dude, the last few days—no, all week—you haven't been . . . right."

Well, that was one way to put it. Haunted by the dark visions of magic that surrounded his home and his town and his own head, racked by dreams that showed Nadia Caldani dying over and over again, avoiding Nadia even though she was the only person he really wanted to see, and knowing that the one responsible for all this pain was the girl he'd believed was his best and only friend: "Not right." Sure.

"This is about Elizabeth, isn't it?" When Mateo turned to stare, Gage shrugged. "You guys were hand in glove all summer; you haven't gone near her for weeks."

"Nope." Once again he thought of the monstrous, unearthly thing Elizabeth really was. Saw the waxen, gilded animal face that shone out from behind her skin. Mateo shuddered. "I'll go near her again sometime. Promise you that."

Mateo was pretty sure the first time he acknowledged who Elizabeth really was, what she could really do, he was going to kill her. Really. With his hands. He had always thought he could never do that, kill someone, except maybe in a war but maybe not even then; now he spent about half his waking hours imagining what it would feel like to get his hands around Elizabeth Pike's throat.

Which was a gross thing to think about. It was like letting a monster sit inside his head and give him notes. But he didn't seem to be able to throw the monster out.

Gage said, "That sounds like, I don't know, what did they used to call it? A lovers' quarrel."

"You still want to ask her out, don't you?" Mateo gulped down some more of his drink; it tasted foul, but that didn't matter. "Stay away from Elizabeth Pike, man. Trust me on this."

Gage held up his hands, as if in surrender. "Hey, I know the guy code. I'm not going anywhere near your ex."

"We were only friends," Mateo said, though the last word stuck in his mouth. All it meant now was that he'd never kissed her. That was the only lie she'd spared him. Why did she stop there? Probably it just would have been too much trouble.

She only took the trouble to pretend to be the one real friend he'd ever known.

"Still. I respect that you need some boundaries there. Okay? But you're not acting like yourself, and now you want to party with the same stupid people I know you hate. You're cutting school. No matter what went down with you and Elizabeth, maybe it's time to get a grip."

Easy for Gage to say—

But then Mateo realized that he might have had one real friend after all.

He and Gage hadn't known each other that long, and this was definitely the longest conversation they'd ever had—but Gage was trying to look out for him. This was not an easy talk to have with someone, but they were having it.

Not that it was any of Gage's business what he did. But— maybe the guy had a point.

Besides, Mateo was past ready to drop this whole scene. The school had called Dad, and he was sick of getting yelled at. He didn't even enjoy drinking like this. It made him sick and stupid, and feeling either way sucked.

Maybe he was just *done*.

"You're right." Mateo sucked in a deep breath that smelled of salt air. "You're totally right. I'm standing around feeling sorry for myself, instead of—"

Instead of spending time with Nadia.

Learning whether he could truly trust her, or any witch.

Finding out what it meant to be her Steadfast, and seeing whether he could help her take Elizabeth down.

"Instead of doing what I should be doing," he finished.

Gage smiled a little. "Can we start with ditching this party? I can drive. We could get some sliders at the White Castle, maybe."

"Yeah. Let's." Mateo tossed his cup into the nearest can. No need to tell Kendall good-bye.

"Come on. Race you!" Gage took off, and Mateo tried

to catch him. When Gage started laughing, it felt for one moment like everything was okay—like Mateo was just a guy, no different from anybody else.

But overhead, the stars twisted in the horrible, roiling sky.

"Draw Four!" Cole slapped down his Uno card, and both Nadia and her dad groaned in mock horror.

While her little brother cackled in glee, Dad said, "You sure you didn't stack the deck?"

"Nope." Cole's feet swung back and forth beneath the dining table's bench. "I'm just that good."

As Dad laughed, Nadia heard her phone chime with a text message, but she ignored it for the moment. Cole hadn't been sleeping well lately—not the nightmares, not like before. But he was restless, getting up two or three times a night to ask for water or turn on random lights. That was a bad sign, one Nadia recognized as well as her father by now. They were concentrating on Cole now, trying to get him back to the good place he'd been in just after the move.

And worrying about Cole meant she didn't have as much time to worry about everything else.

"So tomorrow I thought I'd make chicken soft tacos," she said as she threw down a card. "What do you say to that?"

She'd expected Cole to cheer and Dad to simply agree, but Dad was the one who answered first. "You've been spending too much time in the kitchen lately. You should be going out. Having fun. If you want tacos—why don't we go to that Mexican place in town? La Catrina? That's the one."

Nadia felt it almost like a slap.

"And that guy works there, right?" Dad gave her a look as he played his own card. "Mateo. The superhero."

"He's not a superhero," Nadia insisted, though even now she couldn't forget how Mateo had looked in the first moment she'd seen him, his face illuminated by lightning.

"Ah, but he's not available. I forgot." There was no way she was going to correct Dad on that one; if he found out Mateo wasn't dating anybody, he was likely to suggest Nadia should propose. "Well, we could eat out somewhere else. Drive over to the next town, get some pizza, maybe. If La Catrina is a, I don't know, a sensitive subject."

"Pizza!" Cole crowed, before playing his Reverse card.

Between her brother the cutthroat Uno prodigy and her dad in look-I'm-so-sensitive mode, Nadia thought she needed a break from the table. "Hang on. I'm gonna check my phone."

Obviously the text would be from Verlaine. They weren't friends, exactly—there was something about Verlaine that kept Nadia feeling oddly distant—but they got along, and they were partners in figuring out whatever it was Elizabeth was up to. So this text would be either about the weird patterns of disasters spreading through Captive's Sound and what they might mean—or questions about Novels class. Everything had been quiet today, so Nadia figured it was about Novels class, even though it was weird for Verlaine to be worrying about homework on a Friday night.

Instead, the screen read, *Message From Mateo Perez.*

Nadia sucked in a breath. For a moment she just stared down at the screen. Then she thumbed the message open to see: *Meet me tomorrow at the beach? By my house. My lunch shift ends at 3.*

Nadia wanted to go there tomorrow and just smack him. Mateo didn't get to ignore her for a whole week and then just command her to show up at his convenience. No way.

And yet—seeing the message made Nadia feel as if something tight around her chest had finally gone slack and let her breathe.

Even if she did only show up to give him hell—she knew she'd show.

It was the kind of a Saturday that felt like a Monday. The sky hung low with gray, rain-thick clouds that threatened to burst at any moment, and the gusty wind was a reminder that winter wasn't too far away. Dad took Cole to see some movie with computer-generated frogs or something, so she didn't have to make up an excuse about where she was going.

Of course, she could have just told her father she was meeting Mateo—but that would have led to more Mr. Sensitive. No thanks.

Nadia hugged her shearling jacket around her as she walked from Oceanside Road toward the patch of beach nearest Mateo's house. The homes here weren't like beachfront property she'd seen elsewhere; normally, only the wealthiest could afford houses with ocean views, and the architecture proved it—vast decks of gleaming wood, windows so huge they appeared to be glass walls, that kind of thing. But it was obvious that the homes here were as ordinary and weather-beaten as any others in Captive's Sound.

Apparently there's tons of summer vacation business in towns nearby, Dad had said, back when he was explaining the big move. *But it's never taken off in Captive's Sound, for some reason. That makes it cozier. And more affordable.*

Yeah, Dad probably got a bargain on the house in the town being eaten alive by dark magic. Nadia could imagine the real estate listing. *Cursed Victorian! 3 bd/2 bth, zoned inside soul-sucking net of evil. Act now!*

As she neared Mateo's house, she heard the now-familiar roar of a motorcycle and turned to see him driving up. Nadia hugged herself more tightly and stood very still the whole time he shut off his bike and dismounted. She took not one more step toward him. He'd have to bridge the rest of the distance.

"Hey," Mateo said as he took off his helmet. His expression was hard to read. "Thanks for coming."

"Thanks for asking me." Nadia didn't seem to know what to do with her hands all of a sudden, so she stuffed them in her jacket pockets. "How are you doing?"

Mateo opened his mouth, closed it, then shrugged. "Great. Terrible. Both at once, most of the time."

"Yeah. I know how that feels."

For another moment they just stared at each other. This was worse than the few haunted glances they'd exchanged in the halls at school, on the days when Mateo bothered to show up. Then Mateo finally said, "Come on. Let's walk."

They went to the shoreline, where the sand was no longer loose enough to drag against their shoes but packed hard by the departing tide. The ground underneath was still soft enough to hold the faint impressions of their footsteps, side by side.

"The worst part is what I feel when I see Elizabeth," Mateo said, staring out to sea. "I didn't know I could hate like that. Maybe I have the right to hate her, but inside it feels like—it feels like that sky looks."

He pointed upward. All Nadia could see was an ordinary gray sky, but she knew Mateo's Steadfast ability showed him its true nature. "Describe it to me."

"It boils. With a film across it, a scum—like soup that's gone too hot on the stove. Except whatever this is drains the light. Sucks it in. It's like watching poison poured over us all, over and over again. Be glad you can't see it, Nadia."

She was. But she wouldn't say so. Her spell had done this to him; that meant what he had to see was her responsibility, and always would be.

He continued, "But there's a good part, too."

"Yeah?"

It took Mateo awhile to find the words—a long silence between them that was broken only by the crashing of the waves and the shrieking of gulls. "I don't know if I can make you understand what it's like to know that I'm not crazy. That the visions are true. No matter how evil that reason is, it's real, and now I can fight it. At least, I can if you help me."

Their eyes met; as one, they slowed their steps and simply faced each other. Nadia finally said, "Does that mean you— you trust me?"

"I have to."

It was like another slap in the face, but how could she blame him?

Then Mateo added, "And you'll have to decide whether or not to trust me."

"Why wouldn't I trust you?"

He glanced down at the sand, breaking eye contact, like he was ashamed. "Because I haven't told you everything."

"What else is there to tell me?"

"I've seen you in my dreams. My visions of the future."

Nadia frowned. "You told me that part."

"I didn't tell you the part where I've seen you die."

The ground seemed to drop out from under her. " . . . What?"

"More than one dream. More than one way you might— it might happen." Mateo paced back and forth in front of her, talking with his hands as he struggled for words. "So it's not like I know exactly when, or how, or even for sure. You're not the only one I dream about, either—but you've been showing up more and more, and I know you're in a lot of danger. I knew that before I ever laid eyes on you. Once I thought—I thought if I stayed away from you, if I weren't there to see any of the stuff my dreams said I would see, then you'd be safe. Right? But one of the visions showed you struggling underwater, and I didn't even get what that was until we went diving in the sound. Then I realized what kind of trouble you were in, and what I had to do to help you. So maybe some of the dreams let me protect you. I don't know. All I do know is that I should've told you this a long time ago."

It was creepy. And then some. Nadia took a deep breath, then another, making sure she felt steady.

Mateo now looked like he expected to have to catch her when she fainted. "Are you okay?"

"Yeah."

"I should've said something. I was trying so hard not to believe it—"

"We have to believe in your dreams. That's how you saved me from the wreck, and on the night of the dive." Yes. That was what she had to hold on to. Nothing else mattered. "Your dreams are a curse to you—I know that. But they might be the only thing that keeps me safe."

"Then they're worth it," he said, as if that were as obvious as day following night. Something warm and stealthy turned over inside Nadia's chest.

In truth, though, she wasn't particularly frightened of the visions themselves. Yes, it was unnerving hearing that a guy who could see the future mostly saw her in a whole lot of trouble. But the dreams could be symbolic rather than literal; the one where she had been "floating" rather than drowning proved that.

No one vision worried her as much as the fact that he'd seen lots of ways she might die—that she played such a large part in the dreams he'd had so far. Why should she be so central to whatever was happening here in Captive's Sound—in whatever danger seemed to be approaching? October thirty-first wasn't far away now. That was frightening enough to think about, especially whenever she looked at Verlaine's careful maps and the target drawn over the town. But why would it focus so strongly on her?

Worst of all: He'd talked about his dreams with Elizabeth. Maybe Nadia didn't know why she mattered so much—but by now, Elizabeth might.

Mateo studied her face for a second and seemed to decide they needed to talk about something else. "Okay, apparently I'm your Steadfast. And a Steadfast makes you more powerful, right?"

Changing the subject—definitely a good idea. "Remember that whole scene in chemistry class? Doesn't normally happen after a spell of liberation. So, yeah. When you're closer, my magical power should be, um, amped up."

"Well, come on. Let's find out what you can really do."

Nadia heard the challenge in his voice and, despite her worries, had to smile. A spell, any spell—but what?

Once again she thought of the spells she'd managed to decipher in Goodwife Hale's Book of Shadows. For every one that sounded beyond awesome (a spell for extinguishing or even reversing fire), there was another that wasn't as useful these days (like the one to remove enchantments on your milk cow). But one in particular had stood out to her, precisely because of how much she would have wanted it that night she dove off the lighthouse: a spell for moving water.

"Okay." She took a deep breath and brought her hands in front of her chest, a gesture almost like praying, except that the fingers of one hand curled around the pendant on her bracelet that was made of pearl. "Let's try this."

In her mind, Nadia put together the ingredients:

> *The love of a child.*
> *A living thing rising from the earth.*
> *Hope through grief.*

Each one had to be thought of, then felt so deeply it almost ached—

—and as she concentrated, her eyes shut, she felt Mateo slip his hand between hers. He didn't clutch at her, didn't weave his fingers into hers, just touched her. His skin was warm, his hand slightly rough from hard work.

That should have been the most distracting thing possible. Instead Nadia's thoughts took on an entirely new clarity. It was like the world had gone from black-and-white to color, from a flat photograph to three dimensions, but more, with every sensation and feeling more vibrant to her than ever before—

Cole standing on his chubby baby legs and taking his first steps, not toward his mother or father but toward his big sister—

Spring crocuses pushing their way up through the snow—

"So what do you say?" Dad sitting at their table back in Chicago, in the apartment that always felt so empty without Mom there. "Do you want to stay here, or are you guys okay with moving and

having a fresh start?" Seeing little Cole nod, giving up everything he'd ever known in an instant, and Nadia suddenly realizing she wanted to do the same and find out what was next—

"Oh, my God," Mateo breathed. Nadia opened her eyes.

The ocean in front of them had begun to ripple upward into shimmering walls of water. They outlined a path stretching into the ocean, until those walls of water were several feet high. There before them lay seaweed glistening green, the iridescent shells of oysters, and wet, dark sand—a road for only the two of them to travel. Water spray turned even the weak afternoon sunlight into radiance, as prisms of multicolored light flickered above it all.

It was gorgeous. It was miraculous. Every fear she'd had seemed to melt away in an instant.

"That—that was not supposed to happen," Nadia whispered.

"In a bad way or a good way?" Mateo's hand remained between hers.

"In a very good way. This is amazing."

"This is biblical." Mateo started laughing. "Are you going to tell me Moses was a witch?"

She laughed. "What, do you want to get struck by lightning? Hush." Though she'd occasionally wondered—there were a few spells that would definitely seem miraculous—

No. Better to drop that thought and avoid the whole lightning-strike-from-heaven thing.

Nadia couldn't take her eyes from the incredible phenomenon in front of her, but she could hear the smile in Mateo's voice as he spoke. "Do you want to walk out there? Stand in the middle of the ocean and watch the fish swim by?"

"No. I should let it go. The oysters and things—I don't want them to—to do whatever the opposite of drowning is." They needed the water, so Nadia let go of the charm and relaxed. Almost instantly, the water rushed back down, splashing their legs and soaking her shoes clear through. Although the ripples spread out across the waves, already the ocean looked exactly as it had before.

Nadia turned to Mateo and saw her own delight reflected back to her in his face. The two of them burst out laughing at the same moment. "So it works?" he said. Salt water flecked his hair. "I'm a good Steadfast?"

"I don't know how you're one at all. But yeah, you're good. You're *incredible*. That spell should have moved the water a couple of feet, not—parted it like the Red Sea!" Nadia brushed back her own dampened hair. The wind was colder now that her clothes were wet, but she didn't care. This beach seemed like the only place she could ever want to be, Mateo the only person she'd want to be with. "We'll have to be careful how we practice. You give me so much power, even simple spells could be dangerous."

Mateo's smile faded, and his gaze hardened again. "Enough power to take on Elizabeth?"

God, she wanted to lie about this. But Mateo had been lied to enough already. "She's strong. Stronger than any other witch alive, and her ally is the One Beneath. But— but maybe I don't have to be more powerful than her. Just powerful enough to stop her."

"Say the word. Anything I can do for you, Nadia, I'll do. And I know what's at stake, you know? I know what Elizabeth can do. I'm not afraid. I'm with you, no matter what."

As they looked into each other's eyes, Nadia found herself remembering what they said about a Steadfast—that the power she gave to a witch was in proportion to the potential for trust between the two. The potential for understanding, and for love.

14

"NADIA?"

"Hmmm?" She kept staring out of the living room window, where the sky was darkest. That was the east, the direction of the ocean. All Nadia could see was the image of her and Mateo together, surrounded by sea spray, with the power of that magic coursing through her—and the look of wonder in his eyes—

"Earth to Nadia."

Startled, Nadia turned to see her father giving her a look. "Sorry. I kinda zoned out there."

"You're sure you're okay with being on Cole Patrol tonight? You look like you've got a lot on your mind."

"Of course I'm okay with it. That's my job, right?" Okay, it was past time to get her head out of the clouds. She and Mateo could explore anything—everything—tomorrow and all the days after that.

"Hey." Her father took a seat next to her on the sofa.

Already he was in work mode—the pen tucked behind one ear was a sure sign—but his expression was worried. "It's not your *job*. You're not the nanny. If you have homework, or you and Verlaine were going to do something—"

"I don't, and we weren't. Seriously, Dad, your case is coming up. Go do your lawyer thing. I've got Cole."

"You're sure?"

"Positive." Nadia knew she ought to be grateful he was so worried. Lots of parents dumped stuff on their kids without even asking. But honestly, it was almost irritating. Dad knew she helped out, knew she wanted to do it, so why did he keep being so careful with her? It was like he wanted to make himself feel better about it or something.

Luckily, Cole was having a good night. All he wanted to do was watch *Toy Story 3* for about the zillionth time.

"I hate that bear," Nadia said as she lay on the sofa, watching Cole munch on Cheetos. She'd be scrubbing orange gunk out from under his fingernails.

Cole nodded. "Lots-o is a douche bag."

"Cole!" It was hard to sound all strict when she was trying not to laugh. "Don't use that word!"

"Is it bad?"

"It's bad enough. Did you hear that at school?"

Cole nodded. He looked crushed, poor little guy. "That's what Levi calls our PE teacher."

"Well, don't you call him that. Or anybody else." Nadia was already on the verge of cracking up. "Um, you want some ginger ale?"

"Okay. But—Lots-o is one, isn't he?"

"Yeah. You can *think* it. Just don't say it. That bear's a—let's call him a jerk."

Nadia made it into the hallway before she started giggling. Somebody ought to hear that story. Maybe she could text that to Mateo? It was as good an excuse as any—though she didn't really need an excuse to reach out to him anymore, did she? But her phone was nearly dead.

So on her way to the kitchen, she stepped into Dad's cluttered cubby of a home office. He wasn't in it; instead he was pacing the length of the backyard, over and over, while he talked with his client on the phone, prepping him for a deposition. Dad could never talk on the phone without having at least fifteen feet of walking space. She could barely hear him outside the window, going on about a "hostile work environment" or something like that. Nadia leaned over his desk to plug her phone into the charging station—ten minutes would give her enough juice for the rest of the night—

—and saw, hovering on his laptop screen, an email from William Kamler.

Aka, her mother's divorce lawyer.

This was snooping. Definitely. Which didn't make Nadia even hesitate before reading it all:

Mr. Caldani—

I have communicated your thoughts about visitation to your ex-wife. However, she remains adamant a meeting with the children is not advisable at this time. You point out, correctly, that this goes against the recommendations of the court-appointed psychologist; however, parental visitation can never be forced by any legal order. Ultimately, only Mrs. Caldani can decide when or if she will choose to contact her children again, or allow them to initiate contact with her. Although I am sympathetic to your feelings as a father, my legal duty is to protect my client's personal—

The screen saver came on, blurring the page into blackness, then replacing it with a weird multicolored swirl that bounced around the screen.

Nadia couldn't seem to move. Her gut had turned as cold and heavy as stone.

She'd given her father crap about how he wasn't the person she needed to talk to. But she hadn't realized Dad was practically begging Mom to see her and Cole, or at least call or email once in a while. Even that didn't change anything.

Her hands shaking, Nadia went to the kitchen and poured Cole his ginger ale, then went back into the living room with a smile plastered onto her face. "Here you go, sweetie."

"Sweetie?" Cole wrinkled his nose. "I'm not a sweetie. How come you're talking all weird?"

She curled back onto the sofa and drew her knees up to her chest. If she hugged them against her tightly enough, it made her feel less sick inside. "No reason."

Verlaine realized she didn't get a vote on whether or not Mateo got to come back on board. For one, he was the Steadfast, which meant he brought some mojo to the table.

For two, he was the one Elizabeth had cursed to see the future, which both made him Victim Number One and added to said mojo.

Still, he'd totally ditched them for a whole week. Instead of working on the huge enormous crisis threatening their whole town, he'd been—well, okay, he'd been dealing with massive personal betrayal and renewed grief for his dead mother. Which was actually a valid distraction.

But Verlaine? She'd been working. Carefully she'd put together a file of her findings about the sinkholes, complete with a PowerPoint presentation, and sent it to the city council; even without any mention that magic was responsible, they ought to be able to figure out that something was seriously wrong, something centered on Swindoll Park. Maybe that would be enough to get them to cancel the Halloween carnival or at least move it. But she hadn't heard anything from the council office. Apparently reading mail from high school students wasn't their top priority. Idiots.

Besides, now that Mateo was here in the *Guardian* offices with them, ready to be productive again, Verlaine was ready to give the guy another shot. Then again, was he even here to be productive?

Because he wasn't going through the records she'd spent all weekend pulling. No, he was staring at Nadia all rapt and gooey, like he was seeing a rainbow for the first time, or something about that sappy. And, of course, he was currently engaged in the oh-so-important task of drawing something in pen on the side of Nadia's sneaker—a tree, maybe. Verlaine was torn between thinking it was completely irritating and feeling the familiar ache of wishing that some guy, any guy, would look at her that way.

Anything can change, she reminded herself fiercely.

"Okay," she said. "The big question here is, how do we stop Elizabeth in her tracks?"

Nadia and Mateo shared a look; apparently they hadn't realized that Verlaine intended to take over the meeting. Well, that was what happened when certain persons were too busy being twitterpated to concentrate on the business at hand. Certain other persons had to seize control. And put together the PowerPoint presentations.

She turned her laptop around so that it showed a white screen with the header: *Operation Stop Elizabeth.* That slide dissolved into the next, which had three columns: *A—Face her directly. B—Secretly undermine her plans. C—Provide alternate action/distraction.*

"As you can see, Option A has serious shortcomings," Verlaine said. "Mostly because Elizabeth is powerful enough to squash us all like bugs." The next slide revealed a clip art cartoon she'd found of a smushed bug, complete with *x*s over its eyes and a tongue sticking out of its mouth. "Which means we need to look at Options B or C."

Nadia raised her hand, then stared at it, like she couldn't believe she'd just asked permission to talk. "Uh—I think Option C is a no-go."

Verlaine shook her head. "No, think about it! We get her to believe there's some other powerful witch just out of town, or—maybe a magical artifact she'd like to get her hands on. I don't know what that would be, but you can come up with something, right?"

Still Nadia looked unenthused. "Whatever it is Elizabeth has planned for Halloween night—it's big. It's important to her. And she's been setting this up for a long time. I don't know whether we could think of anything capable of distracting her. I'm not even sure something like that *exists*."

Well, so much for the next slide, which had all Verlaine's ideas about Option C, her personal favorite. Her disappointment must have showed, because Mateo quickly said, "Hey, that leaves us with Option B. We concentrate on what we can do, not what we can't. Right?"

"Right," Nadia said. Mateo smiled at Verlaine, like she had been really smart to bring them to this point. Maybe he was okay after all.

Of course, she hadn't come up with as many choices for Option B—

Then an idea came to her. "Hey, you said a Book of Shadows has its own power, right?"

"Right," Nadia said, looking up at her. Mateo never glanced away from Nadia.

"And the stronger the witch, the stronger her book."

"Eventually, yeah."

Verlaine grinned. "So why don't we steal Elizabeth's Book of Shadows? I mean, she's four hundred and something years old, so her book has to be, like, the most powerful ever."

"*No.*" Nadia held out a hand, as though she were physically going to stop Verlaine from trying. "Don't ever, ever suggest that again. Don't even think about it."

"Why not?" Mateo looked as startled as Verlaine felt. "It sounded like a good idea to me."

But Nadia shook her head as she rose and paced across the room, Mateo's little sketch still only half-finished on her shoe. "Both of you—you have to listen to me. Everything Verlaine said is true. Which means a Book of Shadows that old, that powerful—it probably has power beyond anything we can imagine. It might have . . . consciousness."

Verlaine bit her lip. "You mean, it would know we were there?"

"Possibly. I can't be sure." Nadia raked a hand through her black hair, which gleamed in the afternoon light filtering in through the dusty *Guardian* windows. "Certainly Elizabeth will have protected it, and probably it protects itself. If we go after it, it could hurt us. Physically, mentally. Mateo, you should never even look directly at it. I don't know what it might do. No matter what Elizabeth's doing, going after her Book of Shadows isn't worth the risk."

Mateo considered that in silence, but there was something hovering beneath the surface—Verlaine could see how badly he wanted to speak. Finally he said, "What if we just destroyed the book?"

"How would we do that without finding it?" Verlaine said.

He shrugged. "I could burn her house down. I . . . might have thought about that anyway."

Nadia put one hand on his arm. "Don't."

That was all she said, but the anger seemed to flow away from him.

Did they not know yet that they were crazy about each other? Verlaine had to wonder. But her curiosity was only a little moth darting about in her mind, around this great big flame that felt a lot like fear.

Elizabeth was evil and ancient and up to no good, and all they had to go up against her with was Nadia's power and Mateo's Steadfastness or whatever you would call it, and Verlaine's own . . . newspaper internship. Wow, Elizabeth was probably throwing up from pure terror right now, only not. What were they going to do? Was there any point in doing anything? Should they just try to get their families to take cruises around Halloween? Verlaine tugged at the tips of her hair, then frowned as her fingernail caught in yet another tangle. It was a nasty one, practically matted. One of these days she was going to cut this whole mess away and go for a pixie cut. Anxious and frustrated, Verlaine hopped down from the ladder, her black Converse shoes slapping against the tile floor, and grabbed a pair of scissors to snip the tangle off.

As she did so, Mateo gasped.

Verlaine turned to look at him; so did Nadia, who frowned. "Mateo? What is it?"

"Verlaine's hair," he said.

She stared down at the little tangle still drifting down into the trash can. "It was never going to comb out. Besides, when it's this long, nobody notices if it's a little uneven on the ends."

"I'm not talking about your hairstyle," he said, like that ought to have been obvious, which it probably should have been. "I mean, when you cut it, there was this little . . . shower of sparks. Only for a second. Now it's gone."

"No, there wasn't." Why would there be?

Then it hit Verlaine: Mateo could see things other people couldn't. He could see *magic*.

Nadia's eyes widened. "What color were the sparks?"

"Dark red. Really dark. Nearly black," Mateo answered. "The same as the ones—" His expression changed as he said, more slowly, "The same as the ones I saw the night I became Nadia's Steadfast. They were surrounding you then, too."

"What does that mean?" Verlaine grabbed a handful of her hair and stared at it, like suddenly she'd be able to see the magic for herself. "Did Elizabeth curse me? Or was it something with the Steadfast thing going wrong?"

"With that color, I'm guessing it's old magic," Nadia said, as if that were remotely comforting. "Something that happened a long time ago but still left—traces behind. And red probably means dark magic. Mateo, how come you didn't mention it before?"

"I thought it was just part of the spell you were casting then," Mateo said. "I wouldn't have known the difference then, or even now, if you hadn't just explained."

Nadia stepped closer to Verlaine and stared like she'd never really seen her before. "Verlaine . . . when did your hair go gray?"

"Since I was little. It's almost always been this way." She was the only gray-haired person in her first-grade class photo. "It was brown when I was a baby. Not after that. The only pictures where I have dark hair are the ones when I'm little bitty, with my—"

Verlaine couldn't breathe. She couldn't think. The possibility pushing into her mind didn't leave room for anything else.

Mateo took her arm as if he was afraid she might fall over. "Verlaine? What's wrong?"

"With my parents," Verlaine whispered. "I had dark hair while my parents were alive."

The *Guardian* was always quiet, but now the silence seemed like another presence in the room, something so enormous and ominous that it surrounded them all. Nadia and Mateo exchanged a look before Nadia said, "How did they die?"

Legs trembling, breath weak in her chest, Verlaine braced herself against the front desk. "They said it was viral pneumonia. Had to have been. We—we all went to Uncle Dave's house one night, and apparently everything was fine. Then he didn't hear from them for a couple of days and got worried. He came over and found them; they'd died in their bed. I was in my crib crying. They had been dead for at least a day. It was like they both got so sick so fast they couldn't even call a doctor."

"Oh, Verlaine." Nadia put an arm around her, which was the first time anybody besides her dads had tried to comfort Verlaine in so, so long. But she couldn't really remember her parents, couldn't remember that weekend she'd been trapped in a house with dead people. The pain she felt was for their absence even from her memories—and now, for something else besides.

"It wasn't viral pneumonia, was it?" Verlaine whispered. "Was it magic? Did Elizabeth do something to them? Did she do something to me?"

"I can't say. Not without"—after hesitating, Nadia finished—"visiting the graves."

Verlaine grabbed her books. "I have to go."

"Hey, wait. Don't run off like that. You're upset." Mateo put an arm out, but Verlaine roughly pushed him aside.

"I need to be alone. Okay?" Without waiting for an answer, Verlaine ran out into the chilly gray afternoon. She didn't want to think about Nadia, or Elizabeth, or magic, or her parents. But the reminder blew around her in the whipping wind, silver and gray, a part of Verlaine forever.

"Nobody ever brought it up," Mateo said a few minutes later as he and Nadia walked along the street that led to the heart of downtown . . . at least, as much downtown as Captive's Sound had.

"How? Two healthy people, not old or anything, and they die of the flu overnight without even calling somebody? That didn't strike people as bizarre?"

When Nadia was trying to figure something out, she got this little worried look—so serious—and Mateo already felt like he knew that look by heart.

He said only, "Weirder stuff happens all the time. Especially in Captive's Sound."

Nadia sighed. "I guess that makes sense. Here, people's idea of 'bizarre' might be . . . warped. But I wish Verlaine hadn't run off like that."

"Sometimes you need some space to deal." That was as close as Mateo could get to apologizing for the way he'd acted recently. But Nadia didn't seem to need an apology. When she looked at him with those dark eyes, he felt like she understood everything about him, even the parts he barely understood himself.

He'd missed her so much during the time he tried to stay away. Even though he'd tried not to think about the Craft or the curse or anything like that, it was the subtler things Mateo had missed. That little determined look she got when she focused on a problem. How calm and accepting she was of the craziest things. The way she doodled cubes and pyramids in the margins of her chem notes. How she always looked down at the cafeteria food with fresh despair, its horribleness a surprise to her every single time—like she was always hoping for something better.

When Mateo thought of all those things together, something tightened within his chest, and felt very like the emotion for her that had always welled up in his dreams. . . .

No longer able to meet Nadia's eyes, Mateo turned his head away and looked into the far distance. Verlaine was nowhere to be seen. She must have sprinted for her car, driven off like a bat out of hell. "What do you think happened to her family?"

"I'm not sure. All I know is that she still bears the scars. Whatever that magic was, it still has some kind of hold on her, even now."

"Now? You mean, Verlaine's—is she cursed? Like me?"

"Did you see that halo around her?"

The dark, thorned shape that circled his reflection in the mirror still had the power to turn Mateo's stomach. It always would, he thought. "No. So, not a curse, then."

"But what? I have to figure this out. I'll keep working with Goodwife Hale's book, see if there's anything there." Nadia hesitated. "Which is about five hours of me trying to read something closer to Middle English than anything normal—"

"It's okay," Mateo said, though he realized how badly he didn't want to leave her. "Gotta get my hair cut this afternoon. But—call me tonight? Tell me what you found?"

"I might not find anything."

"Call anyway."

She ducked her head, glancing away from him with a small smile on her full lips, and despite the cold fall wind, Mateo felt warm all over. Nadia's dark eyes rose to meet his again as she said, "Okay."

He simply lifted his hand in a wave as she walked off.

This is why I never fell for Elizabeth, Mateo thought as he watched her go. *Because she's nothing like Nadia.*

Mateo walked into the barbershop more or less on autopilot, hardly seeing anything in front of his eyes. He didn't have to, though; he'd been coming to Ginger Goncalves for his haircuts as long as he could remember. All he did was nod, barely seeing her as he got into the barber chair. She'd know what to do.

He found that if he stared really hard at his shoes, he didn't see anything of the terrible halo in the mirror, not even out of the corner of his eye.

As Ginger used the electric razor at the back of his neck, once again he thought of Verlaine, alone and probably terrified. All these years he'd known her, and yet he'd never bothered talking with her—never dreamed they had so much in common, that magic had scarred both their lives as soon as they'd begun. And though he'd heard the story of her parents' deaths, because old stories never died in small towns, he'd never questioned it. Verlaine's gray hair was like Ginger's muteness: a part of her, a small strangeness that on its own meant nothing, but in a larger pattern—

Wait.

He focused on the reflection in the mirror—hard for him to do, with the loathsome halo writhing around his head—but now, behind him, he could see Ginger.

Ginger, with a shadow of that same writhing energy coiled around her throat.

Ginger, who hadn't spoken since the church fire in 1995.

Nadia had talked about other witches. How there had to have been others in Captive's Sound sometime.

And men couldn't be told about witchcraft, but women could.

Did Ginger have any idea what had happened to her? Did she understand at all?

Mateo had no clue how to bring this up, but he figured he had to try. He cleared his throat, and she glanced up at him with a pleasant smile. It was okay to ask her yes or no questions, even to communicate with short notes. But it was still tough to get this out. "Ginger?"

She raised an eyebrow.

"Do you—do you believe in magic?"

It was vague enough to mean anything. A song lyric. A joke. If Ginger didn't understand, Mateo figured, she'd laugh or shrug. Blow it off.

But Ginger went stiff. Her usual ease had vanished; now her face was pale, and she didn't seem to know what to do.

That meant he was onto something, right? Had to. Mateo decided to venture one more comment, something that would seem totally innocent to anybody who wasn't knee-deep in witchcraft: "I've been thinking a lot about it lately. Hey, you know Elizabeth Pike, right?"

The razor clattered to the linoleum floor, where it buzzed and jittered amid the scraps of his shorn hair. Ginger jerked away, backing up with wide eyes, until she thudded into the far wall.

"Hey—don't be scared." Mateo got up, held out his hands. He felt stupid trying to do this with a black plastic apron around his neck, so he quickly took that off. "It's okay. It is, really."

Ginger slid along the wall to her front desk, like she was

going for the phone to call 911. Did she think he'd gone crazy, like all the Cabots? Or was her fear much deeper—because it was based in the truth?

Mateo tried, "Is this—are you freaking out because—because of—?" He gestured toward her throat.

That was obviously the last straw for Ginger. Grabbing a pen and an appointment card from the desk, she scrawled something, then held it up for Mateo to see: *GET OUT!*

He got out.

Running down the street, beneath the roiling sky and the chained houses—the whole surreal landscape he was learning to recognize as the truth of his hometown—Mateo grabbed his phone out of his pocket and hit Nadia's name. She answered on the second ring. "Hello?"

"Ginger."

"What?"

"Ginger Goncalves. The woman who cuts my hair. Either she's a witch or she knows about them, but either way, she's cursed, too." As he hurried along the sidewalk, free hand balled in the pocket of his letter jacket, Mateo described her version of the halo—the coiled black noose around Ginger's neck. "Maybe I should have asked her about it differently—I don't know."

"You did the best you could," Nadia said. Her voice was soft. "She wouldn't have been able to understand why a guy was talking to her about it. You're the one and only man in the club, remember?"

Mateo thought about that for a second. "You mean,

you're pretty sure Ginger's a witch, too?"

"I always *knew* there would be more in Captive's Sound. Even if Ginger's not a witch herself, she knows about the Craft through . . . her mother, maybe, or a close friend. And she has to know someone who teaches. I've got to talk to her!"

"I'd give her a day or so to calm down. She was about ten seconds from coming after me with the scissors when I got out of there."

"Oh—okay." Obviously it was killing Nadia to wait even a day. But then the whole tone of her voice changed. "But if Elizabeth cursed her, took away her voice—"

Nadia didn't finish the rest. She didn't have to.

If Elizabeth had torn the voice out of one witch, what might she do to Nadia—to all of them—if they got in her way?

The points and edges of the broken glass shimmered in the light from the stove, creating the illusion that Elizabeth sat in a lake of fire. Legs crossed, bottle of water at her side, she carefully drew one finger along the nearest shard until blood beaded up fresh.

With her cut finger, she finished drawing the final arc of her design amid the glass. Then, with the last droplets of blood, Elizabeth completed the final letter of a name neither she nor any other mortal could ever speak aloud:

ASAEL.

The name of a demon. Of a sworn servant and vessel of the

One Beneath. Keeper of his will, walker of his domains—

—and now, her bonded ally.

You summon me again, he said inside her mind. Possessing no earthly body, he could not speak any other way. *It's been a long time. Aren't you an infant yet?*

"I did not summon you for conversation." Elizabeth took a deep gulp of water. Already, her fast-regenerating body was healing the cuts on her fingers, leaving only faint pink lines behind to show where she'd shed the blood for the elaborate pattern in front of her. "I have need of you, Asa."

You taunt me. So, so close to saying my name, and yet you never will. But you could, you could—

"The One Beneath himself is releasing me from his service!" Elizabeth snapped. "I serve him now for loyalty, not as a mere *slave*. So remember your place."

I am his slave, not yours. I will work with you, not for you. There is a difference, Goodwife Pike. Remember it well.

Elizabeth did not need a demon underling to tell her the finer divisions of power among the servants of the One Beneath. She knew her place with him. He treasured her beyond all his others, was freeing her in resignation and understanding. Her last act for him would be her greatest. They would be united again when at last, at long last, her work here was complete.

"You know what I am trying to do," she said. "You know how close I am to success."

On Samhain the end comes.

"Yet there is a strange energy at work here. Another

witch—more powerful than she should be. A shift in the balances."

One you don't understand. Asa sounded positively delighted. *And the other witch is only a girl.*

"She has changed the structure beneath Captive's Sound!" Elizabeth snapped. "Nadia Caldani knows something of what I am, but that alone would not give her such power."

She possesses two things you do not.

Elizabeth refused to ask. If the demon was fool enough to tell her that Nadia possessed faith or hope or love, any such token from a children's story, she'd beg the One Beneath to send him to the deepest torments, and it would be done for her. As a gift. As a blessing.

But in the past century, she'd forgotten how useful Asa could be. *Nadia possesses Goodwife Hale's Book of Shadows.*

How? How had she found it? Elizabeth herself had no need of it—formidable witch though Prudence Hale had been, her knowledge counted as nothing compared to Elizabeth's own. But the book was so old, so powerful that it had served as a kind of anchor of the magical energies in this town. No wonder the balances had been thrown off. Nadia had not only moved it, she had taken possession of it—begun to learn from it.

Then Asa said, *And Nadia possesses a Steadfast.*

Elizabeth frowned. "Who?"

You know a Steadfast is shielded from the eyes of a demon. I cannot see her face. But I sense the presence and the power of a Steadfast behind Nadia's witchcraft.

A Steadfast was normally a woman known well to a witch—a deep friend, a relative, a lover, someone whose loyalty went beyond measure. But Nadia Caldani had only recently come to Captive's Sound. With her were only male relatives, neither of whom could serve as a Steadfast. So she had drawn upon someone new.

"The gray-haired girl," Elizabeth said. She looked at the glow of her stove and smiled.

15

"WHAT HAPPENED TO YOUR HAIR?" DAD THRUST AN apron at Mateo. Obviously Mateo was still On Dad's List—which he expected to live on forever, given how many absences the school had reported. "Never mind, tell me tonight at home. Another three minutes late and I'd have docked your pay!"

"Sorry, Dad." Mateo pulled himself together for the dinner shift. He was almost relieved; after dealing with magic and curses and evil witches and destruction, waiting tables counted as a break. For the next few hours, he wouldn't have to worry about anything more complicated than whether to serve the guacamole on the side. It already looked like it was going to be a crazy night at La Catrina—most of the tables filled even though it was only five p.m.

Mateo glanced over his area on the floor, then paused as he saw who was at the two-top by the back.

He walked to her first. "Hey, Verlaine."

"I didn't come here to talk to you about it," she said very quickly. "I mean, I didn't come here to *not* talk to you. It's just—I feel like I'm not ready to talk about this with anybody. And I didn't want my uncles asking me why I was acting strange. But I didn't want to be alone, either. And I thought I wanted to be near at least one person who would understand why I'm like this. You know?"

Weirdly, he got it. "Yeah."

"And I'm sorry if I was weird with you about—taking off for a while. I get it now. I really, really get it."

Mateo shrugged it off. "You need anything?"

"A virgin piña colada and more of these chips. Way more. And later I might need to go into a veggie-fajita coma." Verlaine leaned back in the booth, her pale skin stark against the red leather. "Did something happen to your hair?"

"I'll check back with you," Mateo promised. He started on his rounds—waters for this table, the next already wanted their nachos yesterday, and then—

—then Ginger came in.

She seemed much more together than she had in the barbershop: calm, steady, even smiling. Ginger came to La Catrina a lot, always ordering by pointing to the menu. But she rarely came alone, and he would never have expected to see her again today.

Their eyes met as she took a seat, and even though she wasn't in his section, Mateo figured he needed to go over and say something. Quickly he dished out the waters and nachos and put in the order for Verlaine's drink; while he had that moment at the bar, he quickly grabbed his phone and texted Nadia. *Ginger's here at La C.*

Keep her there! Nadia sent back almost instantly. *I'm coming over.*

It made more sense for Nadia to talk to her, Mateo figured, but that didn't mean he shouldn't acknowledge what had happened at the barbershop. Besides, that would be part of making sure Ginger stuck around long enough for Nadia to reach La Catrina. But Ginger would want to stick around, wouldn't she? Now that she'd calmed down, she had sought him out; that had to mean she wanted to help, or share what she really knew about Elizabeth. Or maybe she just wanted somebody to finally understand. Mateo knew exactly how that felt.

Maybe Ginger would know a weakness they could exploit—some way for him to start getting back at Elizabeth for all the evil she'd done to him and his family. To Mom.

So the first free moment he had, he went to Ginger's table. She sat there, head held high; once again he saw the sooty, coiling collar of the curse wound around her throat. Mateo imagined he could feel the weight of the thorned halo bearing down on his head.

"Hey there," he said, trying to keep it light. "I think I need to get this haircut finished sometime."

Ginger wrinkled her nose and nodded.

"That bad, huh?" Mateo laughed, but the self-consciousness wasn't totally faked. How weird did he look?

He now avoided mirrors as much as possible, but he'd have to brave one to see precisely how lopsided this was. "Sorry if I, uh, startled you today."

She shook her head and looked up at him, her eyes so sad that it choked off anything else he might have said. Ginger held out her hand, as if she needed someone to hold on to— as if she was as desolate and afraid as Verlaine, or even more.

What must it feel like, not to be able to speak to anyone, not one word, for ten years?

Moved, not caring who could see, Mateo took Ginger's hand and squeezed it tightly.

Lightning-fast, with her other hand, Ginger grabbed his wrist.

The floor fell out from under him. Mateo felt the ground slam against his back, saw the twinkling lights strung along the ceiling rafters, and then he didn't know anything any longer.

"Slower, honey." Nadia's father sat in the passenger seat, leaning a little too close to her. "Technically you don't have a learner's permit in Rhode Island. If the cops stop us—"

"What cops? I think Captive's Sound has, like, one guy. Part-time." Nadia slowed down a little anyway. It wasn't like she couldn't try talking to Ginger later on, if she missed her tonight. And since her dad had insisted the whole family should go to La Catrina for dinner as long as she was headed that way, it wasn't like she'd have much opportunity for an in-depth discussion.

But she could at least make contact with another witch.

Okay, maybe Ginger wasn't a witch. Maybe she was just cursed, the same way Mateo was. That wouldn't explain how she'd recognized Mateo's hints about magic, though—and definitely wouldn't explain away Ginger's panic at the mention of Elizabeth Pike's name. If Ginger knew enough to be afraid, Nadia thought, then she definitely at least knew about witchcraft . . . and few women outside the Craft were ever told about it. So the chances of Ginger being a witch were good. Really good.

Finally, a witch in Captive's Sound who isn't evil. Someone who knows what's going on—someone older, who could maybe teach me all the stuff Mom never got around to—how long can it take to get to La Catrina! This town isn't big enough for a drive this long!

It was hard to be patient.

Then Nadia turned the corner and saw La Catrina—and the ambulance in front of it.

From the backseat, Cole whispered, "Did somebody die?"

"You don't know that," Dad said. "But maybe this isn't the best night to eat out after all."

"But did they die?" Cole's voice had begun to shake. Nadia wanted to turn and comfort him, but she couldn't; fortunately, Dad was right there.

"Hey. Come on, buddy. People have minor accidents all the time. Remember how the ambulance came for us? And we're okay."

"We have to find out if anybody died," Cole insisted, and now it sounded like he was crying.

It's nothing to do with Mateo, Nadia told herself, even as her pulse quickened and her hands tensed on the steering wheel. *Probably somebody choked on some food, or had a heart attack.*

But wouldn't Mateo have texted her about that? Maybe he hadn't had a chance. Maybe he was doing CPR, being a hero again.

Even as she hesitated, unwilling to drive away but unable to think straight, a tall, skinny figure darted out from the crowd of onlookers—Verlaine, her silvery hair streaming behind her. She was running toward them as fast as she could, brilliant green Converses slapping the pavement, and her eyes were wide with terror. Nadia's whole body went cold.

Verlaine called out, "Nadia!" as she waved a hand in the air. Nadia snapped down the window as Verlaine reached them, panting. "It's Mateo. He collapsed."

"You mean—he fainted. Passed out," Nadia said. Those things could happen to anybody who got overheated or didn't eat enough; it didn't mean anything serious. They'd called an ambulance just as a precaution.

Mateo was okay. He had to be.

But Verlaine shook her head. "He's unconscious, still. Mateo's dad is freaking—they're shutting down the restaurant early. Nobody can tell what happened." Verlaine's eyes widened, clearly suggesting that she knew more but couldn't say it aloud in front of other people. She said only, "Oh, hi, Mr. Caldani. Hi, Cole."

Dad nodded, but he spoke to Nadia next. "Honey, why

don't you go with Verlaine to check on Mateo? We owe that guy a lot. I'll get Cole home. He could use some quiet time."

"Are—are you sure?" If Cole needed her—

But Dad had him. And Nadia couldn't take her eyes from the ambulance, from the stretcher she could barely glimpse being slid into the back. The red and blue lights seemed to beat against her eyes, to blind her to the rest of the world.

Before waiting for her dad's reassurance, Nadia threw the car into park and leaped out. "I'll call!" she shouted as she dashed toward the ambulance, Verlaine at her side, without ever looking back.

Her father's "Okay!" behind her was very distant.

They couldn't run fast enough; even as they reached La Catrina, the ambulance doors slammed shut. The paramedics peeled out so fast that the tires squealed. Nadia clutched at Verlaine's arm. "Oh, God. Something's really wrong with him. They're scared."

"It all started when he went to talk to *her*." Verlaine pointed, and at the far edge of the crowd Nadia saw a stout woman in her fifties with long, ash-blond hair. The woman looked deeply worried—and, to Nadia's eyes, guilty. "That's Ginger Goncalves."

Nadia pushed through the still-murmuring crowd, straight for Ginger, whose eyes widened. She turned to go, but Nadia called out, "Ginger! Wait!"

Ginger just walked toward her car faster, but Nadia caught up with her, running too fast to stop easily; she had to catch herself against the side of the car with both hands. Verlaine was right behind her, but she grabbed one of Nadia's arms as if to pull her back. "Nadia, *think*," she whispered. "Whatever she did to Mateo—what if she does it to you, too?"

"She won't," Nadia said loudly. "I bet she can't even if she tries." Every protective spell she'd ever learned seemed to flood into her mind at once, and she raised one hand—the hand with her bracelet, all its pendants and stones promising that the power was hers if she only chose—

But Ginger's eyes widened as she saw the bracelet. Different witches kept their materials close in different ways—jewelry, bands on belts, stones in small sacks kept in pockets or purses—but each way was easy enough to recognize if you knew what you were looking at, and Ginger did.

For a few moments they simply stared at each other. Then Ginger grabbed a pad of paper from her handbag and scrawled a note, which she defiantly held straight in Nadia's face: *You told a man about the Craft.*

"He had to know," Nadia said. But she couldn't explain that Mateo was her Steadfast; Ginger wouldn't believe her, and since even Nadia didn't yet understand how it was possible, she didn't want to get into it, particularly with a witch she wasn't sure she trusted. "Because of the curse on his family."

Ginger shook her head; clearly that wasn't a good enough reason.

Verlaine huffed, "Why are you explaining yourself to her? She's the one who hurt Mateo!"

"I broke one of the First Laws," Nadia said quietly, never

taking her eyes from Ginger's face. The ambulance's siren was too far away now, almost gone. What was happening to Mateo? "I have to answer for that. Always. Forever. But I've never used my powers to harm another human being. Ginger, what did you do to him?"

Ginger's face crumpled, like she might cry. With a shaking hand, she jotted out another note: *It was only a spell of forgetting. Amnesia—for today, maybe a few days before—no more. So he wouldn't know about me.*

Nadia held the note as she and Verlaine read it together. "But that shouldn't have made him collapse. Dizzy for a second, maybe—confused—not anything that would make them call an ambulance."

Quickly Ginger wrote: *I don't know what happened. It wasn't meant to hurt him.*

But already Nadia's mind was working fast. With a warning glance at Verlaine, who seemed to understand she should remain quiet, Nadia said, "I—I have a Steadfast, one who was near you when you cast the spell."

Ginger's eyes widened, and Nadia knew that they'd both seen the same thing. A spell of forgetting, on its own, was simple but strong; it could erase a day's events beyond any recovery. But if a Steadfast amplified that spell—even a Steadfast not sworn to that particular witch—then it could be far more devastating. Mateo would have forgotten everything about himself. Everybody he'd ever known, every place he'd ever been. He probably no longer remembered how to speak or stand.

At this moment, his body might be forgetting how to breathe.

Nadia steadied herself against Verlaine as she said to Ginger, "Drive us to the hospital now. You have to lift that spell on Mateo as soon as possible. If you don't—"

"What?" Verlaine whispered. "What happens? Could Mateo die?"

"I doubt it." If only Nadia could draw any comfort from that. "But he could turn into a vegetable. He might never walk or talk again. Never remember who he is. The person Mateo was—that will be lost, forever."

Elizabeth lifted her head, suddenly alert.

The bonds of the curse on the Cabot family—yet another of the constants of her world, a presence in her life as unchanging and guiding as the North Star—had suddenly fallen slack.

Nadia Caldani cannot have broken the curse. She doesn't have the power. She couldn't. Even as anger rippled through her, Elizabeth realized—no, the curse remained. But the ties that held Mateo close to her, kept him under control . . . some powerful magic had disturbed them. And even through the murk now separating her from him, Elizabeth could tell that Mateo was in serious physical distress. Perhaps even mortal danger, though she couldn't be sure. That stupid girl must have tried some spell beyond her ability, thinking her little Steadfast friend gave her the strength to do anything she wanted.

Well, Mateo Perez couldn't die yet. She wasn't done using him up.

Elizabeth rose lazily from her place on the floor. In her mind, no less sarcastic for the voice being mere thought, the demon spoke: *Will you run to his rescue? Play the noble heroine?*

"Silence, beast." Elizabeth had ceased to see the point of humor some two centuries before; already she was eager to find him an appropriate vessel, the better to house him where she need not hear his endless mockery. "I don't have to run anywhere for a rescue."

She unbuttoned the front of her white dress, then let it fall from her body onto the floor; she wore nothing underneath. Her wood stove was only a few steps away, and as always her bare feet found the slivers of floor not covered with glass. Then, with bare hands, she pulled open the metal door of the wood stove. It took more than heat to burn her now, and besides—what glowed and crackled within was not wood.

No power was more flexible than stolen power. Or—if you knew how to use it properly—sweeter.

The light of stolen love and life painted her thighs and belly, touching them with heat. Unblinking, Elizabeth stared into the glow, picturing Mateo's face.

You are mine, she thought. *No one else can free you. Only me.*

Ginger drove to the hospital so quickly that Nadia found herself bracing her hands against the dashboard. It still didn't feel fast enough. But within minutes the three of them were dashing across the hospital parking lot. From the grim, desperate look on Ginger's face, Nadia could tell how truly she regretted having hurt Mateo.

It didn't matter. Nadia remained so angry with Ginger, so frightened for Mateo, that she wanted to scream.

Mateo will be okay, she reminded herself. *He won't die. They have machines that keep him breathing. Ginger will break the spell, and he'll be fine again in no time.*

Physically, that was true. But what about Mateo's mind? Although he would be able to remember things from now on, would he ever recall anything from his past? Was every moment he'd ever known—every moment *they* had ever known—lost forever?

They ran into the ER waiting room. Nadia hurried to the nurse on duty. "Yes, hi, we're here about Mateo Perez— we're his, um, his friends." Would they even let anybody in to see him? Could Ginger cast the spell from here?

"I'm sorry," the nurse said. "No visitors outside the immediate family."

Nadia glanced over at Ginger, who still looked as likely to bolt as to help Mateo. Before she could think what to do, though, Verlaine shouted—more loudly than Nadia had ever heard her say anything, "This is an outrage!"

Heads turned around the waiting room. The nurse said, "Miss, I understand you're upset, but the same rules apply to you as to anyone else."

Verlaine grabbed out her phone and started recording video. "This is about—about freedom of the press! The public has a right to know what's being served in local restaurants if it's *killing people!*"

Someone across the room, who seemed to be waiting for a doctor to check out a black eye, said, "Wait, restaurants are killing people?"

Everyone started murmuring, and Verlaine used her free hand to start beating on the nurses' station as loudly as she could. "I demand accountability! I demand justice!" Then she shot Nadia a look that clearly meant, *Would you please get a move on?*

"If you don't quiet down, I'm going to have to call security!" the nurse cried; already a security guard was edging toward Verlaine. Nadia started backing away from the fracas, towing Ginger along with her. As everyone focused on Verlaine, who kept on shouting about citizen journalism, Nadia was able to push through the doors that led to the ER itself.

Captive's Sound was so small, and so quiet, that no other patients were in the ER. Both doctors and all the nurses swarmed around a single hospital bed. Amid the sea of tubes and scrubs, Nadia could just see Mateo. He looked so pale, so still. Her heart constricted painfully in her chest.

"Do something," she whispered to Ginger, who nodded.

It was horrible, having to rely on someone else to save Mateo. Though Nadia could have tried something herself, it would be harder for her; the spellcaster herself always had the greatest power over the spell.

But even as Ginger lifted one hand to begin, Mateo suddenly sat upright.

"Whoa—" he groaned. His eyes opened, then shut tightly against what must have seemed like too-bright light. "Whoa, what's going on?"

"Lie back down!" one of the doctors ordered, but Nadia could tell she was relieved, as were all the other medical staff in the room.

Mateo stared past the sea of doctors toward her. "Nadia?"

A nurse finally saw them. "Excuse me, no visitors. You'll have to step outside."

"You're okay, Mateo!" Nadia called to him even as the nurse pushed them both back toward the doors. "You're going to be fine!"

As they were finally edged out, they almost backed into Alejandro Perez, who looked petrified. "Please—my son—"

"He's awake and responsive," the nurse said. "We'll tell you more when we can. Wait out here."

"He's awake?" Mr. Perez repeated. Relief made his face go almost slack. *"Madre de Dios."*

Nadia nodded quickly. "He woke up while they were in there. Sat up and knew who I was and everything."

Apparently Mr. Perez was too overwhelmed to ask himself why she and Ginger would have been in the ER in the first place. "You're sure?"

"It's all going to be okay." It was the kind of thing people said even when they couldn't be sure, so Nadia could get away with it; she did know for sure but couldn't explain how she knew. And Ginger looked as confused as she did. . . .

"I've been working him too hard," Mr. Perez whispered.

"Riding him too hard, after he skipped a week of school. Wanted to—to straighten him out, you know? But Mateo's always been a good kid. The first time he ran a little wild, I drove him to this."

"No, no! It wasn't your fault," Nadia insisted, thinking, *It's mine.* "Please don't blame yourself."

He patted her shoulder absentmindedly. "It was good of you both to come. But I—I need to talk to the doctors now."

"Of course. Go," Nadia said. Next to her, Ginger nodded.

Silently they walked into the parking lot—where Verlaine leaned against Ginger's car, slightly disheveled. They must have tossed her out here for creating a disturbance. As soon as the doors swung shut, she said, "What just happened?"

Nadia didn't answer—she couldn't—and instead turned to Ginger. "Did you do something in the car? Cast a spell?"

Ginger shook her head no and shrugged.

"It doesn't make any sense." Tugging her hair up into a tail with both hands, Nadia breathed out in frustration. "Your spell shouldn't have worn off on its own. Even if it weren't strengthened by his—by there being a Steadfast around."

The answer hit her in a rush: *Elizabeth.*

He was her crystal ball, her window to the future—she still needed him. Elizabeth's dragon claws had been sunk into his family for hundreds of years; why would she let go now?

And she was still so attached to him, still so aware of everything about Mateo, that she'd sensed the spell without even being there.

How deep did that connection go? Would Nadia ever be able to free him? Was that even possible?

Nadia took a deep breath, trying to clear her head. She realized that Ginger had been scribbling something for a few seconds now, just as Ginger finished and held up her note: *You've broken one of the First Laws. You have no right to the Craft.*

"We'll have to agree to disagree on that," Nadia said, but she felt like she was dying inside. It was like all the anger her mother would have felt, all the scorn, was bleeding through Ginger into her—like somehow her mother had left because she knew this would happen, which made no sense but at this moment felt horribly true. She tried to stick to the subject. "Elizabeth did this. You know she did. Just like she's the one who cursed Mateo in the first place—and cursed you."

Ginger only stared, but Nadia knew that was the same as agreeing with her. Verlaine hugged herself and watched them with worried eyes.

"She's planning something." Nadia stepped closer. "Something terrible, this Halloween night at the carnival. I know you don't approve of me. I know you think I've done something awful but—it's not like what Elizabeth does, you get that much, right? You're—" Her voice broke, and a flush of shame warmed her cheeks, but Nadia forced herself to keep going. "You're the only other nonevil witch I know right now. My mother's gone. Elizabeth's a Sorceress. If we don't stop her, I think a lot of people are going to get hurt. And I'm sure Mateo's going to be the first. Please, tell me—what would you do? What are you going to do?"

Ginger jotted one more note, handed it to Nadia, and got into her car. The door was slammed shut in a way that suggested they wouldn't be getting a ride back home.

Nadia looked down at the piece of paper, which said only, *RUN*.

16

MATEO KNEW HE WAS DRUGGED. THE HEAVY, SWEET taste on his tongue and the overpowering weight of his eyelids and his body told him that. It was as though he were sinking through endless fog but couldn't bring himself to care.

Nadia had been here with him. That was the one thing he now knew for sure, the one thing that made the rest of it okay. If she had been here to check on him, then everything must be okay.

He saw nothing now; he didn't care. His hand hurt—one constant pinpoint of pain. *The IV,* he thought, without really caring why there was one jabbed through his skin. Mateo's only real connection with the rest of the world was hearing, though he didn't bother making sense of what he heard.

"—keep him overnight for observation. We'll need to do some tests."

"Of course." That was Dad. Mateo was sure of that much, and it was such a relief to know who Dad was, to remember him. But why a relief? He couldn't put it together right now—not with the fog swirling all around him—"But everything looks normal?"

"His vitals are strong. We're giving him antiseizure medication just in case, but if he doesn't have another episode, he can go home tomorrow morning."

That sounded good, Mateo decided. Now he could let himself fall asleep. But wasn't there a reason he didn't want to go to sleep? He could remember it now if he wanted to—

—but he didn't want to. He relaxed and let the fog swallow him whole.

For a long time there was nothing.

Then he saw Nadia again.

They sat on the back porch of some house on the beach—not Mateo's, but it might have been any of a few dozen strewn along the coast of Captive's Sound. A fire pit flickered from the sand below, and crystal wind chimes sang with the breeze. It was late at night, and the sky was so clear he could see where the stars met the sea. They were curled up on a swing, and Nadia shivered from the chill.

"Don't kiss me," she said.

She was cold, so cold. Despite his own shivering, Mateo shrugged off his jacket and slipped it around her shoulders. Nadia's dark eyes seemed like part of the night that surrounded them, and he couldn't stop wanting to bury his hands in her black hair.

Why was this different?

"You're not dying," he whispered. "Not this time. It's okay for me to be with you."

Nadia smiled up at him as she trailed two fingers along his cheek, a touch that made him feel like he was melting. She smiled even as she said, "I'm dying the whole time this happens."

Mateo laid one hand along her belly; he could feel the warmth of her skin through her shirt. Slowly he slid his hand toward her back, bringing her into his embrace.

She leaned against him and whispered, her breath soft against his lips, "If you kiss me, we're both lost."

It didn't make any sense. Dreams didn't have to make sense.

Just as he bent toward her, though, there was light—"Time to check your vitals!" in a chipper voice—and Mateo wasn't awake but he wasn't dreaming any longer, either. He let the dream go easily; the fog wouldn't let him hold on to anything for long.

At three a.m., about when Verlaine was starting to think she might have calmed down enough to go to sleep, she thought again of Ginger's note.

RUN.

"Forget it," she groaned, throwing back the covers to grab her phone again. Even as she did so, Nadia texted again: *Sorry if I woke you up—can't sleep.*

Me either. Hey, are we considering fleeing as a possibility? I would be good with fleeing. She really should have put that in the PowerPoint as Option D.

Nadia didn't seem to be thinking about escape—at least not enough, in Verlaine's opinion. *Tell me more about that church fire. The one where Ginger lost her voice.*

I was little. I don't remember much about it. As Smuckers jumped up on the bed, Verlaine absentmindedly petted him, trying to remember anything Uncle Gary had ever said about the fire. He was the one who knew pretty much everything that went down around here. *It was the Catholic church—they were in this really old building then, not far from the beach. There was some group meeting in the basement, but just like a women's club or something. Most of them died. Ginger got out but she never talked after that.*

That wasn't a club. I'd bet anything that was a coven.

What? Are you sure?

Ginger's a witch—and that fire can't have been targeted only at her. There are more specific spells you could use against one enemy.

What kind of spells were those? Verlaine wondered if she really wanted to know.

Nadia kept typing. *If Elizabeth only wanted to hurt or warn Ginger, the curse alone would have done it. But the fire striking a whole group of women who met alone . . . to me, that says coven.*

A whole group of witches—right here in town—and Verlaine had never suspected. Someday soon, she figured she wouldn't even be capable of being surprised anymore, but not quite yet. *Why would a coven be meeting in the Catholic church? Isn't that, like, a conflict of interest or something?*

They probably said it was a knit night or a book club or something. It's always easiest to hide in plain sight.

Her phone screen was the only light in her room; the shadows it cast made everything look unfamiliar. Verlaine realized she was shivering and clutched Smuckers closer, though the fat old cat meowed once in protest. *So Elizabeth just goes around destroying other witches in town, whenever, wherever?*

No, because she hasn't come after me, and she could. I wouldn't be able to stop her, Nadia replied. That wasn't exactly reassuring.

Why had she let herself get sucked into this? But Verlaine knew now—witchcraft had played a part in her life long before she'd ever met Nadia Caldani. She wound a strand of her waist-length hair around one finger, over and over, coiling it all; in the phone's light it shone silver.

Uncle Gary and Uncle Dave kept the one formal portrait of her and her parents framed in the hallway, bigger than any of the many pictures they'd all taken together over the years. So she wouldn't forget, they always said, like she remembered back that far to begin with. Verlaine was hardly a year old in that picture, chubby and grinning with her dark curls as her mom and dad hugged her tight. She'd lost everything she could see there—the parents, the baby fat, the dark hair, and even the smile.

Was Elizabeth the one who had taken it all away?

Her phone chimed again in her hand. Verlaine looked down to see Nadia's text: *The witches must have been planning on challenging her. That's why Elizabeth killed them. She must have left Ginger alive but mute as a kind of warning.*

Warning who?

Anyone else who was coming after Elizabeth.

Um, isn't that us? Verlaine was starting to wonder whether "teen runaway" was the worst thing she could put on her college applications.

But as scared as she was, there was no erasing what she'd learned. Her whole life, Verlaine had been wearing the scars Elizabeth had given her; now, at last, she saw them for what they were.

Her uncles said that Mom had a fantastic sense of humor and had crocheted Verlaine's baby blanket herself. That Dad used to sing Beatles songs to her when she was a baby to put her to sleep.

They deserved justice.

And if going after Elizabeth Pike was the only way to make that happen—then no matter how scary it was, no matter how dangerous, Verlaine had to try.

Sorry, Nadia typed. *I didn't mean to scare you.*

Verlaine's reply popped up on her phone almost immediately. *Hey, if I need to be scared, scare me. We know what we're getting into now. Right?*

Right, Nadia said, hoping it was true. But Elizabeth was so ancient—wielded such unfathomable power—that she might be able to come after them in ways Nadia couldn't even begin to guess. Their only hope was that she'd underestimate them, and that could only take them so far.

Besides—how could Elizabeth underestimate her? With so few skills, so little knowledge, no mother, no teacher,

Nadia couldn't be any real challenge to Elizabeth, and they both knew it.

Then she heard a high, wavering cry from her little brother's bedroom.

Cole's awake, she typed quickly. *Gotta go.* Then she dropped her phone and hurried to Cole before he could wake her father. Her bare feet padded against the old wooden floors, the one loose board squeaking underneath as she reached her brother's door. "Hey, buddy. You all right?"

He lay in bed, clutching his covers up to his chin, which was always a sign of bad dreams or at least potential monsters in the closet. "No," he snuffled.

"It's okay. I promise." Nadia came to sit on the side of his bed and ruffled his hair with her fingers. "Was it seeing the ambulance tonight? Nobody got hurt, not really, but I guess that was pretty scary anyway."

"I don't know," Cole said. He looked so small, lying there. These days, when he ran around like crazy and could eat almost half a pizza by himself, Nadia sometimes forgot how little he still was. "But I woke up and I wanted Mommy."

Then he started to cry again—almost like he was ashamed. A little boy in first grade shouldn't have been ashamed of still wanting his mom. And Mom should have been here for him.

Nadia's throat tightened, but she didn't let herself lose it, too. Instead she whispered, "Scoot over, huh?" When he did, she lay down beside him, atop the covers, but still able to hug him tight.

Cole cuddled next to her, even as he said, "I thought I was too big now."

She'd told him that during the summer, mostly to try to get him used to sleeping on his own again; Dad had said they had to help Cole start acting like everything was back to normal. He did now, mostly. So she could make an exception. "Not if you have a bad dream. Nobody's so big that they don't want a hug after they have a bad dream."

"Okay." Cole closed his eyes almost right away; he'd always been quick to soothe, but Nadia knew she'd need to stay until he was fast asleep.

Going after Elizabeth meant risking more than her own safety. More than Verlaine's, more than Mateo's. It meant risking Dad, and Cole.

She looked over at him, with his chubby cheeks and fat little hands; lined up along the wall were his favorite toys, the race cars and the LEGOs and the sock monkey. Despite Mom's abandonment, despite the move and everything they'd been through, his world was still so innocent.

Nadia took a deep breath and tried not to think about Elizabeth, or curses, or the monsters in the closet.

The next day, Mateo impatiently went through the various tests the doctors wanted to run. He had to pretend to be concerned, but since last night was definitely not a "seizure," it was all a huge waste of time.

What he wanted to do was to find out what the hell actually *had* happened to him—what Ginger had done.

Nadia would know. But using cell phones near the hospital machines was forbidden, and since she'd be in school until three p.m., he was stuck for the time being. Hours of bad food, useless tests, and the smell of Lysol awaited.

That, and his dad freaking out nonstop. "You're not using steroids, are you?" he said as he paced the floor. "If you are, you know you can tell me. We'll deal with it together."

Mateo somehow managed not to roll his eyes. "Dad. I'm not using steroids."

"You're going out for baseball again this spring, right? I know that's a lot of pressure."

"Seriously, do you remember where we live? This is Captive's Sound. If you try out, you're on the team. They made a couple people try out last year who didn't want to."

His father didn't seem to hear any of this. "You promise me? Because if something's making you sick, we need to know."

Mateo nearly snapped at him, but he realized how tired Dad looked; probably he hadn't slept. Thinking about how badly Dad had been scared made Mateo feel like crap. "I absolutely promise."

After school was out, Nadia and Verlaine came by—but they got there about five minutes after Gage, who had brought him a flash drive with some TV shows on it and one of those oversize chocolate bars, which at any other time would have been awesome. But as it was, talking about what had really happened was pretty much impossible, and Dad returned long before Gage left. That didn't give Nadia any chance to explain.

He wanted more than an explanation, though. Mateo wanted her near—close to him, beside him—

The dreams, he reminded himself. And hadn't there been one last night? The drugs had dimmed it; Mateo knew he'd had some kind of vision of her again but couldn't recall the details.

And—he realized—he wanted to.

The visions—the ones that had cursed his family for centuries, the same ones that were beginning to ravage his own mind—Mateo wanted them. He needed them. Because they told him when Nadia was in danger, and gave him a chance to keep her safe. He'd said that before, but he'd never felt it as strongly as he did right now. Before he'd been willing to accept the visions of the future; now he *wanted* them.

Nothing was worth more than Nadia's safety. If he had to suffer for it—go crazy for it, be like his mother and grandfather before him—then that was just how it was.

"Hey, are you okay?" Gage looked worried. "You kinda went away for a second there."

Verlaine nodded. "Your eyes did this kind of misty thing." She shot Nadia a look like, *Is that magic?*

Nadia didn't see it; she was looking only at Mateo, and a shadow of the yearning he felt flickered in her eyes, too.

Even Verlaine must have been able to see it, because she hurriedly said, "Gage, Mr. Perez, could I talk to you guys for a second?"

They glanced at each other, then back at Verlaine. Gage shrugged. "Yeah, but why?"

"We're doing a special on this in the *Lightning Rod*. About how even teenagers need to watch their health, because stuff like this can happen to *anyone*." Verlaine's expression was so serious and businesslike that Mateo had to cover his mouth like he was yawning, just to hide the smile. "Mr. Perez, your eyewitness account would of course be the most compelling—and Gage, you're the 'guy on the street,' the average high school student confronting his mortality for the first time."

"Confronting my mortality?" Gage didn't look too thrilled about that.

Dad, though, seized on the idea. "This is definitely something you kids should think about. Come on. We'll get snacks in the cafeteria. *Healthy* snacks!"

"Absolutely," Verlaine said, shepherding them both out the door. "Mmm. Fruit."

As soon as the hospital-room door swung shut, both Mateo and Nadia burst out laughing. "How does she do that?" Nadia said.

"No idea." But already Mateo's attention had returned to Nadia, and to whatever witchcraft had brought him here. "Nadia—what happened? How did you save me?"

She pressed her lips together in a thin line for a moment before answering. "Ginger tried to cast a spell of forgetting. So you wouldn't remember what you'd learned about her. Of course, she didn't know you were a Steadfast. You boosted the power of the spell, and basically—you forgot everything. Your body forgot how to live. It was dangerous, way more than she meant it to be."

It helped a little to know that Ginger hadn't really tried to kill him. They were hardly friends, but still—she'd given him his first haircut, back in the days when he was so little he'd thought it would hurt. "But you made me remember, huh?"

"I was going to try," Nadia said, "but I didn't get the chance. The spell was lifted as soon as I reached you."

"How?"

But he knew. He knew even before Nadia said her name: "Elizabeth."

Why? Why would she *save* him? She was trying to destroy him.

It made him angry, so angry he wanted to stalk out of the hospital right now, go straight to Elizabeth's house, and demand the answers.

He wanted to shake her by the shoulders until her chestnut curls tumbled around her blank, beautiful face. Wanted to scream at her until he didn't have any breath in his lungs. *Why did you curse me? Why did you make me believe you were my friend? Why did you do all that and then save my life?*

The black rage made him tremble, and he lay back on the bed, trying to slow his breathing. If a doctor came in now, they'd think he was having another "seizure" and he'd be stuck in here for another day.

"Hey." Nadia put her hand on his shoulder, but he was

271

so angry he couldn't even appreciate the touch. "Are you all right?"

"Yeah. I mean, no. Physically I guess I'm fine."

Mateo knew he wouldn't have to say the rest.

Nadia's hand slowly slid from his shoulder as she hugged herself. "I'm sorry."

"It's not your fault," he said absently.

"Isn't it?"

He shook his head, but at the moment, his fury eclipsed everything else—even Nadia sitting next to him.

Confronting Elizabeth was the worst thing he could do. If she'd restored his memory, she could probably steal it again. And if she started to wonder how he knew about magic, she'd realize Nadia had broken one of the First Laws to tell him. That could only put Nadia in greater danger.

But he knew he'd never feel complete—not for one second of one day—until he'd had some kind of revenge.

Elizabeth had ruined so many lives. She was trying to ruin his. No way was he going to let her get away with it.

No way in hell.

"So, I heard that they were, like, going to put him in the psych ward, but then they figured out the collapse was, like, physical instead of mental—*who knew*, right? And so they thought maybe he had a brain tumor, and they were going to do emergency surgery, and they were starting to shave his head, and that's why his hair looks like that." Kendall Bender led her crew of girls down the hallway past Nadia, who was stashing her stuff in her locker. "But then he didn't have a tumor and maybe it was a seizure, and I was thinking, maybe there's something in the food, like, at that restaurant? Because I like the burritos there and all but you can never tell with stuff that's, like, you know, *foreign*."

Nadia didn't bother contradicting Kendall. Her mind was too full of what she had to do today. Right now, beyond anything else, she needed to get to Mateo.

All last night, she'd tossed and turned. There was only one thing she could do—only one responsible choice she could make—and as much as she hated it, Nadia knew what she had to do. She couldn't put this conversation off one moment longer.

When she finally saw Mateo, he was walking across the gravel area of the quad. His haircut really was lopsided—Ginger had freaked out midsnip, apparently—but otherwise Mateo looked fine. Amazing, really. When he saw her, his face lit up in a smile that warmed his brown eyes and made something inside her melt.

Just get it out, she told herself. *Walk over there and say it.*

Already Mateo was coming over to her. Brown leaves caught in the wind skittered across the gravel, in front of her feet. Nadia clutched her hoodie more closely around her and tried to find her strength.

"Hey," she managed to say as he reached her. "You're back."

"When you're glad to be at school, it's a bad sign." He grinned at her, but she couldn't find the strength to smile back. Instantly Mateo leaned closer. "What's wrong? Is it Elizabeth?"

"No. I mean, yes, but—not exactly." This wasn't doing either of them any good. Nadia forced herself to meet Mateo's eyes as she said, "I can't do this."

"Can't do what?"

"Challenge Elizabeth. Not if it puts everyone I care about in danger. We have to find some way to convince her we're giving up. And—I don't know how, but we'll figure out a way"—Nadia swallowed hard; this was the worst part—"a way to break the bond between us. You can't be my Steadfast any longer, Mateo."

He stared back at her. She'd imagined that he might be relieved, but instead he looked wounded . . . as wounded as she felt. More than anything, she wanted to take it all back, and tell him that of course they were tied together forever. How could it ever be any other way?

Instead she turned and walked away, refusing to look back.

17

NADIA MANAGED TO AVOID BOTH VERLAINE AND MATEO for the rest of the school day, even though she had to hide in the bathroom instead of eating lunch. It felt cowardly, hiding from them—

—no, all of it felt cowardly, period.

I'm not backing down because I'm scared, Nadia reminded herself. *It's because I'm putting too many people in danger. Dad. Cole. Mateo. Elizabeth's evil—but that doesn't make her my problem.*

That was all true, or true enough. So why did it make her feel so hollow inside?

When the final bell rang, she didn't even bother returning to her locker, just shouldered her heavy backpack and hurried across the grounds, not looking back. The crowd of laughing, carefree people didn't seem to have anything to do with Nadia. Even though she'd learned most of their names by now, worked with a couple of people on school projects, they were still strangers, really. And that was how she wanted it.

But it was so easy to imagine them out on the night of the Halloween carnival, acting crazy in their costumes, laughing like this, until the ground began to shake—

"Nadia!" That was Verlaine behind her. Nadia didn't want to turn around, but she did.

Verlaine and Mateo ran to her, side by side. Why was it surprising to realize they would have talked about this without her? *The whole world doesn't revolve around you,* she told herself. But all she could do was grip her backpack straps tightly and stare at the ground as they came closer.

"Wait up," Verlaine panted, even though Nadia had already stopped walking. "We need to talk to you about this."

Mateo said nothing, only looked at Nadia with those dark eyes—brown with a touch of gold.

Nadia managed to say, "I realize you guys both need to understand what was done to you. And maybe I can help with that. But this whole thing about figuring Elizabeth out, taking her on—that has to stop."

"How can you say that?" Verlaine stomped one Converse-clad foot on the ground. "We're just supposed to let her go on like she has been? Hurting anybody who gets in her way?"

"If we get in her way, then we're next." Although she was talking to Verlaine, Nadia couldn't look away from Mateo's face. "We're all fooling around with stuff we don't under-stand—not even me. My mom"—her voice choked in her throat; she spat the bitter words out—"my mom didn't teach me enough. There's no one else to teach me. I'm not Elizabeth's equal. I'm not even close. To you two, maybe it seems like I know everything there is to know about magic, but I don't. Anything I try to do to Elizabeth is doomed to fail. Do you understand that? Mateo, you—you got hurt two days ago. You could have ended up on a ventilator, in a coma, for the rest of your life. And that was just Ginger coming after you because you knew too much! Because of me. It's nothing compared to what Elizabeth could do. Do you guys get how far over our heads we are here? If you did, there's no way you'd fight me about this. You'd know the only thing to do is to run as far away from Elizabeth as possible."

"How?" Mateo said quietly. "We live here. I'm cursed. There's no getting away from that."

"I don't know," Nadia confessed. "We'll have to figure something out." She'd been up all night asking herself this same question. Dad liked his new job, even if they did scrape by on less money, but she figured he'd still put her and Cole in front of everything else. So if she started talking about how desperately she missed Chicago—and said she wanted to go to Yale or Stanford, someplace crazy expensive—maybe he'd talk to his old law firm and get his job back. It was the only plan she had so far, but it seemed possible.

Verlaine was so thin, so pale—a stretched cobweb of a girl—that Nadia sometimes forgot how tall she was. Now, though, when Verlaine's fury was blazing, there was no forgetting that she towered over her, and even had a few inches on Mateo. "Elizabeth might've killed my parents. She definitely killed Mateo's mom. How can we not take her on? Somebody has to! Do you want to let her get away with it?"

"No!" Nadia shot back. "But she already got away with it! I don't have the power to stop her, and you two—you have to stop believing that I do. You have to stop believing in me."

She started to turn away from them, but Mateo's hand closed around her arm, and just like that, Nadia couldn't move. Feeling him touch her made her want to melt, even though she knew she ought to push him away.

Mateo looked at her steadily as he said, "I can't do that."

"You can walk away from Elizabeth if you have to—you've already started—"

"That's not what I mean." Mateo's thumb brushed along the crook of her elbow, back and forth, the smallest, gentlest touch she could imagine. "You said I had to stop believing in you. Well, I can't."

Nadia refused to cry. She wouldn't. Even if her eyes were blurring and she couldn't get a word out because her breaths were coming hard and fast, even if Mateo kept looking at her like *that*, she wasn't going to cry.

Mateo kept going. "You've already done the impossible. Remember? I'm a Steadfast. Shouldn't happen. But it has. You've already figured out more about Elizabeth than just about anyone else in town ever did. I don't know enough about all this to say whether you could ever be stronger than her, but—I think you could be strong enough. Nadia, you could be strong enough to do anything."

She gulped down something that was either a sob or a laugh, and although she still wanted to pull her arm away, she couldn't bring herself to. She could only look back at Mateo and wish she were anything like the person he thought he saw.

"Okay, so, you two are having a *moment*." Verlaine jerked her backpack onto her shoulders in a huff. "Mateo, good luck getting through to her. Nadia, call me when you're talking sense again." With that, Verlaine stalked off across the grounds, her silvery hair seemingly a tangled part of the gray fall sky.

Once they were alone, Nadia whispered, "Mateo, you aren't listening."

"You're not talking. Your fear is." He breathed out. "Listen. Can we go somewhere? Hang out for a while? We could talk about this better if we weren't about forty feet from cheerleader practice."

"My house. Dad's at his hearing, and Cole's over at a friend's for a while." Nadia realized that she needed to be at home; more than that she needed to be in her attic, surrounded by the tools of her Craft. It was the Craft that had shaped her life so much so far, that had brought Verlaine and Mateo to her. It was the Craft she was coming close to abandoning.

So it was the Craft she needed to confront now—and when she did, she wanted Mateo beside her.

"The last time I was here I thought it was bigger," Mateo said as he stooped his head; the sloping roof of the attic meant that he could only stand up straight at the very center. "Of course, the last time I was here I was seeing my first magic spell. So I guess I got distracted."

Nadia sat cross-legged on one of the oversize pillows on the floor; normally she popped her phone into the dock she kept in the corner, both for the music and to make sure her father and Cole wouldn't overhear anything they shouldn't. Doing that now felt like trying to set a mood or something, though, so she didn't. But that meant Mateo took his seat across from her in a silence that felt heavy and strange.

Yet not awkward. Mateo—even though he was a guy, even though they couldn't agree on what to do or how to do it—he belonged here.

Didn't mean she knew what to say to him.

Their eyes met, and she looked at him from a different angle than before—and then it was hard to meet his eyes. Mateo said, "Okay. Where do we start? You're finally smiling, so I guess we're on the same page."

"It's not that." Nadia tried to cover her mouth with her hand, the better to disguise her smile. "Momentary distraction. Sorry."

"What is it?"

"It's just—" She put this as gently as she could. "Ginger really shortchanged you on that cut."

"Is my whole head still lopsided?" When Nadia nodded, Mateo groaned. "Great. I'm trying to have a serious discussion while I look like an idiot."

"You don't. Look like an idiot, I mean." Nadia hesitated. His hair was the least of their concerns—something for her to focus on instead of the bigger issue—but maybe it was better to get rid of any distractions. Besides, Mateo really did need some help. "Hey. I keep some scissors up here. Let me finish it."

"Cut my hair?"

"Shouldn't be too hard. I could try," she said. "Only if you want me to."

"Yeah. Okay."

Nadia leaned over to one of her toolboxes (she used ones from the hardware store—less suspicious and supersturdy) to get her scissors; Mateo slipped off his letter jacket, revealing the hard lines of his chest and arms beneath a long-sleeved black T-shirt. At first she was startled—by how amazing he looked, how close he was, the fact that he was taking his clothes off—but then she thought, *He doesn't want to get hair all over himself. Obviously. Don't be an idiot.*

But her pulse was pounding as she took the scissors, and grabbed one of her drop cloths to drape around his shoulders.

When she slipped her arms around his neck, he shifted his weight—surprised the same way she had been, she thought, by how close they were. Just thinking that made her cheeks flush hot, and Mateo wasn't looking her straight in the eyes any longer, either. He said only, "You've cut hair before, right?"

"Sure. Plenty of times." No need to tell him that the hair she'd cut had belonged to her old Barbie dolls, which all looked demented afterward.

Nadia tentatively reached toward him, her fingertips barely short of his hair, until finally she ran her hands through it. Mateo's hair felt like warm silk against her palms. At her touch, he closed his eyes. Him reacting like that—it made the silence in the room softer, something that could hold them both.

Carefully Nadia took the scissors in one hand and combed her fingernails through the very back of his hair. Should she just—even it out? That seemed obvious enough. The metallic scrape of the blades against each other made her bite her lower lip, but then the first lock of hair fell away.

There were ways to use locks of hair in love spells—

"Thank you," she said quietly as she made the next snip. "For believing in me. After what you've been through— everything that's happened—I wouldn't blame you if you hated witchcraft. And witches."

"I did, for a little while. Or thought I did. But that was only Elizabeth."

Nadia brushed some hair past his ear, feeling the curve of it against her thumb. She checked the other side of his head and decided to risk another snip. "I know that must have been hard."

"Yeah." Mateo swallowed hard. "I thought she was my best friend. All those great memories I have of us growing up together—it's hard to believe they were only lies." He hesitated. "Do you think she erased other memories? You know. Other people I used to be friends with. So I'd really think she was all I had."

"I don't know."

"I can't decide what would be worse. Her wiping out whatever happy memories I ever had, or whether—whether there weren't any." He breathed out; his shoulders rose and fell, and she paused in her work, only for a moment. Then Nadia bent closer to him to start again.

It was easier, somehow, talking to him when they didn't have to look each other in the eyes. So she kept her concentration on the fringe of dark hair between her fingers as she snipped. "You have the right to feel betrayed." The next words stuck in her throat, but she got them out: "Elizabeth made you think that you loved her."

He hesitated before saying, "It was never like that between us. You get that, right?"

Once again Nadia remembered Elizabeth saying she could make Mateo love her at any moment she chose. Make him believe he'd always loved her. There was no reason for her to do that, Nadia knew, no reason it would increase Elizabeth's control—but she would do it just to be mean. Just to make sure Nadia *hurt*.

"Yeah, you told me," she said briskly. "But there's more than one kind of love. Losing the love of a friend—that's bad enough."

Mateo breathed out. "Sometimes I think the only reason I've been able to keep myself from totally losing it is that she never made me . . . want her. Kiss her. Anything like that. If she had, I couldn't take it."

"You've had too many people using magic to screw with

your head already. That's one more reason to break the Steadfast spell. So your thoughts can be your own again."

"I thought you said you couldn't break that spell—not for a long time, maybe ever."

"Not without—sacrificing my magic."

Nadia knew what that meant. Destroying and burying her Book of Shadows. Removing all the enchantments from the attic. Taking apart her bracelet. Never having the assurance of even a casual spell again. It felt like ripping out her own heart.

But if that was what it took to keep her family safe—and to set Mateo free—

"Then I don't want you to break the spell," Mateo said.

"I'm ready to do it."

"Well, I'm not. This Steadfast thing—what we did that day on the beach, what we were together—it was *amazing*. It felt like I'd been waiting my whole life to be a part of something like that."

Me too, Nadia wanted to say, but the words wouldn't come out. She combed one hand through his hair, shaking out the loose strands, checking her work—hey, this looked pretty good. But her fingers trembled, and her breaths were coming shallow and fast as she struggled against tears.

"Don't take it away from me," Mateo said. "Or from yourself. As scary and as weird as this is, being your Steadfast—I know it's what I was meant to do. Like being a witch is what you're meant to do. It's a part of us. You can't just . . . end it like it never happened."

Nadia sat back and set the scissors down. "You know I'm telling you the truth about how dangerous it is."

"Yeah. I do. You want to protect the people you love. I do, too. But we fall apart or we stand together, right?"

It flowed into her like sunlight, took her tears away. If Mateo could bear the curse, and still have the courage to stand as her Steadfast and take Elizabeth on—how could she do any less? She still owed Dad and Cole all her protection, but with Elizabeth's evil unfolding everywhere around them, the only thing for Nadia to do was fight. At least she wasn't fighting alone.

"I'm sorry," she whispered. "You're right. We stand together."

"Together." Mateo held his hand out, and she took it. When their eyes met again, Nadia flushed with warmth. She kept waiting for him to say something else, but he didn't. Maybe he couldn't, if he felt as shaky as she did. If the feeling of his hand in hers did half as much to him as it did to her—

Once again she remembered Elizabeth standing in the hallway, promising to make Mateo love her if it suited her purposes.

If Nadia leaned forward right now—the way Mateo had begun to—if she kissed him and they were together, would Elizabeth know? She'd sensed the spell of forgetting right away; who could guess how deeply she was wound into Mateo's mind?

If Elizabeth realized Nadia and Mateo were together, she might take Mateo back. She might make him believe that he'd always loved Elizabeth. Could Nadia bear that? Once again she remembered Elizabeth's words to her: *You've loved and lost, haven't you?*

And Mateo had said the only thing keeping him from losing it was the fact that Elizabeth hadn't deceived him in this one, last, terrible way.

Nadia pulled back. Mateo blinked, obviously caught off guard.

"Nadia!" Cole's voice sang from downstairs. "Are you home yet?"

That broke the sudden awkwardness, and both of them started to laugh from embarrassment. "Little brothers," Nadia said. "They have amazing timing."

"Apparently." But even though they were smiling, she could feel the uncertainty still between them.

Mateo wasn't sure how he'd expected this whole weird day to end, but it definitely hadn't involved LEGOs.

"These are big-boy LEGOs," Cole said proudly. "Not the stupid ones for little babies. Dad let me get the real ones a year ago."

"I can see that. Is this the Millennium Falcon we're building?"

"Yeah. Or it can be a castle."

Really it sort of looked like the Leaning Tower of Pisa, even if it had Chewbacca in it. Mateo figured it didn't matter as long as he kept sticking more LEGOs on.

He sat with Cole in the middle of the Caldanis' living

room floor, keeping him busy while Nadia talked things through on the phone with Verlaine. Apparently Cole's friend had gotten sick, which made for an unexpected afternoon of babysitting.

Which was definitely not what he wanted to be doing right now. He wanted to be back in that attic, with Nadia's hand in his—back in that moment so he could find out exactly how she felt about him—

But life got in the way sometimes, and that was just how it was. Mateo didn't mind keeping Cole busy; he was a fun little kid. Also, maybe Mateo was way too old for LEGOs, but that didn't mean he didn't sort of like them still.

And, just as obviously, Nadia needed to talk to Verlaine almost as much as she'd needed to talk to him.

"I'm really sorry," Nadia said into her phone for about the eighteenth time. "I had to think about my dad and Cole, you know? And how they could be affected by—um, by our science project. And where are you?" Then she opened the front curtains. "Oh, okay. Come on in." She put her phone back on the counter. To Mateo she said, "I asked Verlaine to pick up some Slushos, but I don't know. She's still pretty hacked off."

"We can live without Slushos," Mateo said.

Cole sighed. "Speak for yourself." Mateo laughed and ruffled his hair.

Nadia opened the front door as Verlaine came up the steps, gray hair in a ponytail, a scowl on her face, and a tray of Slushos in her hands. "They're all cherry," she said. "Take them or don't."

"Yes!" Cole did his version of an end-zone touchdown dance, while Mateo rose to his feet.

"How are you doing?" he asked her, and just like that, Verlaine's expression softened. They'd spoken only briefly this afternoon—the first time they'd ever had a lengthy conversation without Nadia there, even though they'd known each other almost their whole lives. But that had been enough for him to know how betrayed she felt, and how lonely. As suspicious as she was of Nadia, witchcraft, and the rest of it, this was the one time in Verlaine's life she'd ever been included in something.

How come I never talked to Verlaine before? Mateo wondered. *She's smart. She sees a lot. So why is it like I always forget about her? A six-foot-tall girl with crazy clothes and silver hair—it's not as if she doesn't stand out.*

"I'm okay." Verlaine handed Cole his Slusho and took a slurp from hers. "Better now that I'm not being abandoned to investigate my parents'—I mean, our science project all on my own. Plus the whole thing with, um, with Elizabeth."

"Is Elizabeth your girlfriend?" Cole said to Mateo. He looked all kid-innocent, but there was mischief in his eyes to go with the pink Slusho mustache. "Nadia said she was."

"She's not my girlfriend," Mateo said.

Nadia quickly interjected, "Cole, wouldn't it be fun to play in the yard for a while?"

"I'm not supposed to take snacks outside because of that time I got gravel in my sandwich."

"I wouldn't tell. Just this once!"

Cole grinned as he sat in the nearest chair, kicking his legs back and forth. "Nope. I like it here."

Mateo had always wished he weren't an only child, but now he wasn't so sure about that. They'd have to be careful about how they said things. "So our . . . science project is about the sinkholes in town. And what might be pulling the town out from under our feet."

Nadia gasped, so sharply that Mateo thought she might have hurt herself. He leaned toward her, concerned, but instead she thumped her hand fast against the wall. "Oh, that's it. That's actually it."

Verlaine stared at Mateo, who shrugged. "That's what?"

Nadia grabbed the remote and turned on the television; almost instantly, Cole wandered toward it like a kid hypnotized. Then she gestured them closer and whispered, "Goodwife Hale's—book. She said something about this, about the framework of this town being built on mag—on, uh, magnetism."

"He's not listening!" Verlaine whispered. "Magic. It's built on magic?"

"I think so," Nadia continued. "That's what Elizabeth's doing. She's ripping out that old magic. Pulling the town out from under us."

"With the sinkholes," Mateo said, trying to make sure he had this straight.

"Yes, but it's more than that. The way this town is sick on the inside—and all the curses she's laid, whatever the hell that is buried beneath the chemistry lab—there's magic everywhere here, do you understand?"

"We do now," Verlaine said, "but where are you going with this?"

Looking straight at Mateo, Nadia continued, "You said the magic was a part of us. That it wasn't meant to be taken away. That's true for this whole town. See? Captive's Sound has been cursed and enchanted for so long that it's—it's literally lying on a foundation of magic. Elizabeth's stripping away her own spells. She's removing the framework."

He could kind of see that. "Why?"

"The One Beneath must want it. I don't know what for. They say sometimes he demands death for its own sake." Nadia said that so quietly, so matter-of-factly, that it sent a chill along Mateo's spine. Next to him, Verlaine shuddered. "But now I know some of the spells she must be using. That means—that means I have an idea what to do to stop her."

"This sounds dangerous," Verlaine said.

"It is." Nadia nodded slowly. "But it's worth a try."

Mateo felt the urge to tell her not to do it—whatever it was—to get between her and Elizabeth if he could. But he knew he couldn't. "What are you going to do?"

"I'm going to try to turn the spell back on her," Nadia said, her dark eyes lighting up. "Unmagic her, at least a little bit. We're going to fight fire with fire."

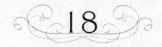

18

"A STEADFAST," ELIZABETH MURMURED.

She stood on the shore, on a patch of beach so rocky that no houses had been built very near. Her legs were thigh-deep in the water; the sharp fragments of shells underneath her bare feet cut into her flesh. Droplets of her blood would be mingling with the seawater even now. The One Beneath could claim the entire sound as her blood soon.

He needs so little to claim us, Asa said. *Does that never seem unjust to you?*

"Silence, beast."

The more she thought about the identity of Nadia Caldani's Steadfast, the less certain she was. Verlaine Laughton was the obvious choice, the only girl she had seen regularly in Nadia's company. Yet she was so new to Nadia's life—such an unusual person to reach out to.

They might have known each other before, Asa chimed in. *Did you ever consider that? People talk via computers now. The witch and Verlaine could have been friends online.*

Elizabeth had never used a computer in her life and did not intend to begin at this late date. As cold sea spray stung her face, she considered the possibility of some past acquaintance between Nadia and Verlaine. It seemed unlikely. They had not greeted each other that first day at school, and their attitude toward each other during the few days Elizabeth had observed them early in the semester—it was more wary than warm. No, they had been strangers before.

Yet what kind of a Steadfast could Verlaine Laughton be? Bereft as she was, could she even hold the power? Elizabeth supposed it was possible—this was something she'd never tested—though she found it surprising.

Must be fun for you. You get so few surprises these days.

Although Elizabeth did not appreciate the demon's attempts at levity, there was truth to what he said. This world felt so old to her—so peculiar and yet so predictable. People wore shapeless, flimsy clothing now, and the women were brazen, and everyone talked to little machines they held in their hands, but they were as venal and selfish as they had ever been. Their hopes were just as craven, their perspective as small. She'd abandoned any attempt to take part in their ordinary affairs many decades ago, beyond her token school attendance to look after the Chamber. Being with ordinary mortals increasingly felt to her like watching small, squabbling children fighting over broken toys.

Even the Craft could no longer fascinate her; she had

mastered it so long ago. This one tiny unanswered question about a Steadfast was the first flicker of uncertainty she had felt in many years, and briefly it entertained her. It was like seeing a butterfly in the desert.

But Verlaine remained the most likely candidate. Perhaps there were others to investigate—that school counselor, for one, Ms. Walsh; she seemed to take an interest in Nadia—but Verlaine Laughton was the correct place to begin.

Satisfied, Elizabeth dipped her hands into the ocean and drank. Even a mouthful of seawater could cause vomiting and hallucinations in most people. She was past all that now. It could not even make her thirstier than she already was, always was. All she needed to do was to see if she could start to taste the blood.

"You should've had your friends stay for dinner," Dad said as he went into the kitchen. "We could have celebrated."

"If you'd called ahead to tell me you won, maybe I would've asked them." Nadia wasn't being entirely honest about that, she knew. Today had been intense for all of them; she figured Mateo and Verlaine probably needed to decompress tonight as much as she did. Her nerves remained on edge. But still—she could imagine a day when they would all hang out at her place, and her father would maybe be in "kind of cool Dad" mode instead of "annoying oversensitive Dad" mode. It could be . . . sort of fun. She could see them here. Especially Mateo. Her lips curled into a soft smile as she remembered how friendly and gentle he'd been with

Cole, down there on the floor like playing with LEGOs was still his favorite thing to do.

If only they could get out from under Elizabeth's influence—if only she could be sure that Mateo could be hers to keep, that there was no chance of having him stolen away—

The clanging of a pan on the stove jolted her back to the here and now. "Hey. What are you doing?"

"Making us some spaghetti." Dad had taken out a glass jar of some sauce from the store. "The pasta—that's going to be on this shelf, right? Yes. Huh, no spaghetti, but we have these tube things, and that works just the same."

"Dad. I'll make dinner."

"Don't be silly." He didn't even slow down, like he wasn't listening to her at all. "I've got this. How hard can it be?"

"That stuff in the jar is from, like, a factory. I can make it from scratch in half an hour, and it'll be ten times better."

"Yeah, I know, but this is all right, isn't it? You've eaten it before. Cole even likes it; he put it in the shopping cart himself."

"That's not the point." Why was he being so annoying? Nadia wanted him out of her kitchen, where he was going to make a mess, plus gross pasta sauce. She tried the buttering-up approach. "You won your big hearing today. So you should take the night off, right? Let us treat you."

"The treat for me is fixing dinner for my family." Dad was starting to look about as ticked off as she felt. "Don't you have some homework to do? You never seem to have any homework."

"*Dad.* Come on." Nadia tried to snatch the packet of rigatoni from him. To her surprise, he grabbed on to it tighter, and for half a second they were in the world's stupidest tug-of-war, she and her father almost fighting over a bag of pasta—

—until it ripped apart, scattering rigatoni all over the kitchen so that it clattered on the counters and the floor, rolled into the living room, even got into Nadia's hair.

She stared at her father, who stared right back, until at the same moment they bent to their knees to start scooping it up. She huffed, "I've got it, okay?"

"No! It's not okay!" Dad wasn't shouting—he never shouted—but he was as close to angry as he ever got.

"Why are you yelling at me? I was just trying to help out! I'm always trying to help out! Most parents would like that, you know, not scream at their kids when they try to be nice—"

"Jesus Christ, are you ever going to let me do anything for you?" Dad's voice broke on the last word, and then he sat back on the floor, right there in the middle of all the pasta, and leaned his head into one hand. For one horrifying second, Nadia thought he was going to cry, but he didn't.

She felt like she was frozen there on her knees, one hand full of uncooked pasta. But slowly she eased herself into a seated position; whatever Dad was waiting for, she felt like she needed to wait it out with him. From the backyard, they could hear Cole yelling out the details of some imaginary battle involving all his action figures.

Finally Dad said, "I know you do a lot for this family, Nadia. You've really stepped up since your mother—since she left. And I appreciate that. I couldn't make it without you."

"Thank you." Her voice seemed very small.

"But you're still my daughter, okay? It's my job to take care of you. It's not your job to take care of me."

He didn't have any idea. Elizabeth's whirlwind was coming for them, for everyone in town, and scary as it was, Nadia's witchcraft might be the only thing that could stop her. If Nadia wasn't taking care of her father, of all of them, who knew what might happen?

Still—she could let the man cook once in a while, if it made him feel better. Even if it meant eating nasty sauce from a jar. "Okay," she said. "I'm sorry I fought with you over the bag. That was stupid."

Dad just sat there, forearms on his knees, staring at nothing in particular. "Never learned to cook. Always left that to your mom. I let that firm take so much of my life—eighty hours a week, ninety, more—and she always said it was all right. She had the home front covered. That was our deal, how it was supposed to work. I thought—I really thought she was okay with it."

Nadia remembered Mom laughing about the "home front." It had been one of her favorite jokes. "I thought she was, too."

He shook his head. "I was a fool. I should've known that couldn't work forever."

"It worked *fine*. Everything was absolutely fine until one day, Mom—it was like she checked out." How else could she even say it? Nadia had known before Mom left that something was wrong, but only for a couple of weeks—a couple of weeks during which Mom had hardly seemed to notice they were even around. "You didn't do anything."

"I don't know. Guess we don't get to know." He sighed and thumped the back of his head once, softly, against the counters, then looked at the kitchen with something like his usual good humor. "Tonight's another pizza night, isn't it?"

"Looks like it."

"You order, and I'll clean up."

"Okay," she said, even though she was sure this meant she'd find lost rigatoni noodles lying around the kitchen for another day or two to come.

"And—we should take a break sometime soon. As a family. Maybe take a weekend away. Go down to New York, maybe. Keep our city-dweller cred current, you know?"

Dad's attempt to talk like a teenager was embarrassing, but not so much that Nadia missed the opportunity. "Can we? Please? We should go soon. Halloween weekend, definitely."

"Halloween? But there's some big carnival here in town, with a haunted house and everything."

"It's supposed to be incredibly lame." Nadia thought fast. "Last year a kid around Cole's age cut his hand open in the haunted house. I heard he needed a dozen stitches. It's really unsafe."

Dad frowned. "Huh. Well, I wouldn't want Cole running around in something like that."

"You should get the tickets to New York tonight. I bet there's tons of fun stuff to do in Manhattan on Halloween. And Cole misses the 'L' so much, probably he'll want to ride the subway the whole time." Little boys had a thing about trains.

"You know what? I think it's a good idea." Dad nodded, satisfied with himself. "This is going to be good for us. I'll get online after dinner tonight."

An incredible tension that had been gripping her heart seemed to release in an instant. Whatever happened on Halloween night, Dad and Cole would be far away. Nadia could come up with an excuse not to go at the last minute—a school project, something like that. Knowing they were safe would let her concentrate. That was one less thing Elizabeth could do to her, one less weapon Elizabeth would have against them. No matter what happened to Nadia, the rest of her family would be okay.

When Dad hugged her before standing up, she hugged him back for a really long time. He seemed to need it.

Reasons to Visit My Parents' Graves Soon
1. Have to know if that hag Elizabeth killed them or not.
2. Should probably take flowers or something because I've never taken anything there and maybe that's kind of awful, and I am somehow being the worst daughter ever to people who aren't even alive.

3. If Elizabeth did this, then revenge is necessary even though she is a megabadass witch from ye olden days and I am a high school senior with a shrieking-alarm key chain as my sole means of self-defense. So some planning time for said revenge is probably necessary.

Reasons Not to Visit My Parents' Graves Soon
1. Not sure I'm ready to deal with that, at all.
2. Already working on stopping Elizabeth in her tracks, so revenge motivation is an unnecessary addition to my plans.
3. Also that's probably the only way to make this apocalypse-averting thing even more stressful than it already is.

Verlaine stared at the lists on her laptop screen and groaned. Even though both lists were short, she knew she could keep adding items all night and still wind up with no clear conclusion.

She had made her usual nest behind the *Guardian* front desk for the Thursday night "late hours," which was something the editor, Mrs. Chew, had come up with to help Verlaine burn more internship credits. Her coffee milk was in its usual glass at her side; the funky Bakelite bracelet she'd found seriously underpriced at the thrift store, the one that was too bulky to wear while typing, made a turquoise ring on the other side of her laptop. Since the newspaper wasn't exactly a hotbed of activity even during regular hours, Verlaine usually found this a good time to update the *Lightning Rod* or get homework out of the way before the weekend.

Or, in this case, to sit around making useless lists that didn't do anything to settle her chaotic mind.

Between two fingers, Verlaine caught the shorter strand of her hair—the one she'd cut the other day. Mateo had sworn he'd seen something, and she believed him. Somewhere, sometime, magic had been worked on her, and the taint of it lingered.

But that doesn't mean it's why Mom and Dad died. Your hair could have turned gray from the shock. That's what Uncle Gary always said. You were alone in that house with them for a day, and it must have been scary as hell. Sometimes she had nightmares about it—not real memories, but her imagination running wild with what it would mean to be trapped in a house with two dead bodies.

If not her parents, though—then what was the magic about?

Sourly Verlaine thought, *Maybe it's all about making me the least popular kid in school. Yeah, I bet that's it. Elizabeth uses her badass witch vibes to figure out who doesn't get to be prom queen.*

"Hello, Verlaine."

She glanced up to see Elizabeth standing right in front of the desk.

About eighty thousand swear words ran through Verlaine's mind all at the same second, which was maybe why none of them came out of her mouth. Instead she just gaped.

Elizabeth didn't seem to notice. She seemed as calm and gentle as ever, a knit cardigan pulled over one of her white dresses. Her windswept chestnut hair fell over one shoulder, and she smiled, unbothered by Verlaine's silence. "These evening hours are a good idea. I wanted to ask about the fee to place a classified ad?"

She couldn't seriously want that, could she? Maybe she did. Maybe evil Sorceresses had their own classified-ad needs. *Help Wanted: Henchman/Underling for part-time service. For Sale: Eye of toad, never used.* "Um, I'm not sure. Let me check."

"If at all possible."

It felt beyond weird to go look this up for Elizabeth Pike, the same as she would have for any other customer. But Verlaine didn't know what else to do. Without Nadia by her side, any confrontation would have been stupid to the point of suicidal. For now, all she could do was act naturally.

So maybe not letting her fingers shake so much while she typed on the keyboard would be a good idea.

"Okay," Verlaine said, a bit too loudly, but Elizabeth didn't react. "As long as you keep the text under five lines, it's seventy-five dollars for one week, one hundred dollars for two. Which is a whole lot cheaper than virtually any other paper in the world, but hey—it's the *Guardian.*"

"Under five lines." Elizabeth's voice sounded distant. "I'll have to think how to word it. Thanks for your help."

"No problem." The only problem, Verlaine thought, had been keeping this fake smile plastered on her face the whole time.

With a nod, Elizabeth turned to go. She walked back out into the night without ever glancing back.

What was that about? Verlaine wondered.

Once she was halfway down the block, Elizabeth reached into her bag and pulled out the turquoise Bakelite bracelet. It gleamed brightly in her palm.

Verlaine must have been wearing it earlier today. It would work.

Although Nadia considered calling Mateo to be with her while she attempted the spell, ultimately she decided against it. For one, it was late—eleven p.m.—so if his father realized he was gone or her father realized he was in her house, it would be tough to explain.

Also, the first time she did this shouldn't be too strong. Spells for removal of magic could be violent or gentle, showy or soft. This needed to be gentle and soft. Nadia was mostly checking to see if it would work—whether she could sneak a sliver of Elizabeth's magic away without her noticing. That was more likely without the boost to her powers that Mateo provided. (Later, when they had to stop her on Halloween, then she'd need him by her side the whole way.)

Finally, this spell was best cast while in the water, and there was no way Nadia was taking another dive in that freezing cold ocean. Much, much better to run a hot bath.

One thing awesome about living in an old-fashioned house was the old-fashioned bathtub. It was white porcelain, so big about four people could sit in it at once, set up on golden claw feet. Nadia had the squeaky taps turned all the way up, which was the only way to fill the tub before the water started getting cold.

Okay, supplies. Quartz dust. Rose petals. And—the razor blade.

Nadia set the stuff on the broad shelf beside the tub and took a deep breath. Then she slipped off her robe and sank into the warm bathwater, which covered her whole body up to her neck. She wore only her bracelet.

The dust swirled into the water, making it cloudy and yet softly sparkly. The rose petals floated on the surface. The razor blade—

—this was harder to do than she'd anticipated. Nadia had never cast any spells that called for her own blood, not before this. But blood mixed in water gave certain kinds of magic an accuracy and intensity that couldn't be matched any other way.

Great. The one time I actually need it to be that time of the month, and it's not.

She bit down on her lip, held out one thumb, and jabbed.

Ow! Owowowowow. But she'd done it. Nadia pressed on the tiny cut in her thumb tip until the first fat drops of blood spattered into the water. First they became strange trails of red, then lightened to pink, then vanished.

By the light of her stove, Elizabeth began her work. When she held the bracelet up to that glow, she could feel the response between them; yes, this would do nicely.

But then a cool draft shivered past her—a kind of chill that had nothing to do with temperature.

Her eyes widened. Nadia—reaching out for her. Attempting to meddle. And she seemed to understand precisely how to do it.

Elizabeth's respect for the girl increased, but she felt no alarm, any more than an elephant would have been afraid of a gnat, even if it knew where to bite.

She set aside Verlaine's bracelet. That could wait.

First she needed to show Nadia Caldani her place.

NADIA SANK DEEPER INTO THE TUB. THE FINE SPARKLY dust was beginning to settle to the bottom of the tub, forming lines of glitter that swirled with the water.

Summon the ingredients, she told herself. *Everything is ready.*

As Simon Caldani finished reading a chapter of *The Trumpet of the Swan* aloud, his son, Cole, said, "Daddy, what's outside?"

"There aren't any monsters outside. Promise."

"I *know.* They're *birds.* But how come there are so many of them?"

Simon rose from the side of Cole's bed to peer out the nearest window. Sure enough, there in the biggest tree of their yard were dozens of birds—hundreds of them? It was hard to tell in the dark, because they were all black. Crows? He'd never realized how large crows were before. More were alighting on the tree every moment, the flapping of their wings audible as a weird rustling sound. The rustling seemed to surround their home on every side.

"It's getting colder," he said. "They're migrating."

"I thought birds went south for the winter," Cole said. He was right, of course. But surely—

"They must be on their way. They'll move on soon." With that, Simon pulled the curtains shut. There was something eerie about it, those masses of birds, and somehow it seemed as if they were all staring at this house. That was the kind of thing that would give Cole nightmares for sure.

Elizabeth lit her candle. She made her own out of tallow fat, the old way, boiling down the dead flesh herself. How it glistened when it melted—and ahh, the smell. There was no replacing that stink, the fetid odor of real magic. Some people prettied it up, but she preferred to know it for what it was.

Holding her hand out flat, Elizabeth pushed it forward until her fingers were in the candle's flame. The first flare of heat hurt, but she had long since learned to ignore pain.

She held it there, and held it there. Her skin turned red, and the thin wisp of smoke rising from the candle began to darken. The tallow scent deepened into the smell of smoldering flesh.

Hotter, Elizabeth thought. Pain-sparked tears welled in her eyes, but they were meaningless. Her fingers had begun to turn black. *Make it hotter.*

Make it boil.

Nadia leaned her head back on the heavy curved rim of the claw-foot tub, breathed in steam and put the ingredients together:

> *Bone through flesh*
> *Something shattered to the sound of a scream*
> *The destruction of a thing beloved*

The air was almost uncomfortably thick with steam now, and Nadia could feel her whole body prickling with heat from the tub—she hadn't turned the cold tap enough—but she knew she had to concentrate.

An X-ray in shadows of blue and gray, revealing the jagged white fault line where her ulna should have showed through strong, and pain lancing its way up her arm while Mom stroked her hair.

The car windows the night of the wreck, splintering into spiderweb patterns as they flipped over and over, as all of them shrieked in sudden terror.

But Nadia couldn't think; the water was so freaking hot— it almost burned.

Her eyes opened wide as she realized the water was getting hotter. Though the taps were off, the water in the tub was heating up second by second, faster all the time, and she gasped aloud to see steam billowing up—oh, God, it stung, it hurt, it was going to start *cooking* her—

Nadia shoved herself out of the tub, flopping over the side

onto the tile floor so hard it knocked the breath out of her. As she lay there in a puddle, skin red and burning, trying to inhale again, the room heated even further and she heard the unmistakable sound of water boiling. She grabbed a towel to hold over her face, coughing into it as the steam thickened until she couldn't see her own toes. The heat was almost overpowering, and for a moment she thought she might pass out.

But she pushed herself to her feet. The doorknob glowed with heat, but she got to the bathroom window—an old-timey little rectangle that swung out from a side hinge, at least in theory. Nadia had never tried to open it before. Desperately she pushed at its wooden frame, but it wouldn't budge; the window had been painted shut, probably almost a century before—

—then it gave. A blast of cold air rushed into the room. Although steam still filled the air, already Nadia could see through it again, and the temperature went from unbearable to merely uncomfortable.

A crow landed immediately outside, the wings flapping so close it startled her, so she yanked the window back until it was only open a crack. It didn't matter; the worst had passed.

She leaned against the beadboard wall, gasping for breath. After a few seconds, she took a washcloth and pulled the glowing-hot metal chain of the stopper out of the tub; what little water hadn't been evaporated began to drain away, leaving trails of glittery quartz dust behind.

She wiped it up, then used the washcloth to undo the lock on the bathroom door.

Elizabeth knew. I wasn't even all the way into the spell, but she still knew. She nearly boiled me to death.

She would have killed me, and this spell—it was so little—

Somehow Nadia struggled into her robe and managed to stay on her feet as she walked out of the bathroom. In the hallway she passed her father, who gave her a look. "Honey, there's steam halfway down the hall. I know girls like their baths, but running the hot-water heater costs money, okay?"

She couldn't give him any answer but a nod.

Elizabeth pulled her hand from the candle. The flesh had been charred away deeply enough in spots for her to see the bone.

You scare me, Asa said. *And I'm from hell.*

"Silence, beast."

She flexed her fingers, ignoring the stark pain this earned her. As Elizabeth watched, the flesh began to bubble, and the skin lightened from black to a charred tan back to its natural pink. The wounds closed over again, restoring her hand to what it had been before.

Immortality had burdened her for so long, but it had its benefits.

Nadia Caldani still lived—Elizabeth could sense that much—but a warning had been delivered. Perhaps it would be heeded, and these pointless distractions would stop. Surely her threat had been clear enough that she needed to take no further action at this time.

Still, she hung Verlaine's bracelet on a hook near the stove, keeping it close, just in case.

"You should have called me," Mateo said. He knew he was repeating himself, but he was almost too freaked out to think straight. "You're safe now. You're okay."

"I'm okay." Nadia's voice trembled. "But I'm not safe. None of us are."

The three of them were sitting on one of the outside picnic tables, theoretically eating lunch outside despite the chill, but their food lay there, ignored. The thought of Elizabeth somehow reaching across town to hurt Nadia, to try to kill her—"I never dreamed about her attacking you that way."

"You weren't with me. That must be why. You can only dream of the future you're going to see." Nadia was trying hard to sound like she was in control again, but he knew better. Besides, what she was saying was no comfort whatsoever. He dreamed of Nadia in constant peril; it was even worse to think that she faced other dangers he'd never see, never have the chance to warn her against.

Verlaine sat across the table from them, huddled in a fake leopard-skin coat with a wide black collar. "How did Elizabeth know you were trying the spell?"

"She must have performed sentry spells—guards around the kind of magic that could damage her plans. Sort of like the barrier around town but more specific."

His memories of the wreck came flooding back. Looking

down at that shattered car, seeing Nadia there, bloodied and trapped in the muck—that was what Elizabeth's barrier had done. Any step outside the margins Elizabeth had set for them could mean death. "If that's how we're going to stop her—but she can sense that we're doing it—"

"I know." Her voice was so tired, so shaky. Mateo wanted to put his arms around her; if they hadn't been in the middle of the quad, with Verlaine only a couple of feet away and people walking by every second, he would have. "I'll have to think of another way, or—or I'll have to wait until Elizabeth's in the middle of her own magic, when she might be too deep in one spell to cast another, or too distracted to notice."

Verlaine chewed on a fingernail. "Waiting until the last possible second doesn't sound like the ideal A-game."

Nadia nodded. "Believe me, I know. But we're so out of our depth here."

For a few seconds they all sat there, depressed and slightly scared—and then Gage suddenly sat down at the table with them. "Hey, guys. What's up?"

"Hey," they all said in unison. Mateo thought they couldn't have sounded sadder if the funeral march had been playing.

"Whoa. You guys look like your dogs just died." Gage paused. "Oh, wait, did somebody's dog actually die? If so, I'm sorry. Way sorry."

"No dead dogs," Mateo said. He managed an expression that might pass for a smile. "What's happening with you?"

"Something that should cheer you guys up, so I'm guessing

I got here in the nick of time. Night before Halloween, my aunt's place on the beach, it's party time. An actual fun party, Mateo—you might want to check one of those out some-time. Not the same jerks standing around being rude to one another while everybody acts cool."

"A party?" Verlaine frowned in confusion, like that was a word in English she didn't know yet. Then again—nobody had ever asked Verlaine to any of the parties before; at least Mateo had never seen her out. Probably she wasn't used to being invited. For his part, Gage only now seemed to have realized he'd asked Verlaine, too, but he didn't seem to mind.

Mateo said, "The jerks are still going to be there, though. They always show up."

"Yeah, but after the first hour they'll blow it off because they're too cool, and then the rest of us can enjoy ourselves."

"Like, Kendall Bender would be there?" Verlaine didn't look reassured. "I can think of more fun things to do than hang out with her. Lots more. Up to and including reorga-nizing my dads' spice rack."

That was weird—Mateo didn't usually think of Kendall as being that bad. Yeah, she was as dumb as a box of hair, and about equally sensitive, but it wasn't like she went out of her way to be mean to anyone. Well, anyone except Jinnie, but those two hated each other and Jinnie *was* one of the jerks.

And Kendall was also mean to Verlaine.

Come to think of it, everybody who didn't ignore Ver-laine was mean to her, even the people who weren't mean to anyone else. Mateo knew he'd always ignored her; Gage had, too. Why had he ignored someone who was—now that he thought about it—actually great? It didn't make any sense.

Before he could really think about it, though, Nadia said, "The night before Halloween, huh?"

The night before disaster struck Captive's Sound if they didn't do something to stop it—yeah, not the ideal time for going out. "Are we, um, busy?"

But Nadia surprised him. "Who knows? If we aren't—it might be good to take our minds off everything for a couple hours."

He could see that. In fact, if Elizabeth was now watching Nadia so closely that she could pounce at any moment, going out might be the only way to throw her off. "So you'll come with me?"

Nadia's eyes met his, and he realized he'd just asked her out for the first time. It wasn't that he hadn't meant to ask her sometime; they'd become so close, so fast, that it was hard for him to remember that they hadn't been out before. That he hadn't even kissed her yet—

She hesitated. That moment in her attic, when he'd thought they might—Mateo had wondered whether she was holding back then but had decided he'd imagined it. Maybe he hadn't.

But Nadia nodded. "Yeah," she said in a small voice. "I'll come."

"In case anybody remembers I'm still here, I'll come, too," Verlaine said.

"Definitely. Come on along." Gage gave them finger

guns, trying to be deliberately dorky so it would be ironic but really just kind of being dorky, before strolling off to invite more people.

Verlaine took her sandwich up. "I like that guy."

"He's okay." Mateo couldn't look away from Nadia for long. "Yeah, Gage is great."

Which he was. But Mateo wasn't thinking about anything but the fact that Nadia had said yes.

The warmth of that moment stayed with him throughout the afternoon. Forget trying to concentrate on classes. Even the sickening haze of magic that clung to so much of Captive's Sound didn't have much hold on him today. He'd spent the last couple of months being either scared or furious; this was the first time he'd truly felt happy. And if he felt like that only knowing that Nadia was going to the party with him, what would it be like when they were together?

Less than a week—

Oh, crap. Chemistry lab.

Walking by that place put the damper on his good mood. He couldn't think of why, exactly, but lately chem lab gave him that creepy feeling like there were eyes watching him from behind, or as though he'd heard an odd sound in the house while showering alone: watchful, jittery, tense.

But it got a whole lot worse when Elizabeth walked into the hall.

She was right next to the Piranha, who didn't seem to notice anything out of the ordinary. To her, Elizabeth probably looked the way Mateo had always thought: clean-scrubbed and natural, with fair freckled skin and chestnut curls.

Now he saw her for herself, a creature thick with something gold and febrile that rippled down her like so many snakes. The glow around her was brilliant, almost blinding, and yet there was nothing beautiful about it.

"Thanks for the extra-credit work," Elizabeth said sweetly.

"No prob." The Piranha grinned at her like an idiot—the same way Mateo used to grin at her himself. "I only wish I had more students as motivated as you!"

As the Piranha wandered off toward the teachers' lounge, Elizabeth began walking toward him. "Mateo." Her voice was so warm and sugary. Like honey. It disgusted him now. "Where have you been hiding lately?"

He'd kept himself from shrinking away, hadn't revealed that he could see her true form. But Mateo knew he couldn't keep up the lie one second more. After what had happened to Nadia, it was impossible to think that anything he did could put her in more danger; Nadia was already in as much danger as she could be.

And just once, he wanted Elizabeth to hear what he thought of her.

He said only, "I know what you are."

She paused, then tilted her head to one side. "What do you mean?"

"I know what you are." Mateo's hands balled into fists. He would never, ever hit a woman, but Elizabeth didn't even count as a woman any longer. "You don't get any more of my dreams. You don't get to pretend we're best friends any

longer. Keep your fake memories and your fake smile to yourself from now on, okay? Don't come near me again, or I swear to God, no matter how much magic you've got, I'll find a way to hurt you. Do you understand me?"

Elizabeth didn't protest. She didn't ask what he was talking about. But she didn't lash out, either. She simply stood up straight—less like the sweet girl who had played at being his friend and more like an equal. Why had he never noticed before how tall she was? She could look him squarely in the eyes. "It's not worth making you forget," she said. "I'm bored with it."

Then she walked away, as smoothly and calmly as ever.

It wasn't the epic revenge he'd dreamed of. Maybe that would have to wait for Halloween night.

But at least he never had to pretend to be Elizabeth Pike's friend ever again.

Nadia Caldani had broken one of the First Laws. She had told a man about magic.

Elizabeth was shocked—and she had for centuries believed herself to be beyond the reach of shock any longer. Even she, who had broken so many of the First Laws, had never broken that one. And a young girl like Nadia had?

She must have recognized the curse, Elizabeth realized as she headed home. *Which I should have anticipated she would do.*

That was no reason to assume that Nadia would then go so far as to tell a male about the Craft. No witch properly schooled would ever have made such an assumption . . . or done such a thing without a compelling reason. Abandoned by her mother and teacher she might have been, but Nadia would have learned this rule from the very first.

Then again—Mateo had stopped telling Elizabeth about his dreams. Nadia had taken away Elizabeth's window into the future, which at this point was more a moral victory than a real one. But still, that could be her motivation.

Was it reason enough to tell him about the Craft? It wouldn't be for most witches. But Nadia was apparently far more ruthless than Elizabeth had realized. Mere girl though she was, primitive though her magical skills might be . . . she was a fighter. A worthy opponent.

Gulping down the last of her water, Elizabeth tossed the bottle onto the floor amid the shards of broken glass. She made her way through her home to the bright light of her stove, by now the only heat in a very cold house. Neither heat nor cold mattered much to her any longer, but some spells worked better by the light of this unearthly fire.

First she went to the ancient, half-rotted chest of drawers leaning against the far wall. Slowly she pried open a small drawer she hadn't gone into for a decade, not since Lauren Cabot had committed suicide.

There, amid the dust and stained wood, was a human finger bone, yellow with age. This she had possessed even longer than her immortality. George Cabot, the first of his family she had known, the first to serve her: This was all that remained of him. It was all she needed to keep the curse going forever.

Elizabeth's first impulse was to crush it. Mateo Perez would never again share his dreams with her; that made the curse useless. He would only have been able to assist her for another few days at the most anyway, and had already done his last and greatest service by showing her how dangerous Nadia had the potential to be . . . by showing her that many of her plans, in the future, would be dedicated to Nadia's destruction. So why not end the curse?

But no. The curse on the Cabots was part of the magic that underlay all her works; by now it was as much a part of Captive's Sound as the beach or the sea. It would be foolish to disrupt that so profoundly, so close to her goal. No, that curse would die only with her.

You could give him a few days to live as an ordinary human, Asa suggested. *A small gift to remember you by.*

"You think I care about mercy, beast?" Elizabeth said as she placed the bone back in its drawer.

I know you better than that.

Ignoring the demon's japes, Elizabeth crossed the room to where a metal hook hung on one wall. If Nadia truly represented some sort of threat, the very first thing to do was to take away Nadia's Steadfast.

Elizabeth's fingers closed around Verlaine's bracelet.

Dear Mr. Laughton and Mr. McFadden,

Congratulations! You have won an all-expenses-paid cruise to beautiful Jamaica. The boat leaves on Friday, October 30—

Verlaine paused at her laptop, not sure this sounded right. Wouldn't people call them if the cruise were leaving so soon? She couldn't disguise her voice on the phone, though, and she didn't think either Nadia or Mateo could really make themselves sound like adults if they made the call for her. Maybe that guy Gage, whose voice was deep—but they weren't friends yet. He wasn't somebody she could ask for a favor like this. Could Mateo ask him, though? Once her dads believed they'd won the cruise, the rest was easy. Her parents had taken a huge life-insurance policy when she was born, meaning that Verlaine had way more money than most people at Rodman, including the teachers. She drove the land yacht and thrifted her clothes and lived off her allowance because that money was for college—but to save her dads' lives, she'd dip into it and buy them the nicest cruise anybody ever took.

Besides, if they didn't manage to stop Elizabeth, chances were she wouldn't make it to college anyway—

She nibbled again at her fingernail. Her nails were starting to look like crap. Tonight she'd paint them again—that would stop her from biting them—but then she'd have to do something else to calm her nerves.

If only she could be sure Uncle Dave and Uncle Gary would be safe on Halloween. Then the rest wouldn't matter. She could concentrate then.

Determined, Verlaine decided to go ahead and book the cruise. Later she'd call Mateo and see what he thought about the plan to get Gage on board. She surfed over to a travel site—then froze.

The pain arced up through her, so sharp that she first thought there was a knife hidden in the keyboard, one that had snapped up to stab her. That was crazy, but that was how it felt. But a split second later, Verlaine saw the white forks of electricity lancing up from the keyboard, searing her hands so that she thought she could see bone.

All she could hear was some high-pitched, hoarse sound all around her—was that her screaming? Her body seemed to twist away from her, one direction and then the other, jerking around wildly while her mind slowed down, second by second.

I'm being electrocuted, she thought, almost dully.

Then something flung her back from the computer, into the far wall, and she couldn't see anymore, couldn't even feel.

AROUND DINNERTIME, DAD ONCE AGAIN PROPOSED THAT they visit La Catrina. "Since Mateo is no longer somebody we're trying to avoid," he said, giving Nadia a playful glance. It was all Nadia could do not to roll her eyes.

"It's his night off. But yeah, we should go." It would be less awkward to eat with her family there when her father wouldn't be watching her with Mateo the whole time. Way less awkward.

"Want to ask that friend of yours along?" He frowned. "Was it Vera? Veronica?"

"Verlaine." She shrugged. "Sure, I guess."

"Something always happens when we try to go to La Catrina," Cole complained. "We never get in."

"Don't be silly. C'mon, guys. Nadia, honey, why don't you tell Verla to meet us there? And invite her dads along, too. I ought to meet them sometime."

Nadia texted: *Hey, come eat at La Catrina with us if you want. My dad says to ask your dads, so—if you don't want to, no prob.*

So she wasn't expecting to see Verlaine, and wasn't surprised not to have heard from her by the time they arrived at the restaurant. But Nadia immediately overheard Verlaine's name—from a table where Kendall was holding court among her friends.

"So, like, Verlaine was in the school library, but I think she was using the computers for something illegal, like downloading movies or something like that, and there's this thing in the library computers that's supposed to stop you if you do something illegal, like it gives you a shock, and that's how they keep guys from watching porn all the time, but this time it malfunctioned and it, like, electrocuted her, and so she's in the hospital, not this one, the good one in Wakefield, and I heard she could die."

"Oh, my God." Nadia looked over at her father. "Can we—"

"Let's go," he said, like it was the only thing to do. Dad could be great like that sometimes.

Nadia had never felt worse in her life than she did when she saw Verlaine's dads in the waiting room at the hospital. Uncle Gary tried to be polite and informative, even though his voice kept shaking; Uncle Dave could only sit there with his head in his hands.

"A coma?" Nadia whispered. "How long does that— would she—?"

"They don't know." Uncle Gary kept weaving his fingers together, clasping his hands, unclasping them, like he was trying to work all his nervousness out that way. "It's not unusual, really. I mean, we hear about comas that go on for—for months or years—"

Uncle Dave made a small sound in the back of his throat, and Cole put a tentative hand on his shoulder. That was when Nadia lost it. Her eyes began to tear up, and she had to lean against her father.

"—but that's not what usually happens!" Uncle Gary added hastily. "Lots of people who've been through some severe shock go into a coma for only a few hours. Then they come to again and they're fine. They're just fine. All 'coma' means is that the person won't wake up. That's all they can tell us about Verlaine right now. She—she can't wake up."

Nadia hugged her father tightly around the waist while she struggled against entirely breaking down. "How did it—" She had to gulp in breaths that threatened to turn into sobs. "What happened?"

Uncle Gary shrugged. "They said her laptop electrocuted her, but a laptop shouldn't even have enough voltage to do that—and the computer was acting fine when the medics got there. I mean, we've shut it down, and Dell is going to be hearing from our lawyers, believe you me, but how could that happen in the first place?"

It hadn't been the computer, or electrocution. It had been magic. Elizabeth.

Why? Why go after Verlaine, and why now? None of this made any sense.

"Can I see her?" she whispered.

Uncle Dave nodded silently.

"Are we going, too?" Cole asked.

Her father said, "Nope. We're going to get Verlaine's dads something to eat."

Nadia went on tiptoe to kiss her father on the cheek—something she hadn't done in what felt like a long time—before she made her way down the hospital corridors. They were all incredibly wide, so stretchers could get through; it made Nadia feel even smaller and more powerless than before.

Then she stepped into Verlaine's room, and that was definitely the worst.

Verlaine was so pale, so still; as she lay there she looked more dead than alive. Machines were hooked up to her hand and her heart even though the little green and blue lines of data they sent up to the screens around her told the doctors nothing. A plastic mask covered Verlaine's nose and mouth, giving her oxygen, making sure she would keep breathing. Otherwise, at any moment, she might stop.

Nadia gripped the metal rail alongside Verlaine's bed. "Hey," she said, but the word hardly even came out. And it was pointless. Obviously Verlaine couldn't hear.

The door opened, and Nadia looked around for a nurse or doctor—but instead, it was Mateo.

It was like she didn't even move, didn't even think. One moment she realized he was there; the next she was in his arms, hugging him as tightly as she could, stifling her tears against the reassuring warmth of his chest. Mateo stroked her hair, whispered wordless sounds of comfort into her ear, and just held her.

When she could speak again, she said, "How did you find out?"

"Kendall Bender was talking at the restaurant, one of the waitresses told my dad, my dad phoned me. I rode my bike out here."

No wonder Mateo looked drawn; a ride that far on his motorcycle in this kind of cold would have to have been exhausting. But of course, he was almost as worried for Verlaine as she was. Nadia could tell that from the way he looked at her in her hospital bed.

He said, "It's like—it's like I didn't realize she was my friend until now."

"I know what you mean." Maybe it was because they'd been so suspicious of each other at first, or because the stuff they'd been dealing with was so intense—but Nadia had never before thought about how funny Verlaine was, or how good some of her ideas had been. How she was one of the only people who had the sense to recognize magic when she saw it and not let anyone talk her into believing it was just a trick of the light.

To have loved and lost. That was what Elizabeth had said, reminding her of the pain of Mom's abandonment. Had Nadia unconsciously used that to keep herself apart not only from Mateo but also from Verlaine? If so, she'd been a fool;

Nadia could see that now. You had to love people while you could, because you never knew how long you had.

Mateo tenderly brushed Nadia's hair back from her face—his fingertips seemed to paint lines of warmth along her cheek and temple—but his gaze remained focused on Verlaine. "I was wondering about this the other day. Wondering why I don't think about Verlaine when she's not there."

That was a harsh way of putting it, but Nadia knew what he meant. Then the realization dawned on her, and her eyes widened. "You mean—the magic you saw, the old magic that was done to her—you think it has something to do with the way we feel about Verlaine?"

"Or the way we don't feel about her. The way people are vicious to her when they aren't to anyone else."

"If that was magic—then—that would explain why it's not working now, keeping us apart from her. Because she's in the hold of an even stronger magic." Nadia's mind started putting the clues together. She hadn't cared for Verlaine, either, when she met her. But then she'd levitated Verlaine's car and encountered her again—magic masking magic long enough to get her to be okay with Verlaine, if not to care about her as she should. As for Mateo, he'd spoken to Verlaine exactly when the Steadfast spell was taking effect . . . that, too, had provided enough of a crack in the wall around Verlaine for him to like her. Everyone else either tormented Verlaine, the way Kendall did, or kept forgetting about her, like Dad or Gage. Only now, in the grip of a spell so powerful that it threatened to end her life, could Verlaine be seen for who she was.

"Why would Elizabeth do that?" Mateo said. "Cast a spell that made people just—not care about Verlaine?"

Nadia shook her head. "It can't be as simple as that. Maybe she's masked in some way? Hidden?"

"From who? And why?"

"Only Elizabeth could tell us."

"When we take Elizabeth down, will it break the spell on Verlaine, too?"

"Maybe. I hope so." That was one more thing to fight for. Nadia took a deep breath, then another, steadying herself.

But then Mateo said, "This is my fault."

"What? No. If it's anyone's fault, it's mine."

"Don't blame yourself. Please—don't." Mateo's dark eyes sought hers. "You beat yourself up too much already. And this is something I did. Nadia—I confronted Elizabeth. She knows I know, which means she has to know you told me. I said she wasn't learning anything from my visions ever again, that I didn't care how much magic she had, and this . . . what she's done to Verlaine . . . that must be her revenge."

"You told her," Nadia repeated dully. Revenge—would Elizabeth do something as extreme as this only for revenge? That seemed wrong to her somehow, but she couldn't analyze it; she could hardly even think about anything other than the fact that Elizabeth had finally done what Nadia had most dreaded from the beginning: She'd hurt someone, badly, because Nadia dared in some small way to defy her.

Who might have been next? Her father? Cole?

Mateo's face was so pale that for a second Nadia thought he might get sick. "I did this."

She tried to fight back the anger welling inside, knowing Mateo wasn't the true target—only the most convenient one. "No. Elizabeth did this."

"I definitely didn't help," Mateo said. Apparently he wasn't willing to cut himself any more slack than that. He was looking only at Verlaine now, and it was to her he spoke next: "I'm sorry."

Nadia could only grip the side of Verlaine's bed and struggle not to cry.

How could she have gotten everything wrong?

"I'm sorry, too," Nadia whispered. But Verlaine couldn't answer.

Elizabeth had worn her chains so long that she'd forgotten how heavy they were. As she stood here in the light of her stove, naked and waiting, she knew she would miss the weight.

But not for long, Asa whispered inside her skull. *Not for long.*

The entire house quaked as the spell began. This was the dismantling of her deepest magic—but she was at last ready to let it go.

She would be released from the keeping of the One Beneath.

"You have given me everything," she whispered. He would hear; He always did. "Every success, every glory. My mistakes were mine alone. My power was only yours."

Heat flooded through her, whipped around her, as

328

tangible and beckoning as a lover's embrace. Her curls tumbled around her face while broken glass began to circle in the whirlwind that surrounded her. It glinted in the stove's orange light.

To think she had only come to the One Beneath out of fear and necessity. She had gone to Him on her knees to plead for the life of her husband—a man she neither loved nor liked, but one whose farmstead had been her lone source of food and shelter. Too many had known of her practice in the Craft, back in those days when secrets were more poorly kept; as a widow, she would quickly have been shunned and left to starve.

But the One Beneath had seen the true potential within. He had raised Elizabeth up, given her the ability to reach beyond any mortal law.

The immortality spell had been the greatest act of love she had ever attempted. Had it succeeded entirely, Elizabeth could have continued in His service for all the ages of man, growing ever stronger, working His will, until the Day of Judgment—when she would stand with Him and find only joy in the hell made for her.

But the spell had behaved in a way she had not predicted.

Instead of ensuring that she would live forever as a witch in full possession of her talents—as the Sorceress the One Beneath needed her to be—the spell had made her slowly, so slowly, turn younger. At first this had satisfied her vanity, but it had not taken Elizabeth long to see where that path would lead.

It led . . . here. To her own adolescence. To the point where, when she became any younger, her abilities would no longer be manifest. She would possess some little magic, but she would be a Sorceress no more.

What lay beyond that was horrible to contemplate. How pitiful to be a child, bereft of the magic that would allow her to manipulate others into allowing her solitude and giving her what she needed to survive. To spend endless decades being patronized, put in homes, questioned and studied, eternally frustrated by the memory of what she had been and never would be again. Ultimately it would end with her as an infant, forever a curiosity to those around her, and her incapable of standing, eating, or saying a single word.

No. That she could not endure.

So long ago Elizabeth had made this pact with the One Beneath. When the dreams of the Cabots ceased to show Elizabeth in their future, it meant that the death of her magic was but a year or two away. Mateo no longer saw her in his dreams. What that meant for the One Beneath—well, that would only be revealed in time. It was not Elizabeth's to know. If she could weaken or injure Nadia before Halloween night, or better yet ensure her death in the coming conflagration, she would; He was owed no less. She could be certain that in the end He would deal with Nadia accordingly.

All that remained for her to do was to free herself from the One Beneath's service, so that she could again die—and, in her death, do Him the greatest service in all the history of time.

The immortality spell would end—only slightly diminished, because the original magic was so strong that it wanted to endure through all eternity. But that tiny fraction of vulnerability would be enough for her to die, if she met a cataclysm great enough. Or caused one.

Together they would destroy the lines that separated her world from His. Her death would be His freedom.

"Shatter me," she whispered. "Hallow me."

The broken glass spun closer and closer. She bit her lip against the first slash—her skin tearing open, blood beading upon her hip—but then the cuts came faster and faster, and the pain was too overwhelming and too glorious to resist. Elizabeth screamed, as long and loud as she could, and it was the most joyful sound she would ever make.

Time blurred. The world went away. She shivered and shuddered—then gasped as the chains fell away.

Elizabeth was free. The One Beneath had released her. Once again she could die.

Tears sprang to her eyes as she knelt upon the floor, put her forehead down in the puddles of her own blood that congealed there. All but the last few cuts had healed, because of her body's lingering regenerative power; she wept only for the loss. "My only liege," she whispered.

He cries for missing you, too, said Asa, in a tone of voice that suggested he would rather not have told her. Demons often resisted their servitude. It did not signify.

Slowly Elizabeth rose to her feet again. She took up one of her bottles of water—but the thirst had diminished. Strange, not to have it there: She almost missed the craving. After a couple of swallows, she used the rest to rinse blood from her skin. Only a couple of scratches needed bandaging. As it had been centuries since she needed anything like that, Elizabeth wound up ripping some old cloths to tie around the cuts. Probably they were not clean—there was something about cleanliness and infection she dimly recalled from the past couple of centuries—but it hardly mattered. Her other magics remained in place, for now.

"Only one errand left," she said to the demon chained within her mind. "Finding you a place."

Eager though I am to depart your company, I feel the need to point out—you haven't exactly done much to stop Nadia Caldani.

Elizabeth shrugged. "She has been taken care of. The boiling will have frightened her, and now she is without her Steadfast."

She is not. Her Steadfast remains by her side.

"That's impossible." Verlaine Laughton had survived Elizabeth's attack through some fluke of modern medical practice, but she had been comatose for the week since and would remain so until the time came to begin breaking the seal of the captive's Chamber. In such a state, Verlaine should have provided little power to Nadia—and none when Nadia left the hospital in Wakefield.

I can tell you only what I know. Nadia still has her Steadfast.

Then it could not have been Verlaine. But who?

A thought came to her and was as quickly rejected. It was ridiculous. Absurd.

And yet, if there was no other possibility—

Elizabeth's eyes widened as she took in the unbelievable truth.

Mateo paused in front of the door. "You're completely sure there's no other leads we can follow."

"Unfortunately, none come to mind." Nadia squared her shoulders, obviously trying to make herself feel strong. The autumn wind caught her dark hair, a strand of it curling along her cheek.

Did she know how vulnerable she looked in moments like this? Mateo could sense in her the fear that drove her onward—for Verlaine, for him, for her family, but never for herself. Yet Nadia had already taught him that vulnerability wasn't the same thing as fragility. As deeply as she had been hurt—could yet be hurt—nothing had broken her.

Besides, you had to respect anyone who was willing to confront Grandma.

When the butler opened the door to the great house on the Hill, Mateo put on his best smile. "Yeah. I've shown up three times in one year. Crazy, huh? It's like I'm ready to move in or something."

" . . . Mrs. Cabot has retired."

It took Mateo a moment to realize that he didn't mean Grandma had quit her job; so far as he knew, she'd never had one. She was just in bed. "Well, we need to see her. It's important." Then he paused, remembering the ghastly scars on his grandmother's face and how badly they must have hurt. More quietly, he added, "Tell her I'm—reasonable. It's okay. My friend just has some questions about our family history that only Grandma can answer."

The butler didn't seem to think much of this, but he showed them into a side parlor and went upstairs. "He has to wake up Grandma," Mateo explained as he took a seat on the long antique sofa, with its wooden frame and gold silk cushions. "That guy should get combat pay."

Nadia didn't sit by his side; instead she paced the length of the parlor, a long, thin room with ornate green-and-white wallpaper and endless overstuffed, heavily carved furniture, all slightly hazy with a layer of dust. At first Mateo thought she felt awkward—and no wonder—but then he realized she was staring at one of the oil paintings on the wall. "I can't believe it," she said. "Have you never seen this?"

"Seen what?" Usually he got in and out of Grandma's house as fast as possible, so he hadn't spent much time studying the wall décor. But as Mateo went to her side, he realized she was pointing at an old family portrait . . . really old, from the looks of it. The faces were flat, the sense of proportion skewed: It reminded him of paintings of George Washington or Benjamin Franklin he'd seen in history textbooks.

"Mateo, look," Nadia insisted. "Really look."

It was almost as if he had to force himself to do it. Why? But slowly the realization crept in as he focused on one figure in the back of the family group, standing slightly to the side— an older woman whose long, curly hair was half-chestnut, half-gray, and there was something about the eyes—

He whispered, "Elizabeth."

Even this far back, she'd always been there, like a leech or a remora on the side of his family, sucking them dry.

"You're important to her." Nadia never took her eyes from the portrait. "All of you. Her magic may be linked to your family in some profound way we haven't yet guessed. The visions—as horrible as they are, as devastating as they can be—that's not all she's done to the Cabots. Not all she's done to you. We've only just started to figure her out."

Mateo's mouth felt dry. The rage spiked within him again, white-hot and blinding, but he refused to give in to it. Going crazy over this, no matter how understandable it might be—that was just what Elizabeth wanted.

The parlor door opened, and the butler said, "Follow me."

He led them back into the music room, where Grandma always saw him when he came. Never once had she invited her grandchild to so much as come upstairs. Despite the fairly early evening hour, she was already in a nightgown, around which she'd bundled a heavy quilted robe. Though her hair was mussed, she remained as haughty as ever. Of course she was angled so that the scarred side of her face was in shadow.

"The butler told me you did not seem crazed," Grandma said, instead of hello. "But I should warn you that he is armed."

"Great to see you, too." Mateo gestured toward Nadia. "This is Nadia Caldani, my—friend." He didn't yet have the right to call her more than that. "Nadia, this is my grandmother. Grandma, Nadia has some questions only you can answer."

"If you are here to ask if it's safe to become romantically involved with a Cabot," Grandma said to Nadia, "the answer is no."

Nadia stepped closer. "What do you know about Elizabeth Pike?"

The question obviously caught Grandma off guard. " . . . Elizabeth Pike? Good Lord. What do you need to know about her?"

"Everything you can remember," Nadia insisted. She was the first person Mateo had ever seen who wasn't intimidated by Grandma at all.

If Grandma hadn't been so completely bewildered by the question, Mateo thought, she would have thrown them both out. Instead she sat there searching for what to say. "She was—fast, we used to say. The kind of young girl who went around throwing herself at men, including my husband. Not that there was anything improper between them. He told me that and . . . I still believe him, despite everything else. But the way she hung around him! It was shameless. And he was weak in the way most men are weak. A pretty young girl paying him attention—well. He never strayed, but he confided in her. Told her of his dreams, his thoughts, that sort of thing. No doubt it propped up his ego. Whatever can that matter now?"

"You'd be surprised," Mateo said. His thoughts tangled

together and buzzed in his head like a swarming hive. Elizabeth had used his grandfather the same way she'd used him.

Nadia nodded. "And how did Elizabeth know your daughter? Mateo's mom?"

"Lauren took that girl on as if she were a little sister, or perhaps even a daughter." Grandma said it automatically, without any curiosity about how someone she remembered as a teenager with Grandpa might still be a teenager years after his death. *She doesn't let us remember,* Mateo thought with a chill. *Elizabeth doesn't let us recognize the evidence in front of our own eyes.* "And Miss Pike was a bad influence. I'm convinced to this day that she was the one who told Lauren it wasn't too late to have a child. Talked her into trying for a test-tube baby."

Mateo could have reeled. It wasn't that Grandma regretted his ever having been born; she'd already made that clear plenty of times. What killed him was that Elizabeth was the *reason he'd been born.* He was her . . . invention. Her possession, in more ways than he could ever have guessed.

"Test-tube baby," Nadia whispered. "That's what they used to call IVF, right? In vitro fertilization?"

"I have no idea what the technology is called." Grandma sniffed. "All I know is, it made possible what should have remained impossible. It allowed a woman past childbearing years to give birth to a son who will carry on the curse of the Cabots."

Nadia turned to Mateo, almost wild with excitement.

"Mateo, don't you see? This is why you're my Steadfast! No man conceived of woman!"

Mateo's eyes widened as he realized what she meant. Technically, his cells first started dividing in a petri dish somewhere. Did that mean he wasn't "conceived of woman," for the purposes of whatever old curse or spell kept men from holding magic? That had to be it.

"What are you blabbing on about?" Grandma said, her good eye narrowed.

Clearly excited by the revelation, Nadia said, "You've actually given us a lot to consider. But there's just one more thing I need to know—did your husband or your daughter ever mention any—weak spots or vulnerabilities Elizabeth Pike might have? Places she absolutely had to go, possessions that were overly important to her?"

"Not that I can recall. Wait. There was one thing—Lauren was forever meeting with her at the school. Elizabeth Pike seemed to positively be attracted to it. At the time I thought it meant she was only a good student. But no teenager enjoys school that much."

This was the first sensible, helpful thing Mateo had ever heard his grandmother say. Too bad it didn't get them very far: They already knew Elizabeth's plans weren't centered on the school, so nothing at Rodman High could have anything to do with it.

Disappointed, Nadia nodded. "Okay. That's all we needed to know. Thank you for talking with us, and sorry we woke you up."

Before they could go, however, Grandma said, "You're a very polite young lady, Miss Caldani. You seem a sensible girl. And yet the connection between you and my grandson is all too clear."

Was it that obvious to everyone? Were they sending off sparks? When Mateo's eyes met Nadia's, and he felt that moment of raw electricity between them, he could believe it.

Grandma continued, "For your own sake, Miss Caldani—stay far away. I paid the price for loving a Cabot man. Trust me, it's not one you want to pay."

"You can't tell me who to love," Nadia said, so steady and sure it took Mateo's breath away. "I can't even make that choice myself. Sometimes, love chooses us."

"Nadia," he said. His voice broke on her name.

Nadia plowed on. "Mrs. Cabot, it's horrible, what happened to you. And believe me, I know the curse is real. But I can fight back in ways you never could. I can give Mateo a chance nobody else can. And I'm not abandoning him, no matter what."

Her hand closed around his, and they walked out together.

His grandmother must have been too astonished to say another word.

The whole way home, as Mateo's motorcycle zoomed along the winding roads of Captive's Sound, Nadia's mind whirled with what she had just learned. As important as the information about Elizabeth was, she kept going back to the revelation about IVF.

Apparently male infants conceived that way were exempt from whatever powers had once bound them from holding magic. That explained why Mateo was now her Steadfast; although Nadia had long since accepted this, she was glad to finally have a reason.

However—thousands and thousands of baby boys had been conceived that way. IVF began back in the 1970s, hadn't it? That meant there were grown men out there capable of holding magic. Were they also capable of performing it? For the first time in all human history, could there be men who were also witches?

Possibly she and Mateo were the first to discover this. No other witch would ever even think to investigate something every magical principle and even the First Laws took for granted.

But if they didn't know this—what else might be out there, waiting to be discovered?

The motorcycle came to a stop half a block away from her home. Nadia felt relieved; she didn't want Dad walking out to say hi. Not now. Not after what she'd said at Mrs. Cabot's house on the Hill.

She took off the helmet, slid off the bike. Mateo slung his leg over so that he stood in front of her. When Nadia handed him the helmet, his fingers closed over hers, and they just stood there, holding it, like they still needed an excuse to touch.

"What do we do now?" Mateo said.

"We prepare to go against Elizabeth." Nadia felt the

weight of responsibility heavy on her again, crushing down. "She's going to attack the town's magic. So we should cover it, each of us. With what I can reveal with my own spells, and what you can see, we ought to be able to determine a lot of the more powerful forces Elizabeth has at work."

"Like whatever she did to Verlaine," Mateo said.

Involuntarily Nadia shuddered. "Once we know more about her spells, we'll know what she's trying to attack. Then maybe I can figure out how to fight her and keep those spells in place."

His dark eyes betrayed his disbelief. "You're going to fight to protect her magic?"

"It's part of this town now, for better or for worse." She caught herself. "Okay, mostly for worse. But Elizabeth is woven into the fabric of Captive's Sound. That means she can rip the place apart. If keeping her magic in place is the only way to stop her, then that's what we do."

"So we'll be fighting for my curse?" Mateo said. But as horrible as that had to sound to him, he only smiled ruefully. "Didn't see that coming."

"Mateo—"

"It's all right." The moonlight caught the warmth in his deep brown hair, painted the lines of his cheekbones and jaw. "If that's what we have to do, then we'll do it. You're the one who told me I was strong enough to bear the curse. Who made me believe it."

The responsibility pushed her down even harder, but Nadia struggled against it. She snatched the helmet from him, hung it on the bike, and grabbed his hands. No more excuses. No more waiting. "Don't do this only because of me."

"I'm not. But I would."

Mateo's fingers wound around hers, so soft and so slow that her skin tingled. At first she wanted to look away, suddenly shy, but when their eyes met, she couldn't imagine turning from him.

His voice was low. "What you said back there—"

"I meant it. I won't abandon you."

"That's not what I was talking about."

They'd never kissed. This was the first time they'd touched like this. Had she rushed it? "Maybe—maybe you feel like it's too soon—"

"I love you, too." Mateo shook his head, as disbelieving as he'd been when he swore to fight to protect his own curse. "I knew from the visions that I would—when I saw you in danger, it didn't just scare me. It ripped my heart out. So I fought how I felt about you. I didn't want the visions to be true, not any part of them, not even the part that told me I'd love anyone as incredible as you. But no matter how hard I pushed you away, you just kept coming. You're relentless, you know that? You wanted to understand me. You wanted to know me. You wanted to save me, and I think you're the only one who can."

And yet every time she'd wanted to give up, Mateo was the one who had given her the courage to go on. He was the one who saved her, not the other way around. Nadia began to tell him so, but even as she looked up at him, he leaned closer, and their lips met.

The night was no longer cold. The wind no longer tore at her hair, shivered across her skin. Nadia only felt Mateo's mouth on hers, his arms pulling her close, and a deep, delicious warmth that seemed to glow inside her.

When they broke the kiss, Nadia had to catch her breath. He whispered, "So. Not too soon."

She smiled at him—but the sadness in his eyes caught her. "What's wrong?"

"Besides the witch who's cursed me and come after you and already suspects we know too much about the upcoming devastation she plans to let loose on the whole town?"

"Okay, yeah, that's enough," she admitted. "But we're together in this, in everything." *Elizabeth can't take that away,* Nadia nearly said, but stopped herself. Elizabeth *could* take it away . . . and had threatened to do exactly that.

By now Elizabeth had to realize that they were close. The only reason she hadn't destroyed Nadia long ago was because Elizabeth didn't acknowledge her as a real threat. But it wouldn't be beyond Elizabeth to take Mateo away out of pure cruelty. To use his pain against Nadia, or to twist the curse into some new, unimaginable horror.

From his expression, she could tell he was thinking the exact same thing. "We have to be careful," Mateo said. "I already tipped her off, but . . . we can keep from making my mistake any worse. Work separately and not together, so we give her less time to figure out what's going on."

"Right. We should." And yet the thought of parting from him, even for the brief time remaining before Halloween, shook Nadia deeply. They could call; they could text. But still—"I don't want to let her take you away from me."

"Gage's party. We'll see each other then. Go over more of what we've learned," Mateo promised. "And—be together. You and me."

"You and me."

Nadia was reading Mateo's latest text message (*Don't know what's glowing dark red around the city library, but it's nasty—like barbed wire made of flame*) when she heard Dad.

"Okay, we're loading up the car." Her father set Cole's Buzz Lightyear backpack next to the door. "You're sure you're set."

"Positive." Nadia tried her best to smile naturally. "Groceries in the pantry, phone numbers for the neighbors, and all your info in the Big Apple."

Dad put his hands on her shoulders. "You're sure you won't come with us, honey? It's sweet of you to want to finish the group project so Verlaine gets full credit, but you know she wouldn't mind if you took a couple days away with us."

"I know. I just—I'll feel better if I get it done."

Was this the last time she'd ever see her dad? Her little brother? For the first time, Nadia asked herself how they'd feel if something happened to her—if they lost her as well as Mom—but no. She couldn't even think about that.

Cole came downstairs with his jacket only half on his

body. "Dad and I are going to do boy stuff," he announced proudly. "We're going to a Knicks game."

"*If* I can get tickets," Dad interjected. He smiled at Nadia. "No parties in the house while I'm gone, okay?"

She should have told him he was being ridiculous, or promised to be good and smiled as they went out the door. Instead Nadia wrapped her arms around her father and held him tight. Although he seemed startled, he returned the hug. When she thought she could talk without crying, she said, "I'll miss you."

"Honey, are you sure you're all right here?"

"Just—being on my own. It's weird. You know."

"Yeah. I do." And he would, wouldn't he? "We can still stay."

"No, we can't!" Cole's voice was almost a shout—and thank goodness, because it made her smile.

"Really, I'm good," Nadia said. "Call me when you get there, okay?"

"You got it."

And with that, Dad and Cole were out the door. Nadia stood at the window watching the car drive off until the taillights had vanished into the dusk.

"All right!" Gage held up both hands above his head; Mateo slapped them as he came in, pretending a cheer he didn't feel. "Now we can get started."

"Looks like the party's started already," Mateo said. There were a couple dozen people there, laughing and talking—including a couple of the Jerk Squad, even Jeremy Prasad, but maybe the fact that they were here early meant they'd clear out early, too.

"Only now gettin' good," Gage promised. "Now, we have certain beverages of the controlled variety. These are available to those who aren't driving or trying to fry their brains into oblivion, mostly because I am sincerely hoping not to have to clean up any puke later on. Do these categories apply to you?"

"Yeah. I walked over." And Mateo didn't feel the need for oblivion any longer. As crappy as he felt about Verlaine—which was about as bad as it got—he wasn't running from his problems any longer. He was going to face them.

And tonight, maybe he could do better than that. Because tonight, he and Nadia—

—what, exactly? He wasn't sure. But if they were facing the ultimate danger tomorrow, that meant Mateo wanted to spend his last night as close to Nadia as he could possibly be.

Can in hand, Mateo wandered onto the porch that faced the sea. A few people were roughhousing down on the sand, but here he was more or less alone. Wind chimes made of blue-green glass sang softly in the breeze.

Somehow this seemed familiar—but he couldn't quite place the memory. Surely he hadn't been to Gage's aunt's house before; he would have remembered that. But whenever he had visited this place, or another house that reminded him of this, he'd had a good time. Mateo felt warm and relaxed for the first time in way too long.

Even as he settled back into the cushions of the swing, though, he heard a soft voice: "Mateo."

Nadia looked so beautiful. She wore a soft white dress that outlined every inch of her, and her black hair gleamed in the moonlight. But nothing was as incredible as her eyes as she drank him in. Mateo felt like he could hardly speak. Yet he managed to whisper, "Nadia."

"Were you waiting for me?"

More than he'd even known. "Yeah. I was."

Mateo held out one hand, and she took it. As Nadia settled into the swing beside him—her thigh against his, her face so close—he swallowed hard.

Tonight, he thought as she cuddled closer to him. *At least we have tonight.*

Behind her mask—the illusion of Nadia only Mateo would see, the one that would make him weak—Elizabeth relaxed into his embrace, and she smiled.

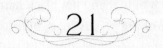

21

DOWN ON THE BEACH, A FIRE PIT FLICKERED, AND A FEW people hung around it—singing along with the music, singing all stupid, voices too high and too low and slightly off-key. He could hear the party going on in the house, everywhere around them, and it didn't matter. Mateo couldn't take his eyes off Nadia.

She curled next to him on the swing, shivering from the cold. Her white dress was too thin for the October night air, sharpened as it was by the ocean so close. Mateo shrugged off his jacket and draped it around her shoulders; as he did, Nadia smiled up at him shyly.

Déjà vu. That was the name for this feeling—the one that told you how you'd done all this before.

But they had important things to talk about, things he needed to discuss now before he got drunk just from the sight of her. "You got the file I sent with all the magic I saw in town. I don't know what most of it means—almost any of it—but at least now you have the info. Do you see a— pattern, anything we can use?"

Nadia thought about that for a moment, then smiled. "Can we maybe not worry about that right now?"

This seemed weird to Mateo, but their brief separation had made him want to see her so badly—and maybe he ought to make that clear before they got to anything else—

"You look amazing," he said. Then he closed his eyes, feeling like he was getting it all wrong. "I mean—I feel weird even thinking about this when Verlaine's still—"

"Shhhh." Nadia put one finger over his lips, which was a way hotter move than he would have thought. "It's okay. Tonight is just for us."

Mateo stroked one hand through her hair, which was as heavy and soft as he'd dreamed. She closed her eyes like— like it felt good, like even that sent shivers through her, and Mateo's heart began to pound.

He trailed two fingers along her belly—her skin was warm through the thin cotton of her dress—and slid his hand around her back, bringing Nadia into his embrace. This was so freaking scary, but why? Nadia was the only girl he'd ever really cared about . . . the only one he'd ever loved. But maybe that didn't make it easier. Maybe it made it even harder to believe that he could be with her.

But he could believe it. To hell with the curse. To hell with Elizabeth and whatever her plans were. He and Nadia had something Elizabeth couldn't take away.

Mateo closed his eyes as he leaned closer.

Against his lips, Nadia whispered, "My Steadfast."

"Your Steadfast. Yours completely," he answered. "Always." And then he drew her into the kiss.

Elizabeth kept her eyes open as Mateo kissed her.

A male Steadfast! It violated every magical law, every principle of the Craft. Even the One Beneath himself should have been unable to accomplish such a feat. And yet Nadia Caldani had done this.

There is a strangeness to her power, Elizabeth thought. Nadia was not stronger than Elizabeth, but her talents could be turned to uncanny purpose. Perhaps it was this that had made her so significant in Mateo's visions of the future. This also was the reason that further steps should be taken to make sure Nadia could not interfere with tomorrow night.

Those steps would be so much easier now that Elizabeth could avail herself of Nadia's Steadfast.

Mateo kept kissing her, his hands clutching her against his body, his lips finding her cheeks and her throat. It was almost amusing to feel her physical response—imagine, being carried away by something as silly and primitive as human sex. She hadn't indulged in so long; no doubt that was why. Elizabeth laughed softly before kissing his mouth again.

A Steadfast gave by far the most power to the witch she . . . or he . . . was bound to. But any witch's spells would gain strength if cast in the proximity of another's Steadfast. Elizabeth would keep Mateo by her side from now until her death. Perhaps he would die with her. That had a sort of poetry—dying with the last of the Cabots in her arms.

"Let's get out of here," she whispered, knowing he would hear it in Nadia's voice, that even now he looked down and saw Nadia's face. The illusion was only for him—anyone else watching saw her as herself, knew that it was Mateo Perez and Elizabeth Pike in a passionate embrace. But that let her make the illusion even more powerful for him, even more compelling. "You and me."

How young he looked, how nervous and hopeful. "Yeah." Mateo swallowed. "We need to talk about how we can use the info we've gotten to go after Elizabeth—"

"There are other things we could do." Elizabeth kissed his neck, and knew now he would follow her no matter what.

Okay, Mateo thought. *We're going to go over all of this. Make our final plans against Elizabeth. That's what we're really doing here. At least, it's what we're doing first. Right?*

Still, something about the way Nadia had kissed him—as if she wanted all of him, body and soul—

The world might end tomorrow, Mateo reminded himself. *Live for tonight.*

His hand tightened around Nadia's. He'd always thought of her as having such small hands. But her palm was square in his, her fingers so long they seemed to wrap around his wrist entirely.

"Where will we go?" he whispered. They were half-way down the beach by now; Gage's party was only a few flickering lights on the horizon behind them.

She gave him a flirtatious glance over her shoulder. "I know a place."

A stray thought wandered in: *Why aren't we going to her house?*

Her father and brother were out of town. Obviously that was their best chance at having privacy as long as they wanted—to talk and plan and—anything else, all night long—

He swallowed hard.

But they were walking in exactly the wrong direction to go to Nadia's home, and besides, if that were where they were headed, she would've said so.

Maybe he should suggest it. "Want to go to your house?"

"I have a better idea." Nadia stepped closer to him. Funny—she was a little taller than he'd realized, too. Maybe his feet were sinking into the sand. She kissed him, slow and deep, and for a few moments all his worries were very far away. When at last their lips parted, and he was gasping for breath, Nadia said, "Bind yourself to me."

"I'm already bound to you. Steadfast, remember?" He slung his hands around her waist.

"This is different. Better. It keeps us close no matter what." She smiled as she added, "Trust me?"

"Of course."

Nadia took his wrists in hers and started whispering some kind of incantation. It was different than any spell he'd seen her cast before, and he felt it immediately—as if unseen cords were wrapping around his hands, tying them together.

Mateo had assumed "close no matter what" was an emotional thing, not a physical one. This was more like . . . well, like she'd handcuffed him. "Um, Nadia?"

He didn't get a chance to object, though, because now they were no longer alone.

"What have we here?" Jeremy Prasad had wandered off from the party, too, apparently; he had a bottle in one hand and his usual arrogant sneer on his face. "Wow, Mateo, I knew you didn't have much luck with girls, but here's a tip: They like it if you actually take them *inside* first."

Mateo wanted to tell Jeremy to get lost, but more than that, he wanted his hands free, and whatever spell Nadia had cast was really strong. Too strong.

Nadia gave Jeremy an appraising look and said simply, "You'll do."

Then she held one hand out, and it was—impossible to describe, something blacker than night, insubstantial and swirling like octopus ink in water, lacing through the air almost faster than he could see and piercing Jeremy's body like so many knives.

Jeremy's face froze in an expression of pain and shock—and then he went limp. He fell face-first into the sand, hard. The bottle landed beside him, and beer glugged out, forming a puddle around one of Jeremy's hands.

Mateo knew, just by looking at him, that Jeremy was dead.

He turned to look at Nadia, realizing even as he did so that this wasn't Nadia. As he watched, horrified, her face and form seemed to melt, like spun sugar dissolving in water. The mask split, peeled off, and washed away, leaving Elizabeth standing there.

She was no longer half-animal, no longer coated in writhing gold. She was only herself, and yet somehow more terrible than ever before.

"I would have kept the illusion for a while," she said, almost apologetic. "You would have enjoyed being with the girl you wanted for a night. I suppose I owed you that much. But I needed to do this. No illusion would have held after you'd seen me take a life."

Mateo wanted to vomit. He wanted to spit the taste of her kisses from his mouth. But even what had been done to him paled in comparison to the fact that Jeremy Prasad's dead body lay only a few feet away. The guy was—he had been a total ass, no question, but he didn't deserve that. He didn't deserve to get murdered, to fall where he'd been standing. Now he lay on the beach like so much trash washed up by the tide.

He knew there was no point in trying to run. Even before she'd bound him to her—Why had he consented to it? Why hadn't he known then that this wasn't Nadia's style, that Nadia would have insisted on making plans first thing?— Elizabeth would have been able to prevent him from getting away. So he said the only thing that mattered. "You have me. So you don't have to go after Nadia. Leave her alone."

Elizabeth shook her head. "It's much too late for that." Then she stooped down to pick up a seashell—a wide, flat one with a sharp, undulating edge. "This will work. The cuts needn't be fine."

Mateo watched, horrified, as she went to Jeremy's body and flipped him over on his back. Jeremy's face—slack and vacant, sand stuck to the skin—was the most gruesome thing he'd ever seen.

Or it was until she brought the corner of the seashell to Jeremy's eyes, and then he couldn't watch any longer.

Gage's party seemed to be in full swing already by the time Nadia arrived. She realized she'd gone slightly overboard; most people were in jeans or cords and sweaters, and she'd put on a black dress with a fairly short skirt. Heels, too. Black played a bigger part in her wardrobe than most people's in town. Probably that was the Chicago city-dweller side coming out. But being overdressed would be worth it to watch Mateo's expression change when he saw her looking like this.

Though of course they were meeting up here primarily to make plans. Everything else came after that.

But it still wouldn't hurt to look good.

She weaved through the crowd of people—couples hanging all over each other, girls trying to get six or seven of them together in one hug for a photo. For a moment she remembered that Verlaine was supposed to be there with her, the first party she'd ever been invited to; the wrongness of what had happened to Verlaine would never stop making Nadia feel slightly sick.

In need of comfort, or at least someone else who understood, she kept searching for Mateo in the dark. He would hate this kind of scene as much as she did—

Nadia smiled as she realized that Mateo would be outside

waiting for her. It was what she would have done, another way they were alike.

So she stepped outside onto the porch that wrapped around the house. Below, in the sand, some people were crumpling up newspaper and throwing it into a fire pit, trying to keep a sputtering blaze going. Only a couple of people hung out on the porch itself, and Nadia made her way around back.

But Mateo wasn't there. Instead, sitting on a broad wooden swing, looking kind of forlorn, was Gage.

She ought to say hi, at least. "Hey. Great party." Hopefully that sounded convincing.

"I guess." Gage shrugged. Apparently he wasn't having a great time.

"Have you seen Mateo?"

Gage's depression seemed to deepen. "Yeah. I saw Mateo."

Nadia went to him. "What do you mean? What's the matter?"

"Oh. *Oh*. This is—awkward." Gage ran one hand over his braids as he sat up straighter. "Um, listen. I don't usually gossip, right? But better you hear this from me than Kendall Bender."

"Hear what?"

"Mateo—I kinda thought you two were—were maybe— you know. But he hooked up with someone else tonight."

It hit her like a slap. That couldn't be true. It *couldn't*.

Gage leaned over, forearms on his knees, to stare down at the porch. "Thing is, he always said he didn't like her that way. And I always had a thing for her. Mateo knew that. Yeah, they were best friends—I should've figured—but still.

After all those months he told me to make my move on Elizabeth, to see him getting together with her at my own party—it got to me, I guess."

"Wait." Nadia grabbed Gage by the shoulders, clearly startling him, but she didn't care. "Are you telling me Mateo left here with *Elizabeth Pike*?"

"Yeah."

"That's impossible."

"Looked pretty possible from where I was standing."

There was no way he would ever have willingly gone with her. Elizabeth had him—whether through a spell or a threat, there was no way to know. But Elizabeth was holding Mateo prisoner. She'd already tried to kill Verlaine. And now—now she had Mateo's Steadfast power to make her even stronger tomorrow night—

"Sucks, doesn't it?" Gage sighed. "But really we should have seen it coming."

"Which way did they go? Tell me!"

"Seriously, don't go after them. You'll only feel worse."

"Gage, this is important."

He couldn't have guessed what she truly meant by that, but his expression changed slightly, like he finally got that this wasn't as simple as a party hookup. "I—I'm not sure. Her house, I'd guess."

Nadia didn't even say thank you, just got up and ran.

Dammit, dammit, why did she pick tonight to wear high heels? Every single step she took on the high, winding coastline road stabbed up through her feet and knees, but Nadia never slowed down. She went up the steps to the main road, wobbled on one heel, and nearly fell—so she stopped only long enough to kick off one shoe, then the other, before taking off running again. Concrete started ripping at her tights, bruising her feet, but it didn't matter.

Next Christmas she was asking for a car.

Mateo's my Steadfast. Not hers. That means he'll give my spells more strength than Elizabeth's. And she won't be expecting me. That's all I've got going for me. Is that going to be enough?

It has to be. I've already lost Verlaine, already let her down, and I can't lose Mateo, too—

Finally Nadia reached the street where Elizabeth lived. She'd been here before—had jealously spied on Mateo and Elizabeth together. That felt so childish now, so pointless. But even then she'd known that approaching Elizabeth's house might be dangerous. Waiting inside could be protective spells, wards, and watchers, omens Nadia might not even recognize.

But Mateo might be inside, too, in danger, and that left her no choice. Nadia went up the steps without hesitation and tried the door. It was unlocked. What she saw was . . . a completely normal, nicely furnished house. Like something out of a Pottery Barn catalog. Not what she'd been expecting.

No. This wasn't right. It had to be a glamour at work.

Nadia touched her bracelet, went through the simple thoughts necessary to construct a spell of disillusion, and watched as the Pottery Barn facade melted. In its place was—a ruin.

Holding her breath, Nadia carefully stepped between the

shards of broken glass and mirrors. Her feet—now effectively bare, as her tights had been all but shredded away—could feel a layer of thick, oily dust underneath. If she put even one foot wrong, though, she'd feel even worse when glass stabbed through her foot.

She heard nothing, but that was meaningless. Elizabeth might have taken Mateo's voice the same way she had Ginger's; even now he could be trying to warn her but unable to speak a word. In any room, around any corner, Elizabeth could be waiting. Watching.

The house was almost entirely dark; the light Nadia found her way by came from an old-fashioned wood stove in one corner of the large front room. Yet the light it cast didn't flicker like flame—it was almost eerily steady, and there was a strange cast to it, as if the yellow were too close to green. And the heat of it almost seemed to sear the skin, though it was a dozen feet away.

Don't look at it, Nadia told herself. Whatever it was, however unnatural that burning might be, that couldn't matter now. All that mattered was finding Mateo if he was here, and getting out again as fast as possible if he wasn't.

Carefully she edged her way along one wall, trying to push some of the broken glass out of the way with her toes. There were the stairs—but they were so rotten, more spiderweb than wood by now, that surely Elizabeth and Mateo couldn't have climbed them.

Here was a back room. Hand trembling, Nadia reached out for the doorknob and turned it slowly, so slowly.

She pushed the door open. Hinges creaked, and her breath caught again in her chest. The stove's light barely reached this room, its heat, either; the chill of the shadows inside turned Nadia's breath to a cloud.

If they're in there, they know you're here. Elizabeth knows. Step inside and find out. At least there was no glass on that floor.

Nadia walked inside. The room was completely empty except for spiderwebs—countless spiderwebs, so thick they'd covered the windows, and a couple of the walls, completely. She breathed out, a sigh of both relief and disappointment. If Elizabeth hadn't brought Mateo to her house, then where might they have gone?

But wait, there was something in the far corner. Nothing Mateo would have left behind, though, just a—

—a book.

Elizabeth's Book of Shadows.

A spiderweb brushed against her arm, making her jump. Nadia flicked it away.

But it stuck. As did another. And another.

The spiderwebs were weaving around her, so fast she couldn't even kick them away, so fast that already Nadia could hardly move. She lunged for the door, but it was too late; already she was tangled in the stuff, spiders crawling among the silvery threads that bound her on every side.

She was trapped. There was no saving Mateo, no saving herself.

Elizabeth had them both now.

22

"COME ON," NADIA WHISPERED, TEARS OF SHEER EXERTION rolling down her face. "Just—a few more inches—"

She reached desperately for the doorway of the room where she was trapped, fingers extended, every joint in her hand and arm aching. If she could only get hold of one of the shards of glass lying right outside, maybe she could start to hack away at the cobwebs surrounding her. Already she could hardly see the lower half of her body, and her left leg was going numb. Nadia had let herself fall to the floor, knowing the glass was her best chance, but now she wondered if she'd wind up mummified here, swaddled in gray filmy stuff, spiders all over her.

Already Nadia had tried to cast spells to liberate herself, but the Book of Shadows's protections were ancient and primal. Her magic skittered across it like a raindrop across the windshield of a car, without any chance of getting in and changing anything.

Worst of all, she felt as if it were *staring* at her. Enjoying her fear and pain.

Nadia clutched desperately at the spiderwebs, trying to pull them away; little legs scrambled through her hair, and she screamed. How long had she been screaming? It seemed like forever, and it seemed like she pulled away handfuls of cobwebs every second, but there were always more around her, bearing her down.

Elizabeth walked into the ocean again; her blood would still be strong here. It would work.

Mateo followed her. He couldn't help it. The frigidity of the waters affected him more than it did her. As the tides splashed over their waists, up toward their shoulders, he said, voice shaking from the severe cold, "Are you—going to—drown us?"

"We will die by fire," she promised. "Silence. I have work to do."

The eyes in her hand were smooth against her palm. They knew her blood, and again they would see.

"You might as well kill me," Mateo said. "That's what you do, isn't it? What you did to Mom, my grandfather, Jeremy. What you tried to do to Verlaine. You use us up and throw us away."

"Yes. But I haven't used you up yet. Your curse is a part of me, Mateo. As long as I live, so does the curse."

Enough distractions. This spell—even for her, this was difficult. Elizabeth had to bring all her concentration to bear, though she knew it would mean her hold on Mateo lessened for a moment. No matter. She knew her duty.

As the eyes drifted away into the tides, she felt the cord between her and Mateo—not break, but bend and stretch, giving him slightly more liberty. He felt it, too, or saw it; he was a Steadfast, after all.

Mateo threw himself at her, bearing them both down underwater. A wave came in, tossing them hard against the shells and sand; Mateo struggled for purchase, trying to get enough grip with his feet to anchor her against the ocean floor and drown her. Elizabeth could have laughed at his foolishness.

Another wave—and this one knocked them both into a roll. Now Mateo dragged her from the water by her wrist and hair before clutching her around the throat with both hands. His knees pressed down on her legs, pinning her.

"I can kill you." His voice shook. "Don't think I can't. After what you did to my mom—I'm going to enjoy killing you."

"No, you won't." She could still whisper. He wasn't even bearing down hard enough to cut off all her air. Angry as he was, justified though he thought himself, Mateo was not the kind of man who could easily take life, not even to end the curse that kept him prisoner. "You'll hate yourself for it."

Mateo paused. Water dripped from his hair, from his eye-lashes. His entire body shook with the tension. "You're right. I will. But if I can protect Nadia—protect everyone—then I have to do it. I have to."

He was talking himself into it. So, he had more resolve than she'd thought.

Too bad he was only a human.

Elizabeth pulled the spell taut again, sent him staggering to the side, then to his knees in the sand. No matter how hard he struggled to rise again, he couldn't. She ruffled his hair as if he were a small boy. "You only had a second," she confided. "And you've lost your chance."

Oh, the despair in his eyes was sweet. Elizabeth warmed herself by it.

The first thing Asa felt was pain.

Not the agonies of hell, not any longer—that would have been familiar to him. No, this felt more like . . . like he'd banged his nose on something.

He had a nose?

He opened his eyes and looked around. Apparently he was lying on a beach, sand all over him (scratchy—he also felt scratchy! Even that was a treat after so long without a body). A puddle next to him smelled strongly of beer.

Pushing himself into a seated position, Asa looked down at the body the Sorceress had provided for him. He was male—not that it mattered so much, but he'd been male before, when he had been what you'd call "alive," so at least he was familiar with the equipment. Apparently he was tall. His skin was a deep, tawny shade of tan.

Something uncomfortably bulky was in his pocket. He pulled out a wallet and flipped through it. Cash—quite a lot of it, if his understanding of human economics was up to date—a set of car keys, a Starbucks card (he'd been wanting to try this coffee he kept hearing about), a Rodman High ID, and what appeared to be a driver's license.

"Jeremy Arun Prasad," Asa read aloud. "Sorry about your untimely death. And thanks for the ride."

Nice voice, really. Not very deep, but—mellifluous. Pleasing to the ear. And even the flat, awkward photos on the ID and driver's license suggested his new form was pleasing to the eye as well. That would make his brief sojourn in the mortal world simpler; such shallow virtues carried more weight than they should here. That was something you could see very clearly from hell.

Carefully he got to his feet. Balance came back to him more easily than he would have thought. Brushing the sand from his clothes and face, Asa wondered how best to begin. He knew his role here—was sworn to it by unbreakable bonds—but the town looked different from above than it did from below. First he had to get his bearings.

"Jeremy!" A tall man with braided hair and even darker skin than his own came jogging up to him. His memories of the people he had seen while observing Mateo Perez supplied the name *Gage Calloway*. "Hey, man, are you all right?"

"Yeah, sure. I just—I think I passed out." The puddle of beer would support that story.

Gage paused. "You gonna be sick? Do you need some coffee or some water or something? I have a strong antipuke policy."

"I feel fine now." *Fine.* What a word for the ecstasy of having legs, arms, a voice, eyes—well, eyes of a sort. They did the job of the real thing. He was whole again. A person again. And this miracle he could only call *fine.*

"Yeah, you look okay, I guess. But I'll give you a ride home."

"What are you doing out here?" Asa thought this time of day—this, with the light beginning to emerge over the water—was sunrise, and that meant it was either too early or too late for most people to be up.

"Some people took my aunt's patio furniture so they could hang out on the beach. I'm still missing a chair. If I don't find it, Aunt Lorraine's gonna kill me. This is the last party I ever have at her place, I swear to God."

It would be, of course. Tonight Gage would probably die, just like most of the residents of Captive's Sound.

Asa felt a wave of pity for the young man, who seemed friendly and kind. He wished he could say, *Get in your car. Go. Drive as far as you can, as fast as you can.*

But Asa belonged to the One Beneath. Working against Him was impossible. If he even tried to speak one word that would go against Elizabeth's plan, so much as attempted to perform an act that might save one of the lives that needed to be ended, not only would he fail, but he would also be immolated in a flame that would make hell look like a top vacation destination. And that fire would outlast even hell, because death was a mercy he would never receive.

Yet at least a few of his actions could be his own, if they

366

were harmless enough. "Come on. I'll help you look for the chair."

Gage stared at him. "Uh, okay. That's—nice of you."

Apparently Jeremy Prasad hadn't spent much of his life being nice for no reason. It hardly mattered. No one here would have time to realize that Jeremy was dead, or who— no, *what*—was walking around in his skin.

So Asa enjoyed what freedom he had, walking along the beach with Gage to look for a plastic patio chair and reveling in the beauty of the last dawn this town would ever see.

Nadia kept struggling. Kept fighting. She pulled the cobwebs from her face, freed one hand, then the other, then the first again. Her feet could kick the tendrils loose for a second before they ensnared her once more. Some of the spiders had found the holes in her tights and were crawling inside them now. Long ago, she'd given up screaming; she couldn't even spare that much breath, and she didn't want to give the Book of Shadows the satisfaction.

No matter how hard I fight, it's not enough, she thought. *Elizabeth's got me, no matter how hard I try.*

How hard I try.

An idea flickered into flame, and Nadia gasped.

A spell like this, meant to entrap—it would naturally wrap itself around someone trying to get away. The harder she fought, the harder it clutched at her.

What if she stopped fighting?

Merely lying still wouldn't work—no spell of protection

could be that easily fooled—but there were other spells that might be more convincing.

Such as a spell that would keep her right here.

Nadia pulled against the cobwebs wound around her upper arms to bring one hand to her bracelet. Two fingers found the quartz charm, and quickly she assembled the ingredients:

> *Love unbreakable.*
> *Hatred implacable.*
> *Hope eternal.*

She had to think it, feel it, believe it more powerfully than ever before —

Hugging her father as he left for New York City with Cole, knowing she might not ever see him again.

The moment she'd realized that Elizabeth had tried to kill Verlaine—then the moment she knew Elizabeth had Mateo in her grasp.

Her own hand reaching for the shards of mirror, hour after hour, despite exhaustion and terror, because there had to be a chance; there had to be.

The spell of encirclement sprang to life around her. Immediately the spiderwebs slithered back. A few of the small crawly guests in the legs of her tights followed suit. The circle spread around her, a soft blue glow, a sphere that was meant to hold her in position against any force. It was what she would have cast the night of the wreck, if she'd had time; it would have kept her and her family almost motionless as the car flipped down around them, protecting them from every blow. Lacking independent thought, Elizabeth's Book of Shadows knew only that another spell now held Nadia in place, that its protections were no longer required, and so the spiderwebs inched away.

No Book of Shadows, not even this one, could know that Nadia controlled the spell herself, that she would be able to use the sphere to move away as she wished.

Her whole body shaking with exhaustion, Nadia began stumbling toward the door. Now she didn't have to worry about the broken glass; the blue sphere around her kept it from touching her feet. She did, however, stop in the middle of the room and rip off the remnants of her tights. A last spider tumbled down and scurried away. She shuddered.

Still Elizabeth's house remained empty. Wherever she had taken Mateo, it wasn't here. But wait—was that daylight outside? She'd been in the grip of a powerful enchantment; time could get lost during an enchantment, making hours seem like days, or years seem like minutes.

I can't have been here all night. Please, no.

Nadia looked out the window and her heart sank. Not only was that daylight—it was late afternoon. No, evening. The sun would be setting any moment. She'd lost nearly twenty-four hours.

The Halloween carnival would already have begun.

She hadn't prepared any more spells. Hadn't thought any more about how to defeat Elizabeth's plan of ripping away the entire magical framework of Captive's Sound. She hadn't even bathed or slept.

Didn't matter. She was out of time.

Nadia saw a pair of Elizabeth's shoes next to the door, simple flats, and quickly slipped them on. She could run in these if she had to, and she had to.

Just then she heard a chiming from her pocket—her phone ringing.

Dad! Nadia thought. Oh, crap, he'd probably tried to call or text a dozen times last night, and she hadn't answered or even heard it over her own screams. Now he was no doubt on his way home to find out what the hell was going on.

But when she looked down at the screen, it was Verlaine's face she saw smiling back. Was one of her dads calling from Verlaine's phone? *Please*, she thought, *please don't let her have gotten worse. Don't let her be*—"Hello?"

"Hey, stranger." The voice was hardly more than a whisper, but it was definitely Verlaine.

"Oh, my God. You're okay!" Nadia could have wept. At least one thing had gone right. "What—where are you?"

"Still in the hospital. Can't talk long." Verlaine's tremulous words made it clear she could hardly talk. "Couple hours ago—just woke up."

"How?" Elizabeth wouldn't have released Verlaine from the spell she'd used to attack her—

—unless she was already beginning. Bit by bit, she was undoing her own magic. A spell here, a spell there, until the great collapse came.

"Managed one thing," Verlaine said. "My dads are here in

Wakefield with me, not in Captive's Sound. Tonight—you and Mateo—"

"Elizabeth has Mateo. I have to get to him, now. But I'm so glad you're all right." At least one of them got out okay. At least in this one small way, Elizabeth hadn't won.

Or—had she? Verlaine's survival, amazing and wonderful as it was, might be only a sign that Elizabeth's final plan was under way, and the end was even closer than Nadia had feared.

But Verlaine was safe. Her dads were safe. Her own father and brother were safe. Gratitude for at least that much flooded through Nadia, giving her courage, pushing back the exhaustion until she knew she could run again.

Verlaine whispered, "Nadia, be careful."

"Good-bye," Nadia said, and hung up. She couldn't have answered any other way. What she had to do now, to go against Elizabeth—*careful* couldn't have anything to do with it.

"Do you know, I've never been to this carnival before?"

Mateo remembered being with her at the Halloween carnival when they were little kids. Remembered them riding the same carousel horse. Giving her his cotton candy. Each memory was just one more of her lies.

He and Elizabeth walked through the carnival, hand in hand. The mere touch of her skin repulsed him, but over the course of the last day, he'd learned how futile it was to try to pull back.

("You consented to the binding spell," she'd told him

sweetly as he'd struggled against her on the beach, his clothes soaked and freezing. "The spells you consent to are always stronger for it.")

They'd dried off by now. To anyone else, they probably looked like a happy couple. He had on his letter jacket and jeans; Elizabeth wore her usual white dress, carefree of the cold. Twinkling lights had been strung from tent to tent, laced around the tree trunks and branches so that they stood out in the darkening twilight. All the little kids and about half of the adults were in costumes—vampires, Transformers, Disney princesses, a couple of ghosts here and there. People were munching on popcorn balls, drinking sodas out of "collector's cups." It was the exact same cheesy carnival it had always been, except this time Elizabeth was here, and she meant to kill them all.

"You think I'm ruthless, don't you?"

"I know you are." He could use his voice when he wasn't trying to defy her; Mateo had learned that today, too.

"If anything less could kill me, I'd do that instead. But it won't. The One Beneath has released me, but the spell's magic isn't that easily undone."

"Wait. You're telling me this whole disaster is just so *you* can die? This is a murder/suicide?"

"Partly."

"Then what's the other part?"

Elizabeth gave him a sidelong glance, more openly flirtatious than he'd ever seen her before. "And ruin the surprise?"

"Oh, hey, Mateo. Hey, Elizabeth." Kendall gave them a

wave; she was wearing something very form-fitting, very short, and very green. "So, Mateo, I want you to know that I thought really hard about what you said about racism and stuff, and, like, perspective is incredibly valuable, and so I didn't go for the sexy geisha thing, and instead I went for sexy Robin Hood."

"You look wonderful," Elizabeth gushed. Why had he never heard the mockery behind her "sweet" voice before?

Kendall preened, striking faux-sexy poses that she probably memorized from the package. "Well, it's sexy *girl* Robin Hood, obviously. Not that there's a whole lot of difference, because really Robin Hood was wearing girl clothes back in the day, and I know they all dressed differently then, but get real, the guy had on leggings."

Mateo wanted to tell her to run. If he could save only one person from this mess, even if that person were Kendall Bender, it would be something. But Elizabeth's spell held his tongue.

"So where are you guys headed?" Kendall said. Her eyes darted down to their joined hands; no doubt she thought this was the gossip scoop of the year.

"The haunted house." Elizabeth leaned against Mateo's shoulder, probably just for the pleasure of knowing how touching her would disgust him. "I like a good scare."

From Rodman High, at least from the top of the football-field bleachers, the carnival in Swindoll Park glittered on the far hill like a swarm of fireflies.

373

Asa sat on the highest rung of the stands, watching the party far away. He would have felt bad for the people celebrating, if there were any point. At least he didn't have to watch them die.

No, his work would keep him right here.

His gaze drifted down to the main school building, specifically to one spot that he'd been told was the location of the chemistry lab.

Nadia made it to the carnival right after dark. She looked around frantically, but so far nothing appeared to be out of the ordinary—and there was no sign of Mateo or Elizabeth.

Chest heaving, exhausted, she braced herself against a nearby picnic table and tried to think. Where would Elizabeth be? Dead center—right at the bull's-eye of the target Verlaine had showed her. But where was that? When they'd looked at it before, Swindoll Park had seemed specific enough, but this park was pretty big, and now it was filled with hundreds of people. She should have downloaded Verlaine's data onto her phone, something like that—

"Whoa. Nadia." Kendall stood in front of her, wearing a pointy hat and some kind of weird green minidress with a jagged hem. "Are you doing, like, a sexy zombie thing? Because it's really more scary than sexy. Just FYI."

Her ripped dress and crazy hair probably would make people stare on any day but Halloween. "Kendall. Hey. No offense—gotta go."

"What, are you looking for Mateo? I mean, I'm not being

insensitive, like, honestly, everybody could tell you were crushed out on him, so I think you should know about him and Elizabeth."

"I've been told." Kendall must have heard the party gossip, too. Nadia pushed her hair back from her face.

"Plus, you know, he's got that crazy gene that runs in his family, and I hear they might have, like, stem cell therapy for it someday, but for now he's bad news. I don't know what Elizabeth's thinking. Taking a guy like that into a haunted house? That is basically asking for a total psychotic break."

Nadia grabbed Kendall's arm. "Did you say they're in the haunted house?"

"They said they were going that way."

All her spells, all her magic, all their desperate efforts to fight Elizabeth, and they'd gotten their single biggest break from Kendall Bender.

"Kendall, *thank you*," Nadia said, and then she took off running toward the gnarled old house with orange lights in all the windows—using her last strength to reach Elizabeth and Mateo, if she could only make it in time.

But then the screams began.

23

MATEO STOOD IN ELIZABETH'S ARMS, WATCHING THE world catch fire.

The walls of the haunted house browned, blackened, sparked into light and heat. People began to shriek; parents snatched up their children and started running for the exits. A guy in a *Scream* mask shouted, "Don't panic!"

Elizabeth never moved. So Mateo couldn't, either. She embraced him tightly, closing her eyes in satisfaction as the fire leaped and crackled around them. "A Steadfast," she whispered. "I'd forgotten how good that feels."

"You're going to burn us alive." Already the smoke stung his eyes and throat, made him cough.

"We won't have a chance to burn," Elizabeth promised, and that was when the ground began to quake.

Nadia ran toward the entrance of the haunted house—but already it was impossible to get in that way, with so many people flooding out. She dashed around to the side instead. The windows there were high, but she could climb in.

As she pried it open, though, a middle-aged man grabbed her around the waist. "Get back from there!" he shouted. "It's dangerous!"

What was she supposed to say? "I know"? Nadia just let herself be pulled back, watched him run off to help others, and then made her leap for the window. It took most of the strength she had left to pull herself up, through, and over, but somehow she made it.

For her reward, she was in a house on fire.

Most everyone inside seemed to have fled by now, but Nadia knew that Elizabeth would still be at the heart of it, and there was no chance she would have let Mateo go. Pulling the neck of her dress over her mouth to filter the smoky air, she dashed up the stairs two at a time.

On the second story, everything seemed to be burning: the walls, the ceiling, even parts of the floor. Nadia squinted against the bright light and the haze of heat—

"Nadia!"

Mateo. He was here. She'd found him in time. Nadia saw him through the blaze—in Elizabeth's arms.

Nadia had made it, she'd made it, they still had a chance—

But even as Mateo drank in the sight of her, memories of his dreams came crashing in. There was that one dream— the one with the fire burning around them both—the one that ended with her dead at his feet.

No, he thought. *This can't be happening. Elizabeth can't win.*

Elizabeth's eyes narrowed. "What is it you think you can do here?"

"I don't know," Nadia shot back, "but we're going to find out."

The ground twisted and bucked beneath them again; floorboards already strained with age and heat began to pop. How much longer could this building stand? Outside, people's screams were only growing louder; the quakes must be starting up out there, too. Elizabeth was going to bring the whole park down, turn it into so much fire and dust. Bury everyone alive.

Yet within him he felt a surge of something almost like hope—not an emotion, though. Something physical. Something real.

Magic, Mateo realized.

He was a Steadfast. *Nadia's* Steadfast. Whatever power Elizabeth stole from him, he had more to give to Nadia, because he belonged to her, completely, in a way that Elizabeth could never match, not with all her curses and all her evil.

Mateo never questioned whether Nadia could be strong enough to defeat Elizabeth. The only question was whether she'd get the chance.

The spell was spreading around them now, so vivid and electric that Nadia could feel it as clearly as she would ever have been able to see it. Deep fault lines throughout Captive's Sound were giving way as Elizabeth took away all the town's dark magic, took it and buried it in the bottomless pit where her soul ought to be.

And no—Nadia wasn't strong enough to stop her.

The trick was not to stop her in the first place.

She'd never have seen this if she hadn't been caught in the cobwebs. The answer there had been to stop fighting, to replace the spell imprisoning her with another that would at least appear to do the same thing.

And yet Goodwife Hale had tried to tell her. In her spidery script, the old witch had written that the strongest opposing force was one that went in the same direction. This was what she'd been trying to say, but what Nadia hadn't understood until now.

So the answer now was not to block Elizabeth or to fight her. Not to do anything to keep Elizabeth from pulling the magic out from under Captive's Sound.

What Nadia had to do was replace the stolen magic with magic of her own.

As the smoke swirled around her, Nadia met Mateo's gaze for one last moment, then closed her eyes. What could be soft enough to slip into all the cracks but strong enough to hold them up?

A spell of liberation. Nothing was as simple, or as powerful, as being free.

> *Helpless laughter.*
> *Washing away what cannot come clean.*
> *A moment of forgiveness.*

Nadia grabbed her bracelet, found the ivory, and dove deep:

Cole calling Lots-o'-Huggin' Bear a douche bag, and having to stagger into the kitchen to hide her laughter.

Trying to clear her mind after reading that letter from Mom's attorney, the one that said she refused to see them no matter how much Dad begged, and watching Toy Story 3 *through eyes that kept filling with tears.*

Sitting on the kitchen floor next to her father, in the middle of a pile of rigatoni noodles, finally understanding why he fought her so hard about every single dinner—he only wanted to do something right for them, just once.

The spell flowed out from her in every direction, almost uncontrollable, the way it had been when she first cast it in chem lab—but stronger now, because that darkness didn't pull at her, and because Mateo was here. Before, they hadn't known how to shape the magic they created together, but now she could feel him beside her.

Like that day on the beach, she thought. *Stronger together than apart.*

So Nadia found the dark places of Elizabeth's magic—from Mateo's map, from her own spells, and from the new levels of power unfolding within her—found the jagged gaps where Elizabeth's dark work had been stolen and filled them once more. She left no hollows behind, made everything stronger than it had been before. The ground shifted beneath them, but already she could tell everything was coming right again—

—everything except the house they stood in, which was being consumed by fire, and even now, the floor started to collapse.

They all toppled sideways. Everyone shouted out—Elizabeth, Mateo, Nadia—and then there seemed to be nothing but smoke and horrible, searing heat. Each breath burned Nadia's lungs, and she reached out blindly for something to steady herself.

She found Mateo's hand.

He grabbed her and pulled her into his arms. As Mateo covered her body with his, trying to shield her from the burning debris falling around them, Nadia wondered if she'd saved Captive's Sound but not their own lives.

Mateo tried to shelter Nadia. Even though it seemed pointless, even though there was no way to run out of this place now, if he could give her a chance, buy her only a couple minutes, then he had to try.

As he cradled her head against his chest and closed his eyes tightly against the stinging smoke, he heard Nadia whispering, "Love unbreakable—hatred implacable—hope—"

The floor gave way. Or the world gave way. All Mateo knew was that there was no up, no down, only the fire and the feeling of Nadia nearly torn from his arms. And—and this strange blue light, which seemed to surround them all of a sudden.

Guess that's heaven, he thought, just before he passed out.

When Mateo opened his eyes again, he did not seem to be in heaven, unless heaven looked a lot like a burned-out version of the caramel-corn stand.

He took a deep breath, then coughed again so hard his ribs ached. But he pushed himself up on his arms to look around. "Nadia?" he whispered.

Mateo couldn't see her. What he did see was the smoldering ruin that had been the haunted house; it had burned down almost to the foundation. And around the ruins—firemen, bystanders, the smoke-stained remnants of the carnival in a town that seemed to be very much still here. Unless someone had been injured in the fire itself, nobody else even seemed to be hurt. Elizabeth's apocalypse hadn't come to pass. Nadia had won.

But had she survived?

He managed to stagger to his feet and start wandering through the debris of the carnival. There were people injured everywhere—minor injuries, to judge by the fact that almost everyone seemed to be conscious and ambulatory—but everything was so chaotic that it would be easy to miss one girl.

But wait.

She might have been a shadow on the ground with her black dress and sooty skin, almost lost in the night. Mateo ran to her, ignoring every ache and cut that told him to stop. As he came closer, the vision from his dream flooded through his mind again: Nadia lying dead at his feet.

It had come true. Elizabeth's curse held. He'd seen the future, and he'd failed to stop it, and now Nadia—

Now Nadia was rolling over onto her back. She looked up at him groggily. "Mateo?"

He fell to his knees and gathered her into his arms. Nothing he'd ever known felt as good as holding her close and knowing she was still alive, still here. The curse might still hold him, but he'd know for the rest of his life that the futures they showed him, no matter how true they were, could be defeated if he only held strong. "You're okay. Nadia, you're okay."

"Everybody—"

"Everybody's fine, I think. You did it."

Nadia gave him a crooked little smile. "We did it."

"Uh-uh. That was all you."

Then he kissed her, with all the desperation and fear he'd felt when he thought she was gone, and all the love, too. Nadia made this soft little sound in her throat, and then kissed him back so hungrily that he forgot everything else in the world.

"You're sure you're all right now?" the old lady said. "Hate to leave you by yourself."

"I'm fine. Thank you." Elizabeth waved the woman off and continued on her way home.

Her body was blackened with grime, and her hair smelled of cinders. But she couldn't stop smiling.

As she reached the porch of her house, the door opened and Asa came out to meet her. "Well, well," he said, in Jeremy Prasad's voice. "I can't help but notice that you're very much still alive. Failure?"

"Not at all. Not if it worked."

Asa nodded once. "It worked."

This went beyond Elizabeth's wildest dreams. She had left the service of the One Beneath, been willing to die for him, because the devastation would be enough to crack the Chamber. And she had ripped out all the magic from Captive's Sound, just long enough to accomplish this one most important task. Nadia had replaced it, though, which meant—

Elizabeth lived. No longer immortal, no longer aging backward, but young, healthy, with her strength and her magic still at the ready. She had not had to die to liberate her lord and master; instead she could swear herself to his service again and help the entire rest of the way.

The disaster she'd created, the one that would have consumed Captive's Sound, had only taken place for one split second. It had destroyed only the first and most important thing she had wanted it to destroy: the bars of the prisoner's cell.

"What does it look like?" she asked Asa. "Our glorious work."

"Like an enormous crevasse ripped through the chemistry lab. Like a huge mess, basically." He crossed his arms and looked at her sourly. "Were you expecting something grander?"

"Its grandeur comes from its purpose."

First the bars are removed. Then the bridge is built. Then the One Beneath can finally enter the mortal world and reign supreme.

Elizabeth had been willing to die to accomplish only

the first of these tasks. Instead, it was done, and thanks to Nadia Caldani's interference, Elizabeth remained alive, well—and ready to take on the next two tasks herself, as soon as possible.

Nadia deserved all her thanks, really. She would have to think of something special.

"The One Beneath is coming," Elizabeth whispered, before she spread her arms wide to the night sky and laughed from pure joy.

EPILOGUE

"SO WHAT'S THIS?" VERLAINE LAY IN HER BED, HER BIG, shaggy cat curled at her feet, as Nadia snuggled next to her and Mateo set the flower-bedecked tray in front of the newly returned patient.

"This," Mateo said, "is the very best Day of the Dead brunch the kitchen of La Catrina could create. Not that the Day of the Dead and brunch really go together so much. But hey, it's a celebration."

"That it is." Nadia still felt utterly exhausted; she hadn't known it was possible to be so tired. Tiny nicks, cuts, and spider bites still stung her legs. Her throat remained raw and tender from the smoke last night. But what did any of that matter? Captive's Sound, and everyone in it, remained in one piece. Elizabeth's evil plan, whatever it had been, seemed to be defeated. Verlaine was back home, still kitten-weak but obviously on the mend. And she and Mateo—

Well, there were plenty of reasons to celebrate.

Verlaine was enjoying being the center of attention for once. "Let's see. We have a Tex-Mex omelet, some pancakes that look like—Mickey Mouse?"

"Those were me," Nadia hastened to add.

"—and this." Verlaine held up a small brilliantly painted skull, not unlike the cheery skeletons that played guitar and danced on the walls of La Catrina. "What is this, a souvenir?"

Mateo said, "Lick it."

After a moment, Verlaine gave Mateo a look. "You're lucky I trust you." Then she held it to her mouth, gave it an experimental taste, and brightened. "Oh, it's sugar!"

"You guys don't know much about the Day of the Dead, do you?" Mateo said. He took his place on the bed with them, on the other side of Verlaine. That meant that he and Nadia weren't next to each other—and right now even a few minutes away from Mateo felt like too long—but Nadia knew as well as he did that what mattered most was making Verlaine feel safe and loved. Though that strange emotional distance remained, suggesting that whatever Elizabeth had done to Verlaine remained as powerful as ever, Nadia remembered how she should feel about Verlaine, and she was going to hold true to it. Mateo continued, "The Day of the Dead is when you're supposed to go to the cemetery and visit your dead relatives."

"Lilies, black, yada yada," Verlaine said.

But Mateo shook his head. "No. It's a cheerful day. A

great day. You don't go there to cry; you go there to celebrate. To remind yourself what you loved about the people
you lost, and have fun with them like you used to when they
were alive. People bring chocolate and *pan de los muertos* and
sugar skulls like this one."

Nadia thought about it. "So all the happy skeletons on the
wall of your dad's restaurant—"

"Exactly." Mateo grinned. "In Spanish, *la catrina* means
'the rich woman.' I think the name was originally to kind
of make fun of Grandma. But the skeleton of a rich woman
with flowers in what ought to be her hair—that's one of the
figures people celebrate on the Day of the Dead. Like all the
other 'happy skeletons.' They're reminders that we all die,
but even death isn't the end. Not if people remember you,
and remember the love you had while you were still here."

"I still think it's kinda morbid," Verlaine said, but she nibbled on the edge of the sugar skull anyway.

Seize the moment, Nadia reminded herself. *Better to have
loved and lost. At least you can remember.* Even remembering
Mom didn't hurt as much any longer.

And, as she looked across at Mateo—grinning at her over
Verlaine's head—Nadia knew the only way you ended up
with any love to remember was by daring to love right now.

She didn't intend to waste any more time.

Smiling brilliantly, Nadia said, "I think it's beautiful."

READ ON FOR A SNEAK PEEK AT
THE SEQUEL TO *SPELLCASTER*

1

NEARLY EVERY GRAVESTONE IN THE CEMETERY OF
Captive's Sound made a promise about forever.

The tombstones said things like *Remembered Evermore* or
Always In Our Hearts. But for all those promises of unending
devotion, nobody seemed to visit very often.

Today, though, three people had arrived.

Nadia Caldani stood directly under the cast-iron gate,
which bent into curves to imitate leaves, roses, and thorns.
Nothing about her wine-red sweater or dark jeans betrayed
the most important secret Nadia had: that she was a witch—
young and only half-trained, but more powerful than she'd
once believed.

Her thick black hair was gathered back into a ponytail,
which revealed the bruise on her temple and the small cuts
along one cheek. Less than thirty-six hours before, she'd
fought the darkest magic she knew of—wielded by Elizabeth,

a sorceress, a servant of the One Beneath. Somehow, against all odds, Nadia had won. She knew she should feel elated. And yet fear still flickered inside her, a fire that wouldn't quite go out.

I got lucky, she thought. *But at least Elizabeth's gone, and we can start picking up the pieces.*

Next to her stood Mateo Perez, letter jacket slung over the black T-shirt and jeans he'd have to wear for his shift at the restaurant later. Nadia knew he'd always thought of himself as an outsider in Captive's Sound, isolated by the curse that followed his family. For a long time, he'd believed he had only one true friend—but that had only been Elizabeth playing games with his mind. Elizabeth had used him, and the curse, for her own purposes.

Nadia had been able to show Mateo what Elizabeth really was. More important, she'd discovered who he really was: someone strong enough to bear the curse. Someone who could serve as her Steadfast, the person who could amplify the strength of her witchcraft. Someone who now could *see* magic at work in the world, both light and dark. She had known within weeks that she needed him beside her, always. They'd kissed for the first time only days before; she felt like she could taste that kiss, feel his lips against hers, every moment.

We have time now, she thought as he looked sideways at Nadia. *All the time in the world. So today isn't about us. It's about Verlaine.*

❧ ❧

Verlaine Laughton leaned against the gate, trying to catch her breath. Her pale hand clung to the cast-iron leaves; around her wrist dangled the white plastic bracelet she'd worn in the hospital and hadn't cut off yet. Though her dads had protested her going out with her friends so soon after being discharged, she'd convinced them she needed it. "Sunshine," she'd said. "Fresh air." That sounded healthy, right?

Now she was about to walk to her parents' graves for the first time in far too long. Through Nadia's magic, and maybe Mateo's abilities as her Steadfast, Verlaine would learn whether their deaths had been caused by dark magic— whether every sorrow in her lonely life, all the way from being orphaned as a baby to having silver-gray hair at age seventeen, was a result of a spell Elizabeth had cast.

Elizabeth's gone forever, Verlaine told herself. *I can't get back at her now no matter what. There's nothing we can do to reverse the spell now that Elizabeth's dead. So what good does it do to find out?*

Nadia put her hand on Verlaine's shoulder. "Are you okay?"

"Yeah." Verlaine straightened to her full height—several inches taller than Nadia, even a couple above Mateo. "I'm fine."

"We don't have to do this now," Mateo said. "We could come back in a few days. There's no rush."

"I know we don't have to do it now." The words rattled out of Verlaine, too fast and too shaky, but determined. "We don't *have* to do it ever. But I want to know. Let's just get it over with."

"All right. Come on." Nadia put her arm around Verlaine, and that human contact helped her feel better.

Nadia had said that the magical resonance around Verlaine was old, going back very nearly to the beginning of her life. If Elizabeth had been responsible for the spell, they would be unable to break it—now that Elizabeth was dead.

But the magic around Verlaine was an especially cruel one. It kept her from being fully noticed or appreciated. The magic kept her from being loved.

It wasn't an absolute barrier. Her family, who had loved her from infancy and thus before the spell, still cared deeply for her. And there had been moments during the past few weeks when other, stronger magical forces had temporarily canceled out the effect of whatever it was that had been done to Verlaine—when she felt like her friends truly cared for her.

Those moments were fleeting, however. Even now, Verlaine knew Nadia was here mostly out of a sense of obligation; when her eyes met Mateo's, she saw the same sense of guilt. It wasn't their fault any more than it was Verlaine's. The magic was to blame.

Even if the curse is forever, I want the truth. Just so I know what I'm dealing with, instead of always wondering why.

They walked slowly along the rocky path that outlined the graveyard. Captive's Sound had clung to this craggy, joyless bit of the Rhode Island coastline since colonial times; several of the tombstones were centuries old, blackened with age, the once-deep carved letters worn to mere scratches by rain and time. The chill of the November wind was sharpened by the salt air as it sent gold leaves skittering past their feet and caught at Verlaine's long, gray hair.

Captive's Sound was somehow fundamentally sick. Rotten at the core, Nadia thought, from all the dark magic that had been worked here over the centuries by Elizabeth Pike. She'd hoped Elizabeth's death might have begun to heal the town. But the trees were still stark and too small, the light more watery and less bright.

Then again, it was only November 2. *Give it time to heal,* Nadia reminded herself.

Verlaine stopped short, her Converse sneakers kicking up dust on the path. "There. My parents are over there."

She pointed at a still-smooth granite block, one of the long tombstones that bracketed dual graves. Nadia helped lead her toward them. She noticed Mateo taking care not to step on any place where a dead person might lie. From some people that would only have been superstition; from Mateo, she knew, it was a sign of respect.

Finally they were at the foot of the graves, looking at an epitaph that read: *Richard and Maisie Laughton, beloved children, loving parents.*

Gone from us too soon.

"They don't have any flowers." Verlaine's voice was small. "I used to want to bring them when I was little, but it always made Uncle Dave cry. He was close to my mom; he said she was his best friend, always. Coming here hurt him so much that I quit asking. But now they haven't had flowers for years and years."

"It's okay," Mateo said. "They know you still love them."

"Do they? We proved magic exists, and witches exist, and also crazy-ass sorceresses who sit near you in chemistry class, but we don't know anything about heaven, last I checked." Verlaine wiped at her face, though she wasn't crying; it was as though she was trying to focus herself, Nadia thought. "Or is that in your Book of Shadows, Nadia? Proof that there's an afterlife?"

"Nope. That's as mysterious to you as it is to me." Nadia decided the best way to comfort Verlaine at this point was to stay focused on the task at hand. "Verlaine, I want you to go stand between the two graves."

The effect was immediate. Verlaine steadied just at the thought of having something constructive to do. "Up by the gravestone? Or does it matter?"

"It doesn't, but there might be some, uh, physical impact. So standing farther back is good." She glanced over her shoulder. "Getting a little distance is a good idea for you, too, Mateo."

He smiled at her, and it was one of those moments where it hit her all over again—how somehow this wonderful guy had come into her life exactly when she was trying to shut everyone out. Mateo had beaten down the doors. Burned the fences. Picked the lock on the gate. "Distance," he said. "Got it. You don't need a Steadfast for this?"

"I always need my Steadfast," Nadia said softly. "But you'll be more than close enough."

Verlaine positioned herself between her parents' graves, a strange look on her face as she gazed down at the place where her mother lay. Her usual vintage look was less polished today, but she'd put on acid-washed jeans and a poufy white sweater for an eighties vibe. All Nadia could think was how pale and thin she looked. Like a ghost among the graves. "Here?"

"That works." Nadia lifted her hand and took hold of her wrist—specifically, the quartz charm that dangled from her bracelet. The bracelet wasn't just a piece of jewelry; it was her way of keeping the primal elements she needed for her witchcraft close at every moment.

But the elements alone weren't the magic. They only grounded Nadia, made her ready. For magic, she needed the spell.

For revealing magic done long ago:

Fear conquered.
Love betrayed.
Secrets laid bare.

Those were the ingredients. Now, to give them power. Nadia closed her eyes and thought of the deepest, most emotionally resonant memories that fulfilled each—

Standing with Mateo in the Halloween carnival fire, aware the house was about to collapse around them, facing Elizabeth's magic and fighting back with her own.

"It's better this way," Mom said at the doorway, suitcase in hand, not even looking Nadia directly in the face before she left her daughter behind forever.

Meeting Elizabeth's eyes across the chemistry lab as one of Nadia's spells went haywire, and Elizabeth's mocking smile, her utter lack of surprise, revealing that she was another witch—but horribly, undoubtedly, a Sorceress.

Nadia opened her eyes to see a bottle-green mist drifting around them—centered on the graves, and on Verlaine. A soft sound rustled through the air, like silk on silk. Verlaine's long, silver hair began to drift around her, as though she were underwater.

"It's cold," Verlaine whispered.

"Stay very still." Nadia held up one hand as a warning. Verlaine's eyes went wide, but she didn't move.

The mist swirled a little faster, then froze in place—literally. One moment it was vapor; the next moment, greenish crystals of ice sleeted down around them. Verlaine winced and covered her head as the ice rattled on her parents' gravestones. It instantly melted, running through the carved letters to drip down onto the brownish grass below.

Verlaine peeked through her fingers. ". . . That's it?"

Nadia nodded. Mateo stepped closer to them, and when she turned toward him, what she already suspected was confirmed in his eyes.

"What did it look like to you?" she asked. Mateo, as her Steadfast, possessed a window into magic that even she could never match.

"Dark red metallic . . . streaks, I guess." He struggled, obviously trying to find the right words. "Like they were raining down in this greenish mist."

"We saw the mist, too. That was a freebie." Verlaine

walked toward them, her steps unsteady. Nadia wasn't sure whether that was from the lingering effects of what Elizabeth had done to her last week or the emotions she had to be feeling. "So. Dark red. That's old magic, right? What did the spell tell you, Nadia?"

Best to say it as quickly and cleanly as possible, Nadia decided. "It's not just an echo of an old spell. Whatever spell this was—it was cast a long time ago, but it's still at work. It's linked to your parents' deaths. It's unquestionably dark magic. And"—the next was just Nadia's judgment call, but she was certain—"yes, Elizabeth was the one responsible."

Verlaine didn't react at first. Her pale face remained almost expressionless, and except for her wind-tossed hair, she didn't move.

Mateo took a step closer to her. "Verlaine? Are you okay?"

"I could at least have brought some flowers." With that, Verlaine crossed her arms and let her head droop, drawing into herself.

Verlaine had told them the story of how her parents had died—and even to her it was only a story, one she'd been told, because she was still a baby when it happened. She'd been found wailing in her crib; her parents' dead bodies lay in their bedroom, both apparently so severely and suddenly ill that they'd been unable even to call for help before they perished. Now they knew Elizabeth was the one responsible. Elizabeth would have been there that day, ignoring baby Verlaine's cries as she looked down on her two victims.

But why? Had Verlaine's mother been a witch, too,

someone Elizabeth destroyed for opposing her? If Elizabeth had killed the father out of spite, why leave Verlaine alive? Had Elizabeth kept people from caring about Verlaine so that, perhaps, nobody would investigate her parents' deaths?

None of it made sense. Next Nadia would try spells to find out what had been done—that much, maybe, she could manage. However, she'd never be able to tell Verlaine why Elizabeth did it. That had died with Elizabeth.

She thought again of Mom walking out the door, leaving her family for good. Sometimes Nadia thought the worst part of it all was not knowing why.

Mateo took her hand as they both stepped closer to Verlaine. The touch was still new enough to send a thrill along Nadia's skin. "Hey," Mateo said quietly to Verlaine. "Are you okay?"

"Next time I'll run by Jasmine's first." Verlaine brushed back her silvery hair; her hand was still bruised from the hospital IV. "That's the florist in town, Nadia. I forgot you were new here and you might not know. I can run by there and pick up a dozen roses. Two dozen. Or—how many roses do you think they might have at any one time?"

Nadia wanted to tell Verlaine that everything would be okay, but she didn't want to give her friend false hope. "Listen. I want to try something."

"Another spell?"

"Yeah. I want to find out exactly what was done to you, and whether there's some way to reverse it."

Verlaine glanced up at that. "*Can* you reverse it?"

"Maybe. We won't know until we try." Nadia gave her an encouraging smile. As long as they remained near the bodies of her parents—the first victims of the spell, and thus the ones who bore the deepest marks of magic—Nadia thought they had a shot.

She raised her hand to her bracelet, ready to begin her next spell—

Verlaine screamed. Mateo grabbed Nadia and pulled her back—only moments before her hair stood on end. It was as if lightning struck, but instead of a second's flash of lightning, a column of fire swirled up in front of them, twisting and writhing with its heat. The roar of it deafened Nadia, and she staggered into Mateo's arms.

"My parents!" Verlaine cried. The flames danced on their graves. No, not danced—*consumed*. As Nadia watched in horror, the graves caved in, as though the coffins and bodies within them had instantly disappeared.

The fire vanished as quickly as it had come. For a few moments they all stood there, staring at the scorched earth, their quickened breathing the only break from the silence.

"What—" Verlaine had to stop and take a deeper breath before she could finish. "Nadia, what did you do?"

"That wasn't me," Nadia said.

From behind them came a voice: "No. It was me."

They all turned as one. Standing beneath a stone angel was Elizabeth.

Alive and well.

Elizabeth smiled. "Just who I was looking for."

11

THE DAZZLING SERIES CONTINUES

Nadia, Mateo, and Verlaine have saved Captive's Sound from the dark Sorceress Elizabeth . . . or so they thought. With Mateo as her Steadfast, Nadia's magic is more powerful than ever. But there is still so much she doesn't know about the craft, leaving her open and vulnerable to a darker magic . . . which has begun to call Nadia's name.